Praise
Ned Kelly Award

'Temple is as dark and m
as any James Ellroy or Elmore Leonard with whom you
might kill the small or sad hours.'
Peter Craven, *Age*

'Another world-class crime novel from Peter Temple.'
Canberra Times

'Temple's work is spare, deeply ironic; his wit, like the
local beer, as cold as a dental anaesthetic…For this
Melbourne-born reviewer, the only thing better than a
Temple novel is a Carlton win.'
Graeme Blundell, *Australian*

Praise for *White Dog*
Ned Kelly Award for best crime novel 2003

'A brilliant novel.'
Australian

'Says more about contemporary Australia than most of the
so-called literary fiction churned out by writing programs.
And I'm looking forward to the next one.'
Sydney Morning Herald

'There's not much left that counts for a hill of beans in this crazy
world, but one safe bet is a new book by Peter Temple.' *Age*

'A cracker of a yarn…*White Dog* can be horribly violent, raw
and profane at times, but equally sharp, witty and wise as well.'
Australian Bookseller & Publisher

'Peter Temple is the man—the lay-down misère best crime writer
in the country…Lively, cracking prose, spiky wit and crisp, action-
packed stories which dazzle and grip…A joy-ride of a book.'
Adelaide Advertiser

Praise for *The Broken Shore*

'A towering achievement that brings alive a ferocious landscape and a motley assortment of clashing characters. The sense of place is stifling in its intensity, and seldom has a waltz of the damned proven so hypnotic. Indispensable.' *Guardian*

'A stone classic. Hard as nails and horrible, but read page one and I challenge you not to finish it.' *Independent*

'The first of Peter Temple's books to be published in the UK and at last we can see why he is acclaimed as one of Australia's leading crime writers…This is a very fine book. Characterisation, dialogue and the quality of the prose are all top-class.' *Telegraph* (UK)

'Although The Broken Shore might have been written with the intention of crossing the restrictive boundaries of genre, it might well be the best crime novel published in this country.' Graeme Blundell, *Australian*

'If you only read one crime novel this year, read *The Broken Shore*. It's not just a good yarn—there are plenty of those—what Peter Temple achieves here is much, much more… *The Broken Shore* might just be a great Australian novel, irrespective of genre.' Sue Turnbull, *Age*

'Powerful…taut…compelling…fascinating…Highly recommended.' *Canberra Times*

'Serious, unflinching, relentless—and often hilarious.' *Australian Bookseller & Publisher*

'Great plot, believable, fallible characters and some terrific dialogue.' *Sun-Herald*

OTHER NOVELS BY PETER TEMPLE

An Iron Rose
Shooting Star
The Broken Shore

THE JACK IRISH NOVELS

Bad Debts
Black Tide
Dead Point
White Dog

PETER TEMPLE

THE JACK IRISH DOUBLE

DEAD POINT
+ WHITE DOG

Text Publishing Melbourne Australia

The Text Publishing Company
Swann House
22 William Street
Melbourne Victoria 3000
Australia

Design by Chong Weng-ho
Printed and bound in Australia by Griffin Press

National Library of Australia
Cataloguing-in-Publication entry

Temple, Peter, 1946-

The Jack Irish double : dead point + white dog / Peter Temple.

ISBN: 9781921351884 (pbk.)

Irish, Jack (Fictitious character)
Private investigators--Fiction.
Crime--Fiction.
Temple, Peter, 1946- Dead point.
Temple, Peter. 1946- White dog.

A823.3

DEAD POINT

For Gerhard and Karin,
dear friends, for all the good times:
Kom dans, Klaradyn.

On a grey, whipped Wednesday in early winter, men in long coats came out and shot Renoir where he stood, noble, unbalanced, a foreleg hanging. In the terminating jolt of the bolt, many dreams died.

Later, in the car, Cameron Delray sat behind the wheel, looked straight ahead and made no move to get going. Harry Strang, head deep in his old racing overcoat, held his knuckles to his forehead. After a while, he said, 'Act of God, no bloody insurance for that.'

I was in shock, rubbing my hands together, trying to comfort myself. Most of them you can lose easily and there are fifty reasons why. This was the one we couldn't lose. If the ground was firm. If the horse didn't miss the start, and this horse was not going to miss the start, it was the best-schooled horse in the world, if it didn't miss the start, it could street the small field by at least six lengths, probably ten.

And nobody knew that except us.

The ground was firm. It didn't miss the start.

All Renoir had to do was run 1000 metres. On lazy days, not pushed, we had clocked him doing that in around 57 seconds. Only one horse running against him had come close to such a time. Afterwards, that creature swabbed positive for Melazanine and hadn't run under 65 since.

So that didn't count. Drug-assisted times don't count.

The day before, Harry Strang, walking next to Kathy Gale, big hand holding her elbow, said, 'Can't win with you up, he can't win. Just mind you get him out with em, keep him away from em, don't touch him, he'll do the rest.'

All Kathy had to do was get the horse to jump cleanly out of gate number six, just urge him on, one bend, it didn't matter about looking for the short path, being out wide meant nothing, he could beat them if he ran on the grandstand rail, the horse was ten lengths better than any of the competition. Just go for the judge.

Renoir, black as the grave, stood in the stall with the patient air of a Clydesdale, no sign of nerves. The VE 4000 showed me a calm, intelligent eye and Kathy Gale's face, her mouth, the upper teeth resting on the plumped pillow of the lower lip, the tooth next to the canine that jutted slightly, that broke the rank of her seagull-white choppers.

I saw Kathy put out a hand and rub Renoir under his left ear. It twitched. He liked that; she had done it to him hundreds of times. They stood in the gate, a horse and a small rider, at their ease, friends, together greatly superior to the men and animals on either side of them. And when she urged him, he would respond with a great thrust of dark and gleaming thighs.

The race caller said, 'Three to come in, very serious plunge on Renoir for a horse with one place from nine starts, never run this distance. He's shrunk from 30–1 to outright favourite, 4–5 on, pressure of the money, started as a trickle. Not just the bookmakers either. TAB pool is astonishing for a pretty ordinary autumn race.'

A pool swollen by our money, ours and the money of all the price-watchers who got on with us in the last moments before betting closed.

'Last one goes in, that's Redzone,' said the caller, 'the line's good, light flashing…'

The moment.

The gates opened and they came out together, eight abreast, but only for a moment because Renoir needed no more than half-a-dozen strides to draw away, a length, two, three. Then Kathy settled him, didn't let him bolt, used what she knew about sitting on horses to manage him. Just before the bend, she looked over her shoulder, just a jerk of the head, saw the inadequate herd well behind her, and she took the horse over to the rail. In the straight, Renoir's dominance was complete. With three hundred to go, he was six lengths clear and Kathy was riding him hands and heels, copybook riding, and drawing further ahead with each stride.

'Well, isn't this easy,' said the caller. 'Renoir's thrashing this field, drilling the bookies who got caught early, he's in another league altogether and Kathy Gale isn't even…'

I had Kathy and Renoir in perfect focus, all grace and power, an unbidden smile on my face, and then I saw her head drop and her arms in their silken sleeves go forward to clutch the lovely black neck and I saw shining horse and rider falling, falling, falling, all gainliness gone, all grace and power departed in a split second of agony.

They fell and she lay still and he, the proud and lovely creature, struggled to stand and the field had plenty of space in which to part and ride around them so that some undeserving twosome could be declared winners.

Now, in the car, Harry took his hands from his face and fastened his seatbelt. 'Home,' he said, 'have a bit of Bolly, thank the stars the Lord didn't taketh away the girl.'

On the way, on the hideous tollway, in post-adrenalin shock, I was thinking about life, the brevity, the silliness, my life in particular, the fragility of life, how unfair it was that the huge burden should be carried on such slender and brittle supports, when Cam said, driving with two fingers in a suicidal rush of trucks and boofheads, petrolheads, 'The giveth is we got average fifteen with the books, just on ten on the tote.'

I sat up, heart pumping as if from a dream of flight, enraged and irrational. 'You put money on that?' I said. 'A fucking thing not fit to lick Renoir's boots, shoes, whatever, hooves, bloody hooves…'

Harry had his head back, against the headrest. 'Jack,' he said, sadly, 'they don't have races with only one horse.'

I slumped in my seat, a child gently chastised. How often do you have to be told some things?

Lyn, the fourth Mrs Harry Strang, opened a French door at the side of the mellow red-brick house as we came up the gravel path from the carriage-house. She had the sexy look of someone who'd been running, followed by a hot shower and a rough towelling. Her right hand came up, fell. She knew. She was once a trainer's wife, she knew.

'Had better days,' said Harry without being asked anything. 'Might have the bubbly in the study, love.'

In the awesome room, we stood with our backs to the five-metre-high wall of books that held everything ever published on horses and horse racing and looked out across the terrace and the lawn and the yew hedges to the naked maples moving like things possessed.

There was a knock. Cam opened the door in the library wall and Mrs Aldridge came in with a tray. I saw the delicacies, salivated. I'd had them before and they featured in my dreams. Ethereal capsules, a shell of champagne batter just puffed in hot oil. Inside, the teeth would meet a fresh oyster wrapped in tissue-thin smoked salmon.

Lyn Strang followed, three flutes on a silver tray, a bottle of Bollinger, uncorked, stoppered with a sterling silver device.

Harry looked at his two women. 'What would I do?' he said, head to one side. I had never seen him like that.

'Stuff yourself with all the wrong things,' said Mrs Aldridge, sharply. She left the room.

Harry looked at Lyn. 'Glass short,' he said.

'No,' said Lyn. 'Can't bear racing post-mortems.'

She touched his cheek, smiled, a brisk nurse smile, and left.

Harry poured. Cam and I waited for the toast, Harry always proposed a toast to the next time. It didn't come. He sipped, and we sipped. My eyes met Cam's.

'Well,' Harry said, putting his glass down on the tray, looking out at his garden, 'I'm thinkin of givin it away.'

I didn't want to hear this. It had been in my mind from the moment he said, 'What would I do?'

'An act of God,' said Cam. He was holding his flute to the light, studying the minute bubbles. 'Whoever that is. There'll be better days.'

'Not today's stuff,' said Harry, still not looking at us. 'That's the business. The punt's the punt, can't cop it, drop it. The commissioner, that's what makes me think it's time to shut the shop.'

'We'll fix the Cynthia thing,' said Cam. 'We're workin on that.'

I wanted to second Cam's statements but I didn't believe them and I couldn't find a quick reassuring lie.

Harry picked up his glass, had a generous sip, shook his head, pretended to cheer up. 'Got to be good for ya, don't ya reckon?' he said.

'We'll fix the Cynthia thing,' repeated Cam.

Cynthia had been the commission agent for four big plunges, marshalling teams of old-age pensioners, young-age pensioners, the bored, a retired bank manager, two strippers gone to flab, an ageing hooker relishing undemanding vertical work.

The most recent plunge had been a simple matter involving a nightclub owner who believed, correctly, that a non-performing horse he secretly owned through his sister-in-law's cousin would show unexpected ability in a feature race at Flemington.

Afterwards, Cynthia had collected the large sum her platoon of punters had taken off the bookies. She was in her old Mazda, driving to meet Cam, cruising down a narrow Yarraville street, when a four-wheel drive forced her to the kerb. Two men got out, asked for the money. She said she didn't think that was on, and, in full view of an old man on sticks and a woman on a bicycle, one of the men punched her in the face six or seven times, held her by the hair, turned her head and broke her jaw and her nose and impacted her cheekbones. When they were gone, she got Cam on her mobile, speaking thickly through the blood and the crushed cartilage, then lost consciousness.

Cam more or less drove across country to reach her, ignoring traffic lights and stop signs and other vehicles, took her to Footscray General. The number the woman on the bicycle had written down belonged to a vehicle stolen less than an hour earlier. It was found in the city, in Latrobe Street, just after 6 p.m.

Cynthia now had less than forty per cent sight in one eye. We weren't going to be able to fix Cynthia. And the Cynthia thing wasn't any easier.

'Can't get over that,' said Harry. 'Not a thing used to happen. Bash a woman like that, bastards'd do anythin.'

I knew what he was thinking. He was thinking about his women: his wife, thirty years his junior, the final fling, and his housekeeper of thirty-five years, a person who left England for him, left home and kin to look after a broken-bodied jockey. He was thinking about Lyn and Mrs Aldridge because he loved them and he was fearful for them. Not for himself, not for Harry Strang, the champion jockey of whom an English racing writer once wrote, 'In his presence, agitated English horses become calm and calm English jockeys lose their composure.'

Cam knew too. He finished his glass, poured for us, for himself. 'Just run-through boys,' he said, his face expressionless. 'Too clever for banks, too lazy for drugs. Somebody told em about Cyn, one of her troops would be right. We'll get there, sort it out.'

We wouldn't. Cam and I had already been over Cynthia's troops. All we found was that one had gone to Queensland suddenly. So did we. We joined the woman at her ailing aunt's bedside. She was so shocked and showed so little evidence of new-found riches that Cam slipped her two $100 notes when we left.

'Won't make any quick decision,' said Harry. 'Nothin comin up, sleep on it for a bit.'

We finished the bottle and didn't move on to the customary second one. Harry came to the front gate with us, out in the blustery night, trees thrashing, held me back, fingers like a bulldog clip on my left bicep.

'Two knocks in a row, Jack,' he said, 'you'll be hurtin. Not a write-off, though. Get twenty-five, thirty cents in the dollar back, thereabouts.'

'Can't drop it, cop it,' I said. 'Isn't that right?'

He squeezed my arm, more pain. 'Remember the Bank of Strang, cash advances for the creditworthy. Also, a little legal matter, need some consultin. Next week suit?'

'Day and night,' I said.

'Cam'll make a time.'

He let go. We looked at each other. 'Harry,' I said, no mental activity preceding what followed, pure emotion. 'Cynthia. We'll take care of that.'

The front door of the house opened. Over Harry's head, I saw Lyn Strang, short, strong, warm peach-coloured light on her hair and shoulders, a carpet of peach laid around her shadow on the broad verandah. 'I wanted to say goodbye. I was upstairs,' she said, something in her tone, not relief but something like that.

In the street, beyond the high red-brick wall, Cam started the transport we'd come in, a much-modified vehicle apparently known to some as an eight-bore streetslut. It made a feline noise, the sort of sound a prehistoric giant sabre-toothed tiger might have made.

I raised my hand at Lyn. She waved back.

'We'll fix it,' I said to Harry, repeating the stupid, unfulfillable promise.

'Wouldn't surprise me,' Harry said, no confidence in his voice. 'Pair of bright fellas like yerselves.'

Cam drove me to my place of residence, the old boot factory in North Fitzroy, early Saturday night traffic. Lots of taxis, sober people going out for a good time. He double-parked outside, turned down Bryan Ferry on the eight-bore's many speakers.

'The big man's a worry,' he said. He lit a Gitane with his Zippo, rolled down his window. 'Seen it comin for a while.'

Cold air and the pungent Gallic smoke sent a tremor of craving through me. 'There's nowhere else to go on Cynthia,' I said.

'Cyril,' said Cam. 'Come at it from Cyril's end.'

We dealt with Cynthia through Cyril Wootton, professional middleman, dead-end and cut-out, collector of non-enforceable debts, finder of witnesses, skips, shoot-throughs and no-shows, and my occasional employer.

'Cyril's deeply shonky,' I said, 'but this, no.'

Cam sighed smoke. 'Can't leave him out,' he said. 'Can't leave anythin out.' He turned his head and looked at me, black eyes saying something, wanting me to agree to the unsaid.

I opened the door. 'I'll talk to him tomorrow.'

'Me too?'

'No.'

I was getting out when Cam said, 'Jack, this trot, it'll end, don't be shy.'

He too was offering to lend me money.

'Thanks,' I said. 'Could come to that.'

I watched him drive away, slowly in the quiet street, the deep, feral sound of eight cylinders entering the blood-stream, agitating it.

There wasn't anything else to do but light the fire in a clean grate, prepared on a nervous race-day morning with scrunched paper, kindling, a few sticks of bone-dry wood, cut and split and chopped and delivered by Harry Strang's man in Avoca. He was the owner of a calm grey mare called Breckinridge, a horse now burdened only by the weight of children. It had been four lengths clear when it won the Ballarat Cup at 30–1, and from then on some people got their wood free and I got mine at a discount.

There was a time when I thought I'd never go back to the boot factory. Having your home blown up by people who want to kill you can have that effect. But when the time came to decide, I couldn't let an explosion rob me of the place I'd shared with someone I loved beyond the telling of it. I packed my bags and left the converted stable I'd been living in, grown used to, and went back to where I'd kissed Isabel goodbye on the day a mad client of mine murdered her in a carpark. I walked up the stairs, unlocked the front door, went down the passage to the big, empty living room, looked around, opened a window, and I was home.

Ignite the fire, watch that Avoca kindling go up like a cypress hedge. Now, to the kitchen. What follows Bollinger and oysters in champagne batter? Perhaps a slice of sirloin, a thick slice, moist and ruddy in the centre, served with a cream, mustard and finely-chopped caper sauce, some small vegetables on the side. Yes, but the kitchen wasn't going to run to that. Next. Open the fridge. There was a piece of corned beef. A corned-beef, cheddar and pickle sandwich and a glass, glasses, of Heathcote shiraz, that was what it was going to run to.

How old can corned beef get before it kills you? I sniffed and pondered, studied the iridescent surface of the chunk of meat and, sadly, decided that risk outweighed reward. Now it was cheddar and pickle, mature cheddar, not mature when bought but now most certainly. And then it flashed through my mind that it was bread that made the Earl of Sandwich's innovation possible, you needed bread. Next.

I thought briefly about getting out the Studebaker Lark, agonised, then rang Lester at the Vietnamese takeaway in St Georges Road. Lester answered, a non-committal sound with which I was familiar. He was a client. I'd sorted out a small matter that troubled him. For an immoderate fee, in cash, a woman lawyer in Richmond had done the paperwork needed to bring his aged mother into the country. Then a man came around and told Lester that it would cost $150 a week, also in cash, to keep his mother from being sent back. The money would be passed on to a corrupt official in Canberra.

Lester had been paying for three years when he consulted me, referred by someone he wouldn't name. I made some inquiries, then spoke to the Richmond solicitor on the telephone. She had no idea what I was talking about, she said, highly offended and haughty. I didn't say anything for a while, then I said I'd appreciate a bank cheque for $23,400 payable to Lester, delivered to me by hand inside the hour.

She laughed, a series of starter-motor sounds. 'Or what?' she said.

'Or you can practise law in Sierra Leone,' I said. 'How's that for an or?'

A silence. 'Your name again?'

'Irish, Jack Irish.'

Another silence. 'Are you the one who killed that ex-cop and the other guy?'

My turn to be silent, then I said, 'I wasn't charged with anything.'

The cheque arrived inside an hour. I took it around to the takeaway and gave it to Lester's wife.

A few days later, Lester knocked on my office door. He was carrying a sports bag and he didn't appear overjoyed. 'How much?' he said. 'You?'

I wrote out a bill for $120. He studied it, looked at me, studied it again. Then he unzipped his bag and put wads of notes on my table, fifties, twenties, perhaps five or six thousand dollars, more, in used notes.

Temptation had run its scarlet fingernails down my scrotum. What did it matter? A success fee, that's all it was. Merchant bankers took success fees. But I wasn't a merchant banker. People like that grabbed what they could within the law. In my insignificant way, I represented the law. I was a sworn officer of the court. I was a thread in an ancient fabric that made social existence possible.

I *was* the law.

Sufficiently psyched up by these thoughts, I leaned across the tailor's table, plucked two soiled fifties and a twenty, pushed the rest back his way.

'Lester,' I said, 'not all lawyers are the same.'

Now I said, 'Lester, it's Jack. Any chance of Bruce dropping off some food?'

'How many?'

'One.'

'Fifteen minutes,' he said. 'Jack, you want prawns?'

'Lester, I need prawns.'

13

A glass later, the buzzer sounded and I went downstairs and opened the door to bright-eyed Bruce, the elder of Lester's two teenage sons. He'd come on his bike, cardboard box on the carrier. I tried to give him some gold coins but he was under instructions. 'No thanks,' he said. 'My dad says no-one's allowed to take money from you.'

Virtue may be its own reward, but there are other possible spin-offs.

I said, 'I wish that were a universal principle, Bruce.'

He smiled, he got it. No shonky lawyer was ever going to get fat on this new Australian.

Upstairs, the phone rang. I made haste up the old, squeaking stairs, both hands on the food box. Lyall had been known to ring on a Wednesday night, Thursday night, any night, from any time zone, usually from some troubled place, satellite phone borrowed from the CNN person or a UN person or, once, from the head of the Chechen mafia.

'Irish,' I said, winded. It was a handy name, you could say it as a sigh, one syllable, a longer surname would have had to become double-barrelled.

'Jack, Jack,' said Cyril Wootton, his resigned voice. 'Whatever became of obligation, of sense of duty?'

My breath came back in a reasonable time. Recently I'd been running around Edinburgh Gardens in the early morning, going up Falconer Street and down Delbridge to Queen's Parade, running and walking, limping really, streets empty, sometimes a dero lying on the pavement, clenched like a fist against the cold, the occasional pale young man with dark eye sockets and a stiff-legged walk, and always the three women at the tram stop, head-scarves, smoking and talking quietly, perhaps the last sweatshop workers to live in the gentrified suburb.

'Got no idea, Cyril,' I said. 'I don't follow the greyhounds. Never bet on anything that's trying to catch something else, that's the principle. Good names, though.'

In the moment before he spoke again, I heard the sounds of his midweek haunt, a pub in Kew he stopped off at to slake the thirst he developed after leaving the Windsor in Spring Street.

It was a raffish spot for Kew: two financial advisers had once fought to tears in the toilet, and the legend was that three pairs of women's underpants were found in the beer garden after a local real-estate agency's Christmas party in 1986.

Wootton expelled breath. 'There is considerable anxiety,' he said. 'I am under pressure to produce results. And you cannot be contacted.'

I felt some contrition. I hadn't done any serious looking for Robbie Colburne, occasional barman.

'Feelers are out, Cyril,' I said.

'What feelers?'

'He's not using his vehicle, that narrows things.'

'Narrows? There was no belief in Cyril's voice. 'Are you saying he hasn't gone anywhere?'

'Within limits.'

The trawl through the airlines hadn't produced the name but that meant nothing. You could give any name if you paid cash to fly or you could travel by bus or taxi or a friend could give you a lift or you could ride your bicycle out of town, rollerblade, run, walk, limp.

'Quite,' he said in his assumed Coldstream Guards officer's voice. 'Is he spending?'

'He's a part-time barman. What would he have to spend?'

'So you've got nothing to show for three days?'

'Cyril,' I said, 'I'm probably being over sensitive, but, at this moment, my inclination is to say bugger off, get someone else. Silly, but that's my state of mind.'

While Wootton weighed up his options, I listened to a surf of witty real-estate and financial-advice banter, the women shrieking, the men baying like hounds, randy hounds.

'Jack,' he said, 'it's serious.'

Even against that background of happy parasites at play, I recognised a Wootton plea.

'Tomorrow,' I said. 'My total attention to this matter.'

He caught my tone, knew that I was in earnest. 'Yes. Give me a ring, old chap.' I'd be giving him more than a ring. I'd be paying him a visit, and the thought gave me no pleasure.

By ten, I was in bed, betwixt fresh linen sheets, steaming Milo on the bedside table, classical FM on the radio. In my hands, I held a novel about young Americans undergoing rites of passage in Venezuela.

All alone at the end of the day. Lyall no doubt in some godforsaken country.

Outside, a cold rain was falling on the city. I didn't need to go out to know that. I could feel it in my heart.

I woke before daylight without need of an alarm, splashed my face, put on the saggy old grey tracksuit and went shuffling through the park, around the streets. In Delbridge Street, an insane Jack Russell terrier threw himself against his front gate with a hideous bark-shriek, catching me by heart-stopping surprise for the fiftieth time. The dog would have to die. There was no other way.

Back home, I lay in the huge cast-iron bath for an hour, drinking tea, tapping off cold water, running in hot, reading the *Age*, ruminating on creeping flab and aching knees and other matters of the corpus. Then I dressed in sober business clothing and drove to Meaker's in Brunswick Street for breakfast. Meaker's had been the writing on the wall for working-class Brunswick Street when it opened in the late 1970s, serving breakfast at all hours to people with vague artistic leanings who didn't know what time it was and couldn't afford to eat at home because of the infrastructure required. Now the whole street provided that service and lots, lots more.

'The look I like,' said Carmel, the newest waiter. Despite having the appearance of a 14-year-old waif, she had been married twice and now, sensibly, had retired from dud men, any men, and was the companion of a sleek home-wares buyer for a shop called Noir. I knew this because she had told me, unbidden and unencouraged, when we met by chance early one evening soon after her debut at Meaker's. Much has been learned, not all of it life-affirming, at the Brunswick

Street laundromat. Something about the place—its tropical warmth, the sullen chugging of the machines, the way the newly cleansed garments swirl and flirt and twine in the perforated stainless-steel drums—encourages intimate revelations.

Down there on the left bank of the river Brunswick, Carmel spoke freely about her life and aspirations. Then her companion arrived to fetch her, a severely edited person, nothing more could be subtracted from her dress or manner or speech without her being rendered partially unclothed or immobile or incomprehensible.

'Good tie that,' said Carmel now.

I said thank you.

'My first only ever used his ties to tie me up,' said Carmel. 'Mind you, they were school ties, greasy, ballpoint marks and bits of food on them. He went to Wesley.'

'That's really the only use for old Wesley ties,' I said. 'Melbourne Grammar boys sometimes tie theirs around their waists when they're naked or use them to commit suicide.'

Carmel nodded. 'Or for scarfing,' she said. 'Like that singer. What can I get you?'

'Just toast and tea,' I said. 'Italian breakfast tea.'

'One latte,' she said.

Afterwards, I caught a tram into the city, stood all the way to Collins Street with the barely awake and the glowing pre-dawn joggers, the perfectly made up and the bloodily shaven, the hanging out and the merely hungry.

Offloaded, I took myself up the stairs of the stone build-ing to face Mrs Davenport. I found the bureau chief to Cyril Wootton, CEO of Belvedere Investments, in her usual rigid position behind a desk in the firm's panelled reception room.

'Corporal Wootton fronted yet?' I asked. I'd known the man when he was a redistributor of military stores, an illegal wholesaler of Vegemite and Tim Tams and Tooheys beer, a saboteur of the war effort in Vietnam.

The silver-haired exemplar drew breath and it pinched her nostrils. Nothing else ever moved. There was no knowing her age; she had mummified her face through discipline. 'I'm afraid Mr Wootton's engaged,' she said. 'Would you like to wait indefinitely or make an appointment?'

Mrs Davenport knew precisely how dubious Wootton was, how thin and swaying was the rope he walked, and yet she had no difficulty in presenting herself as if she were Moralist-in-Residence at the Centre for Applied Ethics.

'The former,' I said, 'I'll just sit down and look at you and puzzle over how a person so coldly beautiful can also be so warm and caring.'

She left the room, came back inside ten seconds and said, 'Mr Wootton will see you.'

Wootton was behind his big oak desk, palms on the top, every centimetre the bank manager of the 1950s, essence of jovial probity, careful with the bank's money but decent and understanding, a man who never failed to count that air shot on the golf course that no-one saw. He pointed to the client's chair.

'Early for you. Reforming your habits?'

I didn't sit down. I went close to the desk, loomed over him.

'Cynthia.'

He frowned. 'Yes?'

'Cam thinks you might be the one.'

Wootton's hand went to his collar, fingers inserted above the tie knot, four fingers, not much room there.

'Fuck, Jack,' he said, 'are you…?'

I didn't say anything, just kept looking into the brown eyes of Corporal Wootton, a corporal of stores. There wasn't much to see.

'Jesus,' he said, emotion in his voice, 'he can't be bloody serious. Jesus, Jack, he's not serious? Don't tell me Harry…'

'Cyril,' I said, 'if you are the one, say so now. I'll give you two hours to arrange to give the money back, plus a hundred and fifty grand for Cynthia's pain and suffering. And that's letting you off lightly. You then disappear. Forever. I'll try to keep Cam from coming after you. Try, that's all I can do.'

He looked at me in despair, mouth opening and closing. 'No, Jack,' he said, 'no, no, no. You can kill me but no, never, I don't know anything about it, she's a friend of mine. I would never…Cam's mad, I'd never ever do anything…'

He tailed off, closed his eyes, squeezed them tight, shook his head like a dog with a grass seed in an ear.

'Say so now, Cyril. You don't want to wait for other circumstances. Hanged through the Achilles tendon from a meat hook, those circumstances.'

'I swear. I swear. No. Jesus, no.'

I sat down. 'I'll take your word on that,' I said. 'I hope that's not a foolish thing to do.'

Cyril opened his eyes, blinked rapidly, straightened his pin-striped shoulders, regained some composure. 'Don't take my word,' he said. 'I don't want you to take my word. Tell Cam to check me out, every last thing.'

'I'll tell him I believe you when you say you had nothing to do with it.'

Cyril looked away, stroked his tie, a regimental tie, though certainly not the tie of his regiment. 'Do you?' he said.

'For the moment.'

His head turned. 'I should bloody well hope so,' he said in a cub-lion growling tone, recovering rapidly. 'This your idea of fun?'

'Of kindness, more,' I said. 'It was me or Cam. Or worse. Both. But I'd be lying if I said I didn't enjoy your snivelling.'

'Christ,' he said, sniffed, 'threatening me, you're supposed to be a lawyer.'

'Things not always incompatible. I'm going to tell Cam I don't think you need shaking. That's an act of faith. If I'm wrong, Cyril, I'll be there to see you dropped into that compactor in Hopper's Crossing. They say it makes a noise like a dog chewing chicken bones.'

'Jack.' He cocked his head in pain.

'Moving on then. I can't look for this Colburne prick on what you've given me. What's the story?'

Cyril composed himself in an instant. 'In that matter, your services are no longer required.'

I shook my head. 'What's this, revenge? Don't be petulant, Cyril.'

He pointed to a copy of the *Herald Sun* on his desk. 'Page five,' he said, an expression of distaste on his face.

I opened the paper at the page. The first item in a single-column collection of briefs had the headline: *Body in garage.*

The story said: *A man was yesterday found dead in a car in a garage in Rintail Street, Abbotsford. Police identified him as Robert Gregory Colburne, 26, a casual barman.*

The story went on to say that police were treating the death as accidental but were keen to talk to anyone who had seen Colburne recently.

'There endeth the lesson,' said Wootton, cold as the widow's lips. 'Now, if you'll excuse me, I have matters to attend to. People depend upon my understanding the concept of urgency.'

I saw no reason to prolong this encounter or to say goodbye. Time would heal. Or not. At the door, turning the big fluted brass knob, I heard Wootton clear his throat.

'In his own vehicle,' he said, 'in his own garage.'

I continued on my way. As I passed Mrs Davenport in the anteroom, her nostrils contracted fractionally. 'This has been prepared for you, Mr Irish,' she said.

I stopped. She held out a hand, pearl-coloured nails, perfect ovals, and young hands, hands far too young. What secrets had this woman learned during her long stint in the pay of a specialist in sexually-transmitted diseases? I shuddered inwardly, took the envelope she was offering and left the premises.

On the tram, enjoying the presence of a few teenage drug dealers heading for Fitzroy, I opened Mrs Davenport's envelope: a cheque for three days' work at the usual rate.

Out loud, I said, 'Cyril, oh Cyril.'

One of the adolescent drugporteurs not on his mobile heard my utterance, misunderstood completely, turned, made the selling signal.

I gave him the look and the continental flicking fuck-off sign. Although he was probably untravelled, he got the message.

As I had received Cyril Wootton's message. That he behaved honourably even when I did not.

Detective Sergeant Warren Bowman had the good-humoured manner of a man in sales, not any old sales, specialised sales, motor spares or plumbing supplies or bearings, some secure line of work where the pros know stock numbers off by heart and the customers expect them to say things like 'Almost got me there, mate' and 'We have the technology'.

'They're sayin it's an ordinary OD,' he said.

We were sitting in the Studebaker Lark just off St Kilda Road, the day turned irritable, periods of sunshine, sudden snarls of rain. Detective Sergeant Bowman was speaking to me courtesy of another policeman, Senior Sergeant Barry Tregear, someone I'd known since I was a boy sent to fight abroad for my country. At the request of some other country, the way it had always been for Australia.

'Family doesn't want to know that,' I said, lying.

Warren turned his long head and appraised me. He had bushy black eyebrows that he brought together and parted: quick, slow, slow, quick, an eyebrow Morse code.

'Yeah, well, not always your best judge,' he said, dot, dot, dash. 'The family.'

'No. Funny place to OD.'

Dot, dash. 'Well, they don't set out to OD.'

'Shooting up in his garage? Be more comfortable in his unit.'

Dash, dot. 'No knowin. It's like suicide. Go a long way, some of em. Mountains, some, they like to go to high places.

But there's others want to creep away. Toppin's a bit like hide and seek, know what I mean? Some kids always go for the wardrobe.'

Expertise in dark matters. Warren knew these stock numbers.

A couple walked by, young, handsome in black clothing, arguing, heads flicking, spurts of words. He stopped, she stopped, he raised a hand, inquiring. She knocked it away in contempt, walked. The man waited for a few seconds, turned and came back towards us, jaw moving, small chewing movements.

'He's bin screwin around,' said Warren. 'Some blokes got no idea when they're lucky.' There was a stain of resentment on his tone.

'So Robbie went into his garage, locked the door, got into his car, shot up, that's it?'

He nodded.

'The fit's there?'

A nod.

'Tracks?'

'Yeah. User.'

'User ODs alone in his Porsche parked in his garage. That would be unusual, wouldn't it?'

Warren shifted in his seat, looked at me, dash, dot, dash, took his lower lip between thumb and forefinger, gave it a tug. 'I'm in the box here, am I?'

You forget that people are doing you a favour, at some risk to their careers.

'Sorry,' I said. 'Get carried away.'

He kept looking at me, a long dash.

The angry young woman in black was coming back, in a hurry, full of regret, hoping to catch the man. Her calf-length coat was unbuttoned and it flapped open at every stride, long legs flashing, pale legs.

'Jesus, women,' said Warren, tone pure resentment now. 'Fucking looks, all the bastard's got is looks.'

'For some things,' I said, 'all you need is looks. The key to the garage, he have that on him?'

He said nothing.

I looked upon the empty winter street, trees pen-and-ink lines against the sky, first hint of closure now, the imperceptible dimming of the light that some part of the cortex recognises.

Nothing more to be gained from this encounter. I said my thanks. Warren didn't seem eager to leave the comfort of the old, squat American V-8 beast.

I said, 'Warren, Robbie, any form?'

He shook his head.

'A person of interest?'

He didn't congratulate me on my intelligence, opened his door. 'Thought you'd never ask,' he said. 'As I understand it, definitely. The car that attended, they called in, next thing two drug squad heavies are there, the uniform boys are back on the road.'

I said, 'I'm not cross-examining here but are you still saying they actually believe this bloke's an OD?'

Warren turned to me, a shrug, his eyebrows went dot, dash, dot, dash above the friendly salesman's eyes. 'Believe?' he said. 'I dunno what they believe. Believe in a Big Mac and large fries. They *say* there's nothin says anythin else. What they *believe* I haven't got a clue, mate.'

'Any chance of a snap of the bloke?' Cyril didn't have one.

He sighed. 'I'll see. Duty calls. Cheers.'

I watched him go. He crossed the street, walked down some distance, crossed back and went to his car. He didn't drive off immediately, waited a while. A cautious man. Still, there was every reason to be cautious if the drug squad was involved in the matter of Robbie Colburne.

The Prince of Prussia was busy for a Thursday evening, any evening, at least twelve customers. To the left of the street door, a table of young people in black and shades of grey lowered the average age of the patrons by about 25 years. As I came in the person nearest to me, a cropped-haired blonde, said, 'I mean, he's too *exhausted* for sex and then I get up to pee, it's like 2.30 a.m., he's on the net perving at this bondage porn. Extreme bondage. It's his net-pal in Canada tied up like a salami. How gross is that?'

'Well, the net's essentially a passive medium,' said the woman next to her.

'This was active,' said the blonde. 'He was interacting. I know interacting when I see it.'

I didn't move, looked around the room. The Fitzroy Youth Club were in position at the far end of the bar, within easy reach of the door marked GENTS.

At the black and grey table, a shaven-headed man, scalp the colour of the underside of an old tortoise, said, 'I can tell you guys worse.'

I couldn't go without knowing worse, couldn't move.

'I had this partner,' said the man, fat finger pushing at his round dark glasses, 'he comes home, he's faceless, right, he's with this Arab taxi driver and he goes: "Meet Ahmed or whatever, he's your co-driver for the night."'

A thin woman with a beaky nose leaned forward, shook her head and made a contemptuous sound. 'Worse? Jesus, grow up, I'll give you worse.'

Conquering my desire to hear baldy's poignant tale eclipsed by some other speakable act of sexual unmannerliness, I moved to join the three men at the end of the battered bar. They were not young, not shaven-headed, not in black or fashionable shades of grey. They were ancient and in colours from the chewing tobacco, snuff and washed-out old mauve cardigan end of the spectrum. Of depravity, they could know a great deal: more than 230 years of experience sat in this brown corner.

'So, Jack,' said Norm O'Neill, nodding at my reflection in the speckled mirror we faced, 'deignin to grace us with your presence.'

I said, 'I don't have anywhere else to go.'

'Had to take a taxi,' said Eric Tanner, the man next to him. 'Bloody fortune. Extortionists.'

'I was up north,' I said.

It was expected that the Lark would convey the men to St Kilda games, with a stop on the way to place a few bets. Once it had been to Fitzroy games but we didn't have Fitzroy anymore, Fitzroy didn't suit the national league's plans, so they took the club around the back and drilled it between the eyes. Now we supported St Kilda, my idea, a misguided attempt to cheer up the lads, give them something new to argue about, something to do on weekends.

'Up *where*?' said Norm, as though I'd invented a new compass point. He adjusted the fit of the spectacles on his promethean nose.

'Queensland,' I said. 'Went to see my daughter.'

The heads turned to me. 'Daughter?' said the wizened Wilbur Ong. 'Since when've you had a daughter?'

'A while,' I said. 'She's twenty-one.' Somehow the subject

of my daughter hadn't come up in years of talking football and horses.

'Well, this is bloody news to me,' said Norm, aggrieved. He stared at me. 'Now you've got a girl. And the young fella playin for Fremantle that's the bloody spit of Bill? Wouldn't know anythin about that, would ya?'

'Not a thing,' I said. 'I swear.'

Bill Irish, my father, dead these many years, was a Fitzroy Football Club hero of the late 1940s, a patron of this pub. He had undoubtedly at some time stood where I was standing, resting his stonemason's boot on the same brass rail. And his father's workman's boot had probably been there before his. Daniel Irish was also a Fitzroy player, career cut off in its prime by a Collingwood hoon jumping on his arm accidentally. Twice. Given these male genes, old Fitzroy supporters didn't understand why I hadn't played football, didn't understand and didn't forgive.

'Played shockin, your team,' said Eric. 'The fellas got problems findin the general direction of goal.'

'Not to mention what bloody happens when they do,' said Norm. 'That bugger looks like he's outta Pentridge on day release, he misses four, couldn't reliably piss inta the sea.'

Wilbur nodded. 'Dunno about this coach either. Five goals behind, he lets the flower girls give up, talks to em all kind and gentle. Decent coach'd give em the red-hot poker up the backside.' He paused. 'Disgrace, I reckon, this team of yours.'

The trio's eyes were on me, unblinking bird eyes, the eyes of eagle fledglings, ruthless, demanding. Even in the closing stages, Julius Caesar faced a friendlier looking audience. Better looking too, I had no doubt.

'So now it's *my* team?' I said. 'Well, so be it. That's that then. I'll stick with my team. You lot can go back to not having a team. Or go for the Brisbane Lions. No, go for Collingwood, that's a nice team, run by television money.'

The bird eyes all flicked away. Then Norm's came back.

'Steady on,' he said. 'Man's entitled to give his team a bit of a buttocking.'

'A man who's got a team, yes. Men who don't have a team can't.' Out of the corner of my eye, I saw Stan the publican gliding across from serving the shaven-headed man.

'Jack, my boy.' His smug mood was upon him.

'Stanley. What've you done to your hair?'

Stan ran five pork sausages over his scalp. He'd had the sparse pubic springs shorn to a uniform height. 'Today's look,' he said. 'Got to keep up.'

'Very fetching look,' I said. 'It was big in the Gulag archipelago.'

'The what?'

'Nothing. I see the clientele's going upmarket.'

Stan gave his conspiratorial nod, leaned across the bar. 'Drink vodka,' he said, winked at me. 'Stolly. They're in new technology. The IT crowd.'

'Who?' said Norm O'Neill. 'Eyeties? All in Carlton, the eyetalians. Accident of history. Coulda settled in Fitzroy. Makes you think, don't it? We'da had Serge Silvagni, lotta grit that bloke, then his young fella, always rated that Steven high, I have.'

'Barassi, he's an eyetalian,' said Wilbur Ong. 'Go back a bit, them Barassis, though. Not convicts but a fair way back.' He sighed. 'We coulda had Barass.'

'Barassi come from Castlemaine,' said Eric Tanner. 'Jeez, there's a lotta ignorance around here.'

Stan looked at the Youth Club and shook his head. 'IT.

Information technology. You blokes think the flush dunny's new technology.' He turned back to me, coughed a polite cough. 'Word's gettin around,' he said. 'These people, they're on the cyberfrontier. On the other hand, they like a bit of tradition. Well, you want a bit of tradition, the Prince's the place.'

'Tradition?' I said. 'Really? Tradition of beer tasting like soap? Tradition of toasted cheese sandwiches that fight with your teeth? Tradition of needing gumboots to go to the toilet? That's what they're after, is it? Well, Stanley, you're in the pound seats.'

Stan shrugged. 'Jack, too critical, always bin your problem. Take the world as you find it, my old man always said.'

'Morris never in his life said anything like that,' I said. 'Morris can't stand the world as he finds it. And what's this past tense? Either Morris is alive or he's been phoning me every day from the afterlife.'

Stan's father owned the Prince and five small commercial properties around the suburbs. I acted for him in his endlessly problematic dealings with his tenants and he sent me instructions daily from his retirement villa in Queensland.

'On that subject,' said Stan. He leaned his head closer. 'Listen, Jack, the wife's talkin to someone the other day, he reckons I could get power of attorney for the old bloke, no problem. Eighty-eight, infirm of mind, that sort of thing.'

'Could we get a round here?' I said. 'The old technology crowd. Soapy beer will be fine.'

Stan didn't move. 'Course you'd still do the legal stuff, don't worry about that.'

I put my face within five centimetres of his. 'Stanley,

when I detect any signs of mental infirmity in Morris, you'll be the first to know. As things stand, the message is more likely to go in the other direction.'

Stan worked this out, sighed, went to get the beer. I settled down to a serious discussion with the repentant Youth Club of the Saints' chances against West Coast on Friday night. Perfect hatred of the non-Victorians drove out any fears about the ability of our side to orientate themselves towards goal.

I drove home through a cold drizzle, the Lark's erratic wipers smearing the lights. It was just after seven, the truce time, day people retreating, night people not ready to advance. At the Queen's Parade lights, I punched the radio, got a boring man talking about tax reform, punched again, got a silly pair of teenagers talking about bad exam experiences, punched.

A voice said: *Should the new government have scrapped its predecessor's granting of a licence for a privately run ski resort and casino at Cannon Ridge? Let's hear your views on 1300 3333, that's 1300 3333. I'm Linda Hillier, talking with you on 3KB, Melbourne's station for the new century.*

It was a voice I hadn't heard for a long time. Drivers behind me began to hoot. I came back to the present and got the Lark moving, turned left. Outside the boot factory, parked under a dripping elm, I listened to Linda Hillier and her callers. She had the talkback touch: silk and steel, kiss them and kick them. Touch had always been her strong point. Early in our relationship, we'd sat in this car at this spot, glued at the mouth, hands going about their business, the business hands want to go about.

But that was long ago.

I killed the radio and lugged the shopping bags upstairs.

32

Each year, the eventide falls faster and only sound and activity can hold the gate. I lit the fire, put on some Mahler, loud, got busy cooking, rang Cyril Wootton's numbers, all of them. I found him in the last refuge of the scoundrel: home.

'My God,' he said, 'where are you, what's that ghastly noise?'

I turned down the volume. 'The person. There's room for speculation here.'

'Matter's closed. You've been remunerated.' The clipped military tone was blurred by a long day of duplicity and substance abuse.

'Time on the meter, as you well know. Tell the client your information is that the official explanation doesn't hold up.'

I could hear him suck his teeth.

'Get back to you, old fruit,' he said.

Back was five minutes. 'The client would like a meeting. Maximum discretion is required.'

'And who,' I said, 'is better equipped to provide that?'

Then I rang Cam's latest number. A woman answered, light voice, not a voice I knew. 'I'll see if Mr Delray is in the mood for callers,' she said.

Cam came on. 'Jack.' He'd been close enough to hear my voice. What did that mean? Silly question.

'I'd cross Cyril off the list,' I said. 'There are things you can't fake.'

'Glad to hear it. Monday morning, free early? Eight-fifteen? We could eat.'

'What meal is that, your time?'

'Too soon to know yet. Pick you up where?'

'Charlie's. He's away. I've been slacking. Bring something.'

I ate in front of the television, watching the first part of a

British drama about a middle-aged artist with an unsympathetic wife, a doctor. The man hit the singing sauce closer to breakfast than lunch, rooted the nanny in the mid-afternoon lull and, before dinner, wine glass in hand, delivered a withering attack on bureaucrats, multinationals, cultural imperialists, and people he didn't like much.

I identified strongly. Not much later, I went to bed and succumbed to the arms of Milo. One day these crumbly grains will be a listed substance, prescription only, traded on cold streets, the price floating on the surging sea of supply and demand.

'Do you know who I am?' the man in the perfect dark suit asked.

I nodded. My inclination on seeing him had been to leave and, later, to chastise Wootton severely for not warning me. 'What would you like me to call you?'

He hesitated for an instant. 'Colin will be fine.'

The waiter arrived, a plump young woman in black, not fully alert yet. In that condition, we were companions.

'Weak latte for me, please,' said Mr Justice Colin Loder.

'Short black.'

The judge was short and trim. His curly dark hair was razor-cut, parted at the left with the aid of a ruler. He looked as if he'd gone to sleep before 9 p.m. the night before, and come to our meeting fresh from swimming five kilometres followed by a full-body massage. I envied that in a man.

We were sitting at the window table in a cafe called Zanouff's in Kensington, in Bellair Street, across the road from the station. You could see the trains taking the condemned into the city.

'Don't judges have flunkeys they send out on business like this?'

'Good flunkeys are hard to find these days,' he said.

Colin Loder put his elbows on the table, put his fingertips together. Steepling they called it in the body-language trade. 'You have something to tell me about Robert's death.'

'I don't think it was an accidental overdose.'

A deadpan look. 'Why would you know better than the police?'

I gave him a dose of steepling. He noticed. 'It's hard to know what the police know,' I said. 'You can't find out from what they say.'

He unsteepled, moved his mouth, almost a smile. 'Like politicians. What do *you* know?'

'I don't like the proposition that someone doesn't come home for days and when he does, he accidentally overdoses in his garage.'

Colin Loder's black eyes were on me. 'But it's possible, isn't it?'

I said, 'Yesterday I was told that the police were interested in Robbie before his death.'

He touched his chin with a finger, brushed the blue cleft. 'Told by?'

I looked at him, letting him know I wasn't going to answer, my expression telling him, you're not in your court now, Mr Justice Loder.

He held my gaze and then his mouth moved, a tiny twitch of the ruby lips. He'd got it.

'What does interested mean?' he said. 'Exactly?'

'It's an inexact term.'

'Here we go,' said the plump serving person, striving to be cheerful. 'Weak latte and a short.'

We watched a train leave the station.

Colin Loder sipped, put his cup down. He wasn't going to lift it again. He wasn't meeting me for coffee, probably didn't drink coffee, for health and fitness reasons.

I tried mine. Terrible. 'Would you know about police interest in Robbie?'

He raised an eyebrow. 'No, I wouldn't know about that.'

Spots of rain on the tarmac outside. I wanted to end this encounter, drive to Meaker's and there drink decent coffee and dwell on more interesting matters. For example, the form for Cranbourne.

'Well, I thought I should express my doubts to you,' I said. 'I've done that. And the coroner will probably agree with the police.'

I stood up. He didn't.

'It's Jack Irish?'

'Yes.' He knew that.

'Someone said he couldn't understand how you kept your practising certificate.'

'Someone?'

'I mentioned your name to someone.'

'Tell someone I'm of a lovable disposition and my legal clients don't complain,' I said. 'That's how I keep my practising certificate. Nice meeting you.'

He held up a placatory hand, a pink-palmed soft hand. 'Sit down, Jack.'

Reluctantly, I did.

'I'm sorry,' the judge said. 'That was impertinent of me. And I'm sure your doubts are well founded.'

I didn't want an apology. I wanted a reason to leave.

'Well, obviously we need to know more,' he said.

'I don't think there's anything more I can do.'

He looked down. 'I'd deem it a kindness.'

Pleading is hard to bear, even a judge's pleading. 'It would save lots of money if someone gave me Robbie's history,' I said.

'This may sound strange, but I don't know anything about him. Just that he came from Sydney and was a casual barman at The Green Hill.'

'I'll tell you what I know about Robbie,' I said. 'He lived alone in a one-bedroom unit. The neighbours liked him. He put in a light bulb for the old lady downstairs, took her garbage out a few times. He wasn't seen often but he came and went without any noise. That's it.'

Loder nodded. 'Did he have a drug habit?'

'Hard to tell. Not one that left marks on him. Can I be impertinent and ask why you wanted him found if you don't know anything about him?'

He sighed. 'He's related to someone. The person turned to me for help. People think…people in my position can reverse gravity, change the orbit of the earth.'

'So this relative could tell you or me about him?'

'No. The person hadn't been in touch with Robert for a long time. Then she met him again, briefly, and then she lost touch. And so she came to me and I contacted Cyril Wootton.'

'May I ask why you didn't consult the police? My understanding is that they come when people in your position call.'

'I chose to hire someone to find Robert.' A pause. 'Which brings us to where we are now.'

I looked at the street. A man in a raincoat was approaching, something on a string leading him. It looked like a hairy loaf of bread.

We had a short time of not speaking. The rain was getting harder. I heard him run his hands over his temples, the faintest sound of palms over freshly shorn hair, an electric hiss.

'This could turn out to be a complete waste of money,' I said. 'It probably will.'

'If the police won't consider other possibilities, then we must.' He looked at his watch. His wrists were hairy, wiry hairs peeping out under the Rolex. 'I must run,' he said. 'Enjoy your coffee.'

He dropped a note on the counter, didn't wait for change. I watched him walk briskly in the direction of Macaulay Road.

The green hill was once in the worst part of South Melbourne. Now there was no worst part: the whole area was a pulsating real-estate opportunity. Even the most charmless flat-roofed 1950s yellow-brick sign-writer's shop could be transformed into a minimalist open-plan dwelling suitable for thrusting young e-people.

In defiance of the weather, many of these people were sitting at tables outside The Green Hill, a three-storey Victorian pile. Perhaps the telephone reception was bad inside: at least half of them were talking on mobiles so small that they appeared to be speaking to their fists. As I approached, a short-haired and skeletal waiter wearing a long black apron came out and served coffees to two men, both on the phone. I got to him at the glass double doors.

'The bar,' I said. 'How do I find the bar?'

He tilted his head, eyed me. His skin had a shiny water-resistant look. 'Bar X? Che's Bar? Or Down the Pub?'

Too much choice. 'I need to talk to someone about a casual barman who worked here.'

'Human Resources.' He pointed. 'In there, up the stairs, door's straight ahead.'

Economical.

I went into a lobby, an empty room with a marble-tiled floor, dark wood-panelled walls, a single painting lit by a spotlight: it was an early Tucker, an angry painting, a political painting, from the heart. At least they hadn't hung it in Bar X. Doors to the left and right were unlabelled. The staircase was to the right, a splendid thing of hand-carved steam-bent cedar and barley sugar turnings. I ascended.

The door opposite was open. I knocked anyway.

'In, in,' said a male voice.

He was at a long table, a stainless-steel top on black metal trestles, fingers on a keyboard, monitors, printers and other hardware on his flanks.

'Gerald,' he said, smiling, a round-headed man around thirty, balding, olive-skinned, in a collarless white shirt.

'Me or you?'

'You're not Gerald?'

'No.'

His smile went. 'We're currently only hiring in kitchen. And if your CV shines.'

'Glitters,' I said, 'but not currently in the market. You employed a casual barman called Robert Colburne.'

He sat back. 'Police? You've been here.'

'No. I represent his family.'

Represent is a good word. It suggests.

'I'll tell you what I told the cops. Colburne worked here for five weeks, three shifts a week. A few times we called him in to fill a hole. He was fine, he was tidy, people liked him. But nobody here knows him, knew him. Outside work, that is.' He held up his palms.

'He had another job, did he?'

He shrugged. 'Don't know.' Pause. 'How come his family don't know?'

'Drifted apart, lost touch.'

'The cops wanted to find the next of kin. Has the family been in touch?'

'I presume so. Did Robbie come with references?'

'References only mean anything for kitchen staff in this

business. He said he'd worked all over the place. Queensland. We gave him a one-hour trial. He knew what he was doing.'

'Anyone around who worked with him? Just so that I can tell the family I talked to a colleague.'

There was a slight unease about him, something more than having his time wasted. He cleared his throat, picked up a slim telephone handset. 'I'll see.'

He tapped three numbers. 'Janice, call up Robbie Colburne's last three shifts, see if anyone on them's here now.'

We waited. He didn't look at me, looked at the computer screen on his right. Figures in columns, a payroll possibly.

'Okay, thanks.' He put the handset down. 'Down the Pub. Ask for Dieter.'

'Thanks. I appreciate your help.'

He didn't say anything, didn't smile, just nodded, looked at the screen again.

You couldn't get into Down the Pub from the street. Entry was through a heavy studded door in a narrow lane separating The Green Hill from its neighbour. No need for passing trade here. Beyond the door was a vestibule and then you passed through small-paned glass doors into a long room where lamps in mirrored wall niches cast a warm and calm yellow light. The walls were wood panelled to the ceiling, there were booths and tables with leather chairs, and the oak bar with brass fittings was like an altar to drink.

The place was almost empty: two couples in a booth, three men at a table, two lingering male drinkers at the bar. I stood at the counter as far from them as possible. The barman stopped polishing a glass and was in front of me in an instant.

'Sir,' he said. He was tall with wavy dark hair and a neat beard.

'I'm looking for Dieter.'

'I am Dieter.' A German accent.

'Jack Irish,' I said. We shook hands. 'You knew Robbie Colburne?'

'Not too well, a colleague for a short time,' he said. 'It's very sad. Are you family?'

'He lost contact with his family.'

Dieter recognised the evasion. 'So you're not family?'

'No. I'm acting for the family.' I was, at a small remove.

'Acting? I don't…'

'I'm a lawyer.'

'Legal business?'

'Sort of, yes. There's an estate involved.' There had to be.

He nodded. 'I saw him here only. A friendly person, a person easy to work with. Yes. Not like some.'

'Friends?'

'Friends?'

'Barmen have friends. They make friends.'

'Oh, friends? I don't know. He was friendly to everyone. But that's part of the job.'

'So he didn't have any personal friends come in?'

'Excuse me, sir.' Alerted by something, he left me to pour a glass of red from an open bottle. I glimpsed the label: a Burgundy, a Pommard. Dieter took the drink over to the florid man at the opposite end of the bar and came back.

'Robbie's friends,' I said.

'Yes. No. Not here at work.'

A voice behind me said, 'Now Dieter, the guest hasn't got a drink, what's goin on?'

It was an Irish voice, a lovely purring, lilting Irish voice.

The owner was a man in a tweed suit, a pale, handsome man in his mid-thirties with dense black curly hair, red lips and perfect teeth. He had his hand out to me and he was smiling.

'Xavier Doyle,' he said. 'I'm the publican here and I don't know your face and I want to do somethin about that.'

'Jack Irish,' I said.

'Irish? There's a name to make a man sing. What'll you be drinkin? First one's on the house, first and a few too many in the middle says the accountant. Got no heart, these counters of beans.'

He was a man you could like without thinking about it.

'A beer,' I said.

'Not just a beer in this establishment.' He waved. 'Dieter, my fine Teutonic friend, a couple of pints of the Shamrock, there's a good lad.'

'Sir.' Dieter slid off.

Doyle leaned his back against the bar, patted my arm. 'Now Jack, the feller upstairs says you're askin about young Robbie. There's a tragedy for you. Why would a young feller like that get into the drugs? We'll never know, that's the answer, isn't it ?'

'Someone who knew him well might know.'

'I can't say that I did, Jack. I wish I could. You'd like to know all your staff well, wouldn't you? But there's near sixty work here and they're comin and goin, grass's always greener, and the competition always out to poach em.' He paused, a sad look. 'So, no, I can't say I knew Robbie well. But an excellent worker, top of the class, we'd a put him on permanent at the drop.'

The beers came, silver tankards topped with two fingers of foam.

'Let's get in front of some of this Irish gold,' said Doyle. He had a way of holding your eyes, as if looking into them gave him great pleasure.

We drank. It wasn't bad stuff. I wiped off my foam moustache. 'Robbie didn't want a full-time job?'

'Bernie asked him but he said he had other commitments.'

'Another job?'

'Entirely possible. How'd you like this beer?'

'I like it.' I drank some more. He drank, wiped his lips with a red handkerchief drawn from his top pocket.

'Next time you come we'll be drinkin The Green Hill pinot noir. We're takin delivery of vintage number one in a coupla days. From our own little estate out there on the Mornington. Nectar, I tell you, a drop fit for a crowned head.'

He waved at the barman.

'Some of them pecan nuts, Dieter lad. Now Jack, you're in the legal line the boyo says. That's the solicitorin, is it? Or are you one of them fellers wears a ferret on his head?'

'Solicitor.'

Dieter positioned a silver bowl of pecan nuts.

'Good few of your kind drop in here,' said Doyle. 'Corporate, a lot of em, the Lord knows what they do. How'd you get involved in this unfortunate affair?'

I chewed a nut. 'His relatives,' I said. 'Lost touch with him, now they want to know a bit more about his life.'

Doyle nodded. 'Perfectly understandable.' He flashed a cuff, looked at his watch. 'Day's flyin away from me. Jack, it's a pleasure to meet you. We'll be seein more of you now? Promise me that.'

'Promise,' I said. 'Xavier.'

'Call me Ex,' he says. 'It's what they call me.' He turned his head to Dieter. 'Fix this feller in your mind,' he said, 'and take proper care of him.'

He was at the inside door when he turned and came back. 'Next week we're launchin this little cookbook we've knocked out, Jack. *The Green Hill Food* it's called. Lots of the legal brotherhood comin. And the sisterhood, mind you. Your presence is required. Got a card on you?

On the way out, I waved goodbye to Dieter. He was standing at a hatch talking to a young woman on the other side. They were both looking at me. He waved back, a polite wave.

Outside, in the rain, the meter had long expired and the Stud had a note under the driver's wiper. It read: 'If you ever consider selling this, ring me.' There was a name and a number and, after it, in parentheses, the words Traffic Inspector. Such is luck.

'Kashboli?' I said, studying the menu. 'What does Kashboli mean?'

'Where have you been, Jack?' asked Andrew Greer, my former law partner and friend since law school. 'Kashmiri plus Bolivian. Two interesting cuisines.'

I loosened my tie. 'With absolutely fuck-all in common.'

'Exactly. Until united by fusion cuisine.'

We were sitting in the window of Kashboli, an eating and drinking place on lower Lygon Street whose premises had previously housed a famous Carlton drycleaning establishment. Where a bar with a mosaic top now stood, garments were once handed over, precious garments, mainly Italian men's items handed over by Italian women—dinner jackets the men had proposed in, wedding suits, good linen trousers, dark single-vent jackets, many let out a bit at the seams by the skilled fingers of loved ones. It had been my drycleaner when I was a five-suit man practising criminal law with Andrew in nearby Drummond Street.

'Hello, young lovers, wherever you are.'

A seriously big man, big and fat man, in loose white garments, shaven skull, no neck, head like a nipple with features, had appeared behind the bar, sang the line in a singing pose, chin raised, hands up, palms outwards.

Andrew gave him a wave. So did all the other patrons, late-working trade unionists from headquarters down the road by the grim and dedicated look of them.

'Our host, Ronnie Krumm,' said Drew.

'Is that Kashmiri Ronnie Krumm or Bolivian Ronnie Krumm?'

'Neither. Ronnie's from Perth, travelled widely in search of the new. I understand the family's in hardware, very big in the hardware.'

'Hardware, software, Ronnie's big all over. What's the fat content of Kashboli tucker?'

Drew was intent on the menu. 'Excessive but only good fats. Premium, I'm told. No finer fats available. Well, what's your fancy or will you be guided?'

'Be my trained labrador.'

Drew ordered what appeared to be a form of fish stew. It came in minutes, a minefield of a dish. You chewed uneventfully and then you bit on anti-personnel chillies and your eyes lit up from behind. Fortunately, it came with a glass of a sweet off-white substance, a neutralising agent, possibly crushed antacid tablets in a sugar solution.

'Interesting,' I said, recovering. 'Fusion brings electrocution. Tell me about The Green Hill.'

Drew was savouring the Kashboli fish and chilli stew with no sign of strain, no resort to the pale liquid.

'The Green Hill? He raised his glass of Bolivian cabernet to the light, his eyes narrowed, the long face took on a stained-glass religious look. 'Not your kind of place. Very few geriatrics arguing about football at The Green.'

'Tell me,' I said.

'Thinking of taking someone? A date, is it?'

'With destiny. It's for a Wootton client. And I've been there. This afternoon.'

'Shit. Boring. How is the love life?'

'She's taking pictures in Europe. Not enough time between assignments.'

'To do what?'

'Fly home for twenty-whatever hours and go back the next week.'

'Serious concern?'

'I suppose.'

'Extremely fetching person. In a mildly intimidating sort of way. Not talkative exactly,' said Drew.

'No. Well, she can be. Depends.'

'Yes. All life depends. It's pendant.'

'The Green Hill?'

'Testimony to one man's dream,' Drew said. 'Xavier Doyle, heard of him?'

'I met him. Very affable. He shouted me a pint of Shamrock, told me to call him Ex.'

'Radiates charm, Mr Doyle. Gave character for a bloke of mine, waiter at The Green, stark naked outside the National Gallery on New Year's Eve, pointed his bum at a cop. By the time Doyle was finished, I thought the mago was going to award the lad compensation.'

Ronnie Krumm was coming our way, a white tent with a large shining head where the flagpole should be, hipping his was through the tables.

'Everything all right?'' he said. 'Not too hot for you?'

'Was this a hot one?' said Drew. 'Ronnie Krumm, Jack Irish. Jack used to be my law partner.'

I shook Ronnie's fleshy hand.

'And you eat together,' said Ronnie. 'Amaazing. I'm still trying to kill my ex-partner.'

'I never heard you say that,' said Drew. 'Call me when you succeed, I'll see what I can do.'

Ronnie winked and moved on to one of the tables of trade unionists.

'Yes,' said Drew. 'Xavier Doyle, the boy's a dreamer and a doer. Cook from Dublin, guitar player, he sees the huge old place, used to be a temperance pub, falling down. So he finds the money to buy it, plus megabucks for renovations.'

'How do you do that?' I tried to defuse a bite of stew with a big swig of the Bolivian.

'I don't know exactly. They say he won over Mike Cundall. And Mrs Cundall, no doubt. And now he's in with little Sam Cundall and the Sydney sharks, tendering for ski resorts and casinos.'

The Cundall family were in commercial property, carparks, mortgage lending, internet dream factories, many other things. They also gave away large sums and, by all accounts, turned on a good party.

'Cannon Ridge. How do you know he's in that?'

Drew was looking into his glass. 'Because I know things. So what's the interest in The Green?'

'Someone called Robbie Colburne was a casual barman there. Dead of an overdose.'

He drank, rolled the wine in his mouth, squinted. 'Bolivian,' he said in wonder. 'Excellent. Half the price of an equivalent local drop. And made by Aussie mercenaries. What happened to loyalty? Patriotism?'

'You sound like Cyril.'

'Now there's a patriot. Fought abroad for his country.'

'Which broad was that?'

He gave me the Greer frown. 'Very weak, Jack. It's all that buggering around with carpentry. You don't do enough law. Keeps the mind alert. So what's the problem with a dead waiter? The more the merrier, I say. Did he have a ponytail?'

'A barman. I'm told the cops were interested in him.'

'Always interested in barmen, the cops. Source of free

drinks. I ran into your sister the other day.' His eyes were not on me; they were on something behind me.

'It's usually the other way around,' I said. 'Did she mention that she's uninsurable?'

'At lunch with my friends the Pratchetts.'

Dick Pratchett QC was the doyen of the criminal bar, a huge bearded man who cross-examined in a hoarse whisper and sometimes waited for answers with his eyes closed. Juries loved him and so did many murderers and lesser criminals roaming free.

I said, 'Ah. The trophy bride. Rosa's friend.'

Pratchett had recently married my sister Rosa's doubles partner, a woman a good 20 years his junior. Strike three.

'An attractive person,' said Drew, still not looking at me. 'Intelligent to boot.'

'If you like booting. Her predecessor's IQ just topped her chest size. Considerable for a chest but only for a chest.'

'Rosa, I'm talking about your sister.' Drew met my eyes, looked uneasy. 'We're having lunch on Sunday.'

'My sister. That's an entirely different matter.'

Rosa was rich, spoilt beyond redemption. But it wasn't the money that did it. It was being the focus of three adults' lives. My maternal grandparents' money had all gone to her and she used it to do nothing. Unless shopping, playing tennis, having brief affairs with unsuitable men and agonising over life constituted doing something.

I let Drew wait. Then I said, 'She usually lunches with young men. Spunks. Studs. Studs in their ears, studs elsewhere.'

He still wasn't too keen to hold my gaze, looked over my shoulder again. 'More of a meeting of minds, this. No objection is there?'

I studied him, shook my head. 'Really, Drew, you can look at me when you raise matters like this.'

He looked at me. 'Well?'

'It's your life.'

'What's that mean? Of course it's my fucking life. Don't you approve?'

'Approval doesn't come into it.'

'So you don't approve?'

'Forget this approval stuff. You're not asking for my permission, are you?

'Well, no. Yes, I suppose I am.'

'Don't. I don't give permissions.'

A long silence. I thought he was going to get up and leave, let me pay for the explosive fish stew.

'So,' he said. 'Not a good idea, you think.'

We fingered our glasses.

'Fucking awful idea,' I said. 'From my point of view.'

Drew filled our glasses. 'Exactly why is that?'

I'd never been called upon to do something like this. Since her mid-teens, Rosa had always had two photographs beside her bed: a photograph of Bill Irish, the father she never knew, and one of me, in tennis clothes, the older brother to whom she told everything, whether he wanted to hear it or not.

In short, I knew too much.

'The risk is,' I said, 'the risk is that between the two of you you'll end up creating some fucking vast, treeless, mined no-go area. For me.'

'For you?'

'For me. This is about me. You're asking me.'

'What about me?'

'How can I say this? You're a divorced prick looking for

love and affection. Rosa, on the other hand, is only looking for romance. Do I have to say more?'

Drew considered this statement, looking at me. Then he said, 'No, your honour.' He emptied his glass. 'Let's get the other half.'

Over at the trade union table, an argument had broken out between a short-haired woman with thick-lensed glasses and a man with a wispy beard. 'The question isn't whether it's a women's issue,' said the man, 'it's whether it's a union issue.'

The woman looked at the ceiling and said through tight lips, 'This is so fucking unbelievably eighties, it makes me want to puke.'

'A lot to be said for the eighties,' Drew said, signalling to a waiter. 'Bernie Quinlan kicked 116 in '83.'

'That was '84.'

'No, he only kicked 105 in '84.'

There was a moment of non-recognition, then the old woman said, 'Mr Irish, yeah, wait on.'

I heard the boards complain as she went back down the passage. Through the crack in the door came a smell of cat pee, pine-scented disinfectant, paint and food cooked to disintegration.

The old planks signalled Mrs Nugent's return. She opened the door, revealing that she was wearing a yellow plastic raincoat. 'Paintin,' she said. 'The kitchen. Here.' She offered me a suitcase. 'Good clothes, mind you give em to the boy's rellies.'

'Have no fear,' I said. 'It was the landlord, was it?'

I'd left my card with Robbie Colburne's neighbour and she'd been on the answering machine when I got back from The Green Hill.

'Yeah. Come round yesterdee. Give me $20 to clean up the place. Take anythin I liked, give the rest to the Salvos, throw it away.' She hesitated. 'Money's money.' A further hesitation. 'The towels and that, the kitchen stuff. Kept that.'

'Right thing to do,' I said. 'Didn't find anything with an address on it? Letter, anything?'

She shook her head. 'Them others coulda taken anythin like that.'

'Others? Police?'

'Police? Yeah, spose. Who else? Young blokes.'

'Not in uniform?'

Mrs Nugent looked at me with fowl eyes. 'Been in

uniform I wouldn't have to bloody spose, would I? Haven't gone that stupid.'

'No. Sorry. They take anything away?'

'Dunno.'

I got out my wallet. She held up a hand, palm outwards.

'Don't want no money. Just give the suitcase to the family. Tell em the neighbour says he was a nice young bloke. Had manners. Musta bin brought up right. Only saw him the coupla times in the beginnin, don't know he actually lived here.'

'I'll tell them,' I said. 'Thank you, Mrs Nugent.'

'And tell 'em I'm sorry.'

I was at the stairs, carrying the soft-sided black nylon suitcase, when the thought came to me. Mrs Nugent opened the door as if she'd been standing just inside it.

'Sorry,' I said. 'His car. Is it still in the garage?'

'Nah. Someone come and took it. Old Percy downstairs seen him.'

Percy wasn't at home. I drove the short distance from Abbotsford to my office in Carrigan's Lane. The greening brass plate said: *John Irish, Barrister & Solicitor.* As I put the suitcase on the old tailor's worktable that served as my desk, the feeling of guilt that had been with me for a while stabbed me. I should not have taken it from Mrs Nugent. I did not represent Robbie's family. I was just sniffing around for Cyril Wootton, and was being paid by someone who was probably not being entirely candid.

Take it back? And confess what? No. As for the client, who was I to worry? I was no stranger to economy in truth, economy and selectivity.

I opened the suitcase.

Robbie Colburne travelled light: leather toilet bag, two

55

pairs of black trousers, a pair of chinos, three black tee-shirts, three white shirts, a black jacket, a tweed jacket, a black leather jacket, a nylon windbreaker, an expensive-feeling woollen jumper, a pair of shiny black shoes, a pair of runners, old running shorts, a washed-out grey tee-shirt, black socks, underpants. And, on a wooden coathanger, a dinner suit, dress shirt, and black bow tie.

Nothing in the suitcase pockets. I looked at the shirts. Nice, superfine cotton by the feel, no labels. I picked up the black jacket, stroked it. It was light and soft—wool and cashmere, perhaps, no label. The tweed jacket was newish, beautifully cut. No label.

I opened the single-breasted dinner jacket. A product of Canali of Italy. A small label on the inside pocket said Charles Stuart. I knew Charles Stuart, they were men's outfitters in William Street in the city, men's outfitters to the big end of town. If you didn't fit that demographic, crossing the threshold of Charles Stuart's was a post-death experi-ence: a buffed-up person wearing three grand's worth of the shop's stock examined you from top to toe, weighed up your clothing and footwear history, registered all your sartorial sins, made a judgment, came closer and said, lips like a cash-machine slot, 'May I help you, sir?'

I examined the shoes: Italian. I unzipped the toilet bag. It held a silver razor in a slim stainless-steel case, a bottle of Neale's Yard shaving oil, French deodorant, a toothbrush, French toothpaste, nail clippers, a Bakelite comb. I opened the shaving oil and sniffed. An expensive smell, clean. I inspected the toothpaste, squeezed some onto a fingertip, held it to my nose. Lavender.

Robbie Colburne might have been living in a one-bedroom flat in a low-rent block and working as a casual barman but his effects all shouted money and style.

That observation didn't advance things much. I repacked the suitcase, feeling the outside of pockets as I went. The dinner suit was last. I ran my hand over the jacket's outside pockets, felt something at the left hip. I lifted the flap, tried to insert cautious fingers, couldn't. It was a dummy pocket. Of course. What tailor would allow the line of a dinner jacket to be spoiled by something stuffed into a hip pocket?

Through the cloth, I felt the object again. Something the length of a pen cap, flat, no thicker than a stick of chewing gum. I opened the jacket and found the small inside pocket, a sturdy pocket designed to hold a single key, extracted the object. It was a plastic stick, dark-blue, a recessed button on one side. a hole in the front. I pressed the button. A red light glowed in the hole for a second or two. I did it again. The light went off even when the button remained depressed.

Today's mystery object. Nothing to identify it, say what it was for.

I put the device in my wallet, zipped the suitcase, put it in the small back room, sat at my table and eyed the unopened mail. Once letters held promise. Now I couldn't think of anyone who'd write an undemanding letter to me, pen your actual personal letter, fingers holding a writing instrument, hand touching paper. I thought about letters I'd read by fast-dying light, sniffed, imagined I'd caught a scent, held up, looked for a touch of sweat or the smear of a tear. Even, hoping against hope, the ghostly imprint of a kiss, just a touch of lips, leaving a mark.

Just a touch of lips. Lips left their mark, they all did, like branding irons, you felt them forever.

There was nothing left that I had to do or wanted to do. Midday Saturday. Once it had been the peak of the week.

I went to the window and looked at the street. Rain on the tarmac, oilslick-shiny pools in the bluestone gutters. Across the way, outside the clothing factory, a man in a four-wheel-drive had tried to shoot me one night.

The phone rang.

'Jack Irish.'

A sigh. 'Tried the boot factory, the furniture place, the mobile. Then I found this other number with Jack written next to it.'

Lyall. The dry, precise voice made the room seem brighter; no, the clouds must have thinned.

'I don't think we've ever conversed at my professional premises,' I said. 'Do you wish to consult me professionally?'

'I'm in Santa Barbara,' she said.

'Santa Barbara. What kind of trouble have they got there?'

'Understanding a sentence that doesn't mention Steven Spielberg or money. The ones I've met, anyway. I'm staying with Bradley.'

Staying with Bradley was fine from my point of view. Bradley was a former housemate of Lyall's, a film director. That wasn't what made him fine from my point of view. What made him fine was that he was gay.

'Extend my regards.'

'Brad's come out of the closet,' she said, voice low, serious.

'How many times can you do that?'

'It turns out,' she said, 'he's not gay.'

'They've done tests?'

She laughed. I'd been taken with her laugh from the outset, but it wasn't that laugh now. It was her laugh with something subtracted.

'He says he's never been gay, he's not even bi. He's been

58

celibate for twelve years. I just assumed that because he didn't want to screw me or any other woman he was gay.'

'Not an unreasonable assumption,' I said. I still remembered her exact words on that wintry night when we were still near-strangers.

I was in love with him for years. Never mentioned it. No point. He's gay. Huge loss to womankind.

I felt the weight of realisation, of knowing, on my shoulders, a dead weight, a bag of lead sinkers. A silence ensued.

'Jack.'

'Yes.' I could hear the soundless sound of her gathering courage.

'I'm attached, no, I'm in love with both of you. It's very difficult.'

'Torn between two lovers, acting like a fool,' I said. 'The old song. Or is it feeling like a fool? I've got something on the stove.' There are times when you will say anything.

'Jack.'

'Yes.'

'Don't dump me so quickly. This isn't easy. I've agonised over this.'

I said, without thought, 'Lyall, you're in Santa Barbie Doll or wherever and you're fucking Bradley, he's first-up from a spell, and you'd like to tell me about that and how difficult it is for you. Consider me told.'

Silence. Not even a hum from the copper wire that lay down there in the deep Pacific blackness consorting with the bottom-crawling sea life.

'Told,' she said. Click.

I sat there for a while, thinking that I needed a drink, needing a drink. Then I talked to myself for a while, recited the mantra about the black tunnel, and went home. There were things to do. It was time to clear the decks, to confront places long avoided. I cleaned the apartment from beginning to end, a ferocious attack on dirt in which I dusted pelmets and picture rails and skirting boards, washed floors, vacuumed carpets, defrosted the freezer, scrubbed the refrigerator, the stovetop, the oven. Then I turned on my grocery cupboard, threw out ancient spices, old flour, rusted cans of food I couldn't remember buying. Next, I laid into my clothes. Frayed shirts, unloved shirts, shapeless underwear, two old sweaters, lonely socks, a dark suit turning green, a jacket I'd never liked—they all went into a garbage bag and thence to the boot of the Stud. The Salvos could turn them into usable fibres. Then I stuffed two laundry bags with soiled clothes and sheets and table napkins and towels and delivered them into the cleansing hands of the Brunswick Street laundry. Next stop, King & Godfree in Lygon Street, where I bought exotic food and drink without regard for my penury.

At home, at the top of the stairs, a bag in each hand, the manic energy suddenly left me. I steeled myself for one final effort: pour cider over pork sausages in pot, put in oven. Halve tomatoes, quarter potatoes, put on tray, pour on olive oil, put in oven under sausages. Set oven on low. Open bottle of Carlsberg, lie on sofa, read the *Age*. Later on, I ate, drank a bottle of Cotes du Rhone grenache, watched the Saints get thrashed by West Coast, didn't care, a lot, wanted the phone to ring so much that it felt like a bodily ache.

In bed, I resisted the urge to burrow beneath the pillows and breathe carbon dioxide. I read my book. There should be a set number of endings in each life. No-one should have more. Experts could decide how many and enshrine that in the Charter of Human Rights.

But it would be too late for me.

I woke up thinking about Lyall and determinedly switched thoughts to my daughter, Claire. She was pregnant to Eric, her Scandinavian fishing boat skipper. Before my recent visit, I hadn't seen her for more than two years and, in full adult, barefoot, tropical bloom, she was shockingly different. She'd looked like my mother. My mother young and happy. I could not remember seeing my mother either young or happy, but I knew from the photographs that this was how she had looked. Claire was now very beautiful and my first sight of her had left me wrong-footed, unabled.

I had no guilt to carry in regard to Claire. Well, less guilt perhaps. It is all a matter of degree.

Her mother, my first wife, Frances, had left Claire's place in Queensland only hours before I'd arrived. She was still married to the man she'd left me for long ago, a surgeon, thin and pinstriped Richard, and Claire had two half-siblings, boys I'd encountered three or four times a year while Claire was growing up. Richard was your normal medical specialist: straight As for maths and science, no personality that would show up on any test. Nevertheless, he'd clearly touched something in Frances when he'd operated to fix an old tennis injury. Soon after, she departed without warning from the conjugal dwelling, taking with her one-year-old Claire. The next day, Richard arrived at my old law office in Carlton.

'Mr Wiggins to see you, Mr Irish,' said the secretary.

He was as pink and clean as a newly bathed baby and

wearing a suit worth more than I was making in a fortnight, gross. Primed to the eyebrows, hardly inside the door, he said, spitting it out, 'I'm here to tell you I'm in love with Frances and plan to marry her when she's free.'

I was late for court, looking for things. 'Steady on,' I said. 'Now what Frances is that?'

He coughed. 'Your, ah, wife. Frances.'

I said, 'Right, that Frances. You plan to do what with her?'

'Jack,' he said, 'I know this is a painful…'

'Wiggins,' I said. 'Aren't you her surgeon?'

Richard touched his razor-abrased chin. 'I did first meet Frances as a patient, yes, but…'

'Professional misconduct,' I said. 'I think your future lies in medical missionary work. Leper colonies, that kind of thing.'

His lips twitched. 'Jack, I assure you that I have not in any way contravened—'

'What's your first name?' I interrupted.

'Richard.' He saw hope, shot a cuff, put out a slim white-marble hand.

I ignored it. 'Save the assurances for the disciplinary hearing, sunshine. Now, I'm busy, so see yourself out will you?'

He gathered his dignity, head to one side. 'Unless the patient is the complainant, Jack, there really isn't…'

I was putting papers into my briefcase. 'Wiggy,' I said, 'you cut the flesh, I'll do the legal argument. In case she turns out not worth sacrificing a career for, try the sister. Some of the blokes prefer her.'

Cruel. Cruel and unnecessary, but the wounded animal is without compunction.

On this chilly Melbourne morning, many years later, time

having healed some wounds, put fragile scabs over others, inflicted new ones, I drove down Carrigan's Lane, its sole streetlight making gleams on the bluestone gutter. It was still dark as I unlocked the side door to Taub's Cabinetmaking, clicked on the lights, noted the bulbs gone: three. Charlie wouldn't have fluorescent lighting and no day passed there without me risking my life up a ladder replacing incandescent bulbs.

The workshop was as Charlie had left it on the day he flew to Perth to attend the marriage of his youngest granddaughter to someone in the quarry business. His idea had been to be back inside 24 hours but he had been prevailed upon to spend ten days with another grandchild and his family.

Before he left, Charlie said to the workshop, not to me, 'For what do I need a holiday?'

I was under a three-metre-long table, made of red cedar cut in northern New South Wales before World War One. Charlie bought the timber in 1962, wrote the date on it in pencil. I was examining the perfect fit of the wooden buttons that fixed the tabletop to the frame and would allow the timber to move seasonally for a few centuries until it stabilised.

'You'll probably never want to come back,' I said. 'It's still warm. Hot. More than hot.'

He banged a huge fist on the tabletop directly above my head, causing me to feel that I was fainting.

'Hot? You tell me what's hot good for. One thing, you tell me.'

I crawled out, tympana still vibrating, got to my feet, braced myself against the table. 'People go outside and do things, go to the beach, swim.'

Charlie made his pitying noise, a sort of snort enhanced with nasal sounds. 'Exactly,' he said. 'They waste time. You think Mozart went to the beach? You hear that Liszt was a lot of the time swimming? What use is swimming, anyway?'

'It keeps you from drowning,' I said. 'In deep water.'

He rolled his cheroot between thumb and two fingers, puffed at it, shook his head in a worried way. 'Jack, Jack,' he said, 'don't go in the deep water, how can you drown? What use is swimming then?'

'I need some time on that,' I said. 'What do I do while you're away?'

He turned away, walked off towards his machines to touch them goodbye, said over his shoulder, 'Pack up and deliver the library, the lady's waiting.'

I followed him. 'Me? Are you mad? Mrs Purbrick's paying a fortune for Charlie Taub.'

'I told you already, Charlie Taub the woman got. You put a couple screws in the wall, that's it. When I come back, I check.'

'Charlie, that's not a good idea. I could ruin your reputation.'

He wound the blade of a table saw up, wound it down, an action serving no purpose. 'So ruin,' he said, subject closed. He turned his head in my direction. A new subject. 'The one with the horsetail, you know?'

I knew. The property developer who'd turned the old chutney factory in Carrigan's Lane into four desirable inner-city New York-style loft apartments, lifestyle choice plus once-in-a-lifetime blue-chip investment opportunity not to miss.

'I know,' I said, with an icepick in my heart.

'Six hundred thousand dollars.' Charlie pointed around the space.

'An offer?'

'From the agent. Clive, Clive somebody.'

'Clive Miller,' I said. The repulsive Clive, gone on from accepting fellatio in lieu of rent and from dudding poor tenants out of their rental bonds to sitting on boards and living in the best part of Kew. Clive Miller embodied the recent history of Fitzroy.

'That one. Nine hundred pounds I paid. One hundred and fifty cash down, five quid a week.'

'So?' I said.

Charlie straightened, ran a hand the size of an oven glove over the burnished surface of the cabinet, tested the stability of the fence.

'So?' I repeated, wanting to know, at that moment.

'So?' Charlie said. 'So?'

'Are you selling?'

'Selling?' The large head turned around, eyes under thatch bundles regarded me. 'My workshop? So I can go to Perth and learn to swim? So I don't drown?'

'Just asking,' I said, trying as nonchalantly as possible to get oxygen to my gasping little lung sacs.

Now I walked around the workshop, touched a few machines, just to comfort them, spent five minutes studying Mrs Purbrick's library. It was pure Charlie Taub: classical elements—pilasters, mouldings, cornices—but pared of all showiness. The eye was drawn first to the beauty of the wood, then to the perfect balance of the design, its under-statement and severity, and then, perhaps, to the craft of the joiner.

The ensemble, missing only its top and bottom

trimmings, stood assembled in a corner of the workshop. It had been sanded, grain-sealed, shellacked and polished by Charlie's finishing man, the voluble Arthur McKinley, retired coffin-maker. That work had taken six weeks. To reach the stage where the finishing could begin had taken a mere eight months because Charlie had set aside three days a week for the library. Progress might have been even faster had he had someone other than me to assist him. But speed had never been a concern for Charlie. He didn't hear clients' questions about how long a job would take.

Once, in the early days, entrusted with a small table, anxious about my progress, I asked, 'When does this have to be finished?'

Charlie had been rough-planing an 18-inch walnut board with a block plane, working at an angle to the grain to avoid tear-out. The thick plane steel, sixty years old at least, honed and strapped, could clean shave a Gulf Country feral pig. With each stroke, long translucent shavings whispered through the plane's throat, bending back with the grace of a ballerina's arm.

'When it's finished,' he said, 'that's when.'

I went to the storeroom at the back and got out the packing blankets, World War Two army blankets Charlie had bought in the 1950s. Then I disassembled the library. There was not a screw in it; secret wooden locking wedges held it together. By 8.30 a.m., I'd finished wrapping and taping the pieces. I was waiting for the water to boil and thinking about my anchovy-paste sandwich when I heard the vehicle outside.

Cam was in his stockbroker gear—chalk-striped charcoal suit, blue shirt, silk jacquard tie—and carrying a dark-blue cardboard box. He put it on the steel trolley Charlie used as a table.

'Breakfast,' he said and opened the box. 'Scrambled eggs and barbecued pork New Orleans-style on Greek bread. Coffee. Blue Mountain.'

Fusion cooking was completely out of control. What chance did an anchovy-paste sandwich and a cup of tea stand? We got going, sitting on the chairs Charlie had rescued from a skip. The pork melted in the mouth, the scrambled eggs had a faint mustard and cream taste.

'Southern barbecued pork? Greek bread?'

'Good?'

'That's not strong enough. Who's the cook?'

'Greek bloke in Brunswick, used to live in New Orleans. He's got a brick oven out the back, looks like a rocket ship. Fat rocket ship. Little pig's in about eight at night, comes from his brother in the bush, the neighbour comes off shift at 4 a.m., checks it. Bit of bastin. Ready at seven.'

'Write down the address.'

He nodded, looked at me reflectively, tongue running over his upper teeth. 'Talked to Cyn again. She's gettin better, not so vague now.

'That's good.'

We chewed in silence.

'The one, he's got a tatt down the middle finger. Right hand.'

'What kind?'

'The Saint.'

'No, don't say that.' The stick figure with the halo was St Kilda's emblem.

'She says she was at the stove, it came to her. The head and the halo. Halo bigger than the head.'

I took the cap off the coffee cup.

'Can't drink it without sugar. Needs sugar,' said Cam.

'No.' I sipped. This was coffee, Harry Palmer coffee, sugar ruined it. 'That's it?'

'No. Ring each side she thinks, gold.'

'She should go back to the jacks.'

Cam opened his coffee, added sugar from two little paper bags, stirred with the plastic implement, tasted. 'She's not happy to do that.'

Our eyes conversed. I said, 'Yes. Leave it with me. It's an exceedingly long shot and I've exhausted my welcome. But.'

He nodded, not looking at me, eyes on his coffee. 'Can't find any other way.'

'The vehicle,' I said. 'I've been thinking about the vehicle.'

'The vehicle?'

'From a carpark.'

'A carpark.' Cam looked up, into the distance, turned the eyes on me, yellow eyes, the sinews bracketing his mouth showing. Nothing more to be said.

'Do the tatt,' he said, 'then we'll do the carpark.'

'This breakfast, I owe you.'

'Dinner. Owe me dinner.'

When he'd gone I made a call about the tattoo. The man at the other end groaned.

'Jesus, fuck,' he said. 'Use the phone book.'

'Robbery with violence, maybe serious assault. Not inside on February 20.'

'Use half the phone book. Tomorrow it'll have to be. Six-thirty.'

'Not fucking bad,' said the driver.

It was 10.40 a.m. and we were in the furniture van outside the wrought-iron double gates of Mrs Purbrick's neo-Georgian mansion in Kooyong. The greasy rain on Punt Road had turned to a soft, clean mist here, further testimony to the preferential treatment handed out to the extremely rich.

The driver's name was Boz and she was a film grip, an occupation whose essence, as I understood it, was the moving of things. When not gripping films, she used this skill to cart stuff around in her vintage van. I'd met her through Kelvin McCoy, a conman artist and former client of mine who leased the building across the street from my office. Boz transported McCoy's appalling creations to his gallery in the city. He had not been receptive to my suggestion that, on these missions, the Boz vehicle should display a Hazardous Waste sign.

'There's a side door,' I said. 'Just beyond, it's probably best.' I'd hired her for the day; one person couldn't move the library bits around.

I got out and pressed the button in the wall, could have smoked a full cigarette before David, Mrs Purbrick's personal assistant, came down the gravelled driveway. His hair was wet and he bore the telltale signs of someone not long vertical.

'My dear Jack,' he said. 'Apologies in full. I was on the phone, dealing with this most dreadful rug trader. Can you believe the man's tried the old switcheroo on us?'

'The switcheroo? That's impertinent,' I said.

'My word.' He held up a key. 'I have to unlock these now. It turns out all the high-tech electronic rubbish can't keep out a 12-year-old armed with an old remote control. So much for maximum security.'

The gates swung open on silent hinges. Boz drove in and lined up the truck with the side steps to within a centimetre.

She got out, broken-nosed, six foot two, near-shaven-headed, a woman in khaki bib-and-braces overalls and a white sleeveless tee-shirt.

I introduced her to David.

'I can see you work out,' he said admiringly.

'Work out?' said Boz. 'Work out shit, I'm a manual labourer.'

David was suitably taken aback. 'Well,' he said. 'Well, I'll leave you to it.'

It took us half an hour to move the pieces of the library into its home, an empty room with deep windows looking onto the side garden.

Then the real work began.

We started with the plinths, six of them. Their fit was snug but allowed for wood movement. More important were the levels. I worked my way around the room with a long spirit level and a box of maple shims. Fortunately, the floor was true; only three thin shims needed.

Next came the base cupboards, fixed to the plinths with Charlie's hidden locking wedges. Then we put the shelf cabinets on the bases, again fixing them with secret wedges. As instructed, I screwed each cabinet to the wall with two screws that went through prepared slots. Then I slid into place the decorative cover strips that hid the expansion gaps. Finally, I attached the cornices and the skirtings.

The room was transformed. Boz and I stood looking at it. We'd worked well together, said little as we turned a bare room into a library: woodwork softly glowing, bevelled glass catching the light. With books, a library table, a few chairs, the room would be complete.

'You blokes know what you're doing,' said Boz. 'It's beautiful. Best thing I ever carted.'

'Did your bit,' I said.

I walked around, tested a few locks, opened and closed a few doors and drawers, admired the fit, even admired my hand-cut dovetail joints and raised panels. This piece of furniture would be giving pleasure long after everyone alive on this day was gone, I thought. It was not a bad thing to have helped create.

A voice said, 'Oh my God, I'm dreaming. Heaven, this room is absolute heaven.'

Mrs Purbrick, owner of the house, danced into the room, head thrown back, came around me, pirouetted with arms above her head, finished leaning back against me. It would have been girlish had not Mrs Purbrick's girlhood been somewhere in the early 1960s. She was a short blonde with a formidable bosom, all of her lifted, tucked, sucked, puffed, abraded, peeled, implanted, stripped and buffed, and, today, packaged in a short-skirted dark-grey business suit.

'Mr Taub will check the installation when he gets back,' I said. 'This is Boz Bylsma, who did the hard work today.'

Mrs Purbrick was walking around the room touching the woodwork. Her eyes flicked to Boz, summed her up, nodded. She stopped, put her head back and shouted, 'Daavid.'

David appeared. He had clearly been waiting in the passage. He looked around the room. 'Marvellous,' he said.

'Quite marvellous. In exquisite taste.' He tugged at an earlobe. 'An island of good taste.'

Mrs Purbrick fixed him with her gaze. 'I want the books in by the end of tomorrow,' she said. 'Is that clear, darling?'

'Clear? What could be clearer? Any preferences? Leatherbound Mills & Boon? Collected works of Danielle Steel? I believe there's a special on Jeffrey Archer.'

'Use your *exquisite* taste,' Mrs Purbrick said. With difficulty, she raised her eyebrows and showed her top teeth. The teeth were perfect. Some cosmetic dentist probably lay warm and slack beside a pool in Tuscany on the proceeds of that achievement.

'How I wish that that were a standing instruction,' said David, not quite tossing his head.

Mrs Purbrick tried to narrow her eyes at him. 'On your way, you dear little man.'

'Well, that's it from us,' I said. 'On behalf of Mr Taub, I wish you well to use this library.'

Mrs Purbrick came over to me, came close, the torpedoes prodding my bottom ribs, put a short-fingered hand on my cheek. 'You are so old-fashioned and courteous, I can't believe men like you still exist.'

I caught the eyes of Boz, we were even-height, eyes level, some distance above Mrs Purbrick. She was expressionless, then she blinked, just a blink.

'Frozen in time,' I said.

Mrs Purbrick moved her hand down to my chest, traced a circle with a stubby finger. 'I'm going to have to have people for drinks to show off the library, make them envious. You'll be getting an invitation, you and Mr Taub. Nothing fancy, just drinkies after five. Mike and Ros Cundall will be coming. I'm sure you know them.'

'Not in the flesh, no.'

'Lovely people. And I'm sure they need a library. God knows, they've got everything else. I was at Sam's birthday party a few weeks ago, that's the son and heir, charming young man. In the recreation wing. Wing, mark you, it's like a resort, two bars, the pool, billiard tables, gymnasium, sauna. And then there's this games room—electronic shooting things, old pinball machines, you name it, my dear.'

'A library would certainly complete the facilities,' I said. 'I look forward to receiving your invitation.'

Mrs Purbrick saw us to the side door. On the way, she ran a hand over my buttocks, no more than an appraisal, the touch a trainer might give a horse's rump at the sales. It had been a while since anyone had done that to me.

'You will come for drinks, won't you, Jack?'

'It'll require legislation to keep me away.'

'And make sure the darling Mr Taub comes.'

Going back across the river, the empty van bouncing and squeaking, I studied Boz's forearms. Long, sinews showing, just a sheen of pale hair.

'So,' she said. 'Hangin out with the rich and famous. I was on a film set where Sam Cundall was big-notin himself.'

'In films too, is he?'

'Had money in it. Just for tax. And the possibility of sex. Dud film.'

'I haven't been to drinks for years,' I said. 'I'll have to go if the invite comes through. Charlie could use another library job.'

Boz gave me an unbelieving look. 'What about this Cannon Ridge business?' she said. 'Reckon it's bent?'

We talked about the politics of the state. She had no respect for anyone. Outside Charlie's, she said, not looking at me, 'That was quick. Short-time. What d'ya reckon?'

'The deal's the deal.'

She looked at me, left hand went over her stubble. 'No. Make me a lesser offer.'

I thought about it. 'You pay for a late lunch.'

Dodging drug dealers and their customers, we walked to a Lebanese place in Smith Street where they knew me.

Seated in the window, I said, 'How's the film business?'

Boz shook her head. 'Shithouse. I'm thinkin of givin it away. There's a bloke called Sewell moves a lot of art and antiques, wants to pack it in, sell the business. Problem is I can't work out what I'd be buyin.'

'How's that?'

'It's about 90 per cent goodwill, no contracts or anythin, just customers he's had for 20 years. They could take one look at me and say so long Maryanne.'

'You know that number? Tell him you want to go through the books. Work out the percentage of turnover from each of the regular customers. Then go and see them and ask if they'll carry on hiring the firm if you buy it.'

She looked at me, fork poised. 'I could do that?'

'If he says no, walk away. How old's this bloke?'

Through the window, a few metres away, I could see a boy of about 13, a thin boy, face sharpened by the street, peachfuzz on his chin. He was someone's child, lost into the world like a puppy into an open drain, now waiting for something, someone, agitated, scratching, licking his lips, rubbing his small nose. The person came, older, bigger, stood close to him, obscured him.

'Fifty maybe, around there,' said Boz.

The boy was gone. Two girls, older, late teens, dirty hair, faces pierced in three places, were on the spot, heads moving, looking in different directions. One clutched a plastic bag.

'You'll need a restraint of trade in the contract,' I said.

'Pardon?'

'How old are you?'

'Am I asking a stupid question?'

'No. I'm just losing touch with ages. I need a baseline.'

'Thirty-six. A week ago.'

'Happy birthday.'

'Thank you.'

Her eyes were the colour of wet slate.

'Restraint of trade. It stops him selling you the business and then starting a new one in opposition to you. He's young enough to try that.'

'Jesus,' she said, 'I know fuck-all about business.'

'Do the looking at the books bit,' I said, 'then come and see me about the contract. I'm cheap.'

'McCoy says living opposite your office is a risk.'

She'd been told the story.

'McCoy likes to generalise. He's had one unfortunate experience in the street. No-one forced him to throw his chainsaw into a passing vehicle.'

She paid and we walked back to Charlie's in half-hearted rain. I went around to the driver's side of the van with her. Her hair held drops of water. She brushed a hand over her scalp, dispelled the moisture. 'Got any other libraries to put in, I'm your person,' she said, getting into the cab. 'I like your libraries.'

'The person of choice. You will be that person.'

She looked down at me. 'Jack,' she said, 'not to fuck about, I suppose you're taken.'

So plain a question.

'At this moment in time,' I said, 'no.'

'I'm the same. Well, give me a ring. Business or social.'
She started the engine. 'Here's looking down at you, kid.'

I watched her take the top-heavy old van around the tight corner, stood for a while, thinking. Boz.

No. The world was already too much with me.

At the office, the answering machine was signalling me.

Jack, it's Morris. Listen, I want a letter to Krysis. The neighbour says the bastard's storing stuff in the garage again. Tell him he's trespassing and we'll kick his arse. Today, Jack, do it today. Cheers.

Morris, father of Stan the publican.

Jack, Morris again. I forgot to say the prick's pushed the offer up another thirty grand. I told him not interested. He says he wants to talk to you. Tell him your instructions are he should piss off and stop wasting my time. Okay? Cheers.

Ditto. Someone wanted to buy his two adjoining properties in Brunswick, a more than generous offer as I understood it, but Morris couldn't contemplate life without them.

Don't let them tell you Robbie Colburne was just a casual barman.

A woman. Them? Who would they be? Xavier Doyle and company?

Jack, the Brunswick Street one, that lease finishes next month. Bastard rang the other day, wants to talk. Don't want to know him, he's out.

Morris, again. His Brunswick Street tenant was indeed deserving of the slipper, an habitual non-payer.

I sat down and gave Robbie Colburne some thought. Queensland. He'd told The Green Hill he'd worked in Queensland. I rang a man in Sydney called D.J. Olivier. He said he'd ring me back. As far as my assets went, my credibility with D.J. ranked just behind my half of the boot factory. Then I opened my mail, threw most of the contents into the bin, took that into the back room and emptied it into a green garbage bag. After that, I made a cup of tea and sat at my table to read the latest issue of the *Law Institute Journal*. There were many things of interest in it, even some I understood, including recent findings of the legal profession tribunal regarding professional misconduct. Accounts of the venality of some of my colleagues left me greatly distressed. Distressed but not surprised.

I went to my window. Heavier rain now, steady plinks on the pools in the gutter. The lights were on in McCoy's abode across the street, presumably to assist him in committing some disgusting act on canvas. Or elsewhere.

The phone rang.

'Here's a number,' said D.J. Olivier. 'It's good for an hour or so.'

I drove around to the Prince, parked in the loading zone around the corner. Inside, I found no youthful pioneers of the cyberfrontier energising themselves with the fermented juice of radiated Russian potatoes. The nicotine-dark chamber held only a mildly alcoholic accountant called George Mersh, who played seven games for Fitzroy, and Wilbur Ong and Norm O'Neill, both strangers to the cyber and approaching a frontier from which no-one returned.

They saw me, mouths opened like demanding chicks spotting the parent bird.

I heard the words unspoken, raised a hand. The mouths closed.

'Not today,' I said. 'I don't want to hear about it today.'

We would speak of the Saints' inglorious performance but not while the memory was so fresh. Raw. I rapped on the counter and opened the flap.

Stan appeared.

'The phone,' I said.

'Your professional uses his mobile,' he said, and smirked.

'It's the new asbestos. Don't you read the papers, Stan? Worse than stuffing bits of asbestos into your ear.'

His eyed opened wide, then a knowing look came over his face. 'What do you take me for?'

'An enigma wrapped in a mystery. Three beers. And have something yourself. Have, what is it, a Wally?'

He shook his head. 'Jesus, Jack. Stolly. Really.'

I went into the pub's office/archive. The telephone was under one of Stan's jumpers, which I moved with a rolled-up newspaper. Cautiously. Then I cleaned the handset with a paper napkin I found marking a place in a paperback called *Get a New e-Life: Cybertactics for Small Business*, and dialled.

'Done the immediate stuff,' said D.J. Olivier. 'Queensland, driver's licence, issued 1992, renewed January 1996, and most recently six weeks ago. Otherwise, he's not on the books.'

Robert Gregory Colburne had no tax file number and was not registered with Medicare.

'MasterCard, six weeks old, limit ten grand, it's 600-odd in credit.'

'Address?'

'Brissie. Red Hill. 'Also for electoral roll. No phone in the name now or ever. There's just one possible lippy smudge on this collar.'

'Yes?'

'The name got a passport in 1996. Departed Sydney, April '96, but there's no mention of a return arrival.'

'How can that be?'

'Well, sometimes they come back in a sailing boat, tramp steamer, fucking hang-glider, land in Broome, Top End,

Tassie somewhere, there's not always a record gets on file. Till they try to leave through Customs again, nothing shows.'

'Anything else?'

'No traces at the moment between April '96 and the licence renewal and credit card issue six weeks ago. Oh and he enrolled at Sydney Uni in '91. Seems to have dropped out in the first year. He's not there in '92.'

'What school?'

'Walkley. Up there somewhere to buggery over the mountains. You go through Bathurst. I think.'

I thanked D.J. and joined Wilbur and Norm. The subject of St Kilda could not be postponed. We had a fact-free exchange of views. The new development today was that both students of the game found some positive things to say about the Saints' appalling performance. Most of them would have escaped less scholarly eyes. It had been that way with Fitzroy through the many dark seasons, the times without comfort or hope, all our enemies grown taller and swifter, their hands bigger and stickier, their boots crafted to kick impossible bananas and their foul blows, trips and gouges apparently invisible to umpires.

Cheered, I left before the IT crowd arrived. If they were ever coming back. As I turned the corner, the rain paused. The air was cold, deceptively clean-smelling. I could hear water running in the gutters, a flow of toxic liquid heading for the river and the bay.

On the way home, Linda Hillier was on the radio, where I'd left her, on 3KB.

Congratulations. You're listening to Melbourne's smartest station, and that says something about you.

Tonight we're talking about drugs. Heroin users complained on radio this morning that they were treated like second-class citizens. Well, the man I'm about to talk to, the Reverend Allen O'Halloran, says that's what they are. What's your view? The number to call is, and bookmark it in what passes for your phone's mind…

One day, I would phone in. One day when I had the words to speak to Linda.

At home. A fire. No, too much effort. I put on the heating, went to the kitchen, began the defrosting of Sunday's stew and opened a bottle of the exemplary Mill Hill chardonnay. Then I slumped in the armchair, switched on the television for the news.

Innocents dying, the guilty walking free, nature mocking the frailty of human habitations, a hijacking, a royal birth, a supermodel on drug charges, a politician caught out in a lie, a cat's incredible sewer journey, the death of a revered pornographer and the legal battle over his archive of people doing things. Sport. And weather, a map, a man who knew about weather: cold, rain, the possibility of periods without the latter.

Watching this necklace of images strung in some electronic bunker, a part of my mind that bicycled along dull streets and sat on benches overlooking nothing was thinking about Robbie Colburne.

What to make of Robbie? Gets into university. Drops out. Runs up debts. Departs for foreign shores in 1996. Not recorded as coming back. Four years later, back nevertheless, renews his driver's licence and, notwithstanding his credit history, gets a credit card with a $10,000 limit. Appears in Melbourne with a small but expensive wardrobe, gets a casual job as a barman, dies of a drug overdose.

A short but puzzling life.

Someone had to know more about Robbie. Someone had to be able to put some coherence into this narrative. It was just a question of who. The woman who left the message on the answering machine knew something. But I didn't know who she was.

I rang Cyril Wootton on his latest mobile number. The numbers changed all the time.

'You wish to make contact with me?' he said. 'How unusual. That's twice in a few days. The hole in the ozone layer, El Pino, to what do I owe this?'

'Niño. El Niño. Pina Colada. Expensive, this thing.'

'How much?'

'Yes or no. I'm happier with no.' I didn't want to go travelling.

'Yes, if properly accounted for.'

'Was it not ever thus?'

'Ever thus my arse,' said Wootton.

'Really, Cyril,' I said, 'at times your vocabulary is at odds with your appearance. Your carefully cultivated appearance.'

The town of Walkley was a long and narrow blanket thrown over the spine of a ridge running out the back of the Great Dividing Range. To get there, you drove out of Sydney and on through hard country, high, gaunt, dry. Everywhere black rock broke the thin skin of soil, erosion gullies furrowed the slopes. The light was white and offended my city eyes.

I drove around until I found the school, it wasn't difficult, parked the hired Corolla outside the only brick building. The wind was a shock, buffeting, frozen hands pressing against my face.

A sign took me past murmuring classrooms to the principal's office. In the anteroom, a stone-faced woman, big, sat on a stool behind a counter. She looked at me and asked, 'You're not Telstra, are you?'

'No.'

'Bastards. Kin I do for you?'

'Carly?'

'Yes.'

'I spoke to you yesterday. Jack Irish. The lawyer from Melbourne.'

'Oh.' She looked less stony. 'Well. Melbourne. My little sister lives in Doncaster.'

'I'm told it's a great place to live. Does she like it?'

Wince, shrug of big shoulders.

'He's a paramedic. She met him in Bali. This bloke with them, he was dancing, fell over. Heart. Young, too. Everyone panicked. Denzil just went over, pushed everyone away, sat on the bloke, got the ticker going.'

'Saved his life.'

'No. Well, for a bit. Anyway, Carol's down there with him. In Doncaster. Supposed to get married but it's bin six years.'

'It's a big step. Giving it a lot of thought.'

'Yeah.' She passed a hand over her right temple. 'That or he's got somethin else goin.'

Time to move on from Doncaster. 'The principal's in?'

Carly rose with difficulty and went to the door at the back of the room, knocked, waited, opened it and put her head in.

'The man from Melbourne's here,' she said. 'Mr Irish. He rang yesterday.'

She waved me in.

The principal was behind a bare desk in a big, light room with school photographs on one wall and a large whiteboard covered with diagrams and lists on another. He stood up and put out a hand.

'David Pengelly.'

'Jack Irish.'

We shook hands and sat down. He had wispy hair combed across his scalp and a thin, worried face, the face of a farmer forever anxious about weather and weeds and the bank.

'Long way to come.'

'Excuse for a drive. I had business in Sydney.'

'Carly says you're asking about a student.'

'He would have finished about ten years ago. Robert Gregory Colburne.'

'What's it in connection with?'

'He died suddenly. No-one knows anything about his

family, next of kin. I was asked to look into it.' All true.

Pengelly scratched his scalp with one finger, taking care not to disturb hair. 'Ten years,' he said. 'That's a problem.'

I waited.

'The records used to be in a demountable out the back,' he said, pointing. 'Burnt down in '94, my first year here. Couldn't save anything. Kids. Year 12s, just after the exams.'

'Anyone still on the staff from 1990?'

He pulled a face. 'Ann Pescott. That'd be about it. Been packing it in, all the senior ones.'

'Could I talk to her? It would only take a minute.'

Silence while he studied me. Then he got up and went to the door. 'Carly, ask Ann Pescott to step in for a minute, will you?'

He came back. 'Died suddenly?'

'Drugs,' I said. 'Accidental.'

'Not much accidental about drugs. I used to teach in Sydney, in the west. Kids shooting up in the toilet block. Got away first chance I could.' He looked out of the window at a sad stand of eucalypts moving in the wind. 'Can't get away from it though. Can't get away from anything, can you?'

'No, I suppose not.'

'No.' He was studying me again. 'I wanted to be a lawyer. Had the marks. My parents didn't have the money.'

I didn't have anything to say to that. There was a knock at the door and a woman in her forties came in, not confidently. I stood up.

'Ann, this is Mr Irish, a lawyer,' said Pengelly. 'It's about a kid from years ago. What was the name?'

I shook hands with Ann Pescott. She had an intelligent face, lines of disappointment, nervousness in her eyes: cared too much, waited too long.

'Robert Gregory Colburne. He started at Sydney University in 1991, so 1990 would probably…'

Her face was blank. 'No,' she said. 'Colburne, I don't remember a Colburne. But I didn't have the seniors then.' Her eyes apologised for failing me. 'Sorry.'

'He'd have been a bright student.'

'No. He didn't come through me.' She swallowed. 'Must have arrived in eleven or twelve. There were a few new kids around from Forestry around then.'

'Forestry?'

'Conservation and Forestry, whatever it was called then, changes its name every year. They sent a whole lot of people up here from Sydney. Regionalisation I think it was called. Total disaster, city people, they all hated it and then the government changed and they all went back.'

'So people around here would remember them?'

She shrugged. 'Well, yes. Some. I suppose.'

'Where should I start?'

A siren sounded, a harsh noise.

Ann Pescott's eyes went to Mr Pengelly.

'They'll probably find their own way out,' he said. 'Animals generally do when the door's open.'

'Terry Baine at the newsagents,' she said. 'He would have been around in 1990. And they know everything, the Baines.'

I thanked Mr Pengelly and Ann Pescott for their time, together and separately. He seemed sad to see me go. I understood. On my way out, I thanked Carly.

'Got a card?' she said. 'You never know. My sister might need a lawyer in Melbourne.'

'You never know.' Relationships made in Bali are not known for their durability. Six years was probably some sort of record.

I parked outside the newsagent in the main street. There wasn't a great deal going on in Walkley. A bullbarred ute rumbled by. Two men were talking outside the bank, faces and hats shaped by hands and wind and rain and gravity. A shop door opened and a child in a stroller came out, followed by a woman inside many handknitted garments. I could see only the tip of the child's nose, a tiny pink nipple.

Two customers were in the shop, browsing the rack of magazines. The man behind the counter, fat advancing, hair receding, was staring at a computer monitor, frowning, rapping keys. He saw me in his peripheral vision, didn't look around.

'Sometimes I think it's a blessing the old bloke's gone,' he said. 'Christ knows what he'da made of this crap.'

'Terry Blaine?'

He turned his head. 'Help you?'

I introduced myself.

'Melbourne.' He beamed at me. 'There the other day. For the Grand Prix. Stayed at the Regency, me and me brother, nothin but the best. Casino, you name it. Treat for the wives.'

'They like motor racing?'

'Nah. They went shoppin. Had to take the credit cards off em after the first day, mind. Outta control. So what's yer business up here?'

'I'm trying to find the family of someone who died in Melbourne recently. He finished school here.'

'Yeah? Who's that?'

'Robert Colburne.'

Jesus,' he said. 'Robbo.'

'Remember him?'

'Oh yeah. What happened?'

'Drugs. Accidental overdose.'

Terry whistled, shook his head. 'Robbo. Mad, bad and dangerous to know.'

'Knew him well?'

'Yeah. A bit. Came in Year Eleven. Clever bloke, very smart. Went to uni after. Him and Janice Eller were the only ones.'

'Know his family?'

'Only Mrs Reilly.'

'A relation?'

'His auntie. She went back to England, oh, six, seven years ago. Robbo said his mum and dad split up when he was a kid, left him with someone. Then his dad got some tropical wog, PNG, I can't remember, he died. His mum didn't want to know him, she was in England, I think.'

He paused, sniffed. 'Mind you, Robbo was a bit of a bullshitter. Bit of the poof in him, too. Arty-farty.'

'So Robbie wasn't part of the Forestry move up here?'

'Nah. Just came the same year.'

A projectile-nosed woman with a scarf tied over her narrow head came to the counter, copy of *New Knitting* in hand.

'Sellin things today?' she said. 'Or just natterin?'

Terry didn't look at her, took the magazine and passed a barcode reader over it. It appeared not to work. He sighed, jabbed at the till keyboard.

'Voted for this government, mate,' he said. 'Make no secret of it, never have. I can tell you, never again. This GST…no, don't get me goin on the subject.'

'Shockin, the price of this,' the woman said. 'You put it up every second month.'

'Don't blame me,' said Terry. 'That's the pound done that, pound and the GST. Beats me how the pound can be worth more than the dollar. I need that explained to me. That's four twenty-five change. Thank you, Mrs Lucas.'

'Profiteerin goin on, no doubt in my mind.'

He watched her go, slit-eyed. 'Old bitch,' he said. 'Shit I have to put up with.'

'So there's no family around that you know of?'

'Nah.'

'He didn't come back here?'

'Nah. I heard he dropped out of uni, Janice Eller's mum told me that.'

I said, 'I might talk to Janice Eller. How would I do that?'

He blinked, ran a knuckle over his pink lower lip. 'Dead, mate,' he said. 'Thredbo.'

Thredbo was a one-word Australian story, a tragedy on the snowfields, a large piece of hillside coming unstuck, people dying under collapsed buildings.

'What about her family?'

'Only had a mum. She died.'

Not your most profitable expedition, this trip to Walkley. Nothing gained and nothing in prospect but an indigestible meal and a night in some sagging motel bed.

'Anyone around here who'd know anything about Robbie?'

He shook his head. 'Nah, don't think so. This girl came up here from Sydney with the Forestry, hung around Robbo. What was her name? My mate Sim had a thing for her...Sandra someone.'

'Your mate around?'

'Gone barra fishin, way up there in the Territory, lucky bugger. Should be back soon.'

I got out a card. 'I'd appreciate it if you could ask him to give me a ring.'

I got as far as Lithgow. I'd got as far as Lithgow once before, in the largely blank period after my second wife, Isabel, was murdered by a client of mine. At least I think it was Lithgow. I wasn't paying much attention in those days, only sober for as long as it took me to drive from one town to another, any town with a pub to any other town with a pub. If it was Lithgow I remembered, some kind of miners' strike was going on and, in the pub, a drunk miner accused me of being a journalist from Sydney. I didn't deny it, didn't care to, just had a fight with him.

No pub fights on this visit. I drove into the cold valley town, breathed the coal smoke from the fires, bought two stubbies of Boag and a bottle of mineral water from a drive-in bottle shop, found a place that made hamburgers and got one with the lot, except the egg. In a room at an unlovely brick-veneer motel, I drank the beer and ate my supper in front of a television set that changed channels on its own. Then, tired in many ways, I went to bed with my book, *Dying High: Lies About a Climber's Life*, bought on impulse months before, grabbed on my way out to get a taxi to the airport. There is something about the stupidity of climbing mountains that appeals. Perhaps it's the clinging by the fingertips to inhospitable surfaces. I could claim some experience in this area.

In the night, I was woken by the sounds of quick sex close by, intimately close, centimetres away, just beyond the plasterboard wall. Startled, for a moment unsure of where

I was, saddened when I remembered, I wrapped the sour foam pillow around my head, lay thinking about Robbie Colburne. Then I moved on to Cynthia and her attacker with the Saint tattoo, drifted off, listening to the trucks hissing, groaning, whining on the highway, thinking about my life, why equilibrium escaped me, why I couldn't find a steady state, chose to ask questions of strangers, lie down in beds too short, turn and turn again between cold, slithery, electric nylon sheets.

I rose just after dawn, creaks in my knees, happy to be going. I'd only had brief times in my life when I wasn't happy to be going. Sneakily, shamefully happy. Cleansed in a cramped, stained fibreglass chamber, I went outside. In the coal valley, the air was freezing. White breath hung on the face of a man walking two small dogs, clung to a few pale shiftworkers coughing on the first of the day. They were all I saw on my way to the steep, winding road out of the valley. There was a moment on the heights when I could look back: nothing to see, the place gone, buried in sallow, yellow dawn-mist.

On the plane home, I sat next to a middle-aged dentist from Collaroy. Shortly after take-off, and without the slightest encouragement, he told me that he was leaving his wife and two children, aged eleven and thirteen, to be with a Melbourne person he had met at a cosmetic dentistry conference in Hawaii.

'These things happen,' I said. Another man grateful to be going.

'I wasn't looking for it to happen. It just happened. Like a…like a bolt of lightning. Can you understand that?'

'Without any difficulty.' I got out my book, found my place.

'Well, you don't do something like this lightly, do you?'

'No. You wouldn't.'

The dentist leaned over, looked at me from close range. I suppose they get used to doing that, a life of looking into people's mouths. After a while, you lose the feeling of intruding.

'I feel like I'm on a personal journey,' he said. 'The road less travelled.'

I looked at him briefly, a mistake.

'Know what I mean?' he said, licked his lips.

'Yes.'

Complicit, I didn't say that it was not so much a personal journey on a road less travelled as a trip in a crammed bus on a six-lane freeway. All I wanted to do was read. This would stop me thinking about the distinctly unhealthy coughing note I'd detected in the port engine.

My companion went on exploring metaphors for his condition all the way to Melbourne. From time to time, I fed him a new one to keep him from asking me questions.

Home. The comforting feel of one's own tarmac.

On the way from the airport, I got off the suicidal freeway before the tollway began, perversely took to choked Bell Street, and at length found my way to St Georges Road and Brunswick Street. It was early afternoon, overcast. I lucked on a parking spot near Meaker's, went in and ordered a toasted chicken sandwich from Carmel, the worldly child.

'Tell him it's for Jack,' I said. 'That sometimes stops him leaving the bones in.'

'I'll write it down,' she said. 'I'm too scared to speak to him.'

Enzio the cook was subject to mood swings. From bad to much, much worse, and back. I'd almost finished reading the form for Mornington when his squat figure emerged from the kitchen, scowled at the room, came over and put a plate down in front of me: big sourdough slices containing Enzio's secret filling of chicken, red capsicum, ricotta and other unidentifiable stuff, the whole flattened under a hot weight. I felt saliva start.

Enzio sat down, looked around, pointed his blunt and unshaven chin at me. 'Listen,' he said. 'Hair transplants. What you think?'

'Can we talk about this later? Hair and food don't mix.'

He ignored my plea. 'This woman,' he said, 'she likes hair.'

'A new woman?'

'At the market. Her husband died. She talks about his hair all the time, lovely hair, strong hair.' He ran his hand over the surviving strands on his scalp. Unlovely, unstrong.

I looked at my sandwich. The point about a toasted sandwich is that it is eaten warm.

'Talks where? Where are you when she talks about hair?'

He jerked his head. 'Where you think? Where you talk this kind of talk?'

I gave him the lawyerly eye. 'Enzio, if this woman wanted hair, she wouldn't be talking to you in bed about hair. She's feeling guilty because she's having such a good time. Her hairy husband, all he had was hair. That's all she can find to say about him. You, on the other hand, you've got something else.'

I paused, bent my head closer. 'It's not hair she wants, Enzio. Get me?'

The ends of Enzio's mouth bent down, slowly, a sinister, knowing look.

'Fuck hair,' he said. He made a gesture with his right forearm that brooked no misinterpretation.

'Exactly. Now get back to work.'

He left. In the doorway to the kitchen, he turned. Our eyes met. He gave me a confident nod. Several nods.

Next patient, Dr Irish. Would that all problems admitted of such effortless solutions. In particular, my problems. The sandwich was still warm. Halfway, I signalled for the coffee, the short signal, thumb and index fingers a centimetre apart.

Carmel brought the potent eggcup of coffee and a yellow A4 envelope. 'Enzio says this came yesterday.' She touched the tip of her tongue to her upper lip, a kissable upper lip. 'He's whistling,' she said. 'Is there a secret?'

'Make them come to you,' I said. 'Never use force.'

She nodded, no expression. 'Thank you. I believe some call you the cookmaster.'

'The knowing do,' I said.

Carmel was clearing the table next to the door as I left. 'Your work here will never be done,' she said.

The office was cold and I noticed dust. How could anyone trust a solicitor whose office was dusty? I put on the blow heater and the smell of hot dust filled the room. How had this dust problem crept up on me?

Cyril Wootton on the answering machine, twice, a Wootton urgent but not irascible, which was unusual. My sister, Rosa, mildly exasperated, which was not. Drew Greer, saying unkind, mocking things about St Kilda's perform-ance against West Coast. Sad but to be expected from someone rendered agnostic by the death of Fitzroy. And Mrs Purbrick.

Jack, darling, such short notice but you must come for drinks tomorrow, six-ish, no excuses accepted.

It's business, I thought. And my chance to meet the Cundalls. Everyone else had.

I rang Cyril.

'As always, Mr Wootton will be delighted to have made contact with you,' said Mrs Davenport. Every day, she sounded more like Her Royal Highness Queen Elizabeth II.

'But do we ever really make contact, Mrs Davenport? We talk, we may even touch, but do we make contact? I mean, in the sense of…'

'Putting you through,' she said.

'Jesus, Jack,' said Wootton, 'mobile that's not switched on, what the fuck is the purpose…'

'Silence is the purpose, Cyril. The silence in which to do one's work.'

He gave me a silence. Then he made a noise, not so much animal as vegetable, the noise a sad carrot or potato might make, the noise of something deeply, hopelessly embedded in mud.

'The client would like a progress report,' he said.

Spoilt rotten, judges. Associates and clerks and tipstaffs and witnesses and defendants and jurors and learned counsel in silly wigs, all hanging on their every word, many of them hanging and fawning.

'Tell the client I'll report when there's something worth reporting.'

Wootton whistled, put the phone down. He'd be one of the fawners. I'd have to ask Cyril how it was that Mr Justice Colin Loder brought the problem of Robbie Colburne to him.

I sat down and thought about my progress. Nil, really. Robbie left the country and didn't appear to have come back. That was about it. It was strange but there were possible explanations.

Time to go home. Dawn in cold Lithgow seemed days away.

Halfway to my car, I heard a car slowing behind me, looked around, flight-or-fight coming into play: a red Alfa, new, two men in it. At an unthreatening crawl, it drew level, and the passenger window slid down.

'Jack Irish?'

The man was young, sleek dark hair, a mole beside his mouth. He was wearing a grey polo-neck and a soft-looking black leather jacket without a collar:

I nodded, kept walking.

'For you,' he said, holding out a brown paper bag. 'From a friend.'

Without thinking, I took it. The car pulled away, braked before it took the sharp corner, a double pulse of red light in the gloomy day.

The bag held a video cassette, new, unlabelled. Courtesy, presumably, of Detective Sergeant Warren Bowman.

At home, I half-filled the bath, drowsed in it for a long time with a glass of single malt, the end of a bottle given to me by Lyall, bought duty-free in some airport servicing a trouble spot. Or Santa bloody Barbara. It was peaceful in the big room, a bedroom when I bought the building. Once upon a time, a fire had sometimes been lit in the brick hearth on a cold Sunday afternoon, one person had read in the bath, the other had sat in the armchair.

I thought more about Robert Colburne. The judge was paying to find out what had really happened to him if he hadn't accidentally overdosed. He said he was acting on behalf of someone who knew Robbie, lost touch with him for a long time, then made contact again in Melbourne.

I didn't like the feel of that story, the distance it placed between Mr Justice Loder and Robbie.

Musing in the claw-footed bath, a bath big enough for two, if they arranged themselves.

I dismissed that memory, rose and donned unironed but clean garments and began the preparation of a modest meal.

I drank some red wine, moved roughly-chopped onion around for a while, kept away from the hot spot that the famous and expensive French frying pan wasn't supposed to have. The French are the finest conpeople in the world. I added garlic and mushrooms, a tin of tomatoes.

The video. Delivered by hand by men in an expensive car. Undercover cops? I switched off the gas, took my glass to the sitting room and plugged in the cassette, went to the couch and used the remote. The video flickered briefly, began.

A young man got out of a cab. This would be Robbie Colburne. He was tall and slim and, from on high and zooming in and out on him, the camera caught a certain athletic insouciance: chin up, arms moving freely, first two fingers extended pistol-like. It was night but made day by spotlights recessed into the building on his left. Light gleamed on his cheekbones, on his straight black hair combed back. He was handsome, all in black, a jacket worn over a tee-shirt.

The camera followed him to where he disappeared beneath a cantilevered porch bearing the name of the building, incised in polished concrete: CATHEXIS.

Daylight this time, someone sitting at a table on the pavement from across a busy street, traffic blocking vision for seconds at a time. Then a new camera angle, nothing obscuring the man now but the camera unsteady. He had a small glass on a saucer, the shortest of short blacks, drank a teaspoonful, looked around, newspaper in his hand, a half-amused look. He was dark, balding, a fleshy intimidating face.

Early evening, the young man again, Robbie, seen in profile, side on, waiting to cross a busy street, finding a break in the traffic, walking diagonally, the confident walk.

Night again. A long shot in bad conditions, rain, a car window coming down, the camera zooming in, the young man behind the wheel, in a dinner suit now, white shirt, black bow tie, saying a few words to someone outside the vehicle.

End of moving pictures.

I'd asked Warren Bowman for a photograph of Robbie.

I'd expected a still, a mortuary picture. Instead, he sent me a collection of surveillance video clips showing Robbie under expensive observation, moving, in the street. Good of him but why? I could ask Detective Sergeant Bowman. But he would probably say that he was just being helpful.

And why did a casual barman like Robbie deserve this kind of photographic attention? Was it because he wasn't just a barman, as my anonymous caller had suggested?

Warren Bowman said senior drug squad officers were on the scene quickly after the uniformed cops reported finding Robbie's body.

Expensive surveillance, two cameras on one occasion. That only happened to persons of great interest. Unless Robbie was an accidental, someone filmed in the surveillance of someone else. But, in that case, he would be someone close to the target; there was no other way he would be caught on camera so many times.

Robbie caught up in the surveillance of someone else. Was that it? The fleshy man?

Back to cooking. Time to add the tuna, get the rice going.

I was eating in front of the television when the phone rang. Cam.

'Little trip in the morning,' he said. 'Won't take long.'

'I got talkin to the bloke at the hotel next door,' Cam said. He wound down his window, flicked his cigarette end out, raised the window. We were in the V-8, passing the Fawkner Crematorium on the Hume, a sunny morning, petrol tanker ahead, Kenworth behind, stream of heavy metal coming the other way.

'What's the connection?'

'Hotel's part-owner of the carpark. Guest parkin. Carpark employs three blokes on eight-hour shifts, hotel provides security. In theory. This fella, he worked there eighteen months.'

'The name again?'

'Rick Chaffee. Two complaints about extra K's appearin on the clock while he was there. One bloke from Adelaide had a logbook, he reckoned someone took his Discovery for a 200K spin.'

Cam edged out for a look, came back in. He was wearing Western District casual attire today, navy-blue brushed-cotton shirt, heavy moleskin trousers, short riding boots. 'On the day, this Chaffee, his story is he was on the phone, he thought he recognised the driver of the Land Cruiser, let him out without checkin ID. Honest mistake.'

'They buy that?'

Cam shrugged. 'What can you prove? Sacked him. Cops run the tape over him, the hotel bloke says. No form to speak of, some kid stuff in WA, he's a WA boy, Mangoup, Banjoup, one of those up towns, they got hundreds. Plus he's got an assault when he was a bouncer in King Street.'

He was steering with his fingertips, head back, index fingers tapping to the music, soft Harry Connick. 'Worth a yarn, I reckon.'

'If the bloke's in this,' I said, 'it'll take more than a yarn.'

Cam's dark eyes lay on me for a moment.

I went back to reading the *Age*. The story at the bottom of page one was headlined: *Call for Cannon Ridge tender probe.*

It opened: *The State Government was last night urged to hold an inquiry into the tendering process that awarded a 100-year lease on the Cannon Ridge snowfield and a mini-casino licence to a company associated with Melbourne's millionaire Cundall family.*

The company, Anaxan Holdings, has a glittering list of shareholders, including some of Australia's Top 100 richest. A spokesman for shortlisted rival bidder WRG Resorts told a press conference yesterday that WRG has evidence that Anaxan knew details of all tenders before the vital second round of bidding.

The Minister for Development, Tony DiAmato, said WRG Resorts had not approached him. 'I have no idea what they're talking about. The previous government awarded this tender. We fought the whole idea of a private snowfield and another casino, everyone knows that. But it's done, it's history.'

Cam said, 'I read that stuff you sent me. The Saint's big with your crim tatt artist.'

I folded the paper. 'That's what my bloke said. Use half the phone book.'

I'd sent him the yellow A4 envelope left for me at Meaker's, sent it by express courier, fat and silent Mr Cripps behind the wheel of his burnished 1976 Holden.

'It's down here,' said Cam.

We turned right off the Hume, drove through a light industrial area, bricks, concrete products, pipes, turned left and went a long way, to the end of an unpaved road. Ahead, a sign on a wavy corrugated-iron fence was falling over. It said, no punctuation, Denver Garden & Building Supplies Plants Sand Soil Gravel Pavers Sleepers. The gate was half-open, drawn back until its sagging tip dug into the ground.

Cam nosed around it, parked in front of a long cement-sheet building, flat-roofed, meagre shelter over the door, one small window. Beside the door, three bags of cement had solidified, fused. We got out.

To the left of the gate was what remained of the Plants division of the business: a copse of birch trees in black plastic root bags, leaning inward, touching, dead; a conifer fallen over but indomitable, roots broken through the seams of the plastic bag and penetrating the packed soil; a row of concrete pots growing couch grass in abundance; some sad roses clinging to life, sparse leaves spotted with yellow.

The sound of a machine came from beyond the building. We walked around, passed an old pale-blue Valiant, buffed up, saw an expanse of dark, wet, rutted ground, big concrete pens holding gravel and sand, mulch, compost, other dark substances, everything untidy, spilling out of the enclosures, crushed into the ground.

The machine was a mid-sized lifter and it was moving rocks from one part of the yard to another, television-sized rocks for adding character to small, flat blocks in the outer suburbs.

We walked towards it and the driver saw us coming, the light glinted on his dark glasses as he looked our way, kept on going to his new pile, dumped the load with a crash, reversed the machine, gunned it back to the mother lode, took the bucket down, stuck it in with a ghastly screech, lifted, rocks falling out, swung around, went back, lifted the bucket to dump.

We were close, in the noise. The man turned his head towards us. Cam raised a hand, palm outward.

Bucket poised, the man cut the motor. He was big, no neck or chin to speak of, peaked cap too small for his long hair, tiny nose, arms like sewer pipes, belly hanging over a wide leather belt.

'Yah?'

'Rick Chaffee,' said Cam. It wasn't a question.

'Want somethin?' The man's voice was reedy, not congruous with the body.

'Few words about the parking garage.'

'What?'

'Curtin parking garage. You worked there.'

'Jacks?'

'No.'

'I'm workin here,' the man said. 'Busy.'

'Be a good idea to talk to us,' Cam said.

'Yah. Why's that?'

'You could be in trouble.'

Chaffee shook his head. 'Not cops?'

'No.'

He swivelled in his seat, stood up on the platform of the machine, towered over us, our heads at his knee-level. 'What's your name?' he said to Cam.

'Bruce,' said Cam.

Chaffee drew on his sinuses, not an engaging sound, and spat to Cam's right.

'Bruce's not a coon name,' Chaffee said. 'You look like you got a bit of coon in you.'

Cam turned his head to me, eyes full of resignation.

103

'Far as I'm concerned,' he said quietly, 'you stayed in the car.'

'We should leave,' I said, more than uneasy, much, much more. 'There are other ways.'

'Won't take long,' Cam said. 'Since we're here.'

He turned back to Chaffee. 'All I want to do is ask you about the Curtin carpark.' Pause. 'Mr Chaffee.'

Chaffee put a hand into an armpit, scratched. 'Busy, boong, fuck off.'

Cam looked down, shook his head, coiled, sprang, hooked his right arm around Chaffee's knees, pulled the big man out of the machine with one twisting movement, brought him over his head and dumped him.

Chaffee made a sound like a kicked dog as he hit the wet ground. He rolled over, balled himself, he was no stranger to being kicked, would try to grab the foot, the leg.

Cam stood back. 'Get up, Ricko,' he said, ordinary tone. 'I'm in a good mood.'

Chaffee got up, wary of a surprise, but when he was on his feet, I could see he liked this turn of events. 'Hey,' he said, taking off the dark glasses, throwing them to one side, his eyes flicking to me. 'Hey, no reason to fucken do that, really fucken stupid. Fucken boong stupid.'

Cam took a step closer, inside the range of the big arms, his hands at shoulder height, loose fists. He was as tall as Chaffee but 20 kilograms lighter. Chaffee put his head to one side.

'Cocky fucken boong,' he said, then grabbed at Cam's shirtfront, lunging, forehead dropped for the butt.

Cam went forward, into the lunge, his right hand travelled upward no more than 10 centimetres, a corkscrewing fist that made contact with Chaffee's nose, brought the man's head up, opened his eyes wide with pain, his arms falling to his sides, cap falling off.

Cam took another pace, in close, hit him again, the same short, twisting punch, this time high in Chaffee's chest, in the left collarbone. I thought I heard it break.

Chaffee went down, on one knee, both hands at his nose, blood running through his fingers. Cam put his hand in the man's hair, pulled him forward, dragged him across the muddy, rutted ground, Chaffee moaning, not resisting.

'Open the car door, Jack,' said Cam, nothing different about his voice. 'Wind the window down. Take the keys out.'

I opened the driver's door of the Valiant, did as I was told. Cam pulled Chaffee up to the open door, dropped his head on the seat, got behind him, kicked him in the backside with his right boot.

'Get in, Mr Chaffee,' he said.

Chaffee crawled in, using the steering wheel to drag himself. Cam helped, gripped the man's wide leather belt in both hands, pushed him in, slammed the door, a solid thunk.

Feeling his knuckles, flexing his fingers like a surgeon about to operate, Cam went over to the lifter, swung himself up, started the motor, gunned it, reversed, swung the machine savagely, came up to the Valiant.

'Ricko,' he shouted.

Chaffee was holding his chest now, his mouth open, blood in it, running over his lower lip. He looked at Cam, fear, wonder, in his eyes.

'Who'd you lend the Cruiser to that day, the one they sacked you for?'

'Dunno what you…' Chaffee coughed blood.

'You know, bubba,' Cam said. 'Ran your own car-hire business at the Curtin. Tell me now. Quick.'

'Know fuck-all about—'

'Your mates nearly killed a woman that day, know that, Ricardo?'

'Nah, don't—'

Cam raised the hopper.

I stood back.

He dumped the full load of stones, big landscaping stones, on the Valiant.

Stones bounced on the roof, one went through the windscreen, stones fell off the sides, rolled onto the bonnet, the boot.

The roof collapsed, the right-hand door pillar buckled, the back doors popped open.

Cam reversed the machine, swinging around, screamed across to a pit of yellow paving sand, dropped the hopper, drove it into the sand, filled it, sand spilling, raised the hopper, reversed and swung, came back.

A last grey volcanic rock toppled off the Valiant roof, rolled down the crazed, opaque, holed windscreen, over the stoved-in bonnet, fell into a puddle.

In the car, Chaffee was making sobbing, wheezing noises, noises of terror. The roof was pressing on his head and he was trying to open his door, jammed by the impact.

'Jesus, Ricky,' said Cam. 'You come through that alive. You're tough, you WA boys.'

He pulled the lever, dropped most of a cubic metre of sand on the Valiant. The springs sagged, sand poured into the car through the hole in the windscreen, filled the depressions, slithered to the ground.

The Valiant was disappearing under rocks and sand.

Chaffee screamed.

'There's more comin, Ricko,' said Cam. 'Then I'm givin you the gravel shower.' He waited. 'The Cruiser. Who'd you lend it to? Last time I'm askin you, fat boy.'

'Artie, Artie, I only know Artie.' Chaffee's voice was weak, he could barely speak.

Cam revved the engine, calmed it.

'More, bubba,' he said, 'more.'

'God'smyfuckenwitness, Artie's all...I'm dyin...'

'Damn straight,' said Cam. He emptied the rest of the sand onto the car, switched off, climbed down, dusted his moleskins, hands brushing. He went over to the wrecked Valiant, tested the door handle, gripped the door pillar in his right hand, and jerked.

The door came open. Cam reached in with both hands and pulled Chaffee out, jerked him out, let him fall into the mud. Paving sand was stuck to the man's blood, blood and sand all over his big chest, it was in his long hair, and he had a mask of yellow sand on his face, new black blood from his nose eroding it, creating thin furrows of blood.

'Dyin,' said Chaffee. 'Help me.'

'You'll be fine,' said Cam. 'WA boy like you, Buggerup, the old home town, take more than a few rocks, bit of sand. What's that word you called me? I forget. Want to say that again? That word?'

Chaffee put his head back, rolled his face away, into the mud, the white of an eye showing. 'Mate,' he said. 'Sorry, mate.'

'Well, that's okay then,' said Cam. 'Sorry is such a good word. Pity more people don't use it. Tell me some more about Artie.'

Chaffee groaned.

On the Hume, cruising, listening to Harry Connick again, I said, 'A really good trip. A short bloke called Artie. Chaffee's probably going to die back there and all we got was a short bloke called Artie.'

Cam was tapping his fingertips. 'Only hit him twice, can't die of that. Short Artie's good too.'

'How's that?'

'How many short Arties can there be? Short Arties with a Saint.'

The answering machine was speaking to a caller as I opened the door of my office. I took the two steps and picked up the phone.

'Ignore those words. Jack Irish.'

'Jack, Gus.'

Augustine, Charlie Taub's granddaughter. Alarm, a stab.

'Charlie?'

'What?'

'He's alright?'

She read my anxiety, laughed her sexy laugh. My shoulders and my chest untightened.

'Never better. He said to tell you he's staying another week. He's playing bowls every day, he's playing in a tournament next week. He said, and I quote, "Tell Jack, hot's good for one thing."'

I sighed.

'Means something, does it, the message?'

'Yes. Exactly as I feared. Will you marry me? Take me to Canberra with you?'

Charlie's granddaughter was a fighter for the oppressed workers and, said the gossip, being courted for a safe federal Labor seat. That or in due course Australia's highest union office.

'I'm not going to Canberra,' she said. 'You've been reading that idiot in the *Age*. Anyway, I don't think harem life would suit you.'

'The zenana. We'd sit around, the boys, playing cards,

crocheting, waiting for you to come home and pick one of us.'

'I may need to give this Canberra business more thought,' she said. 'Stay close to the phone.'

It was just after noon. Much of the day ahead, much already accomplished: a trip down the bright golden Hume, the witnessing of a man having his nose broken, his collar-bone fractured, tonnes of rock dropped on his prized car, followed by a coating of paving sand, enough sand to provide the base for a nice barbecue area.

Moving on. I settled down at my aged Mac and attended to the affairs of my bustling legal practice, to wit, a letter to Stan's father's tenant, Andreas Krysis, asking him to desist from storing things in Morris's garage, which was not part of his lease.

Hunger struck. I went around the corner and bought a salad pita, came back and ate while reading the sports section of the *Age*. The daily bulletin on all football clubs said that, notwithstanding the team's atrocious performance against West Coast, the St Kilda club president was standing firm behind the coach. 'He has our full confidence. We have always said that we are with him for the long haul.'

In football-speak, these sentiments translated as: *Full confidence*—most committee members want to sack the bastard. *The long haul*—until the next game. Saturday at Docklands Stadium was Waterloo for the coach.

I rang Drew. He was in court. I rang my sister.

'So,' Rosa said, 'to what?'

'To what what?'

'Do I owe this honour?'

'I've been away a bit. I went to see Claire.'

'I know that. I talk to her every second day. You may recall that I'm her aunt.'

It was hard for me to grasp that people saw themselves as aunts or uncles. I had neither, had never felt a vacuum in my life.

'Anyway,' she said, 'you've been back for over a week.'

An edge to her voice, not anger, not the usual exasperation. Worse. Knowingness.

'Lunch,' I said. 'It's been a while. Your choice of venue after the cruel things you said about mine last time.'

'Lunch.' She managed to roll the word around in her mouth, endow it with sinister meaning.

'What about The Green Hill?' I said. 'Very fashionable, I'm told. They know me there at the highest levels, the boss shouted me a tankard of Leprechaun ale the other day, Leprechaun, some name like that, very ethnic.'

Silence.

'Andrew Greer stood me up,' she said finally.

The masticating on *lunch* now meant something.

A moment of calculation.

'Drew? What, a legal matter?'

'No. A *lunch*.'

'I didn't know you knew Drew. In a lunching sense.'

Sparring. A spar.

'I don't. I thought I was going to have the opportunity.'

'To do what?'

'Get to know-him in a lunching sense.'

'Well, he's a busy man, things come up, that's the law.'

'Lawyers don't work on Saturdays.'

'The lawyers you know. Lawyers in name only. Accountants in drag. Tax avoidance, mergers and acquisitions. Drew is a criminal lawyer. They never stop, never sleep. Never eat, some of them.'

She knew. She could not know, but she knew. Some

psychic vibration had reached her, bounced off a star, found her.

'I don't know what this is about,' I said. 'What time are we on? What time is it on your side of the river?'

Silence.

'Well, I rang you, so whose prerogative is it to end the conversation? Tricky point of etiquette, not so?'

'Sometimes I hate you,' she said and put the phone down.

On the other hand, she could know if Drew had told her.

I sat back in my captain's chair and my shoulders sagged. Why had I been so stupid as to speak my mind to Drew? What did it matter if he became entangled with Rosa? What was one more clear-felled forest, one more toxic waste dump, one more nuclear test site in my immediate vicinity?

I sat in this mood of despond for a while and then, for want of something to do, I dialled Telstra inquiries. Since the privatised utility wanted to encourage people to use this free service, it took six minutes to get the number of Baine's Newsagency in Walkley.

'Baine's,' said Terry Baine.

'Terry, Jack Irish, I talked to you—'

'Mate, telepathy, mate, on the verge of ringin ya,' he said. 'Got the name of that girl, Sim come in this mornin.'

'How'd the barra go?'

'Yeah, well, big as great whites ya believe the bastard. Sandra Tollman, that's the name.' He spelled it. 'Sim says she married a Forestry bloke. Says he heard that. Christ knows where he'd hear that.'

I said my thanks.

'Got your number, mate. You're on the record. Comin down for the vroom-vroom next year, look you up.'

Adult life was all desire and expectation. Until it was too late. I went home to change for Mrs Purbrick's library-warming.

David, Mrs Purbrick's personal assistant, opened the huge black front door. His smile seemed genuine.

'Jack,' he said, extending his beringed right hand, the hand with the green stones, 'we're delighted you could come.' He dropped his voice. 'I must say I found the muscle you brought with you last time rather intimidating.'

'Just her manner of speech,' I said. 'She works with film people most of the time. I gather they only respond to a rough touch.'

He nodded, serious. 'I've heard that too. They like the firm smack of something or other.'

'The smack and the other, probably.'

David laughed. 'This way. Everyone's in the library telling madame how clever she is.'

We went through the gallery-like hall, through the open double doors into the wide passage, eight-paned skylights high above, parquetry and Persian rugs beneath our feet.

Music was coming from somewhere. Gershwin. We were close to the library door before the voices within became audible.

'Please,' said David, waving me in.

There were at least two dozen people in the room, more women than men, standing close together, laughter and teeth flashing. For a moment, I looked, wished Charlie were there to see his elegant bookcases filled with books, glowing in the lamplight, the people in the room made handsomer, better somehow, by being in the presence of his craftsmanship.

'Jack, Jack. Darling, so distinguished.'

Mrs Purbrick, on heels so high her toes had to bend at near-right angles to touch the ground, in business gear again, a dark suit, jacket worn over an open-necked white shirt unbuttoned for a considerable distance, great mounds beneath, ceremonial mounds. And, in keeping with the after-work nature of the occasion, severe horn-rimmed glasses. She took me by the lapels and brushed me on both cheeks with her inflated lips, the kiss of balloons, turned to face the room.

'Everyone, everyone, meet Jack Irish, who helped Mr Taub build this magnificent library.'

I cringed. There was a polite round of applause. Then I was taken around the room and introduced to people, youngish people, summer-in-Portsea, winter-in-Noosa, week-in-Aspen people. Over someone's shoulder, I recognised the face of Xavier Doyle, the boyish charmer from The Green Hill. He smiled, threaded his way over, patted me on both arms, a form of embrace.

'And here you've bin tellin me you're a legal fella, Jack,' he said. 'Why didn't ya just come right out and say you're an honest workin man?'

'Shyness,' I said.

'You know each other,' said Mrs Purbrick, touching Doyle's cheek. 'How lovely. Two of my favourite men.'

Doyle shook his head at her. 'Now, I won't share you with him, Carla,' he said. 'That's a warnin.'

To me, he said, 'This lovely lady is one of my investors, my angels, a person of faith in The Green Hill and its future.'

'A commodity required in abundant measure.' A tall man in his early sixties, solid, with a full head of wavy grey hair, was at Doyle's side, a head taller. He put out a hand to me. 'Mike Cundall. Congratulations, beautiful piece of work.'

'Thank you, on behalf of Charlie Taub,' I said. 'I'm the helper. Just here as the front man. Charlie's in WA. Also he hasn't worn a suit since his wedding.'

Cundall nodded. He had grey eyes, clever eyes, appraising, in a lined, stoic face. He'd been drinking for a while. 'Carla tells me you're also a lawyer,' he said.

'In a small way.'

'My father was a lawyer who liked woodwork. He made garden things. Benches that fell over. He'd come home from Collins Street, out of his suit and into overalls, straight to the workshop and stay there until dinner.' He looked around, moistened his lips. 'Which he'd devote to shitting on me.'

A bow-tied waiter with a tray of champagne flutes appeared. We armed ourselves.

'Well,' said Cundall, 'this is probably a good moment.' He coughed and raised his glass above his head. People stopped talking.

'Carla's invited us around,' he said, 'to admire her new library. I must say I'm quite stunned by its elegance, stunned and jealous. And we have with us one of the builders of this thing of beauty, Jack Irish. I'd like to propose a toast: to Carla and her library, may it give her much pleasure.'

He raised his glass and everyone followed. A happy murmur.

'Thank you, Mike darling, thank you,' said Mrs Purbrick, waving her glass at the room, 'and thank you all for coming, you busy people, my dear friends.'

Xavier Doyle moved off, winding his way towards two blonde women, tanned, golf and tennis tans. They broke off their conversation, turned to him, faces opening.

'A mind like Paul Getty behind all that Irish boyo crap,' said Mike Cundall. There was no admiration in his tone.

'Nice place, The Green Hill,' I said. 'On the basis of one visit.'

Cundall was lighting a cigarette with a throwaway lighter. 'Do you smoke?' he asked. 'Forget your manners, nobody smokes any more.'

I shook my head.

'Yes. The Green Hill.' He blew smoke out of his nostrils. 'Money shredder, the Amazon dot com of pubs. Thousands of customers, own vineyard, Christ knows what else, sinks ever deeper into the red.'

'You're an investor?'

'Don't insult my intelligence. My wife's thrown money at The Green Hill. Her own money too. Was her money, I should say. It belongs to the ages now.'

The waiter was back. He had a crystal ashtray on his salver.

'I'll put this here, sir,' he said, drawing a thin-legged table closer to us and placing the ashtray. Then he offered more champagne.

'Nice drop,' I said.

'Roederer, sir. The Kristal.'

We lightened his tray. Another bow-tied man arrived with a silver tray of hamburgers, on sticks, exquisite miniatures, each the size of a small stack of twenty-cent coins, to be eaten at a bite.

Cundall twisted his cigarette in the ashtray. 'Smoked salmon's not good enough any more,' he said, 'too common.' He put one hamburger in his mouth, took a second. When he'd finished both, his mouth turned down. 'Instant indigestion these days.'

117

'How's Cannon Ridge going?' I said.

'That's my son,' said Cundall. 'My son and assorted rich boys. Sydney rich boys. The fucking dot com brigade. New economy.' He put down most of the champagne in a swig, held up his glass like an Olympic torch. 'Still, Cannon Ridge's old economy. Real asset, real business, combines leisure and gambling. Boys got a fantastic bargain.'

The waiter arrived. Cundall finished his glass, took another. 'Get me a whisky, will you?' he said to the youth. 'Something drinkable. With Evian. Just a bit.' He looked at me. 'Whisky, Jack?'

'That would be nice.'

'Decent shots,' said Cundall, blinking.

'Sir.'

'Good lad.'

'I see there's some unhappiness about the handling of the tenders,' I said.

'Politics of business,' said Cundall, slurring slightly. 'WRG wants to build a whole fucking town on the Gippsland Lakes. Get the new government in some shit over Cannon, good chance they won't get knocked back on that.'

He eyed me. 'Good practice, anyhow,' he said. 'Always takes a while to sort out a new lot, find out who to pay, who to play.'

'Jack, darling, you haven't met Ros Cundall.' Mrs Purbrick was holding the arm of a tall, dark-haired woman, once beautiful now merely good-looking.

We shook hands.

'I'm very taken with this room,' said Ros Cundall. 'I've always wanted a library. Do you think your Mr Taub would build one for me?'

'At least you can be sure it'll hold its value,' said Mike Cundall. 'Unlike that cocaine palace.'

Ros Cundall didn't look at her husband, made a wry face. 'Mike built a Las Vegas wing onto our house,' she said. 'All it lacks is the bedrooms for the harlots.'

'I thought you could go on using the house for that,' said Mike Cundall.

Mrs Purbrick laughed, an unconvincing trill. 'Oh, you two,' she said, 'so wicked.' She was watching David talking to one of the waiters.

Our whiskies arrived. We made small talk. Then, all at once, everyone was leaving, much brushing of lips on cheeks. Ros Cundall asked me for a card. So did two other people. Charlie might be building libraries full-time in future.

Near the front door, Xavier Doyle came up behind me.

'Jack,' he said. 'Mind I see you down the pub now.'

'Count on it.'

'That Robbie, you find out anythin more about the lad?'

'No,' I said. 'He's a mystery.'

Sandra Tollman had become Sandra Edmonds but was now Sandra Tollman again. She looked up from a tray of seedlings as I came down the greenhouse aisle. I'd found her easily, through her father, who still worked for the forestry department in New South Wales.

'Sandra?'

'Yes.' She was tall, with dark, curly hair cut short, wearing green work clothes.

'I'm Jack Irish.'

She took off a rubber glove and we shook hands. A long, slim hand, strong. I'd spoken to her on the phone at home the night before. She lived outside Colac and worked for a commercial tree nursery.

'I'll take my break,' she said. 'We can talk in the kitchen. The bosses are in town.'

I followed her out of the greenhouse and down a gravel path to a weatherboard building. We went in the back door, into a kitchen with a wooden table.

'Sit down. Tea or coffee?'

'Tea, please.' I sat where I could look out of the window, at a green hill with mist hanging on it.

She switched on the kettle, put teabags in mugs, got a carton of milk out of the fridge, stood waiting for the kettle to boil.

'Nice place to work,' I said.

'It is. I'm lucky. Nice bosses too, easygoing, no problems about starting times, that sort of thing. My little girl spends the afternoons here with me.'

'Rare thing, a nice boss.'

She nodded. 'I've had a few shits.'

The kettle boiled. She poured water into the mugs and sat at the end of the table.

'Robbie hasn't crossed my mind for years,' she said. 'What's this about?'

I hadn't told her on the phone. 'I'm afraid he's dead,' I said. 'Died of a drug overdose.'

She put a hand to her mouth, eyes wide. 'Jesus.'

'I'm trying to piece together his history,' I said. 'No-one seems to know much about him.'

'Well.' She scratched her head, bemused look. 'Well, I haven't seen him since, it must have been 1994. I had a terrific crush on him at school, I thought he was just the most divine thing, it ruined my school work…anyway, yes, 1994.'

'Where was that?'

Two birds were on the windowsill, looking around calmly, lorikeets, their colours startling in the grey day.

'In Sydney, in Paddington, bumped into him. He was with a woman at least ten years older, more maybe, you can't tell with some women.'

'A friend?'

She had dark eyes, clean whites, no guile in her eyes. 'I was walking behind them and the woman put her hand in the back pocket of Robbie's jeans.'

'Not looking for something, you'd say?'

'No.'

'And then you talked?'

'Just for a minute. In the street. The woman walked away, looked in windows.'

'What did Robbie say?'

'Small talk. Said he'd dropped out of uni. But I knew that, someone else told me, a girl in our class.'

I put a teaspoonful of sugar in my tea, stirred. 'Janice Eller.'

Surprise. 'How do you know that?'

'Terry Baine told me about her.'

'Terry Baine. The fat shit.'

'Sim's still carrying a torch for you,' I said.

She smiled, dropped her head, covered her eyes with a hand. 'God, you know everything,' she said. 'I cringe at the memory. Me walking around behind Robbie like a puppy, Sim sending his mates to give me messages. Really dumb messages.'

'I'm sure it was an extremely serious matter at the time,' I said. 'No other contact with Robbie?'

'No.'

I took out the still photograph I'd had printed from the video, the best shot of Robbie Colburne, almost full face, held it between thumb and forefinger. 'This is the person we're talking about?'

Sandra Tollman looked at the picture, looked at me, shocked.

I'd known. In the unfathomable way of knowing, I'd known since I watched the video clips, since D.J. Olivier told me that there was no record of Robbie returning to Australia.

'No,' she said. 'This is Marco.'

'Marco?'

'Robbie's friend.'

'Marco who?'

'Marco Lucia. Does this mean Robbie isn't dead?'

'You're sure this is Marco?'

She took the photograph. 'It's Marco. He doesn't even look much older. When was this taken?'

'Recently.'

'Why did you think it was Robbie?'

'He was calling himself Robert Colburne. He had a driver's licence in the name.'

'So Marco's dead and Robbie's not?'

'Marco's dead. I don't know about Robbie. Possibly alive.' I didn't think that. 'Tell me about Marco.'

'I loved the name. Marco Lucia. He came up from Sydney in the holidays after year eleven to stay with Robbie, second most divine boy I'd ever met. Everyone in Walkley was just so Anglo-Irish. Blaines and Smailes and O'Reillys and McGregors. Marco could've been Robbie's brother, both pale, this black, black hair. Janice thought it was the second coming.'

We looked at each other for a while. She was back there, in Walkley, age seventeen.

'And after the holidays, did you see Marco again?'

'No. It was just those weeks, two weeks, I was in love, teenage love. Janice and I were the class smarties, readers, suddenly Robbie arrives, then his friend, this half-Italian boy, so exotic, they were both so clever and you could talk to them about books and poetry. Very un-Aussie, two boys who weren't petrolheads.'

'Half-Italian?'

'He said his mother wasn't Italian.' She looked out of the window. 'I think his mother left his father, went off to be a hippy, in Nimbin, somewhere like that. His father brought him up. That's all I know about him.'

'Did you know where he came from in Sydney?'

123

'No. Janice would have known. You know about Janice?'

'Yes. You heard nothing more about Marco?'

'No. I ended up at ag college in Orange. Pressure from my father. Not much talk about books and poetry there, I can tell you.'

'Robbie went overseas in 1996. Did you know that?'

She shook her head. 'That day in the street, that was it.'

I finished my tea. 'Thanks,' I said. 'You've been a great help, saved me from wasting more time.'

She walked to the Studebaker with me. 'This is weird, isn't it?' she said.

'Yes.'

'Was Marco an addict? she asked.

'The dead man had needle marks.'

'I'd like to know how it turns out,' she said.

'Me too. I'll let you know.'

'This come out of the blue,' said Harry Strang. 'People I done some transactin with, '87, '88, thereabouts. She's got the full licence, smart lady. He's a bit of a dill. Often that way, mind. Anyway, we had a bit of luck. Here's the turn now, memory serves.'

We were in open country, sere, rocky outcrops, going down a deeply rutted track.

Cam was driving the big BMW. 'Nice around here,' he said. 'No sheep.'

He'd rung me on the mobile on my way back from Colac. I found the pair waiting for me outside the boot factory. I hadn't asked any questions, just fallen asleep before we reached the tollway.

'When did this happen?' I said.

'Awake are you, Jack?' said Harry. 'Admire a man can kip anywhere. Sign of a clear conscience.'

'Sign of someone who wants to escape life,' I said. 'When?'

'After the night racin at the Valley last week,' said Harry. 'Jean's very upset. Said we'd come out and have a word.'

He was silent for a moment. 'Got through to me, possibly not a personal problem we're havin. Get my meanin?'

'This it?' said Cam.

A sign on the fence said: Kingara. David & Jean Hale. We crossed a cattle grid and drove down a lane of young poplars. There were horses in the paddocks on either side. Straight ahead was a bluestone-faced house, long and low with a slate-tiled roof, behind a struggling privet hedge. We parked next to a Holden ute with a history.

'Stretch the legs,' said Harry. 'Meet the lady. Can't hurt you blokes to meet normal people.'

'I dunno,' Cam said. 'Might find you like normal, ruin your whole life.'

As we sat there, a tall woman, slim, thirties, early forties, strong features, long blonde hair pulled back, ears showing, came around the corner of the hedge. She was wearing horse gear: checked shirt, Drizabone vest, jeans, gumboots. At the same moment, a wheaten labrador with the faintly puzzled but amiable look of its kind came through a hole in the hedge, tail wagging.

'Normal,' Cam said. 'I suppose I could like it, somebody shows me how.'

We got out, cold after the car.

'Come with a crowd,' Harry said to the woman. He went over. They shook hands. She put her left hand on his shoulder, leaned forward and kissed him on the cheek.

'Thanks for comin,' she said, voice a little blurred. 'After ten years, you still took the trouble…'

Harry put up a hand. 'No trouble.'

He introduced us. We shook hands and I resented the fact that her hand seemed to linger in Cam's longer than it did in mine. She had light-blue eyes, a little puffy: she'd been crying. I'd seen my own eyes like that in many a mirror, some of them spattered with substances whose composition or origin one did not wish to guess at.

'I've got scones in the oven,' she said. 'Haven't made scones for yonks. You used to like scones, Harry. Still?'

Harry dry-washed his hands. 'Still,' he said. 'Always. Good memory. Lead the way.'

126

On the verandah, Jean paused to take off her gumboots, quick, supple movements, rubber boots off, feet into worn, receptive shoes. We went through a sitting room with a stone fireplace into a big kitchen, smell of baking, cast-iron stove, sash windows in the north wall, painted cabinets and a big pine table, eight chairs. The view was of an old orchard, much older than the house, in need of heavy pruning.

'Live in here,' said Jean. 'Warm. You don't mind the kitchen?'

'That's where you eat scones, kitchen,' said Harry.

The scones were steaming, pale yellow inside. Butter lay on the rough surface for a second, liquefied, sank. Quince jelly, lemon marmalade and Vegemite. I started with the Vegemite, two scones, moved on to the quince jelly, two scones, pretended I'd had enough, consented to eat one with marmalade. Two, three.

Harry and Jean talked horses. Winter sun slanted in from the north-west. We drank tea out of white mugs, tea made in a pot. 'Sorry, no coffee,' Jean said. 'Can't afford proper coffee these days, can't drink the instant stuff.' She looked at Harry. 'Thought we'd be able to afford a new ute after last week, never mind coffee.'

Harry didn't say anything, ate his sixth scone, all with quince jelly. Cam was on his fourth. Jean offered him another one.

'No,' he said. 'Don't stop now, spoiled for life. Come out here and pitch a tent.'

'So,' Harry said, last morsel swallowed with tea. 'What happened?'

She pushed hair off her forehead. Her nails were cut short. 'We lucked onto this horse, Lucan's Thunder. Owners wanted a new trainer. Complete amateurs, the owners. I thought, same old story, it's always the trainer's fault. But it was. Dave knows him a bit, says he's an arsehole. Piss artist. Dougal Mackenzie? He's had one or two in town?'

'The name rings,' said Harry.

'Christ knows what Mackenzie'd been doing with this horse. I'd say very little and then badly. I put in a bit of time with him, got the diet right, you could see early on he was a rung up from the usual.'

'New South form, that right?' Harry retained form the way teachers used to remember pupils.

Jean nodded. 'Griffith, around there. Won two from seven, picnics really, then these owners bought him and gave him to Mackenzie and he was a dud from then on. Six starts, six–zero.' She paused. 'Anyway, when we started gettin some really good times from him, we thought we had a chance for a bit of a collect.'

'Owners inside?' said Harry.

'Yes. We said we'd talk to you, they didn't want to know, didn't want to share it around. Got a bit greedy, I spose.' She looked down, put a hand to her forehead. 'Wouldn't have happened if we'd gone to you.'

We looked at each other. Harry nodded to Cam.

'Doesn't follow, that,' said Cam. 'We got turned over a while back.'

'You?' She looked at Harry.

He nodded.

'Hurt the commissioner bad,' said Cam. 'How'd they do you?'

'Dave's mate put this bunch together. Sandy Corning, he's a local, a really nice bloke, straight as they come. Got these blokes he knows. Did okay to start but then the owners buggered it, the mates, the aunts, nannas, the lot, all shoving money at the books. So in the end, the collect was only about sixty grand after commission.'

'Where?' said Harry.

Jean drank tea. 'Near the course. The Strand, near Mount Alexander, know that part?'

We all nodded.

'Dave didn't want Sandy to carry the money home, they were going to meet on The Strand. Dave was there first. He talked to Sandy on the mobile, Sandy was in the carpark, collectin…'

'Not clever,' said Cam.

'No, well, the whole thing's not clever. This car blocks Sandy near The Strand, the other one's behind him, his door's locked, the animal smashes the window with a sledge-hammer, one of those little ones, y'know?'

We waited.

'Sandy's got the money in this bag, it's a kid's schoolbag. He just offers it to the bloke. No, they pull him out…'

She sniffed, found a tissue, wiped her nose. 'Anyway, the bastards bashed him.'

'How bad?' said Harry.

Jean looked at the table. 'This woman from across the road hadn't come out, she's a nurse, he'd a died there. Rib punctured his lung, jaw broken, nose broken.'

She looked at us. 'He was offerin them the bag.'

We sat in silence.

'Cops say what?' Harry asked.

Jean looked at the table again, shrugged. 'Nothin. Lookin for them.'

More silence.

'You can say anythin,' Harry said.

She sighed. 'Dave's on the piss before lunch, smokin

129

again. Eight years off em, back to sixty a day. Doesn't sleep. I'm scared. We've had it now, goin down the tubes here for three, four years. More. Bloody owners. First they love the trainer, then the trainer's ratshit, horse's better than the trainer…'

'What about the horse?' said Cam.

'Took him off us. The next day. The one bastard rings up, says they've decided they want him with a more experienced trainer. Jesus, I could've…'

She caught herself, put a hand on top of Harry's, rubbed it. 'Last luck we had was with you. Thought that was the start of big things.'

Harry put a hand on hers, briefly, a hand sandwich.

Jean got up, galvanised, brisk. 'Shit, you don't want to hear this. More tea? I can make fresh.'

We shook our heads.

She made the gesture of helplessness. 'Well, that's all.'

Silence. The labrador came into view in the orchard, stately walk, tree to tree, the honorary colonel inspecting the regiment. One tree offended him and he peed on it.

Harry looked at his Piaget, a slim instrument that cost as much as a good used car, put his palms together. 'Bit of urgency creepin in,' he said, getting up.

We all stood up.

I said, 'See you outside in a minute.'

They left and I turned to Jean.

'The blokes Sandy recruited. Locals?'

'From the pub in town. The Railway.'

'Jean,' I said, 'I need the names and addresses of everyone—owners, owners' relatives, Sandy's blokes, everyone this thing touched, don't leave anyone out. Have you got a fax?'

She nodded. I gave her my card.

'Tomorrow?'

'Today,' she said. 'Tonight.'

We went outside. Jean hugged Harry, kissed him on the cheek, shook hands with us, some moisture in her eyes.

On the way back to the city, on the tollway, after the brief rolling bumps of the cattle grid, the trip up the hard, lined track, on the made road, the freeway, Harry said, head back on the leather rest, 'This would not be a personal problem, am I right?'

'Could be personal,' Cam said. 'Could be local, could be global.'

'Put on Willy,' said Harry. 'Haven't had any Willy for a while.'

'This Sandy,' I said. 'He put the team together. In a pub.'

'Oh, sweet Jesus,' said Cam.

Long before they dropped me it was night, Friday night, dripping.

I drove the youth club to the Prince after the game, very little said on the way. Very little needed to be said. A supporter near us had screamed most of it at the coach at three-quarter time, two sentences:

Lookitthescoreboardyafuckenmongrel. Seewhatyafuckendonetous.

Us. Done to *us*. The coach wasn't one of *us*. Coaches were transients and carpetbaggers. And only a few players in any era in any club ever became one of *us*. The supporters were *us*. They were the investors. Gave the club their hearts, dreams, they expected a return. Every game was an annual general meeting.

'That Docklands stadium,' said Eric Tanner. 'That's not a proper footy ground.'

'Like playin in a circus tent,' said Wilbur. 'It's not right.'

I prepared to reverse park. It was going to be tight.

'Loadin zone,' said Wilbur Ong. 'No can do.'

'No can do?' said Eric Tanner. 'No can do? It's bloody Satdee, no bloody loadin goin on.'

'Not the point,' said Wilbur, calmly. 'Loadin zone.'

I went in, put a back wheel on the pavement. I didn't care. 'Well,' said Wilbur. 'A lawyer, Jack, expect to find a bit of respect for the law in a lawyer.'

'Last place you'd find it,' I said. 'Look elsewhere. It's a loading zone. Am I unloading you lot on the Prince or not?'

Wilbur sniffed, faith in the law's majesty undiminished. We departed the vehicle, burst into the Prince in a low-key way.

It was a low-technology evening. In residence, six silent people and a dog. The cybermeisters were hanging out elsewhere this evening, perhaps at The Green Hill in South Melbourne, sipping a Green Hill pinot noir, flipping through The Green Hill cookbook.

Stan came over, very much the happy hangman today. 'My,' he said, 'you boys really know how to pick a team. Yes, I take my hat off to you. These Sainters, they could be the Roys come back in another jumper…'

'This place still serve beer?' said Eric Tanner. 'Mind you, there's some says you haven't bin able to get a beer here since Morrie retired. Not what you'd normally call a beer.'

'Touchy today. Beer comin up.'

When we had our beers in front of us, had a sip, wiped off our moustaches, Norm O'Neill, next to me, said quietly, not a register I knew he commanded, 'Well, made up me mind, Jack.' He looked to his left, at the others. 'Speakin for me, that's all.'

I didn't say anything. There wasn't any defence to mount for the Saints. This was execution day.

'Yes,' said Norm. 'Reckon I'm stickin with the team. Can't give up on a side that's so bad. Be inhuman, like leavin a hurt dog in the street.'

Wilbur nodded. 'The boys'll come good,' he said. 'Sack the coach, that'll be a start.'

'Things wouldn't a bin so bad today,' said Eric, 'if that bloody ump hadn't found a free for the bastards every time they get a hard look.'

I looked into my beer. It had happened. The graft had taken. The donor hearts hadn't rejected the recipient.

'Hero, that Harvey,' I said.

'And Burkie,' said Norm.

133

'What about that Thompson boy?' said Eric. 'Kid's all heart.'

And so it went. The years fell away: we might have been talking about Fitzroy. I signalled for another round. Stan took his time. When he arrived with the first two, he said, 'Gets worse from here too, don't it. Next week, your girls play the mighty Roys.'

Norm put a hand under his cardigan and produced a fixture card, studied it through his thick, smudged lenses. 'Says here,' he said, 'next week St Kilda plays Brisbane.'

'After Brisbane, there's another word,' said Stan. 'Lions. L-I-O-N-S. Brisbane Lions.'

Norm folded the card and put it away. 'Don't say that on my card. And it never bloody will. Only Lions left are right here.' He waved around the room at the photographs. 'And you, Stanley, you're a disgrace to the memory of these great men.'

He looked at me, looked at Eric and Wilbur. 'Am I right? Am I right?'

'You're right,' said Wilbur.

'Damn right,' said Eric.

'Beyond right,' I said.

A chastened Stan brought the other beers and slunk off. We resumed our discussion of the virtues of individual Saints. Then I drove home and set about making Saturday night bearable. Ten minutes into this, the phone rang. Wootton.

'Just checking the out-stations,' he said, full of gin, jovial Saturday-evening Wootton, back from his golf club, stuffed with nuts and little sandwiches and bonhomie. 'Anything to report, old sausage?'

134

'The out-stations? I think you've got a wrong number. Wrong century too.'

'If you have,' he said, 'the client will be at the same spot on the dial tomorrow morning, 9.30 a.m. Precisely.'

The judge was in a zippered white cotton garment that slotted in somewhere between a NASA spacesuit and Colonel Gaddafi's overalls. He ordered orange juice and a toasted wholewheat muffin with honey.

'Breakfast,' he said. 'I'm on my way to tennis. You don't want to eat too much before tennis.'

'Fatal,' I said.

We were back at the window table at Zanouff's in Kensington, the less-hungover weekend breakfast crowd beginning to straggle in.

The juice arrived. Colin Loder drank half the glass at a swig.

'The dead man's name is Marco Lucia,' I said.

'I beg your pardon?'

It was too early for this kind of rubbish, even from a judge. I said, 'You didn't hear me?'

He gave me a surprised look, weighed up the matter. 'I don't know the name, Jack. An expression of surprise.'

I'd rung D.J. Olivier after Wootton's call the night before. D.J. was part of the seven-day-week world, Saturday night was just another night. A woman rang back at 10.30 p.m., found me deep in melancholy and self-loathing.

'The subject,' she said in a private-school voice, 'has no criminal record. Passport issued March 1996, left the country in April that year, returned January 1998. Name mentioned in reports of a criminal case in July 1999. An article in the Brisbane *Courier Mail* in September '99 refers to someone who may be the subject.'

'What's the criminal case?' I said.

'Assault, unlawful detention. Subject was the complainant.'

'And the article?'

'Organised crime in Brisbane and the Gold Coast. Someone interviewed refers to someone of this name as, I quote, Milan's fucking star, unquote.'

Milan's fucking star.

I liked the way she said that. 'Thanks.'

'Our pleasure. Let us know if you need a broader inquiry.'

Mr Justice Loder's muffin arrived, golden honey in a bowl. When the waiter had left, I got out the photograph of 'Robbie' and put it next to his plate. He looked around, unzipped a pocket and took out a spectacles case, put on a handsome gold-rimmed pair, looked at the picture without picking it up.

'Well,' he said, put a finger to his lips. 'As I said, this inquiry is on behalf…'

My hands were palm-down on the table. I kept my eyes on the judge and raised the fingers of the right one. 'I'm working for you,' I said. 'You get the bill.'

He breathed deeply, looked out of the window, closed his eyes for a second. He had long eyelashes. 'You'll understand this isn't easy,' he said.

'I understand.'

He held my eyes for a few seconds. 'I met him in Italy several years ago. In Umbria. I was staying at a friend's house. The friend was away, and this young man arrived on the doorstep with a letter of introduction to my friend from someone in London.'

137

He had the diction of a schooled witness. 'Calling himself?'

'Robbie Colburne. He said his mother was Italian, from the Veneto, and his father was Australian. He spoke good Italian.'

'Eat your muffin,' I said, 'it's getting cold.'

He looked at the plate, broke off a piece of muffin, held it like a dead spider, put it down. 'I think I'll skip the muffin.'

I said, 'I only need the pertinent bits.'

'A relationship developed. I had a week left of my holiday. He said he was planning to spend a few years in Europe. I didn't see him or hear from him again until a month ago. He rang me one night. My wife was away. She's often away.'

Without looking at it again, Loder slid the photograph over to me. 'He was an attractive person. Intelligent, full of life. And a lot of sadness in him.'

'Most people have to settle for one of those things,' I said. 'Generally, the last one.'

Loder smiled, cheered up a little. 'That's what's pertinent,' he said. 'I suppose.'

Zanouff's was filling up, people wearing dark glasses, two couples with trophy children, dressed to be cute, caps worn backwards, expensive running shoes. One of the fathers had a tic in his right eye, a stress tic. He kept touching it but it wouldn't stop.

'You resumed the relationship?'

'Yes.'

'I won't put icing on this,' I said. 'Are you scared of something?'

The judge smiled, made a gesture of openness with his arms, spread his fingers. The smile didn't have any staying

138

power. Nor did the gesture. He gave up, closed his arms, put one hand over the other.

'Something's missing,' he said.

'Robbie?'

'Yes.'

'Of what value?'

A sad smile. 'How do you value a career?'

'Not talking about the degree certificates?'

'No.'

A train was leaving Kensington station, an empty rattle of train, windows flashing sky.

'Anything happened since you noticed the loss?'

He closed his eyes again. 'Nothing. I'm petrified. My dad's still alive.'

'And then there's the dignity of the law,' I said, cruelly.

He revived, face turning stern. 'I suspect that the dignity of the law transcends and outlasts that of its humble servants, Mr Irish.'

A dignified response from the Bench.

'Silly remark, allow me to withdraw it,' I said. 'Let me tell you what I know about Marco Lucia.'

When I'd finished, Loder said, 'Can you be sure it's the same person?'

'Pretty much. Only one person matches.'

We watched another train, saw the faintest tremor in the plate-glass cafe window.

'Your advice,' said the judge.

'Option one is that you save yourself a lot of money by popping around to your local jacks and telling them what you're missing.'

'And read the first rumour in the paper tomorrow? Option two, please.'

'I can keep looking. There's always the possibility of turning up something.'

'Keep looking,' he said.

'The missing item?'

'Photograph album. Red leather.' He gave me his sad smile again. 'You're asking yourself how I could be so stupid.'

'No,' I said. 'I've stopped asking that question. I know the answer.'

He got up. 'Thanks, Jack.' A pause. 'It's silly but I find the fact that you're a colleague strangely comforting.'

A judge calling me a colleague. As he went out, it occurred to me that this was probably the high-water mark of my legal career.

I caught the 6.05 a.m. flight to Brisbane, two hours in the air, hired a car and drove for 90 minutes, never once lost, to reach the imposing gateway to Haven Waters. It was half-way across a 500-metre land bridge just wide enough for two lanes.

A man in a police-style uniform, light blue and dark blue, armed, left the gatehouse, came out into the white-porcelain light.

'G'day,' he said. 'Have to ask for your name, address and purpose of visit, sir.' He was a wiry man, ginger and freck-led, big freckles. Cold and grey climes would have suited him better.

I gave my particulars. He wrote them down on a clipboard. Then he asked for two means of identification. Fighting my instincts, I handed over my driver's licence and my Law Institute card. Forever on another record. One day D.J. Olivier might find me there and a young woman with a private-school voice would tell someone.

'Only take a minute, sir,' he said and went back. I saw him pick up a phone, talk, nod, put it down. There was someone else in the gatehouse, a movement. Expensive, a two-person guard, six shifts, that would cost management two hundred grand a year, plus benefits. Just to check tickets. Perhaps the second person also did patrols, that would ease the strain.

Gates opened. The man was waiting for me inside, gave me a map printed on card, laminated.

'Down this road, sir. At the T-junction, turn left. Then first right, go past the golf clubhouse and the village.'

He was English, I caught that now.

'First residence after the village. The entrance is on your right, first gate. Adriatica, that's the name. It's marked on the map. And the name's on the gate.'

He pressed a small plastic disc, the size of a fat ten-cent coin, onto the windscreen above the registration sticker. 'So that we can find you if you get lost, sir,' he said. 'We'll take it off when you leave. Enjoy your visit, sir.'

Bugged, I drove across the bridge, down a curving road, through a landscape sculpted by bulldozers, blanketed with imported soil, planted with thousands of mature sub-tropical trees, grassed, lavishly watered. Water was always visible, on both sides deep inlets. I saw two fat joggers, a thin runner, half a dozen walkers, a woman in jodhpurs on a high-spirited chestnut horse. Then the golf course was on my left, greens like great dollops of pureed spinach, people on motorised buggies. I watched a man duff a tee shot.

The golf clubhouse was low, sinuous, heavy with flowering creepers, and then the village appeared on my right, a semicircle of whitewashed buildings of different heights, different roof shapes and pitches, a clock tower in the middle, someone's idealised Mediterranean village, water glimpsed beyond the buildings, flashes at the end of narrow lanes. Two small parking areas were as snobbish as stock-broker bikies, European metal only, nothing Japanese here.

This was where big money came to die, water without, guards within.

I found Adriatica behind a white creepered wall broken by bays housing big shrubs, leaves large and polished. Its gate was black wrought iron, ornate metal stems and leaves. It was a gate for cars. No-one arrived on foot in this place; there was nowhere to walk, nowhere to park, no pavement, no kerb, no gutter.

I parked in front of the gates, got out. It was warm. I took off my jacket and approached the gates.

'Take off the coat,' said a voice.

'I'm not wearing a coat. I'm carrying my coat.'

He came into view from the left, a thin man, not young, slicked-back hair, one eyebrow like a furry caterpillar stuck to his forehead. The weapon held at his side, pointing at the ground, was extravagant, a long-barrelled .38.

I said, 'Put that fucking thing away. I've got an appointment to see Mr Filipovic.'

He shrugged, opened the gate.

I walked up a paved driveway to where a path through tropical jungle branched off to the house. The air was dense with exotic scents.

At the front door, a huge studded Moorish creation, another man, young, tee-shirt and jeans, was waiting, holding a device like a cordless telephone. 'Gotta check you over,' he said, then ran the metal detector over me.

'Give him your coat,' he said.

The man with the revolver had come up behind me. I complied.

'Arms up,' said the detector of metal.

I raised them. 'Looking for a wire?' I said. 'Go very carefully.'

He smiled at me, excellent teeth. 'I'm very careful. Loosen your tie, unbutton your shirt, cuffs too.'

You sensed a lack of trust in him.

When he was finished, he said, 'Come in.'

We went through a hallway decorated with oversize

Grecian-style urns, down a passage and into a sitting room the size of a four-car garage. It was full of white leather chairs and sofas and glass-topped tables holding heavy bowls of tortured coloured glass. On the wall above a fireplace hung a huge picture of a red rose lying on stone steps. The blowsy petals held perfectly rendered drops of dew the size of oranges.

Through the open French doors, you looked over a broad deck to where a boat was tied up, at least ten metres of gleaming white craft with a flying bridge. A man was working at the stern, kneeling on the deck, straightening up every few minutes to relieve his back.

'Welcome to my house.'

The man had come into the room from a door to the right of the French doors. He was in his fifties, heavily built, oiled silver hair combed back, wearing only striped shorts and boat shoes. His skin was the colour of fudge and his chest was grey-furred, like the belly of an old dog.

I put out a hand. 'Jack Irish.'

'Milan Filipovic.' He applied a challenging grip and I gave it back.

'Strong hand,' he said. 'Don't work behind a desk all the time, hey?'

'Thanks for seeing me,' I said.

'Not a problem, mate.'

Another man had come into the room, a younger man, strong looking, a bodybuilder, with dark hair cut short. He was in shorts, a golf shirt and boat shoes.

'Steve,' said Milan. 'He works for me.'

Steve didn't offer to shake hands, just smiled, another mouth of first-rate teeth. Something in the local water, perhaps, or a good cosmetic dentist.

'Hey,' said Milan, 'we're jus goin out on the boat, test the engines. Steve, ask that cunt if he's finished?'

Steve went out.

'This place, what you think? Nice, hey?'

'Very nice. Must be good to live on the water.'

'The best. Cost a fucken bomb. What you reckon they want for management, upkeep, security, all that shit?'

'Quite a bit.'

'Forty grand a year. How's that?'

'That's a lot, that's steep.'

He scratched his chest pelt. 'I told em, I don't need your fucken security, look after myself. Little cunt says it's not an option.'

I watched Steve come back. His legs were too short for his torso.

'Ready,' he said.

'Pineapple juice,' said Milan, 'get a coupla litres.'

He led the way to the boat. We passed the man who'd been working on it. 'She's ace, Mr Fil,' he said. 'Runnin smooth.'

'Good boy,' said Milan, patting him on the chest. 'Tell Denny I said cash.'

We were at the centre of a bay, a big expanse of water. The village's long curving boardwalk was on the right, two-storey boathouse-like buildings lining it, people sitting under market umbrellas. Perhaps forty other waterfront houses were in sight, most of them with boats tied up at their landings, big white muscle boats, here and there a yacht supplying some class.

'Like it?' said Milan.

'Top spot,' I said.

'You gotta earn it.' He was first onto the boat.

Steve and the young man who'd searched me arrived, Steve carrying a big pitcher of yellow juice. The young man cast off, went up to the flying bridge, Steve went below.

'Take a seat,' said Milan, waving at the banquettes. They were gently scalloped into individual seats.

I sat down. He sat opposite me, his pectorals sagging, dark nipples peeping out of the dense hair like the noses of inquisitive forest creatures.

The engines fired, a satisfying sound, a growl that made the deck beneath my out-of-place leather soles vibrate. My searcher took the boat away from the landing, howling off at forty-five degrees from the land. In a few minutes, we were passing through a broad opening to the sea, a dead calm sea, blue-black.

Milan got up, climbed the steps to the bridge, muscles showing in the big calves, said something to the helmsman, who throttled back the engines, settled on a modest cruising speed.

Back in his seat, Milan looked at me, opened his arms, palms upward, smiled. 'Fucken paradise, hey? Whatya think?'

I looked around. There wasn't much to see. An endless flat paddock of ocean, a boat here and there. 'Very close to it,' I said. 'You're a lucky man.'

He laughed, ran a hand over the oiled hair. 'Lucky? Jack, listen, mate, I come to this country with fuck-all, I work like a dog, anythin, mate, anythin, cleanin gully traps, that's what I did. Cleaned a gully trap?'

I shook my head. I had, actually, but this wasn't the moment to compare experiences.

'Yeah, well, don't talk lucky to me, mate. Qualified fitter and turner, you think I get a job? No way, they don't want a fucken wog can't speak two words of English.'

146

Steve emerged with the pitcher of yellow juice and two heavy-bottomed tumblers. 'Yellow peril ready to go,' he said.

'Just a small one. I'm driving,' I said. It sounded lame.

Milan laughed as if I'd said something very entertaining. Steve poured two full glasses, handed me one.

'Pineapple and vodka,' said Milan. 'Good for you, builds up acid, cleans the bowel.'

He put back half his glass. 'No, mate, I'm just a fucken Serb. Nobody likes Serbs, right? Be fine if I was a Kosovar. Right? Remember that lot?'

I nodded.

'Everybody bleeding about fucken Kosovars. Mate, they not even Christians. Christian country this, right? Those people are fucken Arabs. Not from Europe. You see the women? Hide their fucken faces. Got no pity, either. Kill children. Right, mate?'

I didn't say anything. What was there to say to six hundred years of breeding?

'So what's this Marco shit?' he said. 'You NCA, Feds, what?'

I shook my head. 'I saw you mentioned in the newspaper. I've got a client who needs some information. That's it.'

Now he had a good laugh. I was becoming funnier every minute.

'Listen, you not from the Feds, okay, you give the Feds a message from me. Okay? Okay?'

'If they ask me, okay.'

'You tell those bastards, Jack, I tol em, they don't listen. They never gonna make this drugs stuff stick on me. I don't deal drugs, I never deal drugs, never will. Not interested. People come to me with offers all the time. I say no. That's right, Steve?'

'Right,' said Steve.

'Right. I'm not sayin I don't know some stupid people, they get involved in this shit. Not sayin that. Everybody knows stupid people. You can have a stupid brother, how's that your blame, hey? But I tell them, keep away from me, keep that shit away from me.' He leaned over, belly creases deepening. 'Jack, you think I'm such a dumb cunt I'm dealin while I've got the fucken Feds on my fucken hammer?'

'It wouldn't be smart, no,' I said.

'Tell em that, Jack, tell em. Tell em to get off my fucken back. Adult entertainment, that's my business. That's fucken all. And property, I got a bit of property. Plus a couple invest-ments. All in the open.' He looked at Steve.

I said, 'Can I ask you about Marco Lucia?'

'You ready?' Milan said to Steve.

'Ready.' Steve went below and came back with a flat case. He opened it and took out a small machine-pistol and two long magazines. A magazine made a snick as it went into the butt.

Milan took the pistol, showed it to me. 'Nice, hey? Ingram. Better than a Glock. Don't trust fucken Austrians.'

Steve shouted something from the bow of the boat. We slowed to walking speed. A blow-up pool toy drifted by: a swan.

Milan stood up, went to the side and fired a short burst at it. The swan collapsed without a sound.

'And another thing, Jack.' Milan turned to me, took on a sad look, a man injured to his core. 'I'm hurt there's no gratitude.'

'Gratitude?'

'Gratitude. What these pricks in Sydney do when their fat boy gets in the shit with whores? They come to Milan, that's what. I squeeze that cunt Papagos for them like a grape, end of problem. So where's the gratitude?'

'You deserve more,' I said.

'Fucken right. You tell them, Jack.'

'Any time I get the chance. About Marco Lucia?'

A blow-up crocodile came by, followed by several big balls, two ducks and Mickey Mouse. Milan went into a firing frenzy, changing magazines in mid-carnage. The objects deflated, slumped on the water.

'Marco,' I said.

Steve appeared. 'Hey, shootin,' he said.

'Pretty boy cunt,' said Milan. 'People say I topped Marco. Bullshit. Wouldn't fucken waste my time. Cut his cock off, that's somethin else. Find him, I sew it up in his mouth.'

'Have to stick half down his fucken throat,' said Steve. He laughed, showing his teeth.

'Gimme another drink. Jack, have another one.'

'No thanks. Why do they say you topped him?'

'He just fucked off, noone seen him, so they say he's dead, they point at me.'

'Why at you?'

Milan eyed me over the top of his glass, lowered it. 'Warm as piss,' he said. 'More ice, Steve. Why?'

'Why do people point at you over Marco?'

'He did some work for me.'

'What kind of work was that?'

Steve was putting ice into Milan's glass with tongs.

'Just work,' said Milan. 'Things I give him to do.'

'Marco's dead,' I said.

Milan looked at Steve, eyes eloquent, looked at me. 'Says who?' he said.

'Drug overdose in Melbourne.'

Milan drank some pineapple juice. 'Melbourne,' he said, as if hearing the name of some remote cattle station. 'What's he doin in Melbourne?'

'Working as a part-time barman.'

I could see a huge powerboat coming our way at speed, foaming bow waves. It slowed, veered away to increase the distance between us when we passed. Perhaps the idea was to lessen the risk of spilling Milan's drink.

The three men and a woman on board all waved. Milan moved a hand at them. 'Everybody knows Milan,' he said.

'Marco was calling himself Robbie Colburne,' I said.

Another exchange of looks.

'Robbie what?' said Milan.

'Colburne.'

'You sure the dead one's Marco?' said Milan.

'I've got a picture. It's in my jacket. Inside pocket.'

Milan looked at Steve. Steve felt around in my jacket, found the photograph, showed it to Milan without looking at it.

'Hey,' said Milan, a broad smile, real pleasure. 'The pole. Marco Polo.'

Now Steve looked. 'Good fucken riddance,' he said. He was smiling too.

'Overdose?' said Milan. 'What?'

'Smack.'

Another boat came from nowhere, rocked us with its wake. 'Arsehole.' Milan shook his head. 'So a needle?'

'Yes.'

Milan puffed out his cheeks. 'Needle's a big fucken surprise to me,' he said. 'What's the Feds' interest?'

This was not progressing. 'What kind of work did Marco do?'

Milan smiled at Steve. Steve smiled back. 'What you reckon, Steve? What kinda work Marco do?'

'I dunno, Milan.'

'Marco's all cock,' said Milan. 'Work it out.'

'If someone wanted to kill him, why would that be?'

Much laughter. Milan held his empty glass out to Steve. 'More,' he said. 'Whattabout you, Jack?'

I shook my head. 'I'm not getting anything here,' I said. 'You want me to pass on messages, you won't answer a simple question.'

Milan considered this, working his tongue over his teeth. Then he leant over. 'Listen, Jack, the cunt's just a big prick and a thief. Maybe he stole somethin, made people angry. He's no fucken loss.'

He straightened up. 'But don't lookit me. You know how I'd a killed Marco? You know?'

I shook my head.

'I bring him out here, I open him up a little, just for blood, tie him to a 200 kilo line. Then I throw him over and I tow the cunt around lookin for sharks. Tow him till all I got on the line is a bit of bone.'

Steve's mobile shrilled. He said a few words, handed it to Milan.

Milan listened. 'Tell him to fucken wait,' he said. 'I'm comin.'

He gave the phone back to Steve. 'Home,' he said.

The first you saw of Haven Waters was the clock tower. What need did these people have of the time?

Tired, the feeling of the whole body being tired, not the earned tiredness of exercise, of physical work, just tired in the bone marrow. I went down the dark passage to the kitchen without bothering to switch on a light. The clock on the microwave said 9.14. I'd been up for seventeen hours, four hours in aircraft seats, three hours driving.

And bubbles of sour pineapple juice kept rising. Milan was right. It built up acid, it would probably clean the bowel. Scouring, they called it in horses.

Milk. I needed milk, drank two glasses, not terribly old. Then I opened a bottle of red and sat on the couch in the sitting room waiting for the place to warm up. Food I had no need of – I never wanted to eat again.

The buzzing of the tired brain.

Marco Lucia. Milan had not spoken well of him. But what had the judge said?

…an attractive person. Intelligent, full of life. And a lot of sadness in him.

There would certainly have been a lot of sadness in Marco if Milan had had his way and towed him around the Queensland coastline as live shark bait. Bleeding bait.

Listen, Jack, this cunt's just a big prick and a thief. Maybe he stole somethin, made people angry. He's no fucken loss.

A big prick and a thief. Would the judge agree with this description? Yes, if I understood the term relationship properly.

Marco Lucia on the run from something in Queensland.

He comes to Melbourne. Many people think Melbourne is a long way from Brisbane.

Marco takes on the identity of his school friend, Robbie Colburne.

How was it possible to do that?

Groaning, I got up and found my notes.

Robbie Colburne and Marco Lucia both left the country in April 1996.

School friends. They'd gone to Europe together. But only Marco came back. Was it the case that Robbie didn't need his identity any longer? Because he was dead?

Marco could've been Robbie's brother, Sandra Tollman had said. Both pale, with black, black hair.

I poured some more wine, put the video in the slot, sank into the couch with the remote in hand.

Marco going into the Cathexis building. The new Melbourne landmark. Hideous but the very edge of architecture.

The unknown man at a pavement table, dark, balding, a fleshy face seen from across a busy street, then a new camera angle, a second camera, unsteady. The man drinking the shortest of short blacks, newspaper in his hand, looking around, half-amused.

Worth trying to identify the man? No, too hard.

Early evening, Marco in right profile, side on, several parked cars between him and the camera. He is waiting to cross a street, a narrow street, vehicles flashing by. He takes a break in the traffic, walking diagonally, the confident walk.

Nothing there.

Marco in his dinner jacket in a car.

I sat in the half-dark thinking about the origin of the

clips. State cops? Feds? I thought about Marco waiting to cross the street, wound back.

Marco waits to cross, waits, a gap, he walks, he's in the middle of the street. Freeze the frame.

To Marco's right, on the other side of the street, is a parked car. There is someone in the driver's seat.

Was Marco walking towards the car?

I looked at the clip in slow motion. Definitely someone in the car, that was all. And the number plate was visible but unreadable.

Too tired to think any more. I needed Milo and my new book, bought at the airport and only just violated. It was called *Love and Football*. The warm, innocent liquid and a brief read of my book, that would be my reward for a long day in the field.

Tomorrow, I'd take the video in to get some enhancements.

In the cracking dawn, I shambled around Edinburgh Gardens and along the pavements of North Fitzroy, nothing on my mind but the signals coming from all regions of my body—distress calls, warnings, entreaties.

Home, I raided my shrinking store of new shirts, stock-piled in more prosperous times, and showered long and hard and hot, adjectives that could be applied to Marco Lucia if I'd got the drift of the exchange between Milan Filipovic and his white-fanged and complaisant colleague.

After a cup of tea and, at the kitchen table, a few more pages of my new book, a moving tale of innocent passions corrupted by corporatism, I departed for Meaker's. There I breakfasted on fat-trimmed bacon and mushrooms on toast, lavish quantities supplied by an Enzio who appeared to have been irradiated. Twice he winked at me from the kitchen door, both times running a hand over his scalp. The message seemed to be that my reading of the widow had been correct: hair she had not been pining for.

At 9 a.m., I was at Vizionbanc in South Melbourne, just around the block from The Green Hill, showing the manager the images I required.

'Eleven,' she said. 'We're a bit slow today. A morning sickness problem.'

The problem of morning sickness I understood perfectly.

I used her phone to ring Mr Cripps, the postman who wouldn't retire, and arranged for him to pick up the prints. This was done through Mrs Cripps, who could relay messages to the puttering Holden without using a mobile phone, a device her rotund husband once told me he abhorred. That was, in fact, the only thing he had ever told me. Telepathy was not ruled out.

On the way back, I passed the casino, even at this early hour vacuuming in hapless poker machine addicts. It was one thing to put your faith in your scientifically arrived at choice of beautiful creature, to be urged to realise its full potential by a small and muscular person. Hoping a flashing and programmed electronic device would give you money was another matter. Entirely.

At my professional chambers, I found that the fax machine had extruded paper: Jean Hale's list of everyone associated with the Lucan's Thunder plunge. Guilt assailed me: I had given the matter no thought.

And, on the answering machine, Mrs Purbrick.

Jack, I'm experimenting with a new caterer and I need a man of taste. Give me a ring soon, darling.

Pause.

I'm in my beautiful library constantly. Devouring books. And Ros Cundall is green with envy.

Would it hurt to be Anne Purbrick's taster? What could she tell me about Xavier Doyle, Robbie's employer?

Drew was next.

Woodmeister, you're listening to a man who's had a mystical experience. I think I'm in love. In lust and in love. Ring and I'll share this with you.

Not Rosa. Please, God, not Rosa.

I read Jean Hale's list. Plumbers and electricians and painters and redundant teachers. It was even worse than I'd expected.

I rang her. The ring went on for a long time. A man answered, gruff. I asked for her. She was outside with horses.

'What's your name?' he said.

'I'm associated with Mr Strang.'

'Right. Sorry, I'll get her.'

Jean Hale came on.

'Jean, Jack Irish. How's Sandy Corning?'

'Better. He's going to be okay. We're going to see him today.'

'Good. Can you ask him to rule out people on the list? People he has complete confidence in?'

'Yes. Sure.'

'And fax it to me again?'

A hoot outside. Mr Cripps. I said goodbye, found a $20 note, went out and exchanged it for a stout envelope.

'Exemplary service, as always,' I said. He nodded, expressionless as a whale. The yellow Holden puttered away, its waxed surface dotted with fat beads of rain. Beading. You'd done the wax job properly when the result was beading. .

Thinking about how little beading had occurred in my life, I returned to my chair and opened the envelope. The cassette and four prints, two enlargements of Robbie crossing the street, two of the man at the pavement table.

The registration number on the car Robbie was walking towards was now readable. And the person in the car was a woman, half her face visible, looking in Robbie's direction over the top of dark glasses.

I studied the fleshy man in the other pictures. There was a reflection in glass behind him, that would be the cafe window, a reflection of writing on something, not a flat surface, the word *asset*.

Asset?

It didn't matter. I strolled around to the Lebanese and rang Eric the Geek, Wootton's attenuated computer ace, prince of hackers. There were redialling sounds and science-fiction lost-in-space noises before he answered.

'Yeah.' Not an interrogative inflection. This was about as expressive as Eric got but the single grunt conjured up his gloomy, damp-jumpered, patchily-shaven presence.

'It's Jack. I need a name.'

I read out the registration number.

'Minute. Number?'

I gave him the number. While waiting, I studied the notices on the board near the phone. House-minding, dog-walking, appliances for sale, a new homemade wanted poster with a photograph of a thin, dark-haired young man described as a heroin addict, missing dogs, cats, a budgie, probably now inside one of the missing cats. The phone rang.

'Jack.'

Return of the cyber-Visigoth.

'Exactly,' I said.

He sniffed, coughed, a cough that needed attention. 'Hang on,' he said.

Keys tapping, silence, more taps, silence. A tap.

'Company car. Syncred Nominees.' He spelled it out. 'Address 27/6 Kelling Street, Crows Nest, Sydney.'

I wrote it down, said thank you, and rang Simone Bendsten, an expert fisher of companies and the people in and around them.

'How's business?'

'Good. Looking up. I owe you. Max's given me a lot of due-diligence research and he's passed me on to another firm.'

Max was a corporate lawyer I'd recommended her to. I told her what I needed.

'Work of minutes, hold on, I'm at the machine.'

More listening to tapping. Outside, a police car pulled up and a cop got out and went out of view. He came back holding a scruffy, emaciated teenager by the arm, shoved him in the back seat. Was I witnessing your actual drug bust? A Mr Big removed from circulation?

'Jack. Two directors. James Martin Toxteth, Colin Leigh Blackiston.'

'Mean anything to you?'

'No. I'll look around. Ring you?'

I gave her the mobile number.

At the office, in the captain's chair, in a patch of sunlight, I looked at the pictures again. Drowsy. Up too early. Too much exercise. The doomed dog had not fronted today. Scared? Somehow cognisant of my murderous instincts? Aware of my total lack of ruth?

People filming Marco or filming the fleshy man or filming the woman in the car?

They were filming Marco. He wasn't the bit player, he was the star.

A fuck star.

Milan and Steve both showed real pleasure at the news of Marco's death. Death of a fuck star.

A star.

An evil star.

And grapples with his evil star.

The sight of my grandfather, my mother's father, came to me, the lean figure sitting in his buttoned chair, quoting Tennyson, every word a universe of meaning.

The old man was referring to my father's evil star. In my childhood, no week went by when the old man did not find an opportunity to speak ill of the dead man. He made it clear that there was something in me of my father that he had a duty to exorcise. I was well into my teens before it dawned on me that the sum total of my father's evils appeared to be beer, the odd punch-up, and fully paid-up membership of the working class and the Communist Party. The last two vices my grandfather found particularly heinous.

I'd had the old man in mind on my first visit to the Prince of Prussia, empty that autumn afternoon, light from the western windows lying on the scuffed floor, on the dented and cigarette-burnt bar, dust motes and my cigarette smoke hanging in the weak sunlight.

Morris had put down my beer that day, eyes fixed on me. 'In mind of Bill Irish when I look at you,' he said. 'Funny.'

'My father,' I said.

Morris studied me for at least 30 seconds, then he said, head on one side, indignant, 'Where the hell've you bin?'

The mobile jerked me out of my reverie. Simone Bendsten. 'Jack. Those directors. James Martin Toxteth is a former merchant banker. Colin Leigh Blackiston was an investment fund manager. They're in business together in a Sydney venture-capital company called Toxteth Blackiston Private Equity. That's about it.'

No illumination there.

'Thanks,' I said. 'Send me the bill.'

'You're in credit here. Buy me a glass of wine one day.'

'That'll be for pleasure. This is work, someone's paying. I'll use my credit another time.'

Back to drowsing. Should I be brave, ring Drew, find out the identity of the love object? It couldn't be Rosa. He'd stood her up. But nobody stood Rosa up. She'd simply have driven around to his office, fronted up to him. Rich, spoilt people were like that. The phone.

'Jack, the other day, you wanted a snap.'

Detective Sergeant Warren Bowman, he of the telegraphic eyebrows.

'I'm grateful,' I said.

'Sorry I've been so long, mate. No luck, can't be done. Cheers.' Click.

After a while, I put the phone back in the cradle.

The two men in the new red Alfa. The one who gave me the video cassette was young, a mole beside his mouth, wearing a collarless black leather jacket.

Not the messengers of Warren Bowman.

I rested my forehead on the tailor's table.

The rest of the day I spent on the half dozen files I had open: a few letters of demand, a complaint about harassment by a landlord, a protest against an unjust parking fine. Then I did my hours and expenses for Cyril Wootton and faxed them to him.

Driving home in the early dusk, I put on the radio, caught the wheedling tones of a drive-time host called Barry Moran, a seminary flop who had joined the legion of other faith-challenged but inordinately sensitive people on radio. Barry was sensitive to the concerns of the young, the old, ordinary people, extraordinary people, the poor, the rich, the short, the tall, the middling, all religious beliefs, and the legitimate concerns of both sides in every dispute. He strove to be fair to everyone but had a tendency to be snappish with people who disagreed with his reasonable views. Unless they were powerful people, in which case his views quickly came to encompass theirs. He was saying:

...The Development Minister Tony DiAmato joins me now. Thanks for coming on the program, Minister. Last week you washed your hands of the Cannon Ridge controversy because the previous government awarded the tender. It's done, it's history, you said. Now this is a tricky one, I know, Minister, but if the tender process was corrupted, don't you have a duty to declare the tender void and hold an inquiry?

I thought about the library-warming, my attempts to make conversation with Mike Cundall. 'Politics of business,' he'd said. 'WRG wants to build a whole fucking town on the Gippsland Lakes. Get the new government in some shit over

Cannon, good chance they won't get knocked back on that.'

Now the Minister cleared his throat.

Barry, we're talking about allegations here. We've had a pretty good look at the documents and we can't find any evidence of corruption.

Barry, ever the unctuous ex-seminarian, said: *That's a reasonable approach. Now Minister, I'd like to put a tricky one to you. WRG Resorts says a member of the tender evaluation panel was quote placed under duress unquote. Now I wouldn't dream of saying the name but every media person in town has heard it. Do you know who the alleged person is?*

The Minister sighed, tired at the end of the day.

No, I don't. And Barry, I'm surprised at a person like you not recognising that WRG's on a fishing expedition. They say they've got evidence. Where is it? They've yet to approach me with it.

Barry, nimble as ever: *Of course, it might well be a fishing expedition, Minister, as you point out. We might take a call. Its Steven from Doncaster.*

A confident voice said: *Hi Barry, love your show. About this Cannon Ridge business, everybody knows that in opposition this government put up a pissweak resistance to the sale of Cannon Ridge. Pissweak. They let the previous government sell off part of our heritage. Why'd you reckon? Because they're in the Cundalls' pockets like everyone else in this town.*

Barry: *Minister?*

DiAmato, weary: *Well, for a start, Anaxan has five major shareholders…*

Caller: *And one's a Cundall. One's all it takes. You know that…*

It went on this way. I parked beneath the trees outside the boot factory, listened for a while, went upstairs and switched on the radio in the kitchen, tuned to Linda's station.

…breaking up is hard to do. That's what the old song says. But do men take it harder than women? Yes, says writer Phil Kashow in her

new book, published today. It's called Healing Your Broken Bits.
*I want your views on the subject. The author's on the line from Sydney.
Hello, Phil…*

I stood in the room listening to the exchange, Linda's
mildly amused tone in dealing with the publicity-hungry
woman. Then, without thought, I went into the sitting room
and dialled the talkback number, pressed the redial button a
dozen times until I got through to the producer.

'Hello, you are?'

'Jack from Fitzroy.'

'And you want to say?'

'I'm a psychotherapist and I'd like to shed a little…'

'Stay on the line please, Jack.'

A wait, listening to people emoting, then Linda's voice.
'Jack from Fitzroy's next. What's your view, Jack?'

'If breaking up is hard, how much harder is making up?
That's the question I'd like to pose to Phil. And to you,
Linda.'

'Excellent point, Jack,' said Phil. 'No simple answer. I deal
with this in chapter sixteen of my book, called "Be proud
and be lonely"…'

She talked rubbish for a good while, then Linda said,
quickly, 'And insofar as that question included me, not hard
at all, Jack from Fitzroy. Moving on, Phil, you say…'

I switched off, found a bottle of Cooper's Sparkling in the
back of the fridge, stood around drinking it, thinking about
Linda, what the remark meant, about who would want to
give me the video of Marco and why. In the way of minds,
I then veered off to Sandy the bashed plunge organiser, to
my sister, to a despondent survey of the clutter of my life. A
life that had no pivot, no fulcrum, no axis, no…

The phone.

'Jack Irish.'

'I'm in the ad break.'

Linda.

'Ad break. I'm in the life break.'

'Where?'

'Donelli's?'

'Shit,' Linda said. 'Doesn't anything change?'

'Not if I can help it.'

'Eight-thirty?'

For a Tuesday night, Donelli's in Smith Street was crowded. It had recently been redecorated, which included knocking a large hole in the wall between the dining room and kitchen. Now it was a theatre-restaurant: diners could watch the fat *faux* Italian patron and chef, Patrick Donelly, fussing around and abusing his staff.

I'd rung to book. The patron spotted me entering and came out to escort me to my table. 'You're a lucky man, Irish,' he said. 'Two servings left of the stuffed squid braised with white wine and tomatoes.'

'That'll be fine,' I said. 'Anything I don't have to watch you both stuff and cook.'

'The watchin's by popular demand,' he said. 'Punters can't get enough of the chef. Sex objects, that's what we are.'

I looked at the man, torso like a wrapped fridge. 'Speaking for myself,' I said, 'I'd rather have sex with the squid. Now, a decent bottle of white. Any of that little Tuscan number left?'

'Two bottles. I was savin them for the cognoscenti.'

I patted him on the white arm, as thick and round as a fire extinguisher. 'Well, they're not coming tonight, Patrick. I'll have theirs.'

'You'll be dinin on the bill, will ya?' he said.

'I think you can take that as read.'

Donelly owed me a large sum, payment for hundreds of hours of skilled labour over a messy legal matter finally resolved in his favour. Since getting actual money from the man was impossible, I'd been extracting my fee in food and drink.

Linda came in the door. Her hair was different, longer, parted in the middle. She was wearing a black raincoat and she took it off to reveal a black polo-neck and jeans. Lean and handsome, that was the same. She came over and kissed me, on the cheek, touch of silk, throat-catching hint of perfume.

'Now this closes the circle,' she said.

Our first social meeting had been at Donelli's, at this table.

We sat down.

'How can circles be circles before they're closed?' I said.

She smiled. 'When I think of the years I've wasted wrestling with that problem.'

My desire was to take her by the hand and go home, but nothing was that simple. Except in beginnings.

'I've ordered squid. Stuffed. Braised with tomatoes and white wine.'

'Sounds good, excellent.' She pushed her hair back. 'Somehow, I never saw you as a talkback caller.'

'I've always wanted to be. Full of potential. Just never heard a talkback host I wanted to talk to.'

We sat looking at each other, smiling, neither of us sure how to proceed.

'How've you been?' she said.

'I've known better. You're looking good.'

'For radio, I'll pass. You're thinner.'

'Worry.'

Silence again. The wine arrived. I waived the tasting ritual.

Linda sipped. 'Nice. I heard you'd taken up with a photographer.'

She'd never been one to step around subjects. I tried the wine. Much too good for the cognoscenti. 'Who told you that?'

'Gavin Legge. He rang me. Trying to get publicity for a book he claims to have written.'

Legge was a journalist, a client of mine in the old days when I was practising criminal law. I'd got him off a charge of assaulting a female restaurateur. He had also introduced me to Linda.

'The Legge is quicker than the eye,' I said. 'But he's out of date. I've moved on. Now I'm seeing a supermodel. She's eighteen. Stalked me, a thing for older men. What about you?'

She made a gesture of dismissal. 'Too much bother. And there's this internet service that home-delivers men— yourfuck dot com. It's all a working woman needs.'

I nodded. 'Do they take them away again?'

Linda frowned. 'They say they're working on that bit. Four in the garage the last time I looked.'

I laughed, she laughed, and the awkwardness was over, the long time apart contracted to nothing. I felt buoyed, light-headed. We talked about things that lay in our common ground, laughing a lot. She'd always been able to make me laugh and I'd had some success with her.

The squid was served by a small and intense young man. It was delicious. Donelly arrived, lifting Linda's hand and bowing his head to kiss it, reverent.

'Deeply honoured, my dear,' he said. 'I remember when ya first graced my establishment in the company of this ruffian. And now the whole kitchen loves ya. Station of choice while we're preparin the finest food in this city.'

'Thank you,' said Linda. 'I appreciate you saying that.'

I realised that people said things like this to her all the time. It was nothing new to her. She was a celebrity. I took the opportunity to order another bottle of the Tuscan.

'And in the circumstances, how could I say no?' said Donelly, shaking his head at my opportunism.

'Exactly.'

Donelly sighed. 'Consortin with this famous lady, Irish,' he said. 'How ya do it, legal extortionist that you are, defies the imagination.'

'She sees in me what is invisible to people like yourself, Patrick,' I said.

He went off, stopping here and there to bestow benedictions on tables of chef groupies, all eager to have sex with him.

'I've been consorting with other famous people,' I said. 'I met Mike Cundall last week. And the beautifully preserved Ros.'

I told her about Mrs Purbrick's library.

'The son and heir's in with a fast crowd,' said Linda. 'Comes from spending too much time in Sydney. Sam's been trying to get out from under Mike for years but everything he touches turns to dog shit. The nasty coke habit and the gambling don't help. Then along came Cannon Ridge.'

'What's the story there?' Linda knew Melbourne.

'The Sydney smarties put together this consortium to tender. It's full of funny money. They brought in Sam because they reckoned the Cundall name could swing the thing. Not an unreasonable assumption. I mean, Mike Cundall used to just front up to see the last Premier, no appointment, shown straight in. And people heard him shouting at the Premier. Now that kind of thing cuts ice in Sydney.'

And Linda knew what cut ice in Sydney. She'd left Melbourne, and me, to be a current affairs television star in Sydney. That was where it all went wrong between us.

'And he did swing it?' I asked.

She forked up the last of her squid and chewed thoughtfully. 'Let's say it was swung,' she said. 'No-one quite knows how. WRG, the other bunch, they thought they had it stitched up. Australian company, experienced resort operators worldwide, went through the probity stuff without a hitch, pitched the tender on the high side to be sure and threw in some sweeteners. Cometh the hour, they find Anaxan has got them covered on all counts. Into shock they went.'

'I heard Barry Moran saying everyone in the media knew the name of a tender panel member who'd been put under duress.'

Linda looked around. 'Said to be a bloke called Rykel. A conservation bureaucrat on the panel. The whisper is that a large sum arrived in his wife's bank account just after the winner was announced. A transfer from a numbered account at the Bank of Funafuti or some such.'

The wine arrived. Then our plates were removed.

'According to Mike Cundall,' I said, 'and Mike tells me things all the time, this leak stuff is just WRG's way of screwing the government into letting it bulldoze a large section of Gippsland. Presumably the section that houses the last known breeding ground of an endangered creature.'

'With tiny pink nose. Yes, Anaxan's got the spin doctors putting out that story. Best in the business. Ponton's. Did you know Gavin Legge works for them now?'

'Openly? He's come out?'

'This mole has lost his value on the inside. Damaged goods is Gav.'

'What's his book called? *Living Off the Land: How to Take With One Hand While Also Taking With the Other?*'

'*Media Relationship Management in the Cyberage.* It's a slim volume.'

'I beg your pardon? Are we talking about the Gavin Legge who offered to get the name of the man who was tiling his shower into the paper? As a contra deal?'

'We are. Ponton's keep people chained up in New York to write a book for every new consultant. It's called WTB cred.'

'What? Wing Tailed Buzzards?'

'Wrote the Book. As in, the expert on the subject. Then they subsidise publication and bribe the reviewers in the business press to say things like succinct and definitive work, brilliant insights, etcetera. All easy, cheap. One decent contract, Pontons are in profit.'

'Shocked, that's all I can say,' I said.

She gave me the Linda eye and half-smile. 'Yes, well, you would be, pottering around as you do exclusively in Christian outreach circles.'

'Have a heart,' I said. 'Not just Christian. I don't discriminate on grounds of faith.'

She raised her glass, serious, put out her left hand and touched my face for an instant. 'To old friends new again.'

We touched glasses. I also thought I felt a leg touch mine and an erotic charge went through me, through the core. I often thought about her athlete's legs. 'That's a good toast,' I said. 'Welcome home.'

'I may never leave Melbourne. Well, maybe not never.'

'No. They say never is now down to six months.'

Donelly appeared, beaming smoked-salmon face moist above his surgical garb. 'You'll be wantin somethin to close with.'

I shook my head. Something about this personal attention was nagging at me. Celebrity-sucking, yes, but there was something else.

'I want the memory of your stuffed squid to stand alone,' said Linda. 'So a short black would be lovely.'

Donelly smiled at Linda, smiled at me, bowed and departed.

I poured the last of the wine, having had the sense to come by cab. 'You're not driving?'

'The station pays for after-work limousines,' said Linda. 'It's in my contract.'

'Good.' We looked at each other, smiles beginning.

'As someone steeped in the lore of Sydney,' I said, 'do the names James Toxteth and Colin Blackiston mean anything to you? They're venture capitalists, but that's all I know.'

'Jamie Toxteth, yes. Are you planning an IT start-up? Involving horses?'

'I'm trying to find out about someone who ran away with someone else's album of naughty snaps, died of smack, turned out not to be who he said he was.'

'This doesn't sound like Jamie Toxteth country to me,' said Linda. 'Jamie plays polo. The Toxteths are landed gentry. They own Mount Toxteth station. It's huge, like a small country. A country of sheep. Prince Charles spent weekends there.'

'He'd like a country of sheep. They have no problem with following the most stupid. What would a woman in Melbourne be doing driving a car owned by a two-dollar company Jamie owns?'

She raised her cup. 'This place is closing. For all I know, women all over Australia drive cars owned by Jamie. I may be the only one left out. This was a lovely evening.'

Linda found her mobile and rang for a cab.

We rose. Linda went to get her coat. I appreciated the way she looked from behind as I strolled towards the waiting Donelly.

'Show me where to sign,' I said. 'And may I say that if I were a squid, you would be my preferred stuffer.'

He ran fingers over his brow, disturbing the long strands of hair that originated well to the west.

'That'll be $38.50,' he said, a light in his eyes, a glow, an unearthly glow. He'd been waiting for this moment for three years. 'Your outrageous bill paid in full plus $38.50. And we'd prefer cash. If it's a cheque, you'll have to leave your watch.'

An era ended, closed. A watershed, a turning point. Dining out would never be the same.

I gave him a $50 note, said, 'I presume there's a discount for cash.'

'Certainly.' Donelly went away, he was gone for a few seconds, and when he returned, he counted out $11.50 in change. Then he said, 'And here's your discount.'

He put half an unshelled peanut in my palm.

'You're being petty, Donelly,' I said. 'Give me the other half.'

Outside, rain and cold had driven everyone except a few drug desperates into shelter. We stood against Donelli's window. 'I'm back at the boot factory,' I said. 'What about you?'

'I bought a place in Carlton. On Drummond Street, near your old office. It's nice, an old building, used to house nuns.'

'I can understand you feeling at home.'

She put a fist under my chin. Her cab arrived. 'I'll drop you,' she said.

Seize the moment? No. Patience. I shook my head. 'Wrong direction. We'll do this again, I hope.'

She opened her hand, touched my lips with three fingers. 'Call me.'

I was at home on my way to bed, in a better mood than I'd known for some time, when the phone rang.

Cam said, 'Somethin we should do tomorrow morning. You okay?'

'Any luck on short Artie with a Saint tatt?' I said.

Cam shook his head. 'That Braybrook address, he was there for three months in '98 after he came out. Three years for serious assault.'

Artie's name was Arthur Gary McGowan, he had form going back sixteen years, and he lived outside the world of telephone books, credit cards, Medicare, voters' rolls, and phone, power, gas and rates bills. He was out there in the cash economy and all we had was an old driver's licence address.

Today, we were in a non-threatening vehicle, a new Subaru Forester, dark green, parked outside the Royal Melbourne Institute of Technology on Swanston Street, just up from the ugliest new facade in the city. The architects had played an end-of-century joke on the university. Needless to say, the university hadn't caught it yet. Universities never do catch the joke until it's too late. Many a French fraud had died laughing while earnest Australian academics were still doing PhDs on his theoretical jokes.

'She finishes at twelve today,' said Cam, eyes on the passersby. 'Fashion, that's what she does. Whatever that is.'

He was talking about Marie, the 18-year-old daughter of Cynthia the commission agent.

I watched the throng of students, many of them the sons and daughters of the old colonial world, the Asian part. We'd closed our factories so that we could exploit the cheap labour their parents provided. Then we had a second cunning and rapacious thought: we could convince them that our universities were intellectual powerhouses and charge huge fees for admitting their children.

It worked.

'What'd Cynthia say?' I said.

'The boy told her Marie's got a habit. Coupla days ago. She says she went wild, grabbed Marie when she came in the house. Marie says it's over, she's clean, clean since Cyn got bashed.'

'That's all?'

He nodded.

'This Cynthia's idea?'

'No. She doesn't make any connection. I never said anythin. There she goes. You start.'

Cam was out of the car, walking round the front, long strides in his moleskins. He caught up with a slim young woman in black jeans and a purple top, said something. She turned her head, smiled, stopped, obviously knew him. He gestured at the car. She nodded, came back with him.

Cam opened the back door for her.

'Hi,' she said.

I turned and said hello. Her spiky hair was the same colour as her top, her lipstick was green, and she had ear and nose rings. The overall effect was innocent, something a five-year-old let loose on her mother's things might achieve.

Cam got in. 'Marie, Jack Irish. Your mum knows him. He's a lawyer.'

'Hi,' she said again. 'I've only got a minute. What's it about?' Her speech was rushed, nervous.

Cam took out his Gitanes, offered her one. She took it, leaned across for a light, had a coughing fit.

'Jeez,' she said, 'what is it?'

'There's somethin milder here somewhere,' said Cam.

'No, it's cool.' She coughed again. 'Just a shock.'

Not turning, I said, 'Marie, we're trying to find out who bashed your mother.'

I could hear her exhale smoke. 'Yeah,' she said. 'Yeah, that's good. It's like a nightmare. Weird.'

I waited a few seconds. 'How long have you had a habit?'

Silence. 'Christ, what's this shit? I'm out of…'

Cam leaned over the seat, draped his arm. 'Marie, listen, it's not about you and drugs, right? It's about who nearly killed your mum. You love your mum, don't you?'

More quiet. Marie began to cry, a sniffle, throat noises.

'Don't you? Love your mum?'

Then she was making crying noises, not loud, and saying, 'Oh, Jesus, oh Jesus…'

We waited.

After a while, I said, 'Tell us about it, Marie.'

She did a lot more sniffing, then she said, 'Mum sent you?'

'No,' said Cam. 'Your mum told me you'd had a problem, but that now you're clean. She's proud of you, your mum.'

The sniffing resumed. Then she said, courage plucked, 'There's nothing to tell, like. What's this—'

I said, 'Last chance, Marie. You could go to jail for this. Conspiracy.'

This time it was a cry from deep down, a wail, then more sobbing. I looked at Cam. He was looking at Marie, flicked his chestnut-brown eyes at me. I thought I detected a hint of compassion. Probably just the light.

We waited.

'I just told this bloke my mum did big-money bets,' she said, sad voice. 'Don't even know how it works—'

'Which bloke?'

A long silence.

'Can't go back now, Marie,' said Cam, gently. 'Which bloke?'

'Around the bike shop. He deals, everyone knows him, it's safe.'

'Why'd you tell him?' Cam said.

Sigh. 'I dunno, I just told him one day.' Sigh. 'Like I thought it was smart, like my mum didn't do ordinary kind of…Just stupid. Mum always said…Oh, shit.'

'You told him that and then what happened?' I asked.

She became matter-of-fact. 'He said, give us the word when you've got a horse. I didn't know anything about that, mum never said a word, all I knew is some days she's got something on at the races, she's phoning people, you can't understand what she's saying to them.'

'You told him you never heard the names of horses?' I said.

'Yeah. Then one day he says, tell me when your mum's going to the races and I'll give you a hit.'

Silence, waiting, Cam leaning over the seat, looking at Marie, tendons like cable in his neck.

'And?'

'That day, I was hanging out, didn't have a cent…'

'You told him,' said Cam.

'Yes.' Tiny voice. 'I'd've cut my wrists before I told him if I knew what…'

'Where's the bike shop?'

'Elizabeth Street.'

Cam started the vehicle and waited to pull out.

'My mum,' said Marie, 'you're going to tell mum?'

'No,' said Cam, getting into the traffic, 'you've got your punishment. This bloke always there?'

178

Marie sniffed. 'Most of the time. He sees you're chasin and he meets you at the Vic Market. Keeps the stash there.'

'We'll drive by. See if you can point him out.'

We went around the corner into LaTrobe Street, turned right into Elizabeth Street.

Marie saw him almost immediately.

'Next to that white car, the bloke on the bike.'

'Sit low,' said Cam.

He was across the street from the motorcycle dealers, sitting on a black BMW, helmet on his lap, talking to someone in the passenger seat of a car. We got a good look at him—tall, curly red-brown hair pulled back in a ponytail, short beard around his mouth.

We took Marie back to Swanston Street. As she was getting out, she said, 'Cam, I'm so scared my mum'll find—'

'Not from us,' said Cam. 'Stay clean or you'll break her heart.'

'I'm staying clean. That's over, over.'

We watched her go, long-legged walk, bag swinging.

'Get that number run?' said Cam.

'Five minutes. Find a public phone.' Cam took out a mobile. 'Safe phone,' he said.

I didn't ask what that meant. I took it and dialled Eric the Geek.

There was a fax from Jean Hale waiting at the office. Two names on the Lucan's Thunder betting team were circled. One was someone called Tim Broeksma. In the margin, Jean had written: *He's new. Sandy doesn't know much about him. A plumber.*

The other name was Lizard Ellyard. There were quotation marks around Lizard.

He's got a firewood business. Bit of a sad case, was in a bad accident, I think. Anyway, he didn't show up on the day so he really shouldn't be on the list.

I drowsed in the captain's chair, mind picking daisies. Cam and I had lunched well at a pub in Abbotsford. It was a place frozen in time like the Prince, except that this pub had been deliberately frozen, used as a television series location for years, and it was in excellent shape. Halfway through the sausages and mash, I felt a hand on my shoulder.

'Straying out of your territory, Mr Irish.'

Boz, in jeans and a jerkin. I introduced her to Cam. She sat down for a few minutes and I told her about Mrs Purbrick's party.

'You'll end up choosing her books, Jack,' said Boz. 'I saw the signs.'

She was getting up to rejoin a table of people, all talking, telling stories, film people if I read the signs, when Cam said, 'I do a fair bit of movin. Got a card?'

Boz shook her head. 'Got a pen?' She wrote her name and phone number on a drink coaster. He put it in an inside pocket.

I saw the signs.

Now, half-asleep in my office, I was thinking again about who had given me the Marco video. The people who'd taken it? I'd assumed it was a cop video—federal, local. That might still be true. But I had to assume that the cops hadn't given it to me.

Who then? And why me? Why would someone other than the cops give me a surveillance video? What could they want from me?

Who else knew that I was interested in Robbie/Marco? My anonymous caller knew. But there was no way to find out who she was. Had the judge told someone? Not likely. The people at The Green Hill knew. But why would they be interested in helping me find out more about a dead man they had employed under another name? And where would they get the video?

This line of thought wasn't going to produce anything. If I knew more about Robbie/Marco, the questions would probably answer themselves.

I got out the enhanced pictures and looked at them again. Trying to identify the woman in the car belonging to Jamie Toxteth and his partner hadn't met with any success. That left the fleshy man at the sidewalk table.

How to begin?

I was looking out of the window. I could see Kelvin McCoy's front door. A young woman came into view, dressed in what from this distance appeared to be a garment fashioned from colourful rags, offcuts from a tie factory perhaps, and carrying a big flat folio bag. At McCoy's portal, she paused, uncertain for a moment. Oh God, she had been invited to show the unwashed charlatan her drawings. I felt I should open my door and shout a warning. Too late, she knocked. A brief wait, the door opened, I glimpsed the brutal shaven head, she was drawn in. The beast would see a lot more than her drawings before the day was out.

Ah well. Life went on.

The fleshy man. In the glass behind him, the cafe window, a reflection of writing on an uneven surface, the word *asset*.

Written on what outside a cafe? What was uneven?

An apron, it was on an apron, a long black apron of the kind favoured by Melbourne cafes. A reflection of a name on a waiter's apron.

Asset?

My stupidity dawned on me.

I walked up to Brunswick Street and weaved and jinked my way along a pavement crowded with young artists, fashion students, actors, directors, scriptwriters, drug dealers, filmmakers, fashionistas, off-duty *baristas*, models, writers of forgotten grunge novels published by Penguin, *Age* lifestyle journalists, internet entrepreneurs, meme-carriers of every description. Many of them were on the phone to like-minded people. Why did people have so much more to communicate these days?

At my destination, a good bookshop next door to what had been a good gun shop with a bad clientele when I came to Fitzroy, I bought a copy of a guide to cheap Melbourne eating places. Cheaper.

Near the office, I heard the phone ringing, ran, wrestled with the lock, got in, panting.

'Jack,' said Wootton, 'the client wants to meet very, very urgently.'

I took the book with me. You never know how long you'll be kept waiting.

The door was huge and studded and the steps before it had hollows worn in them big enough for birds to bathe in. I pressed the button and waited no more than a minute or two.

A tall, thin man in a dark suit opened the door. 'Mr Irish?'

'Yes.'

'Please follow me.'

We went up a curving staircase to a lobby, then down a grand corridor, stopping at a door near the end. The man opened it with a key and ushered me into a panelled reception room with desks and computers, no-one at work. He knocked at a door to the left, listened, opened it, and said, 'Mr Irish, Your Honour.'

He stood back for me to enter and closed the door behind me. I stood in an impressive room: high ceiling, dark panelling, cedar bookcases tight with bound volumes, small oil paintings in gilt frames lit from above. It was exactly the chamber I'd expected a judge to inhabit. Only the computer station was out of place.

Mr Justice Colin Loder, no jacket, was coming around his leather-topped desk. 'Jack,' he said, 'thanks for coming.'

'Your Honour.' We shook hands.

'Colin. I should've said that before. You know too much for formality.'

'Something's happened.'

'Sit down.'

I sat on a chair with buttoned green leather upholstery.

The judge went back to his seat, sat upright, forearms on the desk. A long yellow envelope lay in front of him. He touched each of his cufflinks, modest silver ovals, checked them, pointed at the envelope with his eyes. 'The worst,' he said. 'Worse than I expected. Left downstairs an hour ago.'

I waited. He pushed the envelope over.

'Read it, please.'

It had been opened with a paper-knife. I removed one sheet of white paper, twice folded. A good computer printer had produced half a page of type:

Mr Justice Loder,

The accused in the so-called 'cocaine jackets' hearing before Your Honour are innocent victims of a Federal Police conspiracy. In its eagerness to make up for its incompetence, this agency has often resorted to illegality in the past and has done so again in this matter. As you will know only too well, an option is available to you when this matter resumes. Choosing it will be in keeping with your well-deserved reputation as a defender of the citizen against improper conduct by government agencies. Therefore I am sure Your Honour will see fit to use your discretion to exclude evidence relating to importation, from which it follows that the accused must be acquitted, since without this evidence the prosecution must fail.

In passing, may I say how sad it was to hear of Robbie's death. The album of photographs you lent him, so touching in their intimacy, will be returned to you at the appropriate time. You will not, of course, wish to recuse yourself or to find some other reason for not hearing this matter. Such actions will have the unfortunate consequence of your reputation being damaged beyond salvation.

Naturally there was no signature. I folded the page, put it on the desk, looked into the judge's brown eyes, eyes the colour of strong tea, the bag left too long in the mug.

'Appropriate is a bad word,' I said. 'What's the cocaine jackets?'

'Cocaine concealed in ski jackets. Two men charged. It's what's called a controlled importation. The Federal Police ran the thing using an undercover agent, an informer. I don't think it would be unjudicial of me to describe the operation as a massive cock-up.'

'The demand. Lawyers wouldn't be stupid enough?'

'No. Not even lawyers are that stupid. They wouldn't know about this. This is from people associated with the accused. Trying to make sure it goes their way.'

'What kinds of people are the accused?'

'They're not Mr Bigs, these two, they're mules, really. But they're all the Feds could lay their hands on. Desperation stuff after spending huge amounts of money.'

'Why wouldn't the people higher up simply let them go down?'

He turned his mouth down, raised his hands. 'Don't know. They may know something. And should they get long gaol terms they might agree to co-operate with the police. Could be other reasons. Family, who knows?'

'Distinct legal tone to the letter. Lawyer in there some-where. The finding it suggests, could you make it?'

'Are you familiar with *Ridgeway?*'

'Familiar's probably not the right word.' It was the landmark High Court decision on police entrapment.

'Well, that's what they'll be arguing. And yes, it's a poss-ible finding, depends on what happens when we resume.'

'When's that?'

'Next Thursday.' He sighed, made a resigned face. 'I suppose I should call the police in now, issue a statement to the media. This'll kill my father.'

185

'You could ignore the letter. See what happens. It may be bluff, they may just go away.'

The judge shook his head. He'd aged years in a few hours. 'No, Jack. Any finding I reach would be tainted by this. The well's poisoned.'

'Give me a few days.'

His chin sank a little. 'Any point?'

'We have to assume that Robbie took the album with this or something like this in mind. If I can find out what happened to him, it's possible I'll know who the blackmailer is.'

Another sigh.

'I won't keep you in suspense,' I said. 'If I'm not getting anywhere by Tuesday, I'll pack it in.'

Silence for a while. The sounds of the city didn't reach the room.

'I'll give you a mobile number,' he said. 'It's not in my name. I've borrowed it.' He took out a notebook, flipped through it, wrote down a number on a desk pad, tore off the page and gave it to me. 'I feel as if I've entered the underworld myself.'

I stood up. 'Can I get a transcript of the proceedings?'

The judge stood up too, went to a wooden filing cabinet and found a yellow folder, gave it to me. He walked me to the door. We shook hands.

'We could get lucky,' I said. 'Chin up.'

He smiled. 'Thanks, mate. Thanks for everything.'

'Don't say thanks till you've seen Wootton's bill.'

The thin man was waiting outside to escort me to the side entrance. On the way to Fitzroy, stuck in Little Lonsdale, I picked up the cheap eats guide, flicked through to the index.

There it was, on the first page I scanned.

La Contessa, assetnoC aL in reverse, was a narrow place in Bridge Road, Richmond, that looked as if it had been there longer than those on either side in what was now a smart strip.

Although it was cold and too early for the after-work crowd, the half-dozen tables outside were taken. Inside, there were only a few customers. I found a seat near the kitchen. The man operating the coffee machine was not of the new generation of cafe people; he had the pained expression of someone too long standing to perform a repetitive task: the assembly-line worker's look.

A young man, possibly the son, came out of the kitchen. He was wearing the apron in the picture, a long black apron with La Contessa printed on it. I asked for a short black. When it came, I had the picture out, facing him.

'That's probably you,' I said, tapping on the reflected apron.

He was intrigued, had a good look. 'Yeah,' he said.

'Who's that?' I said, my finger on the fleshy man.

'Alan Bergh,' he said, suspicion starting. 'What's this, what's this about?'

'I'm a lawyer.'

This statement often has the effect of briefly paralysing the brain of the hearer.

'Right.' Uncertain. 'What do you—'

'I'd like to get in touch with Alan.'

'Yeah, well, he's away.'

'Away from where?'

'Where? His office.'

'Where's that?'

He indicated with a thumb. 'Vietcong supermarket. Upstairs.'

He'd learned that from his father. The war in Indochina was not over. The battle for the hearts and minds of the invaders had still to be won.

I didn't pursue the matter. The waiter left, went outside.

The coffee was terrible, sour, third-rate beans, old, probably black market.

'Come again,' said the father, giving me my change.

'Can't wait to.'

I walked in the direction indicated by the son's thumb. Halfway down the block was a business that satisfied his description. Beyond it, a heavyweight door with a mail slot carried the names of two businesses on the first floor: VICACHIN BUSINESS AGENCY and CORESECURE.

The door was locked. I pressed the buzzer on the wall.

'Yes,' said a woman's voice, hissing through holes in a slim stainless-steel box beside the door.

'Client of Coresecure,' I said. 'Here to see Alan.'

'Mr Bergh not here,' said the voice, staccato.

'When's he coming back?'

'Don't know.'

I accepted that, wrote down Vicachin's phone number. Coresecure didn't have one on the door. Then I went home, a slow journey in failing light in the company of irritable people.

Coresecure wasn't in the White Pages. Nor was it in the Yellow Pages in any category I could think of. I packed up for the day, not a great deal to pack, and drove around to

Lester's Vietnamese takeaway in St Georges Road.

Lester was alone in the shop, in the kitchen. When the door made its noise, he looked up and saw me in his strategically placed mirror.

'Early, Jack,' he barked. 'How many?'

'I need a favour,' I said.

'Ask.'

I asked. He nodded, took the piece of paper and went back to the kitchen, held a long, rapid-fire conversation in Vietnamese on the phone.

He came back and returned my slip of paper. 'They talk to you,' he said. 'You can go there tomorrow.'

I drove home in drizzle, tail-lights turning the puddles to blood, listening to Linda on the radio taking calls on Victorians' gambling habits. The daylight was gone before I found my mooring beneath the trees.

Upstairs, I put on the kitchen radio to hear a man say:….*accept that the state's now on a gambling revenue drip and raise the tax till the bastards scream.*

Linda: *You're saying gambling's a fact of life, so get the most public benefit out of it?*

Caller: *Exactly. And this Cannon Ridge casino, the Cundall casino, slug it. Playground for the rich, double the bloody gambling tax.*

Linda: *Thank you, Nathan of Glen Iris. Now there's a challenging point of view, even if the logic may be slightly fuzzy. What's your view, Leanne of Frankston?*

Leanne: *Linda. I'm a compulsive gambler, I've had treatment…*

Enough. She would ring or she wouldn't. It was probably better if she didn't. We could meet from time to time as friends. Old friends. We'd made a good start at that.

Had she rubbed her left leg against my right? Not a rub, but a linger. A touch and then a linger.

How old did you have to be before this kind of rubbish stopped?

I got a fire going, bugger cleaning the grate. Everything was dirty in my life, why worry about a pile of soft, clean ashes?

Now, a drink. I looked in the cupboard. Campari and soda, Linda's end-of-day drink, the bottles not touched since

Linda. I poured a stiff one, settled on the couch to think. The phone rang.

'No doubt,' said Drew, 'I find you poring over your footy memorabilia, sniffing old Fitzroy socks, marvelling at the size of your antecedents' jockstraps, lovingly preserved.'

'Large in their day but dwarfed by those to come,' I said. 'I gather you've found a form of happiness with some unfortunate.'

Tell me that it is not Rosa, please.

He sighed. 'To find joy and to share it, that is life's purpose. You probably have no idea who said that.'

'No. Let me have a stab. You.'

'Spot on. Anyway, you can't dwarf a jockstrap.'

'The courts will decide what you can and cannot do with a jockstrap. Who?'

'A corporate lawyer. International experience. Top-tier firm, I might add. With a personal trainer.'

I gave silent thanks. 'Trains her to do what? Find 48 billable hours in the day? Render the simple incomprehensible? Conspire with the other side to shake their clients down?

I could imagine the pained Drew look.

'Slander your fellow servants of the law if you will,' he said. 'This delightful creature has been slumbering, awaiting the kiss of an awakener.'

'Slumbering? Form?'

'Unraced.'

'Age?'

'I'm not filling in an application here.'

'I'll put it to you again.'

'The thirties. Thirty-five, six. Thereabouts, I suppose.'

'That's quite a slumber. How did this happen?'

'Her secretary was in a bit of strife. Vanessa came

along to give the poor woman moral support. You'll have noticed the effect a commanding physical presence, razor-sharp intellect, and professional brilliance can have on women.'

'I have. How'd you get Vanessa to notice you?'

'I can feel waves of jealousy passing through this instrument.'

'I hope you're talking about the phone. You got the secretary off?'

Drew sighed. 'Actually, no. Could've been worse though.'

'Moving away from your erotic fantasies,' I said, 'as a man of affairs, does the name Alan Bergh mean anything?'

'It does.'

'Tell me.'

'An employers' secret agent, Mr Bergh. Years ago, when the unions could still get up a decent strike. Before a Labor government broke the Builders' Labourers.'

'Does everyone except me know that?'

'Unusually, no. Bergh planted thugs in marches, demos, the blokes at the back who lob the first unopened can of VB at the cops, that sort of thing.'

'How do you know?'

'Appeared for one of his thugs. You were on sabbatical then.'

He was saying that this was in the time, the long time, when I was drunk, half-drunk, getting drunk again, after my wife Isabel's murder.

'The client told you?'

'We were pleading guilty, mate, as befits people shown on television poking what looks like an electric cattle prod up a police horse's bum. A former racehorse. With not unpre-dictable consequences.'

'Took off at great speed?'

'No. Reared and endangered lives, jockey fell off.'

'Surprising. Given a touch of the jigger, your racehorse generally shows a bit of toe, leaves the field behind. That's the idea of jigging them. So the client told you about Bergh?'

'Not him. Another bloke came in. An extremely dubious character. I got the impression that he'd hired my client and was a bit worried about what I'd do in court. I didn't want to discuss the matter with him, so he said, listen, just don't do anything that'll piss off Alan Bergh.'

'And?'

'Over a cheering glass with the labour aristocracy down at the John Curtin, I asked about Bergh. The word was that he did jobs for employers. The nasty work. Not still in business, is he?'

'He's in some business. Haven't worked out what it is yet.'

I was still trying to work it out in the last moments before sleep. I tried to find a thread in everything I knew about Robbie/Marco. Hopeless. It wasn't a fabric, it was a heap. And now there was a sophisticated attempt to blackmail a judge of the Supreme Court sitting in a drug importation case.

Marco was murdered. He was being watched, and then he was murdered. The supplier of the surveillance clips knew that and wanted me to know that. Milan Filipovic hadn't thought it likely that Marco had stuck a too-potent needle in his arm.

'Needle's a big fucken surprise to me,' he'd said.

But Detective Sergeant Warren Bowman said the dead man had needle tracks.

Alan Bergh and the woman in the car belonging to a Sydney high-flier. How did they fit into Marco's life and death?

Sleep claimed me, troubled sleep, full of strange places, peopled with strangers.

Up early stumbling around the streets, back to Richmond in peak-hour morning traffic, thinking about Colin Loder and his dad. That was what worried him most: his dad finding out that he had it off with non-women.

Not his brilliant legal career crashing. Not his wife and children finding out. Just his expectation of his dad's horrified reaction. His dad probably had his suspicions anyway.

Mr Justice Loder should announce that he was being blackmailed because he was gay or bi, had been silly enough to appear on camera.

Was that all Colin was worried about? Consenting adults? Did his album hold photographs that told a different story?

In Bridge Road, I parked in a loading zone and rang the bell at Vicachin Business Agency.

'Yes,' the voice hissed again.

'Lester rang about me. Yesterday.'

The door bolt unlocked.

The stairway was dark. Upstairs, the offices of Coresecure and Vicachin faced each other across a dim corridor. Vicachin's door opened and a young woman, unsmiling, beckoned me into an office, walls decorated with travel posters. She opened an inner door and stood back.

A balding middle-aged man in a black suit and striped shirt was behind a desk. He stood up and put out a hand. 'Call me Tran,' he said, briskly.

'Jack Irish.'

'Sit, Jack.' He sat down and adjusted his glasses. 'Your

friend tells me you want to know about Alan Bergh. There's not much I can tell you.'

He had an American accent.

'He's gone somewhere?'

'Well, he hasn't been in for a couple of weeks.'

'Have you told anyone?'

'No.' He wasn't looking at me, looking down, fiddling with his glasses.

'Something may have happened to him.'

He shrugged. 'I don't like to interfere. Mind my own business.'

'Do you know much about Coresecure, Tran?'

Tran held up his hands. 'God knows. Something to do with company security. I think Alan was a soldier once. He speaks some Vietnamese.'

'Who's the landlord?'

'I collect the rent.'

An answer to a question I hadn't asked. 'That's up to date?'

'Oh yes. Three months in advance.'

'What did you find when you checked his office?'

'Nothing.'

As he said it, he knew he'd been taken, tugged at an ear lobe, perhaps thinking about the mind-my-own-business problem.

'You worry whether someone's collapsed, heart attack, you know,' he said.

'Of course. Would you mind if I had a look?'

Tran's eyes said nothing. 'I don't understand. Your friend says you're a lawyer. What is your interest in Alan?'

'It's complicated. I think it's important to find Alan. Very much in his interests. You can trust me not to involve you in any way.'

A long think.

'I can't let you into his office.'

'You don't have to.'

More thought. Then he opened a drawer at his right and took out two keys on a metal disk, put them on the desk. He stood up, turned his back on me, went to the window. I took the keys.

'Thank you for talking to me, Tran,' I said. 'I imagine a security consultant's office would be guarded by the latest alarm system.'

He turned. 'No. Nothing of value, I suppose. Sorry I couldn't be more help.'

We shook hands and I left. The outer office was empty. I crossed the corridor and unlocked the Coresecure office. Inside, it was dark and musty.

I felt like a burglar.

In many ways, I was a burglar, always intruding, taking things I had no right to.

There was little to take in the Coresecure office. It consisted of two rooms, the front one not used, the back one minimally furnished. There was a desk, nothing on it except a telephone and a box of tissues. The drawers contained printer paper, an ink cartridge and a box of ballpoints. A printer was on a stand next to a filing cabinet, empty. To the right of the desk, a bookshelf held capital city telephone books, copies of an American magazine called *CORPO-RATE SECURITY*, and a dozen or so books, company histories and books about business failures and corporate crime.

The wastepaper basket was empty.

I went behind the desk, picked up the telephone and pressed the redial button.

Nothing. Last call cleared.

Standing behind Alan Bergh's desk, in his boring office, his telephone in my hand, a feeling of disgust, of failure and futility, settled on me. This was not the way an adult should spend time.

I pulled a tissue out of the box, wiped the instrument, replaced it, realised how silly this was for a member of the legal profession, gave the phone an extra rub anyway and went around looking for other things I'd touched. Paranoia satisfied, I clicked off the light.

In the near-dark of the outer room, reaching for the doorknob, I saw the mail basket. The mail was collected downstairs and someone, Tran's assistant no doubt, posted it through Coresecure's slot. It fell into a basket attached to the door.

A burglar. A thief.

I did a quick sort of Coresecure's mail and left, posting the firm's keys through the mail slot after closing the street door.

Back to Fitzroy, to the office. I'd never spent so much time there. I didn't want to be there. I wanted to be at Taub's, making things. Any things.

At my table, I opened the purloined mail. I'd stolen two bank statements, a credit card statement, and a mobile-phone bill.

I read the bank statements. One was for a cash management account holding $66,354. No transactions in the statement period, an interest credit. A cheque account statement showed three deposits adding up to $28,730 and cash withdrawals, two a week, four or five hundred dollars each time. Six cheques had been drawn against the account, the biggest for $3024. The most recent transaction was a cash withdrawal of $500 two weeks earlier and the account was $12,340.80 in credit.

On to the credit card statement.

Alan Bergh spent money on restaurants, hotels, plane tickets and hire cars, bought clothes at expensive shops, and paid the account balance inside the interest-free period. Rich and prudent.

The last account was the mobile-phone bill: four pages detailing how Alan had incurred a debt of $2548.20. The man gave good phone. I got a pen and asterisked the frequently called numbers and the long calls. Then I rang for Mr Cripps. He was at the door inside fifteen minutes.

Coffee.

Urgent, compelling was the need. I walked swiftly, bought the *Age* on the way, found Meaker's near-empty. A new waiter, a thin young man, took my order.

Waiting for my long black, I postponed reading the paper, watched a man taking things out of the back of a van in the loading zone. A sign-writer: Beems Brothers, Sign-writers.

My coffee came. I sipped.

Foul taste of uncleaned machine, reused grind.

Poised to complain, I realised that I didn't recognise the large person lolling against the counter in front of the machine. Fat, in fact.

I raised a hand. There was anxiety in me.

The new waiter came over. 'Something else?'

He had big teeth.

'What's happened to the usual mob?'

'Pardon?'

'The people who usually work here?'

'New management,' he said. 'New staff.'

'What?'

199

'Sold.'

'As of when?'

'Pardon?'

'When did this happen?'

He held up his hands. 'Temp, mate, can't help you there.'

I got up and went to the kitchen door.

'Hey,' said the man at the coffee machine.

I ignored him, looked in. No Enzio. A small fat man was at the stove. He sensed me, turned his head.

'What?' he said.

'Enzio?'

'Who?'

'The cook.'

'Dunno.' He looked away. 'Ask the manager.'

Behind me, the big man said, 'Staff only, mate.'

I didn't look at him, went back to my table, picked up my paper, made for the door. The waiter said loudly, 'Hang on, coffee's not free.'

I turned, he was close. 'That isn't coffee,' I said with venom.

'Lettim go,' said the big man, back behind the counter.

I looked at him.

'Piss off. See ya, buddy. Go somewhere else.'

Walking away, holding a course, the flow of the aimed and the aimless breaking around me, I was compelled to look back. The sign-writer was scraping at the name Meaker's on the window.

A chilling sense of fate's impudence came over me. How could there be no Meaker's in Brunswick Street? How could it simply be taken away?

Hooted at, I crossed the street and went into a place I didn't know, barn-like, atmosphere of a school staffroom.

It had once been a social club. Macedonian? Portuguese? I couldn't remember. The coffee was awful, I was too bemused to care, left most of it, wandered back to the office.

I saw him from a long way off, leaning against the wall next to my door. He saw me too but he looked away, smoked his cigarette, studied the sky, clear today, some high cloud. I was metres away before he turned his head to me.

Enzio, clean-shaven, in a black suit, white shirt, dark-blue tie.

'Jack,' he said.

'What the fuck's going on?'

He took a last drag on his cigarette, ground it savagely underfoot. 'The bastard Willis sold.'

Neil Willis had owned Meaker's for about fifteen years. He also owned two wedding reception caverns out in the suburbs and his stewardship of Meaker's consisted of hiring a succession of untrained managers and scrutinising the takings at night. Enzio was the only constant, and so the cook had always ended up grumpily showing the managers how to run the place.

I unlocked the door and we went in. I took my seat. Enzio stood.

'Sit down,' I said.

He sat, shifted around in the chair, crossed legs, uncrossed.

'What's this suit business?' I'd never seen him in a suit.

He frowned. 'I'm comin to see a lawyer. You dress proper.'

I understood.

'Smoke?'

'Smoke.'

I fetched the ashtray from the sink in the back room. He lit up, exploded smoke.

'Tell me,' I said. 'Tell me.' I closed my eyes.

'Tuesday, Willis come in, business sold, new boss come in tomorrow. No worries about jobs, he says. Bloke wants all staff to stay.'

He took a deep drag, spoke through smoke. 'Yesterday, the cunt come in. I know straight away, I look at the cunt and I know. Before lunch, sacks Helen. Carmel he sack at the door, says she's late. Martina, she's going off, he tells her, customers complain, pick up your pay tomorrow. Closing time, he come in the kitchen, it's me and the boy cleaning up, he says he's looked at the books, there's stealing going on in the kitchen.'

Enzio looked away, looked at my degree certificate on the wall, took a moment to compose himself.

'Fourteen years, Jack,' he said, still studying the wall. 'Steal?' A catch in the voice. 'Like I steal from my mother?'

'I know.' I wanted to give him a pat.

We sat in silence, contemplating ourselves, our histories at Meaker's, perfidy, the callousness of people. But I was coming out of shock, cruising past resentment. Revenge and compensation were now in mind. This was a natural progression and I had some training in it.

'What's the offer?' I said.

'He says, the prick, he's got the money in his hand, he says four weeks pay I give you, lucky you get anything. Don't like it, I get the cops, you can tell them who you sold all the stuff to.'

'Take it?'

Enzio put his head back, looked at me over his cheek-bones, over lines of spiky hairs that survived his shave, a prickly frontier.

'I spit on him,' he said.

Our eyes held for a moment.

'Right. You in the union?'

He shook his head. 'No. Willis wouldn't have the union.'

This wasn't going to be effortless for someone who'd spent most of his legal career in the criminal courts. I might actually have to find out something about employment law. Either that or I farmed this out. Tempting.

But how could I farm out Enzio?

'Okay,' I said. 'We've got no choice but to nail the poor bastard.'

I got out a yellow pad. I'd bought four dozen yellow pads when the stationer in Smith Street went under. 'Now tell me again what happened. Slowly.'

When we'd finished, I went out with him. The day was turning foul, the wind was sharp against the cheek, coming down the street, chasing bits of litter, harrying them like a bully.

'So,' said Enzio. 'You fix it?'

'I'll fix it.'

We shook hands. I watched him go. At the corner, he felt my eyes, turned his head, smiled, raised a hand. I did the same.

Oh, Lord, why hast thou anointed me the fixer of all things? And why hast thou ordained this in a cold season in which too many things need fixing?

There were moments when I wished I could go somewhere quiet and ask sensible questions like these. My office wasn't the place because the phone was ringing. It was Drew.

'What is it with you?' he said. 'You no sooner take an interest in someone and bad things happen to them.'

He didn't have to say the name. I knew.

'Who?'

'Alan Bergh. Found dead in his car at the airport. Execution-style killing, says the paper. Three shots in the head from a .22.' Someone was knocking at the door. I knew who it was. My day for being knowing.

They sat in the client chairs, a soft-looking big man with a moustache, a younger man with a long horse face. Agents Mallia and Bartholomew, Federal Police.

'Let me understand this clearly,' said Mallia. 'You asked this Vietnamese gentleman…'

'I have no idea whether he's a gentleman,' I said. 'Do you?'

'Manner of speech.'

'Offensive manner of speech, if I may say so.'

Mallia coughed, looked at Batholomew, who ran a hand over his head bristles.

'If you say so,' Mallia said. 'You asked him a lot of questions about Bergh?'

'No,' I said. 'I'll say it again. Clearly. I was interested in using the services of Mr Bergh's company. He wasn't in, so I spoke to Mr Ngo. I asked him if he knew when Mr Bergh would be back or where he could be contacted.'

'He says you didn't know what Coresecure did, what its business was.'

'That's a misunderstanding. I asked him how much he knew about Coresecure. At that point, I thought he might have some involvement with the company.'

Equine-faced Batholomew thought he'd chip in. 'You wanted to use Bergh's services. What for?'

'What for?'

'Yes. What for?' He developed a smile, as if he'd been clever.

'Security.'

'Security for?'

'Nothing in particular. Security in general. I wanted a feeling of security. I've always wanted to feel secure. What about you?'

The smile departed.

Mallia stroked his moustache, then, carefully, scratched the arranged hairs on his head. 'You're probably not aware of the powers conferred upon us by—'

I said, 'I'm perfectly aware of them, agent. If you're taking that route, my lawyer can be here in minutes. He's a lawyer's lawyer.'

Mallia shook his head. 'Appreciate your co-operation, that's all, Mr Irish. The man's dead, you were at his office the day before, you'll understand—'

'Why's this a federal matter?'

'I can't disclose that sort of information.' He looked at his large hands, bunches of hair on the first joints. 'How did Coresecure come to your attention?'

'I'd seen the name on the door.'

'In the area a lot?'

'My work takes me everywhere.'

'Yes.' Mallia raised himself from the chair. Batholomew followed his lead.

'You're not unknown to us, Mr Irish,' said Mallia, attempting to give me the narrowed eye.

'Nor your agency to me, agent Mallia,' I said. 'And I can tell you I've derived very little pleasure from the acquaintanceship.'

I didn't rise to see them out.

At the door, Mallia turned. 'Have a good day,' he said. 'Give my regards to His Honour.'

Things were quiet at The Green Hill, no-one braving the elements out front and only one customer in Down the Pub. Dieter the barman wasn't on this morning, in his place a young woman in the establishment's dark-green livery.

'Good morning, sir,' she said. 'What can I serve you?'

'I'm after Xavier Doyle,' I said.

'I'll see if Mr Doyle's in,' she said. 'It's Mr…?'

'Irish. Jack Irish.'

She went to a telephone on the back counter and spoke to someone, came back. 'He'll be along in a moment.'

Doyle appeared from my right, through a door beyond the last booth. He was wearing Donegal tweeds and a yellow shirt.

'Jack,' he said, hand out. He looked like a mildly debauched cherub. 'My oath, you legal fellas are up and about with the sparrers.'

We shook hands. 'Come and have a cup of coffee in the office,' he said. 'Coffee right for you?'

'Perfect.'

'Belinda, lass, lay on a pot of coffee darlin. In me office.'

Doyle took my arm and escorted me back the way he'd come. We went through the door into a flagstoned passage, past two doors to the end. He opened a wide four-panel oak door and waved me in.

It was a big room, as much lounge as office, modern leather armchairs in front of a fireplace, a desk behind them, its top a curved slab of polished redgum holding a squat computer tower, a thin-screened monitor and a keyboard. One wall of the room was a floor-to-ceiling oak cupboard.

We sat in the armchairs, a low table separating us.

'Not a social call, Jack,' Doyle said. 'Am I right?'

'Business,' I said. 'I wanted to ask you a few more things about Robbie. Do you mind?'

'Not at all.' He sat back, laced fingers over a tweed knee. 'But I don't think I know much more to tell.'

'Did you know his real name?'

He ducked his chin. 'Real name? Meanin?'

'His name's Marco Lucia.'

Doyle shook his head. 'That's news to me. What's the reason for another name?'

'I'm not sure. He was involved with some fairly hard people in Queensland, may have been on the run.'

There was a knock at the door. Doyle got up, opened it, took a tray from someone. He put it down on the table, poured coffee dark and fragrant into china cups.

'Sugar?'

I accepted a spoonful.

'Have a bikkie. Bake em ourselves. Almond shortbread.' He chewed. 'Delicious. Well, we certainly didn't do any checkin on Robbie. No-one bothers for casuals. Why would ya?'

The coffee was rich as rum, the biscuit dissolved on the tongue, all butter. I got out the photograph of Alan Bergh. 'Ever seen this man?'

Doyle took it from me, had a good look, frowned. 'Don't think so. Although there's an awful lot of people come through, you'll understand. I can't say he's never bin here, that I can't. But I can't recall the face offhand. No.'

'Good coffee,' I said.

'Our own blend. Fella in Carlton makes it up. So who's the man?' He put the photograph on the table.

I drank some more coffee, not in a hurry. Then I took out my notebook and found the page. 'These numbers.' I read them out, numbers from Alan Bergh's mobile phone bill. 'They're your phones.'

Doyle wiped his lips with a napkin from the tray. His look was of mild amusement. 'Now you're findin out a great deal about us, Jack. Business numbers, those.'

He wasn't amused, not even mildly. The expression was an instinctive one, animal, speaking of wariness, uncertainty.

'The numbers? They're not in any book.'

I pointed at the photograph. 'This man rang those numbers. Thirteen times in a month. Sure you don't know him?'

Doyle was raising his cup to his lips. He didn't complete the movement, replaced the cup on the saucer. 'Now Jack,' he said, 'you won't mind me sayin this is borderin on the impertinent. You'd have to be doin somethin illegal to know enough to ask such questions. Would that be right?'

'You don't know him?'

'I've said that. Can't say it any better.' No Irish charm in the tone now.

'And the thirteen calls?'

He held up his hands. 'I've told you, they're business phones, lots of people use them, a dozen or more.'

'So someone else in the business would know him?'

'Possibly. Or they might be bloody nuisance calls, man might be sellin somethin, who knows? And you haven't answered the question. Who is the fella?'

'Don't know. Friend of Robbie's perhaps.'

'The picture. Where'd you get that?'

'Someone sent it to me,' I said, standing up. 'I won't waste any more of your time. Wonderful coffee. And the biscuits.'

Doyle didn't rise. 'And the calls,' he said. 'Where'd you get that from?'

'They sent me his phone bill with the picture.'

'So you do know his name?'

'It was a photocopy. No name on the pages.'

Doyle stood up. I had the sense that he was composing himself. He smiled the Irish boyo smile. 'Well Jack,' he said, 'it'll be hard for me to find out who he spoke to if I don't know his name. Would y'like to leave the photo? I can show it around?'

'No,' I said. 'I'm pretty much done with this matter.' I took a chance. 'Robbie did more than work in Down the Pub, didn't he?'

A moment's uncertainty, the hint of a smile. 'More?' Pause. 'He had a few shifts in the Snug, if that's what you mean?'

I couldn't show my ignorance, nodded. 'Yes. Who would he serve? In the Snug?'

'It's admittance by invitation. Our special guests, people…' He realised I was fishing. 'Well, if that's all,' he said. 'Always happy to try to help.'

Doyle escorted me to the door into Down the Pub and said goodbye without shaking hands, no more invitations to share in the life of the pub, drink the pinot, cook from the cookbook, no more pats or jovial remarks.

Driving back, I thought about my handling of the interview. Not good. But I was sure of one thing now:

Xavier Doyle could tell me lots more about Robbie/Marco. Perhaps he could even tell me how the Federal Police knew about my dealings with Mr Justice Loder. At the first lights, I got out my list of things to do, found the address and set course.

Alan Bergh had also made five calls to a mobile registered to a Kirstin Deane, whose work address was a women's clothing shop called Anouk in Greville Street, Prahran.

The narrow street was busy, a fashionable crowd on this side of the river, blonded women everywhere, tanned and tucked, fat sucked away and burnt off, eyeing themselves in shop windows, looking at younger specimens with hatred. I lucked on a park in Anouk's block, slid the old Stud in between an Audi and a Mercedes four-wheel drive.

Anouk's was not overstocked with merchandise. The window display was one dress, a mere twirl of fabric, barely enough to clothe six foot of lamp pole. Inside, two more garments were on display, a cloak-like creation of black velvet, and something that resembled a silk apron. Surely this could only be worn over clothing or in the privacy of the home? Against the left-hand wall, box shelves each held one item, shirts perhaps or cashmere sweaters.

A young woman was on the telephone, seated behind a minimalist counter, no more than three pieces of thick plexiglass on which stood several electronic devices. She was mostly leg, skeletal, high cheekbones, much forehead under much hair, and her eyes and eyebrows and mouth were works of art.

I waited. Her eyes were fixed on a mirror across the room and never moved in my direction. She was talking without pause in a flat, grating monotone, words seemingly joined and undecipherable. After a while, I got between her and the mirror, blocked her view of herself.

Then she looked at me. She said a few words to the phone and put it down.

'Help you,' she said, not a question.

'I'm looking for Kirstin Deane.'

'Yeah.'

She knew I wasn't in the market for a silk apron or anything else she was selling. This was not going to be easy.

'It's about someone you know. Alan Bergh.'

Silence. She looked at the street.

'Alan Bergh. You know him.'

Her head jerked back. 'I don't *know* him.'

'He's dead,' I said. 'Shot dead. In a carpark. Know that?'

Kirstin frowned, pulled her eyebrow creations together, a little untidiness of skin appearing between them, an imperfection on a face as tight as a kite in a high wind.

'I've had it with you lot,' she said.

'He phoned you often,' I said. 'Your dead friend Alan.'

She took a deep breath, she still had lung capacity, her emaciated upper body expanded, she opened her mouth and breathed out like a steam train.

'Not my fucking friend,' she said, some life in the voice now. 'I said I don't know who the fuck Alan is. I'm the messenger girl. And I don't wanna know any more of this cop shit, right? Right? I'm finished with Mick, wish I'd never seen the prick in my life and I'll kill him if he ever—'

I held up my right hand. 'Settle down.'

Kirstin's eyes vanished, became slits. 'Don't you fucking tell me to settle down, I'll—'

'Taking messages can get you into deep trouble,' I said, now a kite myself, out on the winds. 'When someone says he doesn't know about the messages, never got a message from you, you're in trouble. Who'd you give the messages to, Kirstin?'

She closed her eyes, punched the plastic counter top repeatedly with both long-fingered fists, symbolically beating someone. 'Tell Olsen I'll kill him. He's not landing me with his shit. You people, you call yourselves ethics squad or fucking whatever, you're trying to cover something up for the cunt, aren't you. Well, forget that, detective whatever the fuck you are. Whofuckingever. Piss off.'

I did, left without a murmur, like a poor person given too much money by a bank machine.

A name. Mick Olsen. A cop called Mick Olsen.

Alan Bergh left messages for Mick Olsen with the engaging Kirstin Deane, super-salesperson. Who thought I was from ethical standards or whatever name it now had, the old police internal affairs section, the dog investigating its own balls someone once said of it, unkindly.

I would have to ask Senior Sergeant Barry Tregear about Mick Olsen.

At the office, the answering machine held three messages: my sister, curt but with a hint of forgiveness, Cam, equally brief but with no hint of anything, and one that said:

Re your accommodation inquiry, please ring at your convenience.

The D.J. Olivier code.

I went to the window. McCoy was at home, lights on in the alleged studio. I crossed the street and knocked. He came to the door wearing a knitted blanket with a hole for his head. Beneath it, his massive legs were bare save for their covering of beard-like hair and his feet looked like parcels badly wrapped with lengths of horse harness.

'So,' he said. 'Don't think I didn't see you spying on me yesterday.'

'Watching that innocent young thing enter this house of horrors,' I said, 'I considered calling the police. I need your phone.'

'She wanted to learn from a master's hand,' he said, leading the way into the studio.

'No chance of that here.'

I stopped at an unfinished canvas of monumental size and awfulness. 'What an inspired way to recycle fowl manure and horse hair,' I said.

'That'll fetch ten grand,' said McCoy. 'Gissa name for it.'

'Stick some chicken bones on it and call it Century of Bones.'

'Century of Bones,' said the hulking fraud approvingly.

'Gotta ring to that. Century of Bones. You can have the call on the house.'

'Calls plus ten per cent,' I said.

The telephone reposed on a tree stump in the far corner of the former sewing sweatshop. I dialled and got D.J. Olivier himself.

'You're a busy lad,' he said. 'This bloke's ex-army, got two convictions for fraud and he ran a building company that took customers for plenty. Now he's tied up with Geddan Associates. Know them?'

'No.' We were talking about a man called Warren Naismith, someone Alan Bergh had phoned regularly.

'Strategic consultants. That's PR, with violence if required. Do the lot.'

'The lot?'

'Fix. Here, New Zealand, Pacific islands. Office in Canada. Rumour says they blackmailed a cabinet minister in Queensland on behalf of a client. Developer client.'

'I didn't know that was necessary in Queensland,' I said. 'Sounds like overkill. And this person, what would he do for them?'

'Low level, a postman, fetch and carry, that sort of thing. Not welcome around the office, that's for sure.'

I said thanks, rang Cam's latest number. He was a long time answering. I told him about Jean Hale's names.

'This bloke Almeida,' he said. 'I've got him.'

I needed a second to place the name. Too many names. Yes. The dealer on the motorbike Marie pointed out to us in Elizabeth Street was called Glenn Almeida.

'At that address?' My inquiry had provided a vehicle registry address in Coburg for Almeida.

'Long gone. New one from the landlords' revenge file,

my real-estate shonk looked him up. He's out there in the hills.'

A rubbing noise, a towelling sound.

'I found this milk bar lady in Coburg,' said Cam. 'Round the corner from Glenn's old address. She knows the boy, knows Artie too. Her kid, he's naughty, studyin at this new place, the Port Phillip college, new slammer, the boy told her Glenn and Artie had the holiday together.'

I tried to think about this. I was heavy with information, underweight on thought. 'We still don't have Artie.'

Cam said, 'Maybe Artie's just the hammer. Maybe Glenn's the man.'

'I don't think so.' I didn't know that I didn't think so until I said it. 'Jean Hale's trouble. How's that fit?'

'Dunno. Might have a look up there in the foothills tomorrow. Free?'

'No,' I said, 'tomorrow's bad.' I felt guilty.

'Come round on my way back. Sawin or lawin?'

'Lawin,' I said. 'What passes for lawin.'

Receiver replaced, I stood for a moment, no energy in me, no wish to do anything except sleep. Then I sucked in some air and began my exit.

McCoy was staring at his canvas, standing well back, hands on where hips would be if pillar boxes had hips. As I approached, he said, 'Century of Bones. What about a skull in the middle there?'

'I don't think you should kill humans for your art,' I said. 'Unless it's yourself. In which case, just mark the spot and I'll be happy to stick it on for you. For your estate.'

'Animal,' he said, distant, deep in whatever process took place behind the opaque eyes. 'Rabbit. Sheep. Maybe dog.'

It was as if I had woken from a dream of toothache to find myself pain free.

'Dog,' I said. 'Dog. I have the perfect dog.'

Outside, the day was at an end, rain had fallen, now a misty yellow light was on the world. The cobblestoned gutter outside my office was painterly, each cobble glistening like the top of a fresh loaf of bread, a top painted with egg and milk.

I set off for home. On the radio, Linda was talking to a man who called himself a life coach.

And what qualifies you to tell other people how to run their lives?

Life coach: *My training. I have a life coach qualification.*

Linda, the amused voice, not insulting, somewhere between curious and dangerous: *Is that from the university of life? School of hard knocks?*

Life coach, serious: *No, from Life Coach College, it's an accredited institution.*

It occurred to me that I needed this man's services or this qualification. And, perhaps, I needed Linda.

No. Well, perhaps. But only on my terms. What would they be? I had no idea, could not think of a single term.

Supper. I could think about supper, the limited range of suppers available. Not so much a range as an item.

I ate pasta and walked around preparing to go to bed early, seek refuge in my bed, take the decision to activate the answering machine and turn the volume down to nought. Incommunicado.

Even to Linda.

And to Lyall.

Perhaps Lyall would ring me one day and say that there

had been a misunderstanding, that Brad had not actually been celibate for all those years and could we take up where we left off?

My shrinking sensible bit said I should not stay awake waiting for this to happen.

The transcript of Mr Justice Loder's trial—I hadn't read it.

I could put on warm and waterproof clothing, leave the apartment and go down to the car, look for the folder, which might be in the office. Or.

I rang Drew at home. 'Are you in a position to talk?' I asked.

'I find myself able to talk in most positions. Is there one I should know about?'

'There's a trial going on before Colin Loder, cocaine smuggling.'

'Ah, the ski jackets debacle.'

'Know about it?'

'As a practitioner of the law, I make a point of knowing about such things. As it happens, I was recently privileged to hear the views of my learned friend Dick Pratchett QC on the subject. Over lunch.'

That was where the Rosa business had begun.

'I remember. Give me the story in as few words as possible.'

'Well,' he said, 'it goes like this. The Feds've got a dog who calls himself Aaron Ross, apparently well known in drug circles. He told them he was asked by someone called Frank Leavis, a mystery man, noone's ever heard of him, to supply six kilos of cocaine. The Feds became dizzy with excitement when they heard this.'

'I get the drift already.'

'Yes, dulled though you are by sniffing wood glue.

Anyway, Ross rounded up Brian Arthur McCallum, a dickhead, and a lad called John Stavros Ionides, an even bigger dunce. I say this as someone who represented him when he was known as John Stephens. Mystery man Leavis hands over a large sum in US and Aussie currency, and the boys take off for South Africa.'

'South Africa? Since when?'

'Apparently it's like Bangkok, Karachi and Beirut all in one. With Russians added. United drugs of the world. But you can bet your last pack of Fitzroy Football Club fundraising condoms that it wasn't McCallum and Johnny Stephens' idea. Couldn't find the place on the map.'

'The Feds' idea?'

'Or someone else's. So off they go with their bag of money, customs instructed not to touch them. In due course, and I have to say this really surprises everyone who knows them, they actually come back with the coke. They're wearing it in matching ski jackets.'

'You can ski in South Africa?'

'Of course not. But would that occur to these dolts? Again, customs usher them through. McCallum rings from the airport. Ross rings mystery man Frank Leavis. Well, he rings a number and leaves a message. In Tullamarine, off Mickleham Road, by arrangement, McCallum and Johnny Stephens meet Mr Ross to hand over. Change of plan, Ross tells them. The client wants you to deliver the stuff to him personally.'

'Feds want to stitch it up tight.'

'Exactly. So Brian and Johnny and Ross and four hundred hyper-excited Feds all end up in the freezing cold at a service station in fucking Brimbank in the middle of the night. But the mystery man is one step ahead of these dunderheads and never shows up.'

I remembered what Colin Loder had said:

I don't think it would be unjudicial of me to describe the operation as a massive cock-up.

'Anyway,' said Drew, 'he didn't miss much. The boofheads are found to be carrying less than two kilos and apparently the marching powder is of a quality that doesn't produce quite as much of the wit, confidence and feelings of general wellbeing the punters expect.'

'So what the prosecution's got are two blokes approached to buy drugs by a police informer who says he was acting on behalf of a mystery man.'

'Yup. And the only person the drugs were delivered to is the informer. Needless to say, the judge will have the Appeal Court much on his mind. Pratchett QC is of the opinion Colin Loder will kick the thing into the street next week.'

'The Feds wouldn't be buying their dog a big bone.'

'Only themselves to blame. My mate Terry says the word is McCallum, dumb though he is, knows more than he's saying.'

'Meaning?'

'He may know something about Leavis, the mystery man.'

'Something the dog doesn't know?'

'Possibly. Brian might have been just smart enough to find out who the real client was. Someone the Feds apparently suspect but can't do anything about.'

'Thank you,' I said. 'Your fund of knowledge obviates the need to buy newspapers or watch television. Not to mention read the learned journals.'

'Honoured to be of service. What's your interest?'

'Purely professional. Highly professional. On that subject, how is the high-achieving personally-trained one?'

'Ravishing. A weekend has been proposed. Windswept beaches, just the cries of the seabirds.'

'As they impale themselves on used syringes.'

With a soothing mug of the warm brown fluid to hand, I went to bed with my novel. But I couldn't concentrate, eyes on the page, mind on Marco and Alan Bergh and the judge. If Brian McCallum knew who put up the money for the drug deal, someone would want to be very sure he didn't go down and then decide to bargain with the Feds. And that someone would have made sure Brian knew he had nothing to fear, knew that he was going to walk.

I gave up on the book, doused the light, and lay awake for a long time, soft rain on the old iron roof, liquid whispers in the downpipes, all around the hoot and squeal and wail of the animal city. Oddly comforting sounds tonight.

In the morning, I was at the door, ready to hip-and-shoulder the day, when the phone rang.

'I find you decent?'

Linda.

'I find you jolly nice too,' I said, 'but I'd like to be seen as, well, more raffish than decent. Can you do that?'

'Work needed on my interrogative inflection. No wonder I'm having so much trouble with interviews.'

We met at a place in Rathdowne Street north. Once, this end of Rathdowne Street boasted only the best pizzas in town and Frank and Maria's coffee shop, the best-loved coffee shop in town. I hadn't tried the pizzas in a while but Frank and Maria's was gone and now there was an eating strip two blocks long.

'Toast,' said Linda after we'd ordered. 'Toast is *with* breakfast. Toast is *part* of breakfast. Toast is not *of itself* breakfast. Are you in love?'

I'd forgotten how the morning suited her.

'I didn't want to say I'd had my breakfast.'

'What was it?'

'Porridge, scrambled eggs and a piece of steak. Sausage or two. Three, actually. Bit of bacon.'

'Right,' she said. 'Mouldy muesli with curdling milk.'

'Yes, I am in love,' I said. 'I feel you understand me.'

She gave me several bits of bacon and half a grilled Roma tomato. We were on the coffee when she said, 'Jamie Toxteth. You were asking about him.'

It took a moment to summon up Jamie Toxteth. 'The polo player.'

The unknown woman in the surveillance clip waiting for Robbie/Marco was in a car owned by a Jamie Toxteth company.

'I was talking to someone in Sydney and I remembered your question.' She drank coffee. 'She said Susan Ayliss worked for Jamie and this Blackiston person before she became a media talent.'

Susan Ayliss had for a time been television's favourite economics commentator, a Canberra academic who made Treasury notes sound like love letters. She had long blonde hair and a slightly pointy nose, and when she looked over her rimless glasses you wanted to be in her tutorial and you wanted to be the one who said something intelligent.

'What became of the perfect creature?'

'She's an eco-consultant, she reinvented herself, did another degree. Became the squeakiest and cleanest consultant in the known universe, the flying darling of eco-consultancy. Whatever the fuck that is.'

'Flying?'

'She flies her own plane. Like Amelia Earwig. Sees the world from a great height. And won't be interviewed because it could compromise her. The woman is beyond publicity. Beyond fucking belief, in fact.'

'I forget why we're talking about her.'

'Before her career change, she had an affair with Jamie. More than an affair. She got divorced. Jamie left his wife, some even richer snorting-nostrilled horse-mounter no doubt. They lived together but in the end Jamie would not actually cut the painter.'

She'd lost me. I didn't care much about the affairs of

Sydney people. 'Not since Van Gogh has a painter been properly cut,' I said. 'Why are you telling me this?'

Linda ignored the question, put marmalade on her last quarter of toast. 'Apparently a poisonous break-up. Susan had become a partner in the firm, she was the one bringing in all the business, and she had to be bought out. My friend says Susie's lawyer nailed Jamie.'

'That's interesting. I'm glad I know that. I've always felt there was something missing in my global picture.'

She smiled at me. 'Including a new car every three years for a good while.'

She bit off a piece of toast. I watched her chewing. I'd always admired her eating. She was a very neat eater, no teeth showed, no crumb stuck or fell.

'Susan Ayliss's got long hair,' I said.

'So?'

'The woman driving the car's got short hair.'

'When last did you see Ms Ayliss?'

'Few years ago. Well, five or six, could be more. Ten.'

Linda put her head on one side and looked at me.

'Okay,' I said. 'It's early.'

'She was on the Cannon Ridge tender panel,' said Linda. 'I can't remember why you were interested in the car?'

'It appears in a video. Probably by accident. Why was she on the panel?'

'I'm told the last Premier got prickly feelings around her.'

'If that was the only qualification, panel meetings would have been at the Melbourne Cricket Ground.'

'She's also Ms Integrity.'

'Integrity plus the pricklies, now that's an unbeatable combo. I've got to go. I work in the hours of daylight.'

226

She leaned forward. 'I sense,' she said, 'that you're withholding. You'll tell me if you chance upon anything of broadcast quality?'

'With what inducement?'

Under the tablecloth, a hand was on my thigh. 'I have inducements to offer.'

'I'm not sure I fully grasp what you mean,' I said.

Her hand moved upwards. The long fingers came into play. I could feel my blood rushing downhill, upper body going pale.

'Grasp?' she said. 'I could fully grasp you right here.'

I looked at her. Her face was impassive, head cocked as if listening to distant sounds. She wasn't wearing lipstick.

'This hasn't happened to me in public for, ah, fifteen years,' I said.

'Is it like Kennedy's death?' she said. 'A whole generation of people know exactly where they were when they heard about it?' She was scratching me, an unbearably erotic feeling.

'It was in a train just outside Birmingham in England. Snow on the ground. Getting dark. I was eating a British Rail sausage roll.'

'Who was the grasper?'

'Let's see now. I think it was someone I knew…'

She removed her hand. 'That's probably the way I'll survive in memory. Just another hand. Oh well, off you go.'

Deep in thought, I drove to Fitzroy.

Finding a phone number for Susan Ayliss wasn't easy. I rang Simone Bendsten. She was back in five minutes.

'Her company's called Ecomenical. She gave a paper at a conference in Canberra last year. Here's the number.'

I rang it. The brisk and pleasant reception person wanted my name and my company and the nature of my business.

'Tell Dr Ayliss my business is Robbie,' I said. 'I'll spell that for you. R-O-B-B-I-E.'

I was early and had no trouble finding parking near the Albert Park Yachting & Angling Club. A cold day, the palms shaking in the wind.

She was early too. A new VW Passat, a trim and potent-looking machine in a Wehrmacht shade of grey, nosed into a space. A woman got out, dark glasses, headscarf. I watched her walk towards the pier, hands in the high pockets of her trench coat.

I sat for a while. Two hardy skateboarders came by, followed by a group of four fit-looking runners, women. I got out and went for a short walk along the esplanade, came back and went out on the pier.

She was looking my way, kept her eyes on me as I approached.

'Mr Irish?'

'Yes.'

'What do you want?' she asked.

'I'd like to ask you about Robbie.'

She made an impatient head movement, the kind of dismissive oh-fuck-off-you-idiot gesture that features in Learn Body Language For Success videos.

'Spit it out,' she said. 'It's cold here.'

'Your choice of venue.'

'I say again, Mr Irish, what do you want?'

'You knew Robbie Colburne?'

'What do you want?'

'You know he's dead?'

'What do you want?'

'You picked him up in your car one evening.'

An exasperated expulsion of air. 'What is this? Can I ask again, for the last time, what do you want?'

'Nothing. Robbie stole something from someone. The owner's disappointed, saddened.'

She fiddled with the scarf, some loss of composure evident.

'What makes you think I picked him up?'

Spots of rain on the pier, felt on my face.

'Someone saw you. That's not important.'

'Who are you?'

'I'm a lawyer acting for the victim.'

She sighed. 'I feel like an absolute prick,' she said. 'No, let me rephrase that before the actress and the bishop are invoked.'

'I could say that never occurred to me.'

She smiled and looked around, took off the dark glasses and the scarf. Her eyes were grey. Susan Ayliss, once the thinking person's academic pin-up, now wore her hair short at the sides and longer on top and she had lines around her mouth and eyes but she could have stepped straight back into that role.

'Christ, I hate scarves,' she said. 'I was once taken at gunpoint to a polo match, and there were all these ghastly nasal women wearing headscarves, like some cult.'

'I blame the Queen,' I said.

'Damn right,' said Susan Ayliss. 'Well, what do you want to know?'

I couldn't read anything in her eyes. She was here because I'd said Robbie's name. Dead Robbie who was Marco, who was not an easy person to understand.

'I hoped you could tell me something about Robbie.'

She turned, put her hands on the railing, no rings, clasped them. 'I know almost nothing about him.'

I leaned on the railing, looked at the view: dishwater sea, seething. In the distance, specks of gulls floated around the Tasmania ferry at Station Pier. 'Robbie Colburne isn't his real name. You know that, of course.'

'No.' Quick.

I kept my eyes away, looked at the ribbed beach.

Two people had appeared on it, a short and a tall, walking close together, heads down like beachcombers. Not quite Gauguin country, Kerferd Road, unless you treasured used Chinese condoms and spent syringes.

'There's only one Robert Colburne on record, but it isn't the dead man.'

'I'm sorry, I—'

'The person in question lifted the identity of Robert Colburne.'

I looked at her. She had a wary expression, as if I had more surprises in store. 'So, who is the person?'

'Marco Lucia is his name.'

Silence, our eyes locked. She looked away. I kept looking.

'Ms Ayliss,' I said, 'Robbie was a blackmailer or he worked for blackmailers. Did you know that?'

Horn player's lines around her mouth, an intake of air. 'Yes.'

'You're right, it is cold out here. My car or yours?'

'No,' she said. 'I'm happier here.'

'Will you tell me how you know he's a blackmailer?'

'I had an affair with him,' she said. 'No, that's nonsense. I had sex with him. On several occasions.'

'And?'

She moved her mouth, another sigh, deeper. 'There was a video.'

It was getting colder, the sky changing colour like a quick-developing bruise.

'Made with your consent?'

'Consent? Well, I didn't object. Not strenuously anyway. Coming after some bottles of Dom.' Pause. 'Are you shocked?'

I looked at her. The wind and the cold had tightened her skin, put colour in her cheeks. She looked a good ten years younger.

'No,' I said. 'Shock went by some time ago. Passed in the night. So you made a video.'

She didn't answer quickly. 'It seemed like harmless fun at the time. Do you know that I was on the Cannon Ridge tender panel?'

'Yes. How did you meet Robbie?'

She raised her hands, long fingers, I hadn't noticed. 'Don't laugh. At the supermarket. I go to the same one almost every night. I'm always late at the office, never anything in the fridge at home. He bumped into me one night. Then I saw him again a day or two later and we said hello and he said something funny. I saw him again another night, we had a few words and he invited me for a drink.'

'It didn't strike you as more than coincidence?'

'No. You go to the same place, you see the same people. And Robbie's got…Robbie had a casual way. Quick and funny, nothing threatening about him. He was also very good looking and he didn't seem to be aware of it.' She looked at me, looked away. 'And I was lonely, Mr Irish. I work all day and then I go home to nothing.'

It hadn't occurred to me that people like Susan Ayliss also knew about loneliness.

'Did he tell you he worked part-time at The Green Hill?'

'Yes. He said he was trying to write a novel, took any job going.'

Silence. I watched the pair inspecting the beach. From time to time, the smaller one would stoop to look at something. Look but not touch. Sensible.

Susan Ayliss put her hands to her ears, rubbed them gently. Her nose wasn't quite as pointy as I remembered. 'Anyway,' she said, 'we ended up at my place and had sex. I hadn't actually had sex like that before. The men of my acquaintance had not prepared me for the experience.'

My thoughts went to Milan Filipovic. I'd asked him what kind of work Marco did.

Marco's all cock. Work it out.

'How was the video made?'

She looked at me, startled. 'By Robbie. Christ, it wasn't a film set.'

'On the first night?'

'Certainly not. I was sober. The third time. He had a tiny camera, a digital thing, you could watch it on a monitor. That's about all there was in this huge apartment. That and the bed.'

In some circumstances, people tell you more than they need to.

'You watched it on a monitor?'

'Yes. Are you enjoying this?'

'And this was where?'

'At a friend's place.'

'Your friend's apartment?'

'No, a friend of his.'

I thought about the surveillance video, the shot of Robbie going into a building.

'Cathexis,' I said.

She was looking away and she jerked her head at me. 'I don't know. I wasn't paying attention at that stage.'

'Who's the friend?'

'No idea.'

'And the blackmail came when?'

Susan tilted her head, smiled a smile with no life in it. 'A man came to my office. He said he had a business proposition. I knew what was coming and I told him to get out. He said wait and he dialled a number on his mobile, said someone wanted to talk to me. It was Robbie. He said he was watching the video.' She was looking down at the rail, shaking her head. 'Shit,' she said. 'Talking about it makes me feel sick.'

'I can understand that. What else did Robbie say?'

'Nothing. I didn't give him a chance. I gave the man the phone back and I said they could give the film to every television station and newspaper in the country, I did not give a damn.'

'That was brave.'

'Brave?'

'You were taking a big risk.'

She shrugged. 'They just picked the wrong person. A film of Susan Ayliss having sex? I don't have family to worry about. All I've got is my professional reputation. Show it. It might improve my social life.'

She was a brave person.

'When the man talked about a business proposition,' I said, 'what did you assume?'

'The Cannon Ridge tender. I wasn't doing anything else worth blackmailing me for.'

'Did the man say which side sent him?'

'No.'

'What did you think?'

'WRG.'

'Who?'

'He asked me if I'd had an offer from Anaxan.'

'Did you tell the panel?'

'No. I'm only stupid once. I hadn't been blackmailed, Cannon Ridge hadn't actually been mentioned.'

'Splitting hairs though.'

Susan Ayliss gave me a look that said something I didn't quite understand. 'Mr Irish, in my life, I've worked very hard for everything. I grew up in foster homes. Fought off men since I was ten, put myself through university cleaning toilets. I can't be blackmailed. But I wasn't going to cut my own throat.'

I found my picture of Alan Bergh. 'Is this the man?'

No hesitation. 'Yes. Who is he?'

'Alan Bergh. The late.'

She sighed and looked away.

'Robbie had a relationship with a man,' I said. 'Does that surprise you?'

'Well,' she said, 'he said he took any work that was going.'

'There's an album of photographs missing.'

'I think we're talking about sex again, not a relationship.'

'Yes. We think the album was passed on to someone. Any idea who that might be?'

A shake of her head. 'No, no idea, not the vaguest.'

'Robbie didn't mention anyone.'

'No. He didn't talk about himself. One of the things I found attractive.'

Rain again, big spots freckling the pier, cold on the face.

'Thanks for talking to me,' I said. 'Did his death surprise you?'

She looked away, at the sea. 'Yes,' she said. 'It made me sad. I was hoping I'd have the chance to kill him myself for making me feel so defiled and so worthless.'

I watched her go, the wind pulling at her trench coat, lifting the shoulder flaps found so useful on the Somme those many years ago, now threatening to levitate Susan Ayliss. She turned her head and looked back, came back.

'I've told you everything I can, Jack,' she said. 'Will you promise me it'll remain confidential?'

'Yes,' I said. 'Susan.'

I liked her even more than I had when she'd been a media star.

I brooded, driving automatically, registering nothing, a danger on the roads. There was nowhere else to go in the matter of Marco/Robbie. I couldn't help the judge. It had all been for nothing, traipsing around the country, the city.

Marco was a blackmailer's bait, bait for all sexual persuasions. The blackmailer could be Alan Bergh, representing other interests. Why else had he been filmed? In any event, both men were dead. The attempt on brave Susan Ayliss had failed, the one on principled Colin Loder would too. Cannon Ridge was a decided matter, another judge would make the finding Colin Loder could not.

This matter was almost at an end.

And yet and yet. Marco was murdered, Alan Bergh was murdered.

I pulled up at lights.

Susan Ayliss had no doubt that the Cannon Ridge tender was the reason for the plot against her. Which side? Anaxan or WRG? The latter would have been eager to add some weight to their side of the seesaw, the other side having a Cundall, son of a man who could walk into the Premier's office and berate him. But they didn't get the weight, their tender failed. That could have left Bergh and Robbie as untidy bits, much too knowing.

Cathexis.

I had been looking at the building, looking at it across the intersection without seeing it. It was austere, all its materials visible, concrete and marble, bronze and glass, steel and copper—rough, smooth, shiny, dull, hard, soft materials. I could see the incised name that Marco was photographed passing.

Cathexis.

The lights changed. I went around the block, found an unlawful park, walked back to the building. A smoked-glass sliding door admitted me to an extravagant, hard-surfaced lobby, a hall that hummed the word Money. Directly ahead were two lift doors, pale timber. Nothing so crass and indiscreet as a list of tenants was in sight. I was glad I was wearing a decent suit. A recent suit, anyway.

A hotel-sized reception counter was at the right, two young women in black on duty behind it. Beyond that was a door marked Security. I couldn't see cameras but they would be on me and the entrance.

'How may I help?' She was English, willowy, blonde, nectarine skin.

'Gone blank. I can't remember the agents for the building.'

'Barwick & Murphy,' she said, smiling. 'Is it something I can help you with?'

'Well, you might.' I took out my notebook, thumbed. 'Here it is. The Doyle apartment. For sale.'

'Doyle?' She looked at the other woman, also blonde but more mature oak than willow. 'Do we have a Doyle?'

The woman was looking at a monitor, didn't turn her head. 'No.'

'Sorry,' said the first blonde. 'It's probably in another of their buildings. They handle dozens.'

'Yes,' I said. 'Thanks anyway.'

I walked away. Another hunch that failed to deliver. Near the door, I thought, what the hell, try another one. I turned and went back, notebook open.

'I think I had the wrong page,' I said. 'It's Cundall, the Cundall apartment that's for sale. If I've got the right building.'

The willowy blonde frowned, turned. 'Jean, do we have a Cundall?'

Mature-oak blonde didn't turn. 'What?'

'It's supposed to be on the market. The gentleman's not sure whether he's at the right building.'

Mature blonde looked around, an annoyed face, deep lines between her eyes, spent a millisecond on me, made a judgment. 'Who says it's on the market?'

'B and M told this gentleman.'

Jean sniffed. 'They told you it was Mrs Cundall's apartment?'

'Yes.'

'That is quite irregular. Twelve two is owned by Dalinsor Nominees.'

'I don't really care who owns it,' I said. 'I'm looking for an apartment.'

'They're supposed to inform us,' said Jean. 'And there are no inspections without a B and M agent.'

'I'll be back with one,' I said. 'One of their top agents. Licensed to sell.'

Walking back to the car, I felt smug for a minute. A hunch that paid off. Or had it? What had I learned by finding out that Ros Cundall owned an apartment in a building Marco had gone into? Nothing. Ros Cundall probably owned apartments in every expensive block in the city.

Marco working at The Green Hill, Marco going into Cathexis, Marco from the Umbrian idyll turning up on Colin Loder's doorstep.

I was beginning to like the Umbrian story less and less.

Too romantic for my taste. And, in the light of what I now knew about Marco and Susan, implausible.

From the car, I rang Colin Loder's borrowed mobile. He wouldn't be in court, it was lunchtime.

'Yes.'

'Jack.'

'Jack.'

'Clarification. Umbria, the person arrives on the door-step, later reappears.'

'Yes?'

'Bullshit, yes?

A pause, a sigh. 'Well. Yes. A story.'

I waited.

'I didn't want it to sound like…well…'

'A pick-up?'

'Yes. Umbria was a fiction.'

'Where then?'

He hesitated. 'A place I've had a few drinks at. So as not to be completely removed from reality. As are most of my colleagues.'

'The Green Hill?'

Pause. 'How exactly did you work that out?'

'Is that in the Snug?'

'Yes. You know it?'

'No. I know Xavier Doyle.'

'Well, the Snug's like a club, I suppose. You have to be with someone who's persona grata.'

'Who were you with?'

'Ros Cundall, Mike Cundall's wife. I'm on a gallery committee with her. She insisted I join her after a meeting. Introduced me to Xavier.'

'Who introduced you to Marco?'

240

'Ros. He was behind the bar. She said, meet Marco before he's famous, he's writing the great Australian novel. Words to that effect.'

This was a small city. But in the end all cities are small.

'Any headway, Jack?' Not a confident voice.

'A little. Get back to you.'

'Thanks.'

Little was the word. I drove back to Fitzroy thinking about the versatility of Marco, the number of lives he'd touched.

I was unlocking the office door, wind pulling at my clothes, when a respectable Subaru drew up, double parked.

Cam.

I got in. It was warm and comfortable, things I had been missing.

'Pretty up there in the hills,' he said, no expression. 'Total waste of time. The address's at the top of a dead end, three houses on the road. Dunno how you deal drugs from a place like that, all that commutin.'

'Anyone home?'

'Woman hangin up washin, two kids hangin on her, cattle dog.

'What now?'

'The plumber and the wood man.'

I went inside, found Jean Hale's faxed list, made haste to quit the dusty ice cave for the clean warmth of the vehicle outside.

'Plumber I wouldn't be hopeful about,' said Cam, eyes on the paper. 'Make too much money. Like doctors. Now wood's another matter. Very seasonal, wood.'

'What's his name?' I said.

'Lizard Ellyard.'

'Lizard Ellyard,' I said. 'Used to be a bikie gang called the Lizards.'

Cam turned his head, interest in the dark eyes.

I found the Hales' number in my book, got out the mobile. Jean answered.

'Jean, Jack. Can you ask your husband or Sandy if they know why this man Ellyard is called Lizard?'

She was gone for several minutes. I heard the labrador bark, a door bang.

'There, Jack?'

'Yes.'

'Dave says Lizard wears an old leather jacket with Lizard on the back. Bought it at an op-shop, he reckons.'

I said thanks.

Cam was looking at me. I told him.

'The Coburg milk bar lady said Artie was a bike person, very noisy,' he said. 'What happened to the Lizards?'

I tried to remember. 'They were in the news, fighting with some other mob.'

'Lizards,' said Cam. 'Not a good name for a gang. Too close to the ground, the lizard.'

Something on television: a smouldering building, fire engines.

'Their clubhouse was attacked,' I said. 'Or they torched the other lot's place.'

'They all do that,' said Cam. 'That's what they do on Sunday night. I might ask around. Listen, the big man said to tell you, eight in the seventh at the Valley on Sunday. Not the house at all, each-way. And pray for rain in the mornin.'

'Getting back into it?'

Cam half smiled. 'Kiwi horse, come for the winter pickins. Trainer's dad's a Pom, rode against Harry in England. This nag loves mud. The big man's picked the suitable outin for him.'

In the office, a male on the answering machine said: *Jack, here's a number.*

I wrote it down, walked to the Lebanese shop and

ordered a salad roll. Then I rang the number, a mobile. Senior Sergeant Barry Tregear answered.

'Working days now?' I said.

'Days, nights, on a taskforce, mate. We're all on taskforces, force of taskforces. Listen, go a beer? I'm about five from that place, y'know?'

He was standing with his back against the counter, a depleted beer in his right hand: a big man in a dark rumpled suit watching two stringy young men playing pool.

'Where'd you get the tan?' I said.

'Holidays, mate. Private-school boys wouldn't understand. Life's all play to you.'

'I'm close to played out.' I found my beer behind him and had a deep drink. Cooper's. 'What taskforce did you draw?'

'Street dealers. War on street dealers. Finished our task, mate, it's a fucken indoor activity.'

'That's when you form a taskforce to drive them onto the streets again.'

'Exactly. We're like the tides. Move shit in and out.' He drank half his glass, burped, a full-blooded burp. 'I reckon they should give McDonald's the franchise to sell drugs. Quality control, clean premises, collect fucking GST. Plus the junkies get a burger with every hit, keep em healthy. McSmack.'

'Leaving you and your colleagues free to drive around at high speeds and shoot people.'

'Yeah. That and the relationship counselling, role modelling.' He eyed me. 'Down in the weights. Dying or a new girlfriend?'

'Exercise, strict diet.'

'Dying then. On the subject, this query of yours. Mick Olsen. Why are you always fucking around with dangerous things?'

One of the pool players wore a bandanna, the other a cap backwards. Bandanna man was going for an impossibly acute angle. We watched. It wasn't impossible after all.

'Fuuuck,' said his opponent.

'The person's a cop,' I said. 'Cops are only supposed to be dangerous to wrongdoers.'

Barry turned his head, had no trouble finding the barmaid's eyes where she stood talking to a fat man in a Bombers beanie and scarf. She tossed her head. The light from the west window spangled off the rings and stones in her nose and ears and eyebrows.

'Mick's a cop in history,' Barry said. 'Resigned a while ago. Now a man of leisure. But dangerous still. You don't even want to know his name.'

'Why?'

'Drug squad. Policing where the shit interfaces with the fans, if you get my meaning.'

'Just the melody.'

'Here ya go.' The multi-pierced one put two new beers on the counter. I paid.

'I say again, dangerous is the word,' said Barry. He was intent on the pool players. Bandanna man was sighting down the length of the table, trying to pot one of three balls in a cluster.

'This bloke's fucken ambitious,' said Barry.

Bandanna picked the nominee out of the group, thudded it into the corner pocket.

'Shit,' said Barry, impassive, appreciative. 'Man with the golden stick.'

'This Olsen,' I said. Mick Olsen had picked up messages from Alan Bergh left with the lovely Kirstin Deane at her minimally stocked boutique.

'The Commissioner's enema. Just the name's a supposi-tory. And there's blokes in the squad want him dead, they say.' He drank. 'Anyhow, Mick's highly deadly, shouldn't speak ill of him.'

'The name Alan Bergh mean anything?'

Barry looked at me briefly, probed a tooth with his tongue, shook his head, went back to watching the pool.

'Bergh made calls to Olsen's girlfriend. To be passed on, I gather.'

'Jack, Mick's in the drug business. Get lots of messages. It's a message business.'

'What's made him history?'

'Done the Feds like a dinner. Unbelievable fuck-up.'

'Coke jackets?' The case before Mr Justice Loder.

He looked at me, a full look, shook his head in a sad way. 'Jack, I don't know. You had a profession. I looked up to you.'

'Did you really?'

'Fuck off.'

'Tell me about Olsen,' I said.

Barry drank some beer.

I drank some. I was starting to like the taste. I put my glass down, pushed it away. Just a few centimetres away. The symbolic distance between the me who would once have knocked back this beer and then woken up somewhere strange with a full beard, and the me now.

'A bloke called Ross set it up,' said Barry. 'Conned the Feds he's got Mr Big on the line, the man's placed a trial order. A controlled delivery scam. Very stylish, made the Canberra boys look like absolute cunts.'

Bandanna's opponent played a two-cushion shot that sank a ball.

'Jeez, luck,' said Barry. 'These two cunts were supposed to

lead to a Mr Big, like you get to the big-time by being such an arsehead that the delivery boys can take the Feds to you.'

'Where's Olsen come in?'

Barry put a hand into his jacket and, without taking out the packet, found a cigarette. He lit it with a plastic lighter, coughed, calmed his throat with a long drink of beer. 'The talk is that Olsen's the brains. He's a smart fella. Nearly finished law at Monash.'

'That's not a sign of smartness,' I said. 'He got what out of this business?'

'Well,' Barry said, looking around the room, 'it appears the Feds helped the boys bring in more stuff than the two k's they find on them, so the extra's what Mick got out. Between the airport and the handover, that vanished.'

'How do they know that?'

Barry shrugged. 'Apparently they heard from the supply end. After. Over here, these Fed dickheads just took it on trust what the boys were carrying. Couldn't have a look in Perth, open their cases. It was on the pricks, in these jackets, world's heaviest fucken ski jackets, must've hung down to their knees.'

'Where'd Olsen's excess go?'

'On sold quick-smart you'd imagine. Same night. But that'd be a contract.'

He finished his beer, wiped his lips with a thumb. 'Got to go, sweep some of Mick's stuff off the fucken streets.'

'There's a small thing,' I said.

'Oh yeah.'

'I need to find out who identified a body.'

'Fuck, Jack, you're a nuisance.'

'Your day will come.'

'I doubt that very fucken much. Shoulda been a crook.

Chose the wrong end of the fucken stick. What body's this?'

I told him, watched him leave. The pool players watched him too. They knew a cop when they saw one. Then they looked at me. I looked back. They found other things to look at.

A new BMW was parked outside my office, illegally. The driver was on the phone, head back on the rest. I recognised the profile, tapped on the window centimetres from his face. His head jerked around.

Gavin Legge, former journalist and master of the contra-deal, now, according to Linda, a spin-physician for an international PR firm. He got out, right hand outstretched.

'Jack, old mate.' Legge exuded warmth. He also exuded prosperity: new pinstriped suit on the chubby body, expensive haircut and a good dye job, rimless glasses to replace the thick-framed, scratched and smeared pair I'd last seen him in.

'Gavin.'

We shook hands.

'I hope you're not looking for legal representation,' I said. 'I've got a new policy of only taking on clients who promise to pay within five years.'

He slapped my arm. 'Man on a mission, I am. Can we talk inside?'

We went in. Legge looked around the unadorned chamber.

'Backstreet law, eh? Down at the level of the people. I admire that.'

'Some slurp champagne from the tainted silver chalice,' I said, 'some choose honour and a stubby.'

Legge laughed, not a convincing effort, and sat down. I went around the desk.

'I won't beat around the bush, Jack, no, that's not our way at all.'

'Our? Have you subdivided yourself? Been cloned? Is there more than one Gavin Legge now? The world may not be ready for that.'

Another feeble attempt at laughter. 'I'm speaking for Ponton's,' he said, crossing his legs, pulling at his trousers. 'I'm with Ponton's now. World's most respected image management consultants. Headhunted.'

'Are you sure they've got the most valuable part? What can I do for you? All of you.'

'Jack, one of our clients is Anaxan. You'll be familiar with Anaxan, they're going to develop Cannon Ridge, multimillion-dollar development, something all Victorians, all Australians, will be proud of, a world-class ski resort and casino, the Aspen of...'

I held up a hand. 'Gavin, I liked you more when you weren't writing the media releases, just sneaking them into the paper.'

He coloured a little. 'Sorry, my enthusiasm carries me away. It's about Alan Bergh. We understand you were interested in Alan Bergh.'

I didn't say anything. I sat back and laced my fingers on the tabletop and looked at him.

'That's correct, isn't it? You were interested in Alan Bergh.'

I didn't reply, kept my eyes on his. He licked his lips, made a smacking noise with them.

'Now, Jack,' he said, hands in action, 'please don't take this amiss, we've known each other a long time and I'd hate to think—'

'Gavin,' I said, 'you have no way of knowing what interests

me unless you've been spying on me. Will you confirm that you're spying on me?'

Hands in the air. 'Jack, Jack, mate, mate, hold on, listen to me for a second, I'll explain. I can explain.'

'Explain. Briefly.'

'Right.' Legge coughed. 'Right. Now, Jack, our client, that's Anaxan, they've been very disturbed, disturbed and disgusted, I might say, by the tactics of WRG, the other tenderer…Are you with me?'

'Yes.'

'Of course you are. Our clients believe that WRG gained information from inside the Cannon Ridge tender panel. Alan Bergh was involved, we're pretty sure of that, an absolute scumbag, Jack, you'll know that.'

'Why are you here, Gavin?' I asked.

A raised hand. 'Out of courtesy, Jack. Courtesy and friendship. Someone told us you were inquiring about Bergh—no, don't get angry, there was no spying involved, pure chance that it came to our ears. And I wanted to tell you to be careful that WRG didn't try to use you, feed you misleading information. That's all there is to it. No more than that. Just an act of friendship. And courtesy.'

'You're saying that Bergh worked for WRG?'

'Absolutely. Dangerous people, Jack.' He looked relieved.

'What's he supposed to have done?'

'Well, I suppose it's pretty much an open secret. Bribed Paul Rykel. Department of Conservation.'

'I thought the story was your clients bribed Rykel? Anaxan.'

Legge nodded sagely. 'That's the story WRG have put out. Total fabrication. Opposite of the truth. Diametric.'

'Forgive my naivety, Gavin, but if WRG had stuff leaked to them, why didn't they win the tender?'

He smiled, eyes narrowing. 'We believe that Rykel told them the panel was sensitive to price. So they thought they could pull it off by just topping us, coming in a few dollars above. Not very smart. The panel put the extra dollars aside, went for an all-Australian company, top-class consortium, broad range of expertise, access to—'

'Quite,' I said. 'Who killed Bergh?'

His look turned conspiratorial. 'I can't speculate on that, Jack. But of course—'

I waited. He smiled, shook his head. 'Let's just say WRG are known for covering their tracks.'

I didn't have anything to lose. 'So WRG went for Rykel. And your mob went for Susan Ayliss.'

Without hesitation, he said, 'Ayliss was WRG's first choice but she gave them the arse. Rykel was second cab and he delivered.'

Legge rose, tugged at his tie. 'Well, Jack, that's all I came to say. WRG are people who will try to use anyone. Use them and spit them out. Take it from an old mate.'

'Thank you for your concern,' I said, 'but I don't know WRG and I don't know that they know me.'

He nodded at me in a way full of meaning. 'They know you, mate. Believe me.'

At the door, I said, 'Good luck in your new career, Gavin. I can't fault Ponton's judgment in hunting your head.'

'Thanks,' he said. 'Next time we'll crack a bottle of the French.'

Rain had beaded on the BMW. I was beginning to hate beading.

At the Prince, the youth club were conducting a panel discussion covering, simultaneously, the certain outcomes of all eight of the weekend's games. I joined in but most of my mind was elsewhere.

'Now, Jack,' said Norm, 'we goin to this bloody Docklands again on Sundee or not?'

Sunday afternoon was St Kilda against Essendon, second from the bottom against the top.

'Going,' I said. 'There'll be a million Bomber fanatics there. They can't get enough blood. The team needs us.'

'Goin then,' said Norm. He turned to the others. 'Sundee's on.'

They raised their glasses.

'We might have a bet on the way,' I said.

All eyes glittered.

'Got the oil?' said Eric. 'Got the oil, Jack?'

I held up my right hand, moved it around in the maybe, maybe not way.

'He's got the oil,' said Wilbur. 'He's got the oil.'

She rang when hope was gone. I was at the freezer, looking at my personal Antarctic, Scott knew no bleaker moment.

'I'm shutting down my week here,' said Linda. 'You'd be on your way out, I suppose. Freshly showered.'

'Well, yes and no. On my way out I have no doubt. Showering I was putting off until later.'

'Yes or no?'

'Yes. Please. There's nothing to eat here.'

Silence.

'Well,' she said, 'we'll cross that little obstacle when we come to it.'

I made the bed, cleaned the toilet, the washbasin, stacked the dirty dishes. For the rest, the place was reasonably clean from my recent manic attack.

The Avoca kindling came to life briskly. I put on Milly Husskind, sad and sexy trailer-park songs, a voice torn at the edges.

A shower, a quick shower.

I was barely in clean denims and an old and faithful shirt when the buzzer went.

Tonight, her hair was drawn back severely and she was dressed for outdoors in a leather jacket, polo-neck sweater and corduroy pants.

'That's a good look,' I said. 'Sort of tough.'

She came in and looked around. 'I am tough. Toughest woman on radio.' She took off her jacket.

'I heard you roughing up that life coach.'

'That was nothing compared with what I did to the woman selling her book on colonic irrigation.'

'Stuck it right up her, I'm sure. I'm opening white wine. I suppose…'

'I'll drink anything.'

Linda followed me into the kitchen and sat on the table while I opened the wine. I brought the glasses over, put them down next to her. She put a hand in my waistband and pulled me over into the fork of her legs.

I looked down at her. 'That's a suggestive thing to do,' I said.

'I'm in a suggestive frame of mind.' She hooked her legs around mine, drew me in tight.

'Nothing wrong with those muscles,' I said, experiencing shortness of breath. I bent down to kiss her neck, her mouth, felt her hands in my hair.

We came apart.

'You're pretty suggestible, aren't you?' she said, moving a long-fingered hand between us. She was flushed, an erotic sight.

'I've got a new mattress,' I said, hoarsely. 'Very hard.'

She took hold of me. 'Hard I like,' she said. 'Harder the better.'

When it was over, Linda lay on her back, her legs over me.

'We never went anywhere,' she said.

'Anywhere? How far away is anywhere?'

'Far. Europe. America.'

'I've been there.'

'Not with me. With the mystery hand on the train, but not with me.'

'How could we go anywhere? I'd barely got a grip on you when you left for Sydney.'

'You encouraged me. I thought you wanted to get rid of me. Not at the time, I didn't think that at the time. It came to me later.'

'I had your interests at heart.' I rolled over, took her chin in my hand. 'What I didn't know,' I said, 'was that once a starfucker, always a starfucker.'

Linda had been married to a doctor, left him for a rock musician.

'Yes,' she said, 'I've fucked the stars. Rock stars, TV personalities. But that's behind me now. I'm going for the lesser lights in the galaxy. Butchers, I want. Newsagents. Seedy suburban solicitors even.'

'As it happens, I can help you there.'

'Yes?' She had her right hand on me.

'Yes, I know an excellent butcher and a…'

In the pre-dawn, misty rain in the streetlights, a much happier person left the boot factory, a rumpled, low-crotched figure fit only to be abroad in darkness. Today, I would vary my route, stumble along...no, the usual route was better. Stick with a known way.

As was always the case, I felt a surge of wellbeing as the recalcitrant muscles and tendons and sinews warmed up and stretched. I prepared myself for the dog ambush, was caught unawares yet again when the calculating beast waited until the last second before launching itself at the fence.

My thoughts turned to gluing the entire dog to a McCoy creation, but my mood was too good to be coloured by the encounter. I stepped up the pace to the point where I could have overtaken one of those scooters for the disabled, the silent machines that carry flags.

Did the drivers ever wish for something more under the pedal, a bit of grunt? Just for emergencies, mark you. An emergency power surge that spun the back wheels, lifted the nose. That would empower the disabled, brighten an entire day.

Thinking these and other innovative thoughts, I cantered in the dark up Napier Street to Freeman, turned left for Brunswick, the sacred ground on my right, the site of the departed Fitzroy Football Club, my sacred ancestral site. Here, Irish men, my antecedents, their founding male genes coming from the Jewish quarter of Hamburg, had on pale and icy afternoons heard the crowd suck the oxygen from the air as they rose to take the screaming mark.

Sucking oxygen myself, I turned right up empty Brunswick, still moving at tram-catching pace, went past the bowling club and turned right for the trip through the gardens. They were in near-darkness, the light from the lamps diffused by the soft rain.

Then the reserves of energy were found to be non-existent. I slowed to a controlled stagger near the lovely tree where a young woman had been found one winter morning, sitting in the comfortable fork. Dead, strangled, dumped.

Where paths met, I was at a walk. Winded.

The walking winded.

Like a real athlete, my head was up, my hands were on my hips. I was always this way by the time I got to this point. Warming down, they called it. How can you warm *down*?

Exhaustion with signs of distress was what it was.

Standing there, panting, I heard something.

The shift of a foot on leaves?

Something out of the corner of my left eye, just a movement of the dark trunk of a tree.

Close, two metres away.

I turned my head, saw the figure take a step towards me, a man, saw light from the high park lamp ahead gleam on something…

Oh Jesus.

At once, a sound like a fist thumping a desk and a flash, a shutter blinking on a white-hot fire, a tug at the tracksuit hood, burning on the back of my head.

Instinctively, I reached for the man, lurched, covered the distance between us, got both hands on an arm as I fell, pulled him down with me.

He hit me on the side of the head with his left hand, lost his footing, fell towards me, half over me. I let go with my right hand, tried to punch him, made contact somewhere, he made a noise, I rolled over, took him with me, I outweighed him, a slim person but strong, I was on top, no face beneath me, a mask, a silk ski mask, mud on it. I tried to hit him in the face with my left hand, then my right, missed both, realised he had no hold on me.

I got to my feet.

He was bringing the weapon up.

I swung a kick at him, connected, turned and ran. Not for home, too far, get out into the open. I ran in the direction of the playground, the barbecue, sliding on the gravel, got off the path, looked back, saw him coming, moving well, I hadn't hurt him.

Why didn't he shoot? Had he lost the weapon?

No, he wanted this to be neat. He'd wanted to shoot me from close range, a clean hit, a professional hit, Alan Bergh had been shot by a professional…

Run, just run.

I could hear him behind me on the path.

He was closing on me. I could hear his running footsteps over the sound of my heart, of the blood in my ears, of my panting.

The children's playground ahead, beyond that the road gleaming wetly in the streetlight, the school, a light on in the school, a cleaner at work…

If I could reach the road.

Just reach the road.

I wasn't going to reach the road before he caught me.

I looked over my shoulder and saw the dark figure close behind, all black, white blurs for eyes. I changed direction to run through the swings, run between the swings, the ground wet and slippery underfoot.

No more breath in my body, slowing down, he was going to run up behind me, shoot me in the back of the head.

Shoot me. Metres from me.

I saw the swings, solid planks suspended on heavy chains.

I was between them, on an isthmus between the troughs worn away by children's swinging feet.

Behind me, I heard his breathing.

He was almost on me.

Going to die.

I grabbed the swing to my left, grabbed the nearest chain, swung the heavy plank, it jumped up awkwardly, twisting.

He was a metre away, in stride, both hands on the pistol.

I brought the swing seat around shoulder-high.

It smashed into his forearms, knocked them sideways, he fired, the flat sound, no muzzle flash seen, the shot way off course.

His momentum brought him up to me, I smelt his breath, sweet, his left hand was off the gun…

His right hand was bringing the gun back towards me, not worried about neatness now, just a desire to kill me.

I had the swing seat in both hands, threw it over his head, grabbed the chains, pulled them together, no thought in any of this, wrapped them around his throat, twisted with all my strength. He had a hand at his throat, both hands, I twisted, twisted, maniacal strength in my arms, in my torso.

He went down on his knees in the swing's depression, making a gargling noise.

I didn't stop twisting, couldn't stop, went on…

When I stopped, I didn't look at him, walked away.

Without a backward glance, I walked home, slowly, little

261

shudders passing though my arms, my shoulders, more like tiny convulsions, spasms, a great feeling of tiredness upon me.

At home, I was sick for a long time, then I rang the police emergency number, told a woman that there was a body in the north playground of the gardens, at the swings, gave her my name, address and telephone number.

It was twenty minutes before they knocked on my door. I was showered, shaved, dressed. My breathing was normal.

He was a weary-looking uniformed cop, blue-chinned, probably at the end of his shift.

'Jack Irish?'

I nodded.

'Rang about the body?'

'Yes.'

He looked at me for a while. 'Reckon it's a good joke?'

'What?'

'Don't fuck with me. We don't appreciate this kind of crap. I can charge you.'

'At the swings.'

'No body at the swings, there's no body in the whole fucken park.'

'Sorry,' I said. 'Must've been a dero having a nap. Sorry.'

When he'd gone, I went to the kitchen and sat at the table, my elbows on it, my head in my hands.

Someone was sent to kill me. Instead, I killed him.

Had I killed him?

Or had he recovered, crawled away? Perhaps someone had taken him away, dead or alive, because it was less trouble that way? It had been at least fifteen minutes before I'd phoned the police, plenty of time to remove the masked man.

I hadn't seen his face. I had wrapped a chain around his neck and tried my best to strangle the life out of him, thought I'd succeeded, and I had no idea what he looked like.

Just the silk-masked face in the near dark, the smell of his toothpaste.

I walked around the apartment aimlessly, made the bed so recently left. Looked at my watch. It was just after 7 a.m.

Who?

Someone who wanted the matter of Marco to stay closed.

Would they try again? They'd have to find another hit man.

Perhaps they had a supply of hit men. Hardly likely.

Who?

The same people who'd murdered Marco?

It was almost certain that WRG had used Bergh to attempt the blackmail of Susan Ayliss. In that case, he'd hired Marco. But the bid had failed, leaving Bergh and Marco as potential embarrassments. Now they were both dead.

And then I came along, asking questions about both men.

Bergh had held the key to everything. He talked to Doyle, to Mick Olsen, drug scam mastermind…

I needed to look at Bergh's phone bill again.

No.

I needed to do nothing. This wasn't worth dying for. Colin Loder would recuse himself from the cocaine jackets trial and, with luck, never hear anything more about his missing album. As for Marco, his death was of no personal concern to me. I had no interest whatsoever in Marco.

Send a message to WRG that I was no longer interested in Bergh or Marco, that was what I needed to do.

Go away for a while. Go far away. Leave now. That would convey the message that I had disengaged from anything that annoyed them.

Ring Cam, ring Linda, ring Wootton, ring Colin Loder on his borrowed mobile. Ring Stan and tell him to pass the message on to the youth club that I'd gone away, wouldn't be picking them up on Sunday. Ring Gus and leave a message for Charlie. Enzio. I'd have to get hold of him.

A life to run away from.

I could do that. I could spend a few weeks with Claire.

No, I couldn't do that. They might not accept my gesture of submission and send someone to Claire's house to look for me. I couldn't go near anyone I knew.

I couldn't run away from this. There wasn't any way to backtrack, to undo.

Bergh's phone bill. Another look at it.

The city hadn't fully woken yet, only those without a choice were astir: the greengrocer on the corner, the newsagent, dry-eyed shiftworkers going home. I was opening my office door in ten minutes.

There hadn't been any malice in the job they'd done, but they didn't care who knew they'd been there.

My one filing cabinet had been emptied, every file taken from its folder and dropped to the floor.

My old Mac's hard drive was gone.

The in-tray where I'd carelessly tossed Bergh's phone bill was empty. So was the out-tray.

There was the faintest glow of light from the back room.

I went to the doorway. The door of the small fridge was open and a rectangle of pale-yellow light lay on the floor.

I switched on the light.

Everything had been taken out of the small sink cupboard—ancient dishwashing liquid, a tin of drain cleaner, a few scouring pads, a bar of yellow soap I'd never seen before, two rolls of paper towels, a box of tea bags, the jar of sugar.

They'd looked in the old microwave, left the door open. I went to the steel back door. It was open. They'd left that way, down the lane, carrying the hard disk.

I locked the door, looked around, feeling light-headed, queasy in the stomach.

What else had been in here?

Robbie's suitcase. I'd put it between the fridge and the sink.

Gone.

If things had gone to plan, I would be dead now, lying in the park, dragged into the bushes, blood seeped into the tanbark, waiting to be found by some early walker's dog. And there would be nothing in my effects to connect me with Marco or Bergh.

I went to the front room, willed myself to tidy up, failed. What was the point?

Eric the Geek had done the Bergh reverse-directory for me. Would he have kept a copy of his findings? Possibly. There was something distinctly retentive about Eric. I got out my wallet to find the card with his number, searched through the pockets, couldn't find it. In exasperation, I pulled out half-a-dozen cards.

A small dark-blue object. For a moment, it meant nothing. Then I remembered.

The small plastic torch-like device from Robbie's jacket, found in the inside key pocket. The device without hint of function.

I held it between finger and thumb, pressed the button, looked at the red light it emitted for a second or so, turned it over. Something had been scratched into the plastic. I held it to the light. Numbers: 2646.

I thought I knew what this thing did.

The Cathexis carpark was in the basement, entered from a concrete driveway on the eastern side of the building. I found a park two blocks away and walked back, a cold wind opening my jacket, no-one in the streets.

I didn't turn in when I reached the driveway. I walked to the far side, then turned right and stayed close to the wall as I made haste to cover the 50 metres to the carpark entrance. The camera above it was stationary, looking down on where drivers would activate the door-opening machinery by communicating with a steel pillar.

Robbie's device was in my hand as I walked. At the carpark's huge door, I did a right-angle turn, went up to the pillar, saw the eye set into it, pointed the small torch and pressed the button.

The carpark door made a noise and began its rise. I was inside long before it reached my height.

No more than two dozen cars were in the brightly lit chamber. Quality not number, all foreign: Mercedes, BMW, Volvo, Saab, Audi, an Alfa, a yellow born-again VW Beetle in the corner.

I looked around. In the centre of the space, a glowing green arrow on a concrete shaft pointed upwards. I was there in seconds.

Another eye.

I pointed and pressed.

The lift door opened.

A big stainless-steel box, carpet on the floor, deep

plum-coloured carpet. No ordinary lift. No floor buttons to press, just a keyboard, an eye and, above it, a green screen. Beside that, two large red rectangular buttons said ASSISTANCE and EMERGENCY.

The green screen had a message: *Welcome to Cathexis. Please enter your code.*

Point and press.

The screen said: *Thank you. Please enter your password.*

My password?

I hadn't thought about a password. Ah, the numbers scratched on the torch. I managed to read them, typed them in: 2646.

The screen said: *Error. Please re-enter password.*

Time to leave. I was turning when I remembered. The apartment was in a company name. The woman at reception had said it. It had crossed my mind that it was an anagram of Rosalind.

Dalinsor Nominees.

It was worth a try. I typed in Dalinsor.

The screen said: *Thank you.*

The lift was moving. I breathed again. Numbers blipped on the screen, stopped at 12. The door opened.

A foyer with a pale rose carpet. Soft lighting came from wall sconces beside four doors. Number 12 was on my right, a security camera set into the wall above it. Plus another electronic eye, another keyboard. How did the residents put up with this? Better to risk burglary.

There was a button. I pressed it. If anyone was home, I had explaining to do.

No response. I pressed again, waited. Then I gave the eye a beam with the torch.

The keyboard lit up and a voice said: 'Entry code, please.'

If the number scratched on the torch didn't work I was going to be trapped up here on the twelfth floor, waiting for security to arrive.

I tapped in 2646.

The voice said: 'Thank you.'

My shoulders sagged. Bolts slid.

I went into a long hallway, unfurnished, looked around for the alarm system. It was behind the door, a steel box with a green light glowing. The entry code had deactivated the alarm.

An open door from the hall led into a huge sitting room, empty except for two leather chairs and a sofa. Outside, on a balcony, the wind was whipping the bare branches of trees in pots. I walked through into a kitchen, stainless steel and granite, sleek, no visible appliances, no signs of habitation. From the sink, you could look out over the city, blurred by the wet glass.

I went back to the hall, found the main bedroom. The bed was the size of a Housing Commission bedroom, bedding on it, striped sheets stripped back.

Facing the bed, a home-cinema-size screen was built into a wall of cupboards, record and stereo equipment beneath it.

Was this where Susan Ayliss had seen herself on screen? Live in action with Marco.

A dressing-room led off the bedroom. I had a look in the cupboards. Two held women's garments, after-dark wear at a glance, and there were underclothes in drawers and women's shoes in a rack. Ros Cundall obviously used the place occasionally.

Beyond the dressing-room was a bathroom that was also a gym and spa and sauna, an antiseptic Nordic-looking place. In a glass-fronted cabinet, glass shelves held cosmetics—jars and tubes, bottles of all shapes and sizes containing pale liquids and golden vials—three perfumes, atomisers, cologne, cottonwool balls, ear buds, mouthwash, toothpaste.

Nothing. I was wasting my time.

I went back to the kitchen, sighted along the granite countertop, saw the faint trails. It took a while to find the fridge but it was empty except for a bottle of Perrier water.

I opened another door off the hallway. A study, built-in shelves along one wall, a modern desk and a chair, nothing in the desk drawers. Tall and narrow cabinets flanked the doorway. On the way out, I opened the door of the right-hand one. Empty. I tried the other one. Empty.

Time to go, to end this trespass.

But I was reluctant to leave. I went back to the sitting room, looked around, walked around the kitchen again opening doors, checked the other bedroom, the main bedroom again, the dressing-room, the bathroom/gym/sauna.

I was turning to leave, leave the room, the apartment, the building, when I saw, on a shelf behind a chrome-plated exercise bicycle, a bag, a leather-look bag, the size of a small toilet bag.

I went over and picked it up, opened it.

It held a camera. A small digital video camera.

The camera that filmed Susan Ayliss?

Now it was time to go.

Leaving Cathexis didn't require any codes. In a few minutes, I was on the wintry street, curiously elated for someone who only hours before had been running for his life in a public park.

The woman at Vizionbanc in South Melbourne took

the camera away and when she came back her tone was apologetic.

'Only one image on it is retrievable,' she said. 'Sometimes everything isn't completely wiped. A beach. Want to see?'

I followed her into a room lit by the glow from half-a-dozen monitors on one wall. She took me to the end one. It showed a beach, a featureless and windy beach by the look of it, sea to the left, low dunes to the right, scrubby vegetation. There were two sets of marks in the sand, possibly footprints. In the distance, at the right of the frame, on the dunes side, there was something solid, just a dark blob.

'What's that?' I pointed.

'Vehicle,' she said. 'Old Land Rover, Land Cruiser, something like that. The boxy shape.'

'That's good,' I said. 'That's a gift.'

'Trained at huge expense by the Defence Department,' she said. 'We pass the savings on to our clients.'

She went to a work station and fiddled at a console. The dark blob now filled the screen. It was a fuzzy image but it was a vehicle, not quite side-on to the camera, definitely a four-wheel drive, grey.

'Land Cruiser,' she said. 'Short wheelbase.'

'Is that the date the picture was taken? On the bottom.'

'Yes.'

'Can I use a phone? Can someone ring me back here?'

She nodded, took me to the reception area.

I rang Eric the Cybergoth, told him what I wanted. Then I looked at the street, the passers-by, at the rain falling on the Stud where it stood in the loading zone. No beading was taking place on its blue-grey skin. The parking persecutor, the grey ghost who left the message for me around the corner from The Green Hill, he would take better care of the Stud. Love it more. Cherish it. Wax it. It would bead for him. I had his number. I should sell it to him.

On the other hand, if he waited a short time, he could buy it much cheaper from my deceased estate.

The phone on the desk rang.

'Jack?'

Eric the Lawless, master of the cybersteppes.

'Yes.'

'There's one.'

'What is it?'

'Land Cruiser. '82. Want the rego?'

'Yes.'

I walked around the corner to a place I'd noticed called Cafe Bonbon, just two seated customers and a person getting a takeaway. I ordered a short black and a cold croissant from the coffee-maker, a saturnine youth in a chef's white top.

There was a used copy of the *Herald-Sun* on top of the unwanted newspaper dump. I took it to a seat, sat down carefully, the day so violently begun taking its toll on my back, my neck, on everything that supported my unworthy skull.

My eyes had been on the front-page headline for a while before the small active section of my brain registered the big words on the page.

DRUGS BUNGLE

LINK TO KILLING

The opening paragraphs said:

Police sources last night linked the murder of a man at Melbourne Airport to the disappearance of cocaine worth more than $2 million in a bungled Federal Police operation.

The dead man, Alan Bergh, 47, of Toorak, is believed to have been involved in a 'controlled importation' of cocaine from South Africa that went badly wrong and allowed smugglers to get away with cocaine worth more than $2 million.

Victorian Police believe that the Federal Police operation was compromised from within. The Federal Police have declined to comment. Sources say the importation was financed by a Melbourne group looking for new drug sources. 'There are well-known identities involved,' a source said. 'They're trying to break away from their usual suppliers. The

Federal Police had a golden chance to nail some dealers to the big end of town and they stuffed it up.'

The story went on to list other strange goings-on in the local drug squad. Bergh's was the only name given. It was all speculation based on information from unnamed sources, but it had the unmistakable feel of a story planted by the cops and dressed up by a journalist.

I looked at the street for a while, something at the edge of thought, then I got up and asked if I could use the phone next to the coffee machine.

Cam answered at the second ring.

'That pilot with the cap,' I said. Harry and Cam used a pilot who wore a baseball cap backwards.

'Yeah.'

'I've got a name. I need to find out if it filed flight plans recently. Local airports.'

A silence lasting just long enough to express wonder.

'What's the name?'

I gave it to him.

'Call you on what?'

'Hold on.'

I found a $5 note, put it on the counter. 'Can someone ring me here?'

'Sure,' said the coffee-maker pushing the money away. 'Twenty-five cents goin out, comin in's free. What's your name?'

I told him, read the number to Cam and went back to my seat, drank my coffee and ate the croissant without tasting either.

I didn't hear the phone but the coffee-maker shouted my name.

'What's that hissing noise?' said Cam.

'Snakes,' I said. 'I'm in the jungle.'

'That'd be right. The name flew from Moorabbin this morning. Filed a flight plan for Sale. One passenger.'

'Any other flights to Sale?' Sale was near the sea. Beaches.

'June 4 there's one. With passenger.'

The picture of the beach was taken on June 5. There was something very wrong here, something I should have considered earlier. I paid my bill and left. As I rounded the corner, cold rain blew into my face and ran down my neck and under my collar.

At the office, a message on the answering machine. Barry Tregear didn't identify himself: *The query. ID was by the bloke we were talking about. The dangerous one.*

I closed my eyes, let my head fall forward.

Mick Olsen had identified Robbie Colburne's body. Mick Olsen, drug cop, the commissioner's suppository, receiver of messages from Alan Bergh, now the late Alan Bergh.

This was even wronger that I'd thought.

I rang inquiries, asked for the Shire of Sale. One last stab. But not in complete darkness.

When I turned off the tarmac, the western sky was the unnatural pink of denture plates. In the east, the light above the lakes was dirty grey and going quickly. I crossed a cattle grid and drove up a dirt road that made its way around boulders and stands of yellow box.

At the top of the hill, I stopped. The road forked and the landscape revealed itself. To the left was a bay, its right shore a narrow heavily-treed peninsula. To the right, the country was open, grazing country, fenced into paddocks, with a belt of trees along the lake shore. The road to the right twisted down a long way to what looked like a cluster of farm buildings surrounded by trees. The left fork went to the peninsula, entered the trees and was lost from sight.

Dead Point, the map called the peninsula.

I was tired, sore everywhere, filled with a feeling of futility, the feeling that I was moving because I was scared to stop. Sharks couldn't stop; they moved or they died. I wasn't a shark. I was an old goldfish in a pond the new owners were filling with rubble, a fish swimming around trying to find water that had oxygen in it. A shaking of the head, a moving of the shoulders, creaks heard in the joining places. Time to move.

I turned left, drove down to the peninsula, in the direction of what I took to be Dead Point. A few hundred metres before the tall trees began, a new fence and a gate between fat posts barred the way. Beyond the fence, hundreds of trees had been planted, gums, waist-high, not planted in lines but in clusters.

I opened the gate, went through, stopped to close it. Door open, leg out, I changed my mind, left the gate ajar, fuck the farming ethic, drove on, down into the trees.

A narrow road, twisting, etched into the land by wheels, dull water in pools, the old gums close and oppressive, blocking the light.

There was a final bend and then a clearing, large, a quarter of a football field, two timber buildings directly ahead, a ramshackle two-storey structure on the right with a set of big doors, one open a metre. The other building, single storey, was weathered but in good condition. A vehicle was parked in front of it.

An old Land Cruiser.

I parked beside it and got out. Clean air. The sea wasn't far away, its chip-salty taste in the nasal passages.

The keys were in the Land Cruiser. No crime out here in the clean air. I followed a worn route, walked down between the buildings, not so much a path as a rut, reached a portico, a new structure, sheltering a door in the single-storey building.

No bell. This wasn't a bell building. No knocker either.

I gave the door a few hits with knuckles, winced in pain.

Nothing.

Used the left hand to do it again.

No sound from within.

Again.

No-one home.

I tried the door handle. The door opened.

A passage. Dark. Doorways ahead, three to the left, one to the right. Outdoor clothes hung on a peg rail beside the righthand door.

I went in, opened the right-hand door.

It was a big room, warm, a combined sitting room and kitchen lined with timber, its age and its history showing in the adzed posts and beams and the oil stains deep in the now-polished floorboards. The eastern side had once had sliding doors and the upper tracks had been left when a wall of glass was installed. In the middle of the room, a fire glowed behind the glass door of a stove.

'Anyone home?' I said loudly.

No sound, then a log spluttered in the firebox.

I walked to the window past a kitchen table with turned legs and through a casual arrangement of old armchairs and a sofa covered with bright rugs. Beyond the sliding glass doors, a new deck and jetty ran to the lake, huge and still and empty, shining like metal in the gloaming.

Look in the other rooms?

At that moment, nothing on earth held less appeal. I went back to the passage, opened the first door.

A tidy room holding four bunks. Empty.

The second door on the left.

I felt my skin tighten, realised my mouth was dry.

For some reason, I knocked and waited. Turned the handle, pushed the door open.

No surprises. Another bedroom, a large bed, made, nothing lying around.

The third door. A bathroom, two toilet bags on the basin cabinet.

I went out the side door, turned left down the path between the buildings. At the end of the dwelling, I stopped and looked around. The two-storey building had been the boat workshop. Out of its yawning front entrance, wide-apart rusty steel trolley tracks ran down to the water's edge and disappeared under water. Boats had been brought up to the tracks and a wheeled cradle run under the keels. Then they had been winched up the incline into the huge shed.

The shed was a half-dark, empty cavern. I went in, feeling the texture of the packed and oily dirt floor underfoot. Now the cradle stood at the end of its track, near the back doors, piled with 44-gallon drums. It was all that remained of the trade plied in this great space, the hard work of repairing boats.

I went back into the house, into the sitting room, looked out of the window.

A sailing boat was coming in to the jetty, sails furled, under power, two people in yellow rainslicks on board, one at the tiller, one leaning on the cabin.

I moved back from the window and watched the person at the tiller take the boat up to the landing at a near right angle, change direction sharply, cut the power, drift the vessel gently side-on to meet the jetty.

The other person stepped off the boat, went to the bow to begin tying up. A man. He was joined on the jetty by his companion, a woman, who secured the stern line, got back on board, closed the cabin, put a cover over the engine. The man waited for her, put out a hand. She took it. On the jetty, they embraced, kissed, I saw her teeth flash as she laughed. They walked towards the house, his right arm around her shoulders, her left arm around his waist.

I sat down in an armchair, the springs compressing unevenly beneath me.

Waited.

I heard them in the passage, laughing. They would be hanging up their yellow rainslicks.

She came into the room first, didn't see me, ruffled her hair with both hands, an attractive sight.

'Warmth, warmth,' she said, turning back, 'I don't understand…'

He was in the doorway and he saw me and she saw it in his eyes.

I stood up.

'Good evening,' I said. 'Susan. Marco.'

'A drink,' said Susan Ayliss. 'We need a drink. Malt, that's what we need. Double single malts.' She went to the long kitchen counter, where bottles stood on a tray.

Marco walked over, tall, slim, colour on his cheekbones from the cold, wearing a polo-neck sweater. He looked a little older in the flesh.

'You've been looking for me,' he said, smiling, putting out his right hand.

I shook it. His handshake made no attempt to impress.

'Not looking for you,' I said. 'It never occurred to me until yesterday that you might not be dead. I've been trying to find out who killed you and who had Colin Loder's album.'

'Drink,' said Susan Ayliss. She had three glasses on a tray, a bottle in her hand. Marco took the bottle and half-filled the glasses.

I took a glass, put it to my lips, welcomed the smell of campfire clothes, the dark taste.

'Let's sit,' said Susan. She put the tray on the coffee table, switched on two table lamps.

We sat, Susan and Marco on the sofa, not people at ease. I drank some more whisky.

'I'd like to know a few things,' I said.

'I don't have the album,' said Marco. 'I'm sorry.'

'Where is it?'

'The person I took it for, he's got it.' He had a gravelly voice, a man with a cold.

I didn't say anything. We sat in silence. A wind was coming up, gusting, rattling the iron roof. Marco put a hand on Susan's knee, a gesture of comfort.

'I don't know what you know,' said Marco. He tasted the whisky. 'Xavier Doyle. At The Green Hill?'

I nodded.

'Doyle's got it. They're in deep with this drug thing the judge's hearing. You know…'

'Yes.'

'The guys who brought the stuff in, they were told they'd walk, some technicality I don't understand. Anyway, the pictures, that's insurance, concentrate the judge's mind.'

'Doyle and who are in deep?'

'And Cundall. They're both in financial shit. Cundall went to South Africa and met this importer. The guy brings it in by the container. So he came back and worked out this wonderful scheme with Doyle.'

'The judge,' I said. 'You knew he had pictures?'

Marco blinked, twice. 'Yes,' he said. 'Doyle knew.' He drank some malt.

'How would he know that?'

'Knows everything, the X.'

'X arranged for Loder to be in the Snug?'

Marco's fingers went over his hair. He looked at Susan, a long look, his eyes came back to me.

'Yes,' he said. 'I let him blow me. Closed my eyes and thought of England.' He smiled, an open smile, careless of anyone's opinions.

'What brought you to Melbourne?' I said. 'The weather?'

Marco didn't hesitate. 'Weather's okay. I like it, very noir. Actually, I came to make a fuckflick with Susan.' He looked at her and smiled, a slow smile. 'Worst gig of my life.'

Susan took his sleeve, punched his arm.

She was in love.

'Who hired you?'

'A bloke called Naismith. In Sydney. And I wouldn't call it hire. I didn't have any choice. People were trying to kill me.'

'Where does Alan Bergh come in?'

'He got on to Naismith, asked him for someone.'

'Who hired Bergh?'

'Doyle. Well, Sam Cundall through Doyle.'

I looked at Susan. She was tense, didn't want to meet my eyes. I said, 'Susan, Cannon Ridge. Can we go over that again?'

She looked into her glass, sniffed it, a delicate indrawing of nostrils, drank. 'I lied to you,' she said in a quiet voice. 'I passed on WRG's tender to Anaxan. I'm not brave. The thought of the video getting out terrified me.'

Between them, Susan and Gavin Legge had convinced me that WRG were the naughty ones. Legge was going to pay a heavy price for his part.

'I don't understand quite how you got from blackmail to this state of affairs,' I said.

Susan put out a hand and touched Marco's hair. He took her hand, kissed her fingers. Victim and blackmailer, now as one.

'Marco came around to apologise,' she said. 'He does that rather well.'

'I fell in love,' said Marco. 'I didn't expect that to happen.'

'Didn't stop the blackmail though.'

He shook his head. 'No, it didn't. I couldn't stop that, Jack. We're all victims some of the time.'

'The dead person? The person with your wallet in your car? He'd be a real victim.'

'He was dead already,' said Marco. 'A druggie. They found him dead. Overdosed in an alley.'

'They? This is Mick Olsen we're talking about?'

Marco blinked. 'Yeah, someone in the cops found him for Mick. One of his mates.'

I thought about the homemade notice in the Lebanese shop, the face of a missing young man. It wasn't hard to find a body in the city. I drank some whisky, remembered I hadn't eaten since the croissant with nothing. When was that? What day?

'Why did Olsen do this?' I said.

'Didn't want anyone looking for Robbie. Robbie does Susan and the judge, then the book's closed on Robbie.' He laughed, cut it short, pained face.

'Someone tried to kill me this morning,' I said.

'Oh shit.' Marco looked down, ran both hands through his hair. 'Fucking Doyle, he's totally paranoid. Mad.'

I stood up. I didn't ask who had murdered Alan Bergh, what the fate of the real Robbie Colburne had been, I didn't want to know. Already I knew more than I wanted to know, much, much more.

'What made you come here?' said Susan. 'How did you find out about us?'

'I didn't. I found the camera in Ros Cundall's apartment. I knew Marco had some connection with the building and you'd told me about a digital camera. So I associated it with the blackmail attempt. When I saw the picture of the beach and the Land Cruiser, I assumed Marco had taken it. But whose vehicle? I had a look under the name of your company and found an '82 Cruiser.'

'And this place? No-one knows I own it.'

'Someone told me you had a plane. I found your flight plans for Sale. With passenger. Then there was the date the picture was taken. It was after Anaxan won the tender. And you'd flown to Sale the day before with a passenger. That's when I began to think that Marco might not be dead. Hearing that Mick Olsen ID'd Robbie's body put the seal on it.'

She was frowning. 'I still don't see how you found this place.'

'The shire council was kind enough to look you up in the rates register.'

'Sounds simple,' said Susan, tight smile.

'Effortless,' I said. 'Thanks for the drink. I've got a long drive.'

Marco didn't look up, didn't get up. 'What now?' he said. 'What happens?'

'I'm going to ask Doyle for the album. And to behave properly. Apart from that, I've lost interest.'

Susan rose, strain on her face, her age showing. 'Jack,' she said, 'I know, I know I can't ask you…'

'I don't care who runs ski resorts and casinos,' I said. 'I don't care who you told what. The matter's closed.'

'Thank you,' she said. She took my left hand in both of hers for a moment. 'Thank you.'

They followed me out, into a clear night, cold, a fast-rising full moon. At the car, I said, 'I wouldn't like Doyle to know I'm coming around for the album.'

Marco had his arm around Susan. He shook his head. 'Never heard of any Doyle. Count on that.'

I didn't say goodbye, swung the Stud in a wide reverse turn, gunned it. I could be home by midnight.

I could be home by midnight.

I was over the crest of the hill, where the road forked, when I heard the helicopter, saw its lights over to my right, heard the menacing chop and whine.

I drove back without lights, the chalky road clear in the early moonlight. At the trees, I turned the car around, faced the way I'd come.

I sat for a moment, put my forehead on the steering wheel. My body had moved a step beyond tiredness and hurt, gone to a stage where I wasn't feeling anything except a strange sort of buzzing in my limbs, an electrical discharge of some kind.

This was not my business. My business was finished. Almost. Soon. Just as soon as I'd put a proposition to Xavier Doyle that would drain the bonhomie from his cherubic, murderous being. Then my life would resume.

Charlie would be back soon.

Libraries. Ros Cundall had phoned. She wanted a library.

We wouldn't be doing a Cundall library.

Good.

A library every now and then was fine but not a diet of libraries. We would be doing other things, sitting in the workshop fragrant with the smell of wood and discussing philosophical matters. His extended stay in Perth would come under examination. The merits of warm weather. Swimming, perhaps.

I lifted my head, rubbed my eyes, got out. Listened.

Far, far away a dog barking, a long strangled sound. The full moon, it stirred dogs in their blood, all their fluids, people too.

It was cold, a wind coming off the lake, off Bass Strait beyond the lake, a cold passage was the strait.

I shut my mind and set off down the track into the trees, into the dark, walking quickly. The wind was animating the gums, rubbing limbs together until they squealed, pushing under loose bark.

Where the road met the clearing, I stopped. Things were as I'd left them minutes before. No sound save the wind in the trees, at work lifting the corrugated iron.

No. A voice.

Someone talking. A low monologue, no individual word distinguishable.

I crossed the space, went down the passage between the buildings, towards the water, the voice getting louder, words becoming distinct.

I knew the voice.

'Horse prick, secret of life, hey? Fuck people, they smile? That's the attitude?'

In the deep shadows, I stopped, leaned forward.

It seemed so close, the dark helicopter, sitting on the water at the end of the rusty cradle tracks, moving in and out on its floats. I thought I could see a pilot.

Two men on the jetty, near the tethered boat, in subtropical clothing, long shorts, boat shoes.

Milan Filipovic and Steve, his short-legged employee.

I couldn't see who Milan was talking to.

'Don't fuck around in there,' Milan said. He had his small sub-machine pistol in his right hand. 'Don't fuck with me, cockboy.'

Susan Ayliss was on her knees in front of him, something around her neck. He was holding her close with his left hand, like a dog on a choke-chain.

To my left, a voice said, 'Got the Pole's gun.'

It was a tall man, heavily built, all in black. He'd come out of the house through a sliding door, stood in the light holding a pistol upright.

'Goodonya, Mick,' said Milan.

Mick Olsen, late of the drug squad, identifier of Robbie's body.

Marco came out of the boat's cabin, carrying something. A bag, a sports bag. He put it on the cabin roof.

'It's all here,' he said.

'Come,' said Milan. He moved his head and his hair was like a silver cap in the moonlight. 'Come here you piece of shit.'

Marco climbed onto the jetty, head down.

'Treat you like a son,' said Milan. 'You steal from me, you whore.'

'I'm sorry,' said Marco.

I could barely hear his voice.

'Get on your knees, cockboy. Put the bag down, get on your fucken knees and say you sorry.'

Marco knelt, head down.

Milan gestured to Olsen with the machine pistol. Olsen came over, took the weapon, gave the pistol to Milan. 'I'm sorry, Milan,' said Marco. 'I'm really sorry.'

Milan went right up to him, dragged Susan with him.

'Okay,' said Milan, 'I forgive you. Look at me.'

Marco looked up slowly. Milan shot him in the face. One shot. He went over backwards, not quickly.

Susan made a noise, a terrible noise.

Milan pulled her head back, stuck the pistol in her mouth and pulled the trigger.

'Okay,' he said, handing the pistol to Steve. 'Wipe it, stick it in her hand. Lovers' fucken quarrel, hey.' He laughed. 'Let's go. I'm thirsty.'

I walked backwards, slowly, very scared, turned, went quickly down the alley. Hide. I should find somewhere to hide until the helicopter left. Somewhere dark, somewhere to hide my head in shame.

I could have done something. Anything. Shouted, distracted Milan.

Where to hide?

I came out between the buildings, saw the big door of the workshop slightly ajar.

Dark. It would be dark in there, in the huge space, high as a church.

I was inside in a second. It was dark, but not dark enough for me, moonlight coming in through the front entrance. I could see the old cradle piled with drums, 44-gallon drums.

The helicopter started.

Drawn forward, I moved up until I could see the helicopter below, at the water's edge.

Milan was standing on a pontoon, getting into the cabin. Steve and Mick Olsen were on land, waiting for him to get in. Steve had the sports bag. From ski jackets to sports bag, I thought. Sporty stuff, the South African cocaine.

I could have done something. Anything.

These men were going to fly away, fly to warm climes, refuel somewhere, Sydney perhaps. They'd be in Milan's sitting room long before midnight, lounging in the white leather chairs and sofas, drinks on the glass-topped tables, having a good laugh. I thought of the huge picture above the fireplace, a picture of a red rose lying on stone steps, its decaying petals holding drops of dew.

I could have done something.

I went to the back of the shed, went behind the cradle, put both hands on the base of the frame, tested.

Too heavy, probably rusted into the tracks.

I pushed again, put some effort into it.

The cradle moved. Moved a few centimetres.

I changed my grip, put my shoulder against a drum, felt the cold metal on my cheek. Put everything I had into my push.

Moving, the cradle was moving. I found more strength, this was pointless, they would come up here and kill me, put the pistol in my hand.

I could have done something.

Push.

The cradle was running, running freely, rumbling along, picking up speed, getting away from me. I stumbled, went to a knee, got up, gave it a final shove…

Steve was the only one outside the helicopter. He was standing on the pontoon, looking up, he'd heard the rumbling sound.

'Go!' he screamed. 'Jesus Christ, go!'

A drum dislodged from the top of the pile, fell forward, hit the concrete, bounced high.

I could see the pilot's face through the open door. He'd seen the cradle.

One pontoon lifted, the helicopter moved.

The drum bounced again, hit Steve, smashed him into the cabin. I heard his scream over the whup of the rotor blades.

The whole cradle slammed into the helicopter, tonnes of metal travelling at speed, a screeching, crushing sound, a string of sparks as the rotors hit metal, drums hitting the top of the cabin, flying into the air.

Sound like a car backfire, another, a flash of orange in the chaos below.

The blast pushed me backwards, took my sight away, took away my hearing. Instinctively, I turned my head away, turned my body, almost fell over. I didn't look again, willed myself to leave the shed, go across to the jetty, to the bodies.

Susan was dead, no pulse in her neck.

I went to Marco, put my hand to his throat, thought I felt something.

No, my own hammering pulse.

I leant down closer, trying to detect breathing.

From his mouth a sweet, clean smell. His toothpaste. French toothpaste.

The second time I'd smelled it today.

I pushed down the neck of the sweater, saw where the swing chain had bruised him.

Then I ran, down the path between the buildings, across the moonpale clearing into the trees, down the dark road, not stopping until I reached the car, got in, couldn't get my breath, fumbled the key.

The engine started.

On the hill crest, I looked back. There was a yellow glow at the end of the peninsula. Dead Point was burning. Mick Olsen's enemies in the drug squad would be pleased. All they'd had to do was slip me some surveillance clips and I did all their dirty work.

Surrounded by the silent faithful, some with tears in their eyes, we were watching a slaughter at the Docklands stadium when the starter at the Valley sent them off: eighteen hundred metres, class six for four-year-olds and upwards, apprentices claiming, going heavy.

I'd said I'd take the youth club to the football. I'd done it.

Four men with small radios held to their heads.

Number eight, the Kiwi horse, was called The Return. We'd stopped at the TAB on the way to invest our money.

'This thing doesn't come with a guarantee,' I said. 'Could run stone motherless last. Be warned.'

Norm O'Neill laughed. The others laughed.

'I don't think I'm getting through to you,' I said. 'I don't want your families coming around to see me.'

They all laughed.

Now, we all heard the caller say: *They've strung out at the thousand, Pelecanos leads by two lengths from Armageddon, Caveat's poking up on the inside, unruly mob following, bit of push and shove, going's terrible…*

He named seven or eight other horses before he got to The Return.

We all looked ahead, mouths downturned, eyes on the game. An Essendon player, bandaged like a burn victim, was about to kick another goal. Some people don't know when to stop.

I closed my eyes, opened them quickly. If I closed

my eyes for long, I would have to be slapped awake by a paramedic, encouraged to breathe.

On the bend, Caveat's gone up to Pelecanos, Armageddon's struggling, Portobelle's edging into it now and coming very wide is The Return.

Four sets of eyes flicked at one another. Too soon to hope.

Hird kicked the goal. A dog could have kicked it. His teammates came up and patted him. Just another career statistic, what did it matter that it broke hearts?

At the four hundred, Caveat and Portobelle, and coming at them in the centre of the track is The Return, the Kiwi, could be a surprise packet here at big odds, very ordinary recent form…

Heads down, no interest in the scene before us.

The Return's coming at them, Portobelle stopping under the big weight, Caveat's a fighter, won't give in, it's The Return and Caveat, it's going to be The Return, she's clear, the Kiwi raider's going away…

Four men stood up, hands in the air, making animal sounds of satisfaction in the midst of the grieving St Kilda faithful, who looked at us, murder in their eyes.

We sat down.

'No surprise, Jack, me boy,' said Norm O'Neill. 'Had the pencil on the animal this mornin. Put me in mind of a certain Kiwi horse…'

'Say the bloody name Dunedin Star and I'll kill you,' said Eric Tanner.

We made the collect on the way back to the Prince. It frightened me to see how much money was handed over to the youth club, fifties dispensed, repeatedly.

In the car, after crossing the city and listening to a great deal of hilarity, I said, primly, 'I'd never have mentioned it if I'd thought you were going to put that kind of money on.'

Silence. Rain on the windscreen. The Stud had had a long day. The Stud and the Stud's owner, who couldn't remember when the day had begun, remembered, and tried to shut it out.

'Jack,' said Wilbur, low voice.

'Yes.'

'It's our bloody money.'

The wipers needed replacing. So did the door seals. The clutch had that certain feeling too.

'Point taken,' I said.

'You bastard,' said Eric. 'Had the oil.'

'Well,' I said, 'the study of class, sectionals, draw, going, trainer, jock, track, barrier, weight, these things help inform a decision.'

'The oil,' said Eric.

I pulled up outside the Prince, a space waiting for us.

'And then there's the oil,' I said.

The men in the back seat attacked me, beat me around the head with rolled-up copies of the *AFL Record*.'

We went in, had a few beers, no e-people in, didn't talk about the Saints' failings, too numerous to count, concentrated on the positives. All two of them. From Stan's office, I rang Linda's home number. Answering machine.

'Jack,' I said. 'I'll be home by six. Do with that information what you will.'

I said goodbye. The lads were in the process of shouting the bar, not an expensive exercise this Sunday evening. In the street, thoughts of sausages and mash and bed uppermost, my mobile rang.

'Listen, I could use a hand.' Cam.

'Now?'

'Yeah. Can't wait.'

I wanted to groan. 'What?'

He told me where he was. I did groan.

'Bring a torch,' he said.

In the unlovable depths of Coolaroo, Cam was waiting for me at the gate of a car wrecker's yard. In the dark, in spotting rain, we walked down an avenue of car bodies. Hundreds of them, piled two and three high.

'Artie lives down the back,' said Cam. He was in biker gear: leather jacket, jeans, boots.

'Where is he?'

'Handcuffed to a Lada Niva. Hasn't been helpful.'

We went around a large shed that served as an office and set off down another passage between wrecked vehicles.

'Don't they have dogs guarding these places?' I said.

'Should be halfway to Albury by now, the dog.'

I didn't ask what he meant.

'How'd you find Artie?'

'Lizard. Big help, Lizard. Given up the wood business. Just today. Gone home to New Zealand. Wouldn't know this shack was here.' He went through a gap in the wall of old twisted metal. In a clearing stood an ancient weatherboard cottage, sagging everywhere as if dropped from the air onto the site. On its verandah stood two bench seats from cars. Pieces of motorcycle covered the rest of the space.

'In the Lizards together, Artie and Almeida and Lizard,' said Cam. 'Lizard reckons Artie's topped three people. Gets carried away.'

'That Lada strong enough?'

'Artie's tired. Engine block fell on his leg.'

'Don't tell me any more. I'm a respected suburban solicitor.'

Cam led the way through the front door of the house. We were assailed by the smell of burnt cooking oil and cat urine with a strong underlay of blocked toilet.

'Well,' said Cam, 'where'd you reckon he'd keep it? Tried all the usual places.'

'Appliances?'

'Only got a beer fridge.'

'With money, they're scared of fire.'

I went from room to disgusting room, shining my new truckstop torch over everything, unwilling to touch anything. The kitchen was the worst, cats lived there, dozens of them.

We went out the back door. Off the porch was a washhouse, the bottom of its door rotted away leaving jagged wooden teeth.

'Looked in there?' I said.

'Yup.'

The door was jammed. Cam opened it with a kick.

It was the cleanest room in the place, just an old concrete laundry sink, a boiler the size of a 400-pound bomb, and grey dust and cobwebs.

I shone the torch on the boiler, tentatively tried the fire door. It opened with a screech, ashes spilling out.

'Course it could be out there somewhere in a wreck,' said Cam. 'Probably is. Boot of some scrap iron.'

I was looking at the boiler's fluepipe. The ceiling collar had come loose, tilted.

'Hold this.' I gave Cam the torch.

The top of the boiler was at shoulder height. I put both hands around the fluepipe just above where it entered the boiler and twisted.

It turned easily.

I lifted.

The fluepipe went up into the roof, its bottom end came out of the boiler.

I pushed it to one side, let it hang from the ceiling, stuck a hand into the hole in the boiler, found something to grip with my fingers, lifted.

The top of the boiler came off.

I dropped it into the sink, put my arm down the boiler, touched something wet, recoiled.

'What?' said Cam.

'Don't know.'

I reached in again, touched the thing.

Plastic, something plastic. Rain had come down the pipe.

I took hold, pulled. It was heavy. I got some of it out. Cam put the torch down, helped pull the rest out.

A heavy-duty garbage bag, grey, closed with a plastic tie.

Cam opened it. I held the torch.

'Sweet Jesus,' said Cam. 'My sweet lord.'

On the way out, down the dark avenue of dead machine bodies, Cam carrying the bag, he said, 'Artie's storin chemicals down the back. Thought I came for em.'

'As in?'

'Amphie cook.'

'That's punishable by law.'

'Law doesn't know. The big man says drop in for a drink. Good day's racin.'

We passed through the gate. Cam put the bag in the boot of the streetslut. I read my notebook by torchlight, found the number.

Cam lounged against his vehicle, looking at me.

A woman answered, no name. I gave her mine. Barry Tregear came on.

'What now?' he said.

'Arranging your promotion,' I said. I gave him the directions. 'The shed on the back boundary,' I said. 'That's where the fun stuff is.'

'Never thought you'd end up my dog.'

'Also there's a bloke chained to a Lada Niva.'

'Cruel and unusual,' said Barry. 'Chained to an old Ford Prefect's bad enough.'

'Help's on the way,' I said to Cam.

I drove to Harry Strang's house in Parkville, got there just after Cam. Lyn Strang let us in, robustly sexy as always, flesh an alluring shade of pink. She left us in the study, standing by the fire. Only the table lamps were on and I could see the flames reflected in the glass doors of the lower bookshelves. Charlie Taub bookshelves, made long before my time.

Harry came in, freshly shaved, hair oiled, brushed, a herringbone sports coat over a fine-checked shirt.

'Jack, Cam,' he said. 'On the little mudeater, Jack?'

'Handsomely,' I said. 'My creditors send their thanks.'

'Pleasure. Element of risk there. Bollie's in order, I reckon.'

Harry was looking at the canvas bag on the floor next to Cam.

'Brought your swag, I see,' he said. 'Always welcome to stay. Plenty of room.'

Cam picked up the bag and put it on the desk. He gestured to me to open it, long fingers, puffy tonight, the knuckles puffy.

I shook my head.

Cam unzipped the bag, opened it.

'Stuff,' he said.

Harry stepped over, looked. He put his hand in and took out a bundle of notes, fifties, put it back, eyes on Cam.

'Ours,' said Cam. 'And the Hales'.'

A smile grew on Harry's face. He looked like a teenager, a naughty teenager, discoverer of sex.

'Well, bugger me,' he said, eyes going back and forth. 'Chance maybe I thought, coupla bright fellas like yerselves.'

He went to the door, opened it, turned back to look at us, left the room.

'Darlin,' we heard him shout, 'forget the Bollie, coupla bottles of the Krug.'

An inaudible response.

'And an emergency one,' shouted Harry. 'No knowin.'

He came back, closed the door. 'Violence,' he said. 'That wouldn't be involved.'

Cam looked at me, looked at Harry, brushed fingers across his lips. 'Not that you'd notice,' he said.

Krug singing in the veins, all fatigue and guilt banished by the tiny silver bubbles, I parked outside the boot factory.

Lights on upstairs. A moment of fright.

Linda's car parked in the shadows. She had a key. As my breath went out, my carefree mood returned.

She was on the sofa, lengthwise, watching television, drinking what was probably Campari and soda.

'This is what it comes to,' she said. 'The little woman at home, washing socks and waiting for the man to come home from drinking pots and pots of beer with the blokes at the pub.'

I took off my coat. 'Did that for a while. Went on to drinking Krug with a sexy woman in a little black dress.'

'You bastard. Come closer.'

I came closer, stood over her.

She put out a hand, ran it over me. 'Just as I thought,' she said. 'You're still excited.'

I leaned down and undid the top button of her shirt. 'No,' I said. 'This is a new excitement. I am capable of several excitements in the same evening.'

'Better damn be,' she said as she pulled me down. 'I've got a newsagent waiting.'

'Butchers are meatier,' I said as I sank.

When the lust was spent, we warmed the duck pies Linda had brought, sent them down with a Mill Hill shiraz. Mid-pie, Linda looked at her watch, found the remote control.

'News, got to have the news,' she said. 'News is my life.'

I said, 'I was taught it was rude to have sex wearing your watch.'

'Not if it's on your wrist.' She blipped through channels, found what she wanted, a dollwoman speaking.

Six people have been found dead at a remote house on the Gippsland lakes. One of them is Susan Ayliss, a member of the panel that decided the multi-million dollar Cannon Ridge ski resort and casino tender.

I saw Dead Point from above. Then the television helicopter went in low. I didn't want to watch.

The item went on for a long time. At the end, dollwoman said: *The Premier has announced a full-scale inquiry into the Cannon Ridge tender process.*

Linda cut the power. She didn't look at me, snuggled down on the sofa, looked at me.

'What would a seedy suburban solicitor know about that?' she said, suspicion in voice and eyes.

'No more than a newsagent. What he hears on the news, reads in the paper.'

She sat up. 'Shit, I forgot. A courier came. It's next to the front door.'

It was a square package, stoutly wrapped, taped like an injured footballer. I took it to the kitchen, performed surgery on it.

An album. An album with a red leather cover. I opened it, paged through it.

Mr Justice Colin Loder was a person of much greater versatility than I'd imagined, a man of wide-ranging interests and exotic tastes. The problem was he didn't photograph well. He had a tendency to slit his eyes.

'What exactly are you doing in there?' said Linda.

'Opening a bottle.'

I closed the album Xavier Doyle had decided he didn't

need, put it in the cupboard with the dud French frying pan that had a hot spot, opened a bottle of Seven Hills.

'I'm not finished with you,' said Linda.

'And nor am I complete.'

I took the bottle and went next door.

'You'll tell me,' she said, athlete's legs on the arm of the sofa, bare. She opened my old dressing gown, revealing more flesh.

'I've taken an oath,' I said. 'You must respect that.'

'Put that down and come here.'

'It's late. I run in the mornings.'

'Come here, sunshine.'

All bad things come to an end. Almost. Now all I had to do was get justice for Enzio and the Meaker's gang. I put this out of my mind for the moment. A long moment, but not long enough.

WHITE DOG

For Anita and Nicholas, with love and thanks.

'I say again,' I said. 'Is this strictly necessary?'

We were on the Tullamarine tollway, now at its early-evening worst, a howling blur of taxis, trucks, cars, trade vehicles, drivers all tired and vicious.

'I don't want to die not knowing,' said Linda Hillier. She was looking exceptionally attractive, as people leaving often do.

'I don't understand that,' I said. 'Why shouldn't you die not knowing? Why is that worse than dying *knowing*? Let's say you're a mountain climber, you get a chance to climb Everest or K-47, AK-47, Special K, an unusually large piece of vertical landscape. You fall off it or into a glacier, you're going to be snap-frozen, like a baby pea. In that instant, you know. Now, why is that better than...'

I felt her eyes on me. I didn't want to risk a glance. I was driving her car, a new Alfa, much too refined a creature for someone only at home with V-8 American brutes, crude things, power without responsibility.

'Jack,' she said. 'They'll probably terminate me in two months, pay out the contract. I'll send for you. We'll take an apartment in Paris, wake late, coffee and croissants, walk around, eat expensive lunches, hit the pleasure mat in the afternoon...'

I closed on a plumber called John Vanderbyl, a blocked-drain specialist towing a trailer holding his video-equipped probing instruments. He was a laggard and himself guilty of clogging so I moved out and left him behind. Then I had to curb the Alfa's instinct to stay in the right lane, overtake everything. Like me, it was a natural front-runner. Unlike me, it could sustain it.

'That's wonderful,' I said. 'You have to lose for me to win. You'll be heartbroken, I'll be impotent. On the other hand, if you win, I stay in Carrigan's Lane wearing a dust mask while you're bouncing on George V's famous mattresses with Nigel, your priapic young Eton-educated production assistant.'

'How do you know about Nigel?' she said.

'An educated guess. If the Poms want an accent, why can't they find a nice girl from Liverpool? Why do they want an Aussie on London radio?'

'They like us. We don't quite get the class system. We don't instinctively defer to upper-class and upper middle-class twits. We understand irony and understatement. Also we can do attack dog.'

Linda was good at being an attack dog. A calm attack dog, though, taking politicians' calves firmly in the mouth without breaking skin, not letting go, giving little shakes from time to time.

A space appeared in the right-hand lane and, for no good reason, I pulled out to overtake a representative of Bottomdollar Carpets, then eclipsed a four-wheel-drive and an old Mitsubishi.

'When we get there,' I said, 'any chance of a final romp?'

She put a hand on my thigh. 'I think not. I want to leave you wanting more.'

'Which has always been the case. Why isn't it enough to be the best in this town?'

How stupid a question. I had turned it over in my mind, which made asking it even more stupid.

Linda was looking out of the side window. 'Naked ambition,' she said. 'Also I feel like a fake, someone who's lucked it.'

'Of course. Anyone can luck it. All you need is a chainsaw brain and a voice like Lauren Bacall. That's after you get a start in the business, which requires great legs, willing hands and passable knockers.'

'Passable? Hold on, mate, these knockers took work. I started knocker exercises at thirteen.'

'Race-fit knockers, I'm sure. You might have given me a bit more notice of this.'

I heard the petulant tone of my voice.

The long fingers squeezed my thigh. 'Wasn't any more to give,' she said. 'They rang, they offered the money, they wanted me soonest.'

'Just like me. Without the offer of money.'

The airport exit loomed.

'There's a lot of food in the boot,' she said. 'Perishables. I was at the Vic Market yesterday.'

'I'll park,' I said.

3

'No. Do an illegal at the international. Don't switch off. I'll get my bag out and be gone in seconds. No farewells, my father said. He couldn't bear goodbyes.'

I thought that I would have liked her father, a farmer crushed by the bank and a tractor, gone without a farewell.

We travelled in silence. It was starting to rain. I couldn't find the wipers.

She showed me how you did it.

'This car?' I said.

'Keep it at your place. Drive it. I'm coming back for this baby. Baby. Also I forgot to switch off the fridge and freezer. Do that for me?'

'Only if you'll promise to keep yourself nice.'

'Of course. And if I don't, you won't hear it from me.'

I went up the ramp and stopped behind a taxi. Linda took my head in both hands and kissed me, hard, pulled back, kissed me again, mouth open a little, a decent kiss.

'More,' I said. 'Baby.'

'Later. Baby. Wish me luck.'

I nodded, not inclined to speak.

She leaned across me, hair against my face, and made the boot rise. She took her travelling bag from the back seat, brushed fingertips across my lips, and she was out, plucked her slim case from the boot, closed the lid. I saw her go through the doors, not a backward glance, gone as if posted.

I drove home with something lodged in my throat, travelled at a measured speed beneath the high, cruel lights, no urge to overtake anything, smelling new leather, hearing the soft sound of the Italian wipers, like the breathing of a sleeping child. At the old boot factory, I parked beneath the oaks. The mobile rang.

'Tomorrow,' said Andrew Greer, my former partner at law, 'I will be attempting to spring a client now languishing in remand. Thereafter your expensive services will be needed.'

Andrew Greer was on his feet, long feet in narrow, shiny black shoes, everything about him long, all the visible things.

'Your worship,' he said, 'the defendant is a person of impeccable reputation who is traumatised by what has happened. There is no risk of her absconding. She will vigorously contest the charge against her and looks forward to the court clearing her name. I ask that she be granted bail on whatever conditions your worship deems fitting.'

The magistrate looked at the prosecutor, who rose. He was a sad man, not at all the state's doberman, more its stiff-legged labrador, looking forward to the day's end, the worn spot by the fireside, the peace of dog as his head came to rest on his paws.

'No objection to bail, your worship,' he said.

I could see by the movement of Drew's head, the way he looked at his client, that he had been expecting a fight.

The magistrate didn't ponder the matter: $60,000, passport surrendered, report once a day. Court adjourned.

Nothing showed on the woman's face except that she blinked rapidly. When she spoke to Drew, she inclined her head towards him, almost touched his chin with her forehead. Her name was Sarah Longmore and she was charged with murdering her former lover nine days before.

I went outside. It was raining in the same half-hearted way it had been when I left my abode after daybreak. The media were on the pavement—print journos and photographers, many of the latter skinheaded, three television reporters touching lacquered hair, camera and sound people, worried about nothing, complaining, smoking, spitting.

A black four-wheel-drive, a small one with tinted windows, arrived and double-parked: the getaway transport.

Drew and the woman came out, both tall, both in black overcoats. She was supposed to be in her mid-thirties. She could have been a seventeen-year-old ballet dancer, sharp cheekbones, short dark hair combed back with a left parting, over-exercised, living on vitamin pills, cigarettes and chocolate.

The media surged. Two wiry short-haired women in casual clothes appeared and shepherded the pair. Sarah Longmore held her chin up, looked straight ahead. For her, no dark glasses, no undignified attempt to hide her face. There was something disciplined about her, the way she kept her shoulders back, the way she held her head. The shepherds were good, clearing a path without bumping, just using their bodies, arms out, pushing backwards. At the kerb, the woman touched Drew's shoulder, put her mouth to his ear and whispered something, went between the parked cars.

7

The passenger door of the four-wheel-drive opened, she slipped in and was gone.

Drew turned to face the scrum, the microphones pointing at him. I saw on his serious face a desire to entertain the cameras, and then I saw him deny the advocate's thespian urge, shake his head. He said a few words, presumably no comment at this time, turned his back and set off across the street. The microphones drooped. They let him go.

I crossed the street too. He was waiting for me. In rain that was now gaining heart, we walked the two blocks to his old Saab in a lucky parking space near Grice Alley. It took many tries to excite the vehicle and, when it groaned, Drew flooded the carburettor and the engine died.

'You'd think you'd have the hang of it by now,' I said. 'This's been going on since the late eighties.'

'It's not a matter of the hang,' said Drew, 'it's a matter of proper observance of a time-honoured ritual.'

We waited, the windows liquid. The car smelled of orange peels and desiccated apple cores, a hint of salty old swimming towel forgotten under a seat, stiff as a dead rabbit.

'My first time in court for a while,' I said.

'Through luck not judgment,' said Drew. 'Bastards took me by surprise. Last I heard, they wanted her kept in the slammer. Good thing I had the escape ready.'

'Was that Bully West?'

Bully was a bouncer, a reformed standover man who did semi-legal odd jobs for Cyril Wootton, my sometime employer. I'd glimpsed Bully's brutal, pitted chin when Sarah Longmore slid into the car.

'It was the Bully,' said Drew. 'Courtesy of Cyril. Alert of you.'

He tried the ignition again and the car started, the engine rough as sacks. All caution, Drew put his head out of his window and looked back. Then he pulled out, into the path of a taxi. Above the rubber scream and the hooting, I thought I could hear the cabdriver swearing, not in English.

After we caught the lights and turned left into Bourke Street, Drew said, 'Shit, where'd he come from?'

'The rear.'

He shook his head. 'Don't be so fucking sanctimonious. Remember a certain left turn near Piedimonte in St George's Road? Hit an island, cracked the sump, we took off. Airborne, cropdusting the grass with engine oil.'

'It wasn't an island,' I said. 'It was a peninsula, and it wasn't there the day before. Also there was no grass. In addition, I could plead youth and inexperience.'

'Ah,' said Drew, 'and how fleeting is the time allowed for that defence.'

'On fleeting, I saw the fleeting touch of the lapel.'

Drew looked down, touched his left lapel. 'Just admiring the finest cloth Mr Buck stocks. Fleece of house-reared Aussie bleaters, hand-woven by toothless crones in the dim crofts of the Alto Adige. She is, of course, without sin in this affair.'

The oxygen was running low in the airtight Swedish vehicle. I tried to wind down my window but the handle didn't work. The side vent resisted but a fist thump ended that and the city smell came in—cold, moist, petrochemical. It carried memories of late nights, arms around waists, kissed ears, kisses behind ears, the shivery feel of a hand not your own in your hip pocket.

We turned left into Elizabeth Street.

'Mickey Franklin was in the shower on a Saturday evening,'

said Drew. 'Five shots, very messy, all over the show, fired through a towel. The one that killed him went in the back of the head, in the hollow, bullet going upwards.'

I tried to wipe the windscreen with my hand, unhappy to be blind to the many dangers we faced. 'And where was the sinless one? In her own words.'

'At the fatal moment, at home in St Kilda watching television.'

'How come they've got the weapon?'

We were at the LaTrobe Street lights. Drew looked at me, ran a finger under his nose. 'They found it in a garbage bin near the scene. Cleaned and wrapped. She knows the thing, a .32 Ruger, never licensed. She says Mickey Franklin lent it to her when she had a couple of break-ins, other strange stuff.'

The engine sounded even worse when we turned right at the lights, making the uneven, misfiring sounds of crippled Spitfires approaching the white cliffs of Dover in old World War II films.

'Echo Bravo Foxtrot to Control,' I said. 'I say, old beast, I rather think this kite's dying on me.'

'Hiccups,' said Drew. 'It's the weather. The weapon is awkward.'

'Awkward, indeed,' I said. 'Found when?'

'The morning after. Yesterday week. They sprang it on her before she called me.'

'Clever devils. Drop me at the office? I've got an engagement.'

He looked straight ahead. 'Where are we engaged today? In the Valley of the Moonee? On the Field of Caul? At Headquarters? Or at some idyllic country paddock, marvelling at what man and horse can together achieve? Assisted only by undetectable kick-arse drugs, diuretics and industrial-strength marching powder.'

'A man with an easement problem is coming in.'

'A man seeking ease,' said Drew. 'Aren't we all? In the old days, your clients were seeking to stay out of the hard hotel.'

'This is better. These clients tend to have their complete ears and comparatively few are tattooed inside their lower lips.'

Drew turned left into Russell Street. 'Ah, the holy ground once more,' he said.

The Melbourne Magistrates' Courts had been in the stone building on our left, police headquarters across the street, all kinds of squads and units in the building nearby.

Trades Hall and its annexe, the John Curtin Hotel, were just down the road. Drew's office was two blocks north. Once it had been the office of the firm of Greer & Irish, Barristers and Solicitors. The Greer and the Irish often walked down Drummond Street to appear for their clients at Russell Street. They also often drank at the Curtin, took pees with a future prime minister, standing side by side, swaying a little, aiming at white disinfectant balls.

But that time ended when my wife, Isabel, was murdered by a client of mine and I developed a powerful urge to destroy myself.

'Strictly speaking, Wootton should tell you,' he said. 'The person who will add his exorbitant margin to what I am sure are your modest billed hours.'

'Tell me what?' I said.

'To swab Mickey. As man of the track, you'll know the swab.'

11

'Cyril already has a swabbing expert. Cheap.'

'We don't need cheap. I can tell you that Cyril's expert failed the police entrance test. Tester couldn't fit two pencils above the eyebrows, one between the eyes.'

In silence, we drove down Victoria Parade and turned into Smith Street, Collingwood. The street seemed to be having a dealer-free day. From time to time, the cops came in numbers and displaced the drug sellers. It was like squeezing a balloon. When the pressure was removed, it returned to its original shape.

'What would I be looking for?' I said.

'Christ knows. Anything.'

I waited and then I said, 'Drew, the force's full of dickheads but they don't generally land up in homicide.'

'It may not be about dickheadedness. It may be about something else.'

'I think your client's reaching parts clients don't normally reach,' I said.

'Fuck off. Where's your sordid little alley?'

'Next sordid little alley after this one. How'd you get involved in the first place?'

'I appeared for her on a little drugs charge. A long, long time ago. Her father came to court. I clearly made an impression on Sir Colin.'

'Cut of your jib, the lapels. Why was he knighted?'

'Services to something or other. Being rich. A complication is that the deceased had moved on to screwing Sir Colin's younger daughter. Sarah's gone into hiding now.'

'What was Mickey's secret? Screwing one Longmore woman would have been success enough for most men.'

'Perhaps just another peak in the range. A climber, a

stranger to the concept of enough. Upwards, ever upwards. I have no fucking idea.'

Drew was nibbling at his lower lip, something he did when unhappy. You notice things like this when you spend too much time with people.

'Sarah wants me to do the trial,' he said. 'Compounding the stupidity of pleading not guilty. When her old man rang, I knew it was a job for Pratchett QC, freed more murderers than the stormers of the Bastille. But no. Me.'

We threaded the lane and parked across the street from my office. I said, 'So, find further ways to harm poor dead Mickey Franklin. That's the task.'

'Dead but not poor,' said Drew.

'We'd just be taking her money, Wootton and I.'

'I have no doubt that you will apply the standards expected of you as an officer of the court.'

'I said that. Take money for no obvious return. Well, things are quiet.'

'She hasn't confided in me, of course.'

'Of course. Nor would you allow her to.'

'Here's the number.' He offered a card.

I put it in my top pocket. 'This enjoyable excursion,' I said, 'would it be billable?'

Drew looked at me, down his nose, shook his head. 'I think the sawdust's getting to you,' he said. 'The man's worth millions.'

I tried the door handle, it resisted. 'A little thing before we part. Any tips on where to go with this?'

Drew was silent for a while. Then he said, 'I'm just a solicitor. As you once were.'

'And still am,' I said. 'Keep your expectations low.'

I fought the door handle, useless. I shouldered the door, it gave. I fell into the wet bluestone gutter.

'Great exit,' said Drew, looking down at me. 'You leave well.'

I rose and went into my office and made the call to Simone Bendsten, comber of the public record.

'Nice car, Jack,' said the man behind the counter at the corner shop. He'd seen me park outside, he didn't miss much.

'Very nice, George,' I said, 'but not mine.'

He nodded, a man who first opened his shop door in the mid-1950s when almost everyone in the suburb caught the tram to work and having a motorbike was a big deal. Now the place was gridlocked with Saabs and BMWs and what people paid for a worker's house could have bought the whole block in 1950.

'Where's that girl?' he said.

I thought about the long-ago day I'd come in with a Claire Irish shoulder-high to a medium-size brown dog and held up my daughter for inspection.

I'd said, 'Claire, this is my friend George.'

'Gorb,' she'd said.

'George,' I said.

'Gorb,' she said, and gripped the finger held out to her by George.

Gorb he would always be.

'Still in Queensland,' I said.

George nodded. 'They all come back. Holiday, it's all right, not bad. Live there, no. Everything stings you.'

I heard the sound, the dangerous murmur, the jostling, gossiping, teasing, scuffling sound of teenagers released from school for lunch.

'Quick,' I said. 'Salad roll.'

I went back to Linda's car, sank into the leather and watched the country's future invade the shop. Longer hair for girls this year, boys in anarchy—shaven, long, greased, bleached, dyed.

A knock on the passenger window, a big hand. I unlocked the door.

'Gone fucken upmarket, have we?' said Senior Sergeant Barry Tregear, sliding in, filling the cabin, bringing the smell of cheese and onion chips, cigarette smoke, Old Spice after-shave. He adjusted his seat, belched.

'Excuse,' he said. 'Early lunch. Following fucken early breakfast.'

He produced a cigarette, put it in his mouth, groped himself, couldn't find anything.

'Fuck,' he said. 'Bastard took my lighter.'

I pushed in the dashboard lighter. It heated in an instant, changed colour.

Barry used the lighter, put it back without looking, slotted it, no hesitation in the hand.

'This cunt in Dandenong,' he said, 'he goes to call on the

ex-de facto, 3 am, he's off his tits. She's out of it in the bedroom with the next cab, give or take a good few. The boy's not happy, goes out to the shed, finds the wood splitter.'

I was watching a teenage embrace, stylised, she wound around him, found a way to push back her hair at the same time.

'Stop now,' I said.

Barry sighed, added a hint of garlic to the stew of scents in the car. 'Two kiddies in the next room. And teddy bears, whole fucken room's full of teddy bears. All sizes. I'm too old for this kind of shit.'

I said, 'You should have stuck to cleansing the streets of drugs.'

He shook his head, sighed again. 'Jesus, that was a good gig. Just walk around and make bear noises at the cunts. They bugger off around the corner, end of story. Now I have to keep up with these fucken shorthairs—they're on a mission from God.'

The teen embrace unwound. He flicked the bottom of a tiny buttock with fingertips as she set off for Gorb's. She turned her head and gave him a look that was not likely to discourage the practice.

I said, 'Sometimes I think you're losing sight of what called you to your work. The burning desire to fight crime wherever you found it.'

'The burning I remember is when you pee,' he said. 'Now there's this woman, they brung her from New South, from traffic, playground patrol, some such shit, wouldn't know a crim from a fucken cardinal. She's clean, that's her qualification. Might as well make Mother fucken Teresa the commissioner.'

'Dead,' I said, 'but she'd probably have recognised a cardinal. Man in a purple dress. Is that right? Purple? For what exactly are you blaming the woman?'

Barry looked at me, incinerated a centimetre of cigarette. 'Everything,' he said. 'I blame women for everything. Next item. This Franklin business.'

'Yes. Lips sealed?'

'Dunno. Can't feel my lips anymore, the dick's not the same either. You reckon there's a link between dick and lips?'

I smoked passively while I thought about the question.

'I have no doubt,' I said, 'that a link will be found. Franklin?'

Barry looked at me, smoked, squinted. 'Mate, under the new hygiene, people get spanked for talking to blokes like you.'

'Live dangerously. More dangerously.'

A jet of smoke hit the windscreen, fanned. 'Well, Drew'll be looking for manslaughter,' he said. 'Looking and fucken hoping.'

'I gather not.'

He eyed me. 'Not? She's Mick's ex-root, they say he was giving it to the sister at the same time. Had the gun, had a key, there's a witness saw her near the place. Plus no backer for the cuddled-up-in-bed-at-home-with-a-book crap. Reasonable case, yes?'

'Well. Purely circumstantial.'

'Nailed, mate. Nailed like Jesus.'

'What's the strength of this witness?'

'I gather she'd seen her before, saw her having a fight with some bloke over a park. Fucken oath, no teachers like that in my day.'

I looked. A tall woman with cropped hair and long legs was exchanging words with some of the teenage loiterers outside Gorb's. It was a joking exchange but you could see that she was an officer talking to the troops.

'Just as well,' I said. 'Out there in Hay you farm boys were already over-excited by the bra ads in the *Women's Weekly*. That and seeing the farm animals doing it.'

'To this day,' said Barry, 'a bra ad can put a bit of strain on the daks. Unfortunately just a bit. Then there was the step-ins.'

Rain on the windscreen, the tiniest drops.

I said, 'A fetching thing, a step-in. So no doubt there?'

Barry had the last of his cigarette, came close to smoking the filter.

There was no chance of him using an ashtray. I pressed the button, his window sank. He didn't look when he flicked the butt. It could have landed in a passing pram.

'Doubt?' he said. 'Well, the doubt's either done him or had him done. It's like a fucken jail. There's three things to get through. Come from outside, you got help or you go home.'

'And Mickey? Talk there?'

Barry sighed again, moved the big shoulders. 'Well, Mick and the Massianis, six years on the job. They say very tight with Steve.'

'I'm slow here.'

'Me too, got to go,' he said, patted me on the shoulder. 'Keeping down in the weights, I see. Good dog. Have a drink one day, no business, okay?' He got out, closed the door, stuck his head back in. 'This, though. The tip-off. Who was that?'

I watched him go, heading for Gorb's, stiff-legged cop walk from too much sitting in cars. The teenagers blocking the door noticed him coming, parted, found reasons not to look at him.

I left my office and walked the short distance to where the dented, pitted and gouged side door of Taub's Cabinet-making was set in a redbrick wall on a lane that led to Smith Street, Collingwood. Opening it released the smell of hide glue.

I was looking directly at a low bench. On it stood the skeleton of a desk, a big and intricate construction, it would be deep enough for two people to lie side by side on its top, long enough for them to be basketball players. Even imprisoned in a steel cage of clamps, even without its sides, top, doors or drawers, you knew it was a special piece of furniture, probably far too good for the person who had commissioned it. It was probably too good for all the people who would sit behind it, dozens of them, because things made by Charlie Taub could last for centuries.

The man was standing behind the desk framework, left

hand resting on the end of a three-metre sash clamp. Somewhere beneath the huge callused fingers was the spindle.

'So,' said Charlie Taub.

'So,' I said. 'So, indeed.'

'A suit?' He raised an eyebrow flecked with sawdust.

'Been to court,' I said. 'For a client.' All true, insofar as it went.

Charlie removed the dead Cuban cheroot from a corner of his mouth and looked at it. 'Very nice,' he said. 'Good. A profession. You have it, you should stay in it. Then an old man can get a proper apprentice, person shows some respect.'

'A strong girl,' I said. 'You told me.'

He put the cheroot back in its corner, waved a racquet-size hand at the desk. 'Just a piece rubbish,' he said. 'Thirty-two joints to glue, who needs help?'

'Not you, certainly. You didn't say you were gluing this up today.'

'You glue when it's time to glue. You're ready, you say, now we're gluing. Then you glue. You don't write a letter, wait for a reply to come.'

'That's a good point,' I said.

Charlie shook his head and went back to work. I walked around and stood behind him to watch him apply his squares—three of them, short, longer, long—to every angle of the desk carcass. Each time, he put his head back, looking for light between steel and wood. Hide glue was slow drying, slow to grip, it gave you a chance to adjust clamps, to ensure that no clamp's pressure was distorting the framework, pushing something out of square. Complicated pieces were glued in stages but eventually the whole thing had to be put together and then it took experience to ensure that it didn't end up as firewood.

Experience was not lacking when Charlie was in charge.

'Hold,' he said.

I went around and prevented the sash clamp from slipping as he released it.

'Down.'

I moved it. Charlie put his head down and sighted along the device. He didn't need a spirit level. He had one in his head. I put my ill-equipped head down and looked. All I could see of him was one old, calculating eyeball.

'Up,' he said. '*Ein ganz klein wenig.*'

I moved it a few millimetres.

'*Ja.*'

Charlie tightened the clamp, tested the angle with a square, grunted.

And so it went, angle by angle, clamp by clamp. When Charlie was satisfied and we were both standing upright, I ran a hand over a strut.

'Nice bit of planing,' I said.

I had done the unskilled work on the desk: ripping stone-dry ash for the frame on the venerable German table saw, planing it by hand with a 28-inch Stanley, sole as flat and smooth as plateglass and polished by wear to the colour of old silver.

Charlie was looking at the skeleton, rubbing his hands together. He made one of his nose sounds. 'A monkey you can teach to plane,' he said.

'That explains my wages,' I said. 'Are you close to finished here?'

A question expressing a hope.

We went through the knocking-off ritual. I swept and dust-panned while Charlie got out of his glue-stiff overalls, put on his stylish green 1962 jacket with the deep hacking flap. Then he fiddled around, put tools back on the racks, repositioned objects on the work benches, patted machines, tested fences, wound blades up and down, wiped them with an oily rag, dropped the rag in a bin.

I removed the rag and found several other oil-impregnated pieces of cloth, one of them a massive pair of Y-front underpants. Charlie believed that cotton garments once worn close to the body gave a special lustre when used for polishing. I put the items into a plastic bag, squeezed the air out of it, tied it, took it outside, crossed the road and deposited it in the bin beside the door of Kelvin McCoy's so-called studio, once a self-respecting clothing factory. There was still a chance that these rags would self-combust during the night but they would not set fire to the largest collection of old furniture timber in the country, destroy irreplaceable machinery, some of it made by craftsmen dead these fifty years, and ruin two lives. Instead, there was the hope that the incendiary bag might set alight McCoy's den of fraud and fornication and purge the earth of a collection of objects more worthless, tasteless and aesthetically offensive than any assembled since the heyday of Andy Warhol's Factory.

Comforted by the possibility of performing a service to the nation, I went back to Taub's and worked on getting Charlie out the door.

We walked to the Prince of Prussia down old streets pinched narrower by the gathering dark.

'The baby,' said Charlie, not looking at me. Eyes on the ground, he touched my arm, the pat of a grizzly bear. 'No one told me.'

It was a month since my daughter had miscarried at a late stage, the baby's father at sea but homeward bound, Eric the Viking's fishing boat running before a tropical cyclone. Claire hadn't been alone though. Her mother was there, my first wife, Frances. She could organise an invasion of Iraq with a few quick calls. She rang Claire's stepfather, pink Richard Wiggins, surgeon to the carriage trade. She also rang Claire's aunt, my feckless sister, Rosa. The pair flew to tropical Queensland on the first available.

She did not ring Claire's father.

Eric the Viking rang me. Within minutes of his storm-tossed barque making a landing, he was at the hospital. Soon after, from Claire's side, he rang me. I talked to her, said what could be said. Nothing.

I didn't go to Queensland. Rosa came back and said she'd thought Frances had rung me. I said it didn't matter, which was a lie. Frances rang and said that, in all the drama, she had forgotten about me and she was abjectly sorry. But I probably wouldn't have gone anyway.

I didn't say anything for a while. The practice of the law teaches restraint, the disciplining of the emotions, the need always to be measured.

Then I said, 'I should kill you, you nickel-plated bitch.' I tried to give this expression of unhappiness some extra bite by banging down the receiver.

But a click is just a click, as time goes by.

Now, I said to Charlie, 'It could be someone has decreed that I'm too young to be a grandfather.'

'To be a father,' he said, all sympathy gone, 'some men, they're not fit at all.'

I pondered this, not for the first time. 'Well, it was only the one,' I said. 'Everyone's entitled to an experiment.'

The Prince was in sight. It was dark now, the old pub's lights lying yellow and comforting on the rough pavement. My father and my grandfather would only have seen that sight if they had looked back at the Prince, bustled out at closing time, bladders distended by as many beers as it was possible to drink between knock-off and 6 pm closing.

Charlie shouldered the door and we entered. No more than a dozen customers. The Prince had been quiet since the dotcom avalanche buried the shaven-headed net visionaries and their geek slaves who had briefly adopted the place. At the bar, in the corner, three heads turned in unison, like fairground clowns, chins lifted, mouths open to receive a ball. The Fitzroy Youth Club was in place.

Charlie raised a hand at the members and, like a thirsty dog to its water, went directly to the bowls table where two fellow trundlers awaited him.

Stan the publican wasn't in view. He was probably behind the scenes assisting his lovely wife, Liz, to microwave a few freeze-dried delicacies for the customers. If so, we would soon hear the sounds: glass breaking, heavy objects falling, grunts, then screams and yelps. In extremis, Stan screamed and then yelped, that was the sequence: first the worse, then the bad.

I joined the Youth Club, put a foot on the brass rail and an elbow on the counter. Its surface was patterned by the rings of glasses beyond number, its round edge scalloped by thousands of burns, cigarettes put down when both hands were needed for a few seconds to explain something.

'Jack,' said Norm O'Neill, not looking at me, giving me the full right profile. On his remarkable nose sat big spectacles that bore the scars of doubling as safety glasses in his workshop. 'You bin scarce.'

'Trying to cut down on the beer,' I said.

They all eyed me with interest.

'Keeps ya healthy, beer,' said Wilbur Ong, nodding, looking vaguely mystical. 'They done tests to show that.'

'What tests?' said Eric Tanner, the man against the wall. 'What'd they test?'

'The human body,' said Wilbur, still nodding, the sage.

'Done me no bloody good, beer,' said Norm. 'Still, the son-in-law's pure as the driven snow, blighter's crook all the time.'

'Where'd ya get this tests crap?' said Eric to Wilbur. 'From the dentist?'

Wilbur's grandson was the rich's dentist of choice. He ran a three-chair operation in Collins Street—one waiting, one injected, one getting a brief fiddle. In his time, he had numbed every gum of importance in the city.

'Read it,' said Wilbur. 'Somewhere. Can't remember where.'

'Does bugger all for the memory, beer, I kin tell you that,' said Eric.

'Speakin of memory,' said Norm. 'Jack, my boy, we have to think about this Saints business again.'

My spirits were not elevated by this utterance. I had convinced the Youth Club to come out of the exile it had gone into when the Fitzroy Football Club was executed and its proud, tattered banners sold to a club in Brisbane. I had led the ancient Lions followers to the St Kilda Football Club, a journey more taxing than moving the Falashas to Israel. I meant well. I thought I was doing the right thing.

'Yes?' I said.

'Yes,' said Norm. 'I don't think these Saints people give the boys enough support. Too critical.'

'You men could set an example,' I said, relieved. 'Men noted for their compassion for losers. Where's Stan?'

Something of substance struck the closed serving hatch between bar and kitchen opposite us. A moment of silence, then I thought I heard the sound of someone being strangled, the noise of a last, agonising intake of breath.

We looked at one another, waited. Silence from the kitchen.

Norm thumped the bar, thrice. 'Stanley, service needed here,' he said at full volume. 'Customers bloody dyin of thirst.'

The door to the office opened and Stan came out, running a hand over his pig-bristled scalp. I thought I saw a flushed patch on his pink cheekbone, an incipient bruise, bluing by closing time, dark in the shaving mirror in the morning.

'No need to get excited,' he said, breathless.

'A round if you please, landlord,' I said.

Stan went to work, casting glances over his shoulder at the service hatch. When he had the glasses down, I said, 'Conjugal bliss behind the scenes, I gather.'

He put both hands on the counter, leaned across, was about to speak.

'Stanleeee!'

Liz at the office door. 'Your father,' she said, in the tone a clergyman might adopt to announce the arrival of his teenage daughter's forty-four-year-old biker boyfriend.

Stan hastened away. He was back inside a minute. 'He's after you,' he said, not pleased.

Nor was I. Stan's father, Morris, ran the Prince for forty-five years before his wife nagged him into retiring to Queensland. Now he sat in his sun-kissed villa hating it and fretting over his Melbourne properties. I handled Morris's dealings with his tenants, and had I used the normal billing practices of city firms over the years, I would now want for nothing.

The Prince's office had not changed since my last visit. It was still running on the Rogerson's Pharmacy calendar of 1979. I went around the desk to the cove where the telephone sat surrounded by dusty paper cliffs. Now I could see a change: a small television set on the filing cabinet. It was on, soundless.

'Morris.'

'Jack, my boy, listen, what's going on down there?'

'Nothing. Signed Enzio's lease yet?'

'Yes, yes, that's not it, I'm taking your word he's reliable, not that I don't always, don't get me wrong. Jack, that's not the point.'

'Morris,' I said, 'what can I do for you? I'm tired.'

'What's going on with Stanley? Shuddup, Zelda, I'm on the phone. Sorry, Jack. He rings every day. He'll get the pub, what's the hurry now?'

'Maybe he wants to do something else, maybe he's tired of running a pub. I don't know.'

'Something else? What else? The little prick doesn't know anything else. He doesn't even know how to run a pub yet.

I think I'll come back, take over.'

'Morris, I'll ask him. Ring me tomorrow.'

'Find out, Jack. Something going on there. The wife if you ask me. I warned him about her.'

'Goodnight, Morris. Post that lease.'

Sarah Longmore on the television, outside court. She looked even younger on screen. I rose and turned up the sound. Drew appeared, looking like a pillar of the law. 'I have no comment at this time,' he said.

I was hardly back in my seat when Stan was opposite.

'Wits' bloody end, Jack,' he said, softly. 'She says I get him to sign it over now or she's off.'

I reflected that some people did not know a golden opportunity when it sounded like the Crack of Doom.

'Off?' I said. 'Off where?'

Stan's eyes flicked to the Youth Club but they weren't listening, they were discussing the value of things their doctors prescribed for them. I detected a certain negativity.

'Taken to visiting the sister in Castlemaine,' Stan said. 'Didn't want to know her before she went to this wedding. Her niece. Now it's up the bloody highway every second day, stays over.'

'Siblings often grow closer over the years,' I said, speaking from no knowledge at all.

Stan shook his head. 'Not a word about the sister. Listen, Jack, it's all smiles before she goes, gives me a kiss, that's a novelty I can tell you. Comes back, she's like a bloody snake, vicious, don't dare open my trap.'

'And you read what into this?'

With a gentle finger, he touched his flushed cheekbone, a tumescence now evident. 'Mate, what do you think.'

It wasn't a question.

'Came back today, did she?'

Sombre nods.

'And you'd like to patch things up, get title to the place?'

'Well, yes.' More nods.

I leaned forward. We were closer than we'd ever been. 'Stanley,' I said. 'Consider this possibility. Morris signs the Prince over to you. The next day, Liz leaves. She wants a divorce. She's got twenty years of sweat equity in this business. You'll have to sell it and give her half.'

Stan's eyes went large, went thin. He shook his head, smiling, not the cheeriest of sights.

'Forget that,' he said. 'She'd be the one walking out. She'd get bugger all.'

I tasted my beer. Not bad for the Prince, where it usually failed any test, no doubt tainted by something living in the pipes.

'Bugger all,' said Stan, eyes willing me to agree. 'That's right, not so? She's the guilty party. Believe me, I'd get the evidence.'

'Stan,' I said, 'where have you been? That stuff went out twenty years ago. It wouldn't matter if you got pictures of Liz with Rickos and his Crazy Cuban Castanet Caballeros, all eight of them, naked except for sombreros.'

'Half,' he said. 'You sure?'

Eric Tanner tapped me on the shoulder while continuing to talk to the members.

'Never mind bloody doctors,' he said. 'What do they know? Bloody drugs. Probably bloody lollies. Gazebo effect. You heard of that, Wilbur? Scientific term. Ask the dentist, he'll tell ya. I say, ya time's ya time.'

31

He turned to me. 'Listen, Jack, we goin to see the Blue Boys cop a hidin this Satdee? In the circus tent.'

'Put your life on it,' I said. 'On second thoughts, put something of value on it.'

Sarah Longmore's studio was in Kensington, on the rough edge, near the Dynon railyards in a cracked and potholed dead-end street with unpaved verges, weeds battling to survive.

Just before a six-metre corrugated iron wall, I turned into a small cinder yard. A yellow Ford ute, better days seen, had its blistered nose to a building—partly brick, partly cinder-block, partly rusted tin. I parked the Lark next to the ute, switched off the wipers, sat listening to the engine note. The machine had been in the oily and expensive hands of Kevin Trapaga, Studebaker fanatic, and it was making the lovely stroked-cat sound, the V-8 cat. This would last for only a short time, so it was important to savour every moment. Then I could go back to driving Linda's Alfa.

With reluctance, I switched off and got out. The day was cold, wet, clamorous. I could hear trains, what sounded like steel being dumped from a height, the regular banging of a stamper of some kind, and, from inside the building, the screeching sound of metal-grinding. A steel-framed sliding door was the only entrance. I put a hand to it and pushed hard. It slid easily, taking me by surprise.

The inside was one huge, dim space, easily ten metres high at the peak. Unlit fluorescent lights hung in two rows from wooden beams, the floor was a patchwork of surfaces—oil-stained concrete, uneven bricks, cracked pavers, a rectangle of wood, bleached and blotched, probably covering an inspection pit.

Objects stood around, welded metal forms, human-like but bigger, one-and-a-half human size perhaps. In the gloomy corner to my right were what could be witches around a suggestion of a pot. The thing nearest the cauldron was carrying something. A piglet? A child?

Close to them were what I first took to be two boxers, angular stainless steel figures close together, the impression of a left being thrown at an averted head. But as I walked, I saw that one figure appeared to be bound and the other had a projection from his hand. He could be cutting the throat of the bound figure.

I looked left and saw a pack of dogs, six or more, attacking something, mounting each other in their lust to get at it. But then I noticed the thighs, the calves, the ankles, the feet. They resembled humans on all fours, humans with long dog heads, engaged in some hungry act.

Did people buy these creations? Where would you put one?

The grinding noise was coming from a lit area behind a pile of metal scrap—two car bodies, a stack of car doors, a large disembowelled machine, possibly a litho printing press, offcuts of steel and aluminium sheeting, a pick-up-sticks pile of rusted steel rods.

I came around the heap.

In a clearing, in a pond of bright light, a person in filthy overalls was kneeling on someone much bigger, face down, arms outstretched, applying a metal grinder to the head.

I took a step back and looked through the empty socket of a car door. There is a sinister, expectant pleasure in watching someone using a tool that spits on protective gear, makes from a small clumsiness a whine of ground bone and sends a lovely arc of warm blood into the air.

There was no clumsiness. Sparks streamed from the felled knight's metal shell until the worker raised the grinder in both hands, held it up like a howling icon, killed it.

Silence.

I stepped around the car skeleton and the person saw me. The yellow helmet visor reflected the glare from a light on a tripod.

'I'm looking for Sarah Longmore,' I said.

The person stood up, pushed up the visor, pulled off a glove by its fingertips. Then she combed her hair with her fingers.

'Jack Irish?'

'Yes.'

'Thanks for coming.'

Sarah Longmore wore no make-up, her short hair stuck up in several directions, her face was dirty, smeared, her eyebrows furry. She didn't look like the dark-suited woman in court. I thought she looked better this way.

'I told Andrew I'd come to see you,' she said, 'but he said that wasn't the way it was done.'

Her accent was hard to place: not Australian, not quite upper-class English.

'Drew's good on the way things are done,' I said. 'This is also more interesting than my place.'

'What time is it? I lose track.'

She pulled at the zip that ran diagonally across her chest, exposed a black T-shirt.

'Just after four,' I said.

'Beer time. There's tea, coffee, water.'

I could stomach a beer. On many days, I felt that a beer would go well with the muesli, then it would be nice to have another one to get the day moving, get things stabilised.

'Beer, thanks,' I said.

'It's in the shed.'

I followed her, walked around the prone cruciform figure to a lean-to in the back corner of the building, a building inside a building, a rough fibro structure with a window and a flue coming out of the roof. The foreman's hut, presumably. Inside, there was a drum wood-burning heater, a formica-topped kitchen table with an electric frying pan and a toaster on it, two kitchen chairs, two 1950s Swedish-style easychairs. A small fridge, new, stood in the corner.

'It's not cold,' she said. 'Is that okay?'

'Fine.'

'I lived in Berlin,' she said. She took two brown bottles off a shelf, put them on the table, uncapped them with a Swiss army knife lying ready. 'The people I was with drank beer all the time. Morning, noon and night. You get a taste for it. Warm German beer.'

She handed me a bottle. Dresdner Pils. I took a swig. A brown-tasting beer, medicinal.

'Well,' she said. 'Sit.'

We sat in the chairs, bottoms too far down, knees too high, held our bottles on the wooden arms.

'Andrew says you're a lawyer who does other things,' she said. 'Finds people, witnesses, things like that. That's odd for a lawyer, isn't it?'

Sarah Longmore looked at you with the eyes of a child. I felt that she might say anything: My dad says you're a stupid prick. Mum says you always hold on to her a bit too long.

'A long story,' I said. 'Are you happy about being questioned?'

'Well, I'll say when I'm not.'

'The plea, that's final?'

She had the beer bottle to her lips, indenting the skin. She lowered it.

'Mr Irish,' she said, 'I've had all the shit I can take in a week. You can go now.'

I nodded. 'The innocent should always plead not guilty. The murder weapon.'

She closed her eyes for a long time, shook her head, opened her eyes. 'Mickey gave it to me. I had a break-in, other strange stuff. He got worried. I didn't want the fucking thing.'

'May I ask what kind of relationship you had with Mickey?'

'Sexual,' she said. 'Are there other kinds?'

'Apparently. Do you know much about his affairs?'

Sarah raised her eyebrows.

'His business affairs.'

She shook her head. 'Not a lot, no.'

You could get to like the taste of Dresdner. Did Bomber

Harris's teenage aircrews hit the brewery, send the fluid flowing through the burning streets, turning to steam?

Now she drank, a decent swig, almost a third of the bottle. 'That's good,' she said. She got up and went to a black leather jacket hanging over a chair, groped it, found a packet. Camel. 'Started again,' she said, stripping the cellophane. 'No non-smokers in ghastly fucking remand, I can tell you. Clean for three years. Do you?'

I shook my head. I had no desire to smoke a cigarette, the hit was so small, you needed another one straight away. But it always saddened me, self-denial, it spoke of times gone.

There was a plastic lighter on the table. She lit, sucked. Her cheeks hollowed, she blew smoke.

'The relationship with Mickey, did that end over your sister?'

She put her head back, wry smile. 'No. I got tired of it. He wasn't fun to be with anymore. Bad moods, always half-pissed.' She tapped ash onto the floor. 'And you'll want to know that the sex had gone to hell too.'

'Seemingly trivial details like that can help,' I said. 'They'll say there was an overlap.'

'Overlap?'

'Mickey was seeing both of you at one point.'

'Screwing you mean?'

'Yes.'

'News to me but it's no surprise.'

I looked away and after a while she sat down and said, 'You radiate disbelief. If I'd found out at the time, it wouldn't have surprised me. Sophie wants everything I've got and Mickey wanted everything, full stop. Until he had it. Then it had no value.'

'How did you meet?'

'At an exhibition about eighteen months ago. He rang me the next day.'

'How long did it last?'

'I packed it in three months ago.'

'Did he ever say anything about being in danger?'

'No. I can't imagine Mickey saying anything like that.'

'Get any feeling that he might be?'

She looked at her short nails. 'No. Well, his driver always sat at the next table. That's all.'

'Did he eat?'

'The driver?'

'Yes.'

'Vegetables. He only ate vegetables.' She smiled.

It was cold in the room. The foreman would have had the drum heater going, the place snug, the dirty window bleeding condensation.

'Do you sell your work?' I said.

Sarah tilted her head, her mouth turned down, a mock-severe look. 'Offer them for sale? No. They're usually commissioned. Do they challenge you?'

I had some beer. 'I find them full of challenge,' I said.

She held up her cigarette, looked at it. 'Good,' she said. 'Then all the fucking cutting and the welding and the grinding haven't been entirely wasted.'

I thought about Charlie Taub. He would think that the cutting and welding and grinding were a complete waste of human effort.

'Andrew will have to cast serious doubt on the prosecution case,' I said. 'If possible, he'll want to offer an alternative explanation for Mickey's murder. That's the difficult part.'

She nodded. 'If I could help, I'd help, Jesus, believe me I'd help.'

'They've got a witness, says she saw you near Mickey's on the night.'

'That's impossible. Perhaps she saw someone she thought was me.'

'She'll say she saw you on another occasion having an argument with a man about a parking spot.'

Sarah frowned, touched her mouth.

'Did something like that happen?'

'Yes. Months ago. This bastard nipped in behind me and took my park. I was reversing. I was enraged, I got out and he told me to piss off. I wouldn't let him get out of his car. Finally, he got scared and reversed.'

'We'll have to get back to this, it's not good,' I said. 'Tell me about the bruise.'

'What?'

Sarah lifted her chin, took a drag, her eyes were on the ceiling, showing her neck, a long column and pale, tendons showing, a shadow visible on the right side.

'They'll say you got the mark from Mickey.'

We sat in the sagging Swedish Modern chairs, looking at each other, hearing the sounds from the world outside, muted by distance and obstruction but still hard and clanging.

The cigarette was over. She got up, went to the stove, opened the door and tossed the butt in.

'I've often had bruises,' she said.

I waited, drank some more beer. There was a new noise now, a siren, intermittent, a lonely sound. Sarah turned.

'I was unloading some stuff from a truck last Wednesday. A bit slipped, caught me in the throat.'

She unzipped her right sleeve, showed me her forearm. On the intimate inner-arm skin below the elbow was a lavender blotch. 'I bruise easily. Banged this against a piece of scrap yesterday. Hardly felt it.'

The siren had stopped. The other noises had gone too, as if its mournful wail had been a signal to desist.

'You came here after court?' I said.

'I'm not letting this fucking unbelievably awful bullshit take over my life. If I don't carry on as normal I'll lose my mind.'

'Andrew will want you to testify,' I said. 'It would be best if he knew about anything that might be damaging.'

Sarah sat down, sank into the chair, legs apart, held the bottle of Dresdner Pils in both hands. I saw the tiny pinch of flesh between her eyes.

'It's not a pure and holy life,' she said. 'I got a conviction for possession. Just dope. Andrew appeared for me. I don't think he remembers.'

'No surprises, that's what makes a defence lawyer happy,' I said. 'Drew wouldn't want you remembering anything under cross-examination.'

'Such as?'

'An extreme example would be a similar death of someone else close to you.'

Sarah closed her eyes and shook her head, slowly, as if in pain. 'No,' she said. 'No.'

'You said you had a break-in. Where was that?'

She opened her eyes. Hazel would be the colour. 'Where I live. At my father's townhouse in St Kilda. I suppose break-in isn't the word. There wasn't any breaking.'

Goodbye, German beer. I drank the last centimetres, put the bottle on the table.

'There were odd things first.'

She shifted in the chair, moved her head. 'About six weeks ago I noticed a woman and then I saw her again, three times in about ten days. Each time she dressed very differently. Her hair was always different.'

'Did she want you to see her?'

'No, it wasn't stalking. The first time she was leaning against a car talking to the person inside, then she was on a mobile, the other time she was in a car across from the gym. She never looked at me.'

My position in the chair was causing pain in the lower back. Could Swedish melancholy be chair-related?

'St Kilda,' I said. 'I'm told it's like a village. Friendly street prostitutes always ready to lend a hand, the milkman carries emergency coke. You'd expect to see the same people, wouldn't you?'

She smiled, not a complete smile. 'I've even got a friendly neighbourhood peeping Tom. Anyway, I didn't see her again.'

'After you told Mickey about her?'

'What?'

Cold was rising from the concrete slab. It had reached my flabby calves, less flabby than before the morning running, perhaps, but not the calves of a young tennis player.

'You didn't see her again after you told Mickey?'

'I didn't tell Mickey,' she said. 'Sophie told him. She was with me the third time. She actually took a photograph of the woman.'

'She happened to have a camera?'

'She always has a camera.'

'Has Sophie been questioned?'

'She was at a party. She has about fifty alibi witnesses.'

'Tell me about the break-in.'

Sarah put out a hand and picked up a watch, a cheap digital item on a plastic strap. 'Jesus,' she said. She stood up fluidly without using her arms. 'Can we carry on tomorrow? I've got to get home and clean up, I'm meeting my father at six.'

I got up too, not fluidly, I didn't know how to exit a 1950s Swedish Modern chair with grace. 'I'll call you tomorrow night,' I said. 'We can find a time that suits you.'

I gave her my card and said goodbye, walked back the way I had come, around the downed knight in his pool of harsh light, around the steel scrapheap, between the execution and the crawling, panting pack of dog-humans. Finally, I passed by the witches preparing to cook a small creature and came to the sliding door and opened it to the dripping world beyond.

Upstairs at the old boot factory, home, I put on lights, heating, walked around, drew in the dust on the mantelpiece. I looked out of the window at the pencil lines of rain across the streetlight, moved books from one pile to another, washed the breakfast things, turned on the radio, the television, switched them off, got Schubert going: *Winterreise*.

The music soothed places in the mind. I poured a whisky and soda, sank into an old leather armchair, the repaired survivor of a bomb blast that disintegrated its two companions and a sofa, bought long ago at the Old Colonists' Club dispersal. Isabel had done the bidding, she had the ability to wait, to move in the smallest increments, to reveal nothing. That was the side of her that made her good at the law, at poker. Her other side cared nothing for calculation, for economy. Without reserve, that side gave away money, time, attention, love. She ministered to her clients, to her untidy siblings, to total strangers. Once a week, she drove across the city to take a steak and onion pie to an old man met at a tramstop who had trouble remembering her name.

This wasn't the time to think about Isabel. Food, I would think about food. I got up and went to the kitchen to study Linda's donation. Meat, vegetables, cheese. At the Victoria Market, she always bought indiscriminately and extravagantly. 'What am I supposed to do?' she once said. 'The vegie man says he loves me, I'm radio spunk number one, bugger the Italian woman on ABC drivetime. Do I say, Thanks, Giorgio, all I want is a big red pepper?'

'A big red pepper, no,' I'd said. 'You don't want to inflame them further. Better to buy a dozen flaccid cabbages.'

Thinking about Linda, I lost interest in cooking and went back to the sitting room. The phone rang.

'Ah, for once found without twenty attempts.'

Cyril Wootton, the plummy tones, made plummier at this hour by his refreshment stop at the Windsor Hotel.

'Is this a business call?' I said. 'My office hours are nine to five.'

'Hah hah,' said Wootton, unamused. 'You're easier to find at that scungepit pub you frequent than you are at the hole you call your office.'

'That's pretty comprehensive, Cyril,' I said. 'In one sentence, you've insulted two of the things I hold most dear.'

'Moving on,' said Wootton, 'I gather Greer's coached you on the project's parameters.'

I sighed. 'Cyril, the management seminars in Mount Eliza. You promised to stop.'

In the background, I heard Mrs Wootton shouting something, not the dulcet tones of a loving spouse calling her partner to the candlelit dinner table. I thought I heard the words 'little prick'.

Cyril coughed. 'Prelim scan in forty-eight, that's from twelve today,' he said. 'Updates every twenty-four. Face-to-face. We have a high confidentiality threshold.'

'You have something,' I said. 'Something worrying. Hearing voices? Often feel dizzy, feel that the floor slopes away from you?'

'Terminating contact,' said Wootton.

'Before you slip back into domestic bliss,' I said, 'the recorded income needs a look.'

'I have no idea what you're talking about. Goodbye.'

I replaced the receiver. The telephone rang.

'This number does not accept frivolous calls,' I said.

'Talk to the person?' said Drew.

'I did.'

'And?'

'Well. Seen the works of art?'

'No. Why?'

'You should. Open a window into the mind of your client.'

Drew made a noise of acceptance. 'She's an artist. They don't have the normal circuit board. Take the cunt from Eltham who stole my wife.'

'I see she's a painter now.'

'Well, it's the mimic thing. Budgie behaviour. These artistic charlatans trigger mimicry in their conquests. Doomed, of course.'

'She's having an exhibition.'

'Why are you telling me this? I don't give a fuck whether she exhibits herself at Flinders Street station at peak hour.'

'The mother of your children, I thought you'd be interested.'

'The children yes, an interest not often reciprocated. Ms Longmore. Tell me.'

'Just a preliminary conversation. She gave me a German beer.'

'And the feeling?'

'Unease. With tinges of lust.'

'Any chance of you approaching this in a professional manner?'

'Pass,' I said. 'I'm seeing her again. Today, she had to break off for an engagement with her father. Lord Longmore. Baron Longmore.'

'Made another date?'

'Drew,' I said, 'it's me, not your plumber. I'm tied up tomorrow, then it's total focus on Franklin, dawn to dusk and beyond, deep into the night.'

'You'll tell me directly?'

'The prelim scan result, yes.'

'The what?'

'You really need to speak to Cyril about management courses.'

'Cyril,' said Drew. 'Jesus. We might eat out tomorrow. I'm sick of in.'

'I stand at the onset of sick of in. I'll ring.'

Thoughts of food again. I got out a sheet of frozen puff pastry and put it on an oven tray. I unsheathed the Japanese knife, too heavy, bevelled only on one side, soft steel blade taking a vicious edge but prone to chipping. It also rusted in hours if not oiled after washing. In all, a dangerous and temperamental implement. I liked it very much. I used it to chop three cloves of garlic to insignificance, sushi slice a Spanish onion, and cut strips of red pepper. Then I samuraied a dozen mushrooms, put them in a pot on low heat with a big piece of butter, the garlic, half-a-dozen pitted olives, torn up, and three anchovy fillets. I put the glass lid on and left the stuff to sauna for a minute while I poured a glass of the night before's red wine.

Put on oven. Tomato paste? A search turned up a small tin of double concentrated, the best. I spread a thin layer on half the thawing pastry. Time to stir the mushroom pot.

Making something is always good for the soul. There is a therapy in making anything that is little remarked upon, probably because the world cares mostly about planning and results. The bit in between, the making, that doesn't rate much mention.

Cheese? No shortage. Linda was out of control at a cheese counter. I grated parmesan, crumbled a little fetta, cut two slices of mozzarella. Smash time. I emptied the contents of the pot into the machine and gave it the chop. Then I scraped out the mixture and spread it over the tomato paste, tastefully arranged strips of prosciutto and the onion and red pepper slices on top, added the cheeses. Last steps. Fold over pastry, trim edges, pinch over, slash top, dot with olive oil and spread with finger, slide the tray into the oven.

Ten to fifteen minutes would do it. I poured wine and went back to the sitting room to listen to Schubert and to think positive thoughts about my life. The second part was not easy but I made the effort, soon aided by the wine and the cheering smell of the pie thing.

I ate, read, watched the late news on television. To bed, sliding between clean sheets, laid that day, heavy cotton sheets, survivors of the blast, unironed, stiff as the linen napkins at the Society restaurant long ago. I sipped Milo, the warm drink that passeth all understanding, and returned to the new book. Marcel, the French protagonist, was in hiding in Instanbul, hunted by four intelligence agencies because he knew too much. I read some pages, not concentrating, and I lapsed into the half-world, thinking that knowing too much was not a condition with which I was familiar. Knowing barely enough, yes, I could be hunted down for that. Too little, yes, but you'd be safe knowing too little. Except that it presented its own problems. My fingers lost their purchase on the book, it fell away from me.

I put the book on the table and switched off the light. There was music playing downstairs, I hadn't noticed it or it had just begun. Too low to identify, just a soothing undertone. Bluesy. The new tenant, not yet seen, driver of the BMW Mini. Promising. I drifted. On the edge of sleep, Sarah Longmore's metal horror came into my mind, the humanoid hunting pack. I pushed the thought away; the world dissolved.

'The breedin,' said Harry Strang. 'People talk like they know what they're gettin. Breedin's a lottery, thank the Lord.'

'Better than pulling the parents out of a hat,' I said. 'I suppose.'

'Dunno,' said Harry. 'That can work. Take Steel Orchid. He comes of a mistake, sendin the wrong mare to the stud, ends up winnin a couple of big ones. Could've been much more, broke down at Rosehill. When was that?'

'Seventy-four,' said Cameron Delray.

'Right. Knew it was around when Whitlam got the arse.'

We were in deepest Gippsland, on a road climbing the front slope of the Dividing Range, a wet morning, trees dripping, the world green, a feeling of being underwater. Cam was driving the four-wheel-drive, a machine designed to encourage men's fantasies of power and domination. So what if I was once Vernon the School Weed, pinned beneath the buttocks of bigger boys in the playground, crushed and starved of air, farted upon? When you look up at me now from your lowly conveyance, you will know that I am Vernon the Omnipotent, the Breaker of Worlds aka Vernon the Hammer. I am also a brilliant financial analyst, married to my former secretary, Wendy, who sits beside me: Wendy the Earthmother, upon whose rippling thighs even Vernon the Hammer is tossed like a keelless dhow in a storm. Behind us, you see Princess Emily…

A buffer stop for this train of thought.

'This creature,' I said. 'Seven years old, I understood Cam to say. Two wins, two places from sixteen outings.'

'Blood's excellent,' said Harry. 'Can't fault it.'

'Fault its attitude without doing scientific tests. You're thinking of buying it?'

'Well,' said Harry, 'someone's thinkin of buyin him.'

We rounded a bend, Cam slowing the brute machine, he was looking for something. This was country without signs. We had left behind the side roads with their small encampments of mailboxes made from oil drums, milk cans, hollowed-out tree stumps, welded up from bits of rusty scrap metal. Sarah Longmore could do an interesting mailbox, something the rural postie would approach with trepidation, use a spade to insert the mail.

'Like horses,' said Harry, looking out of the window. 'Always did, from a young fella. Never saw a jock any good didn't like horses. Well, with notable bloody exception. That prick Crombie, he hated em, loved givin em the stick. Ride though, the little bastard. Glue on his boots. Always had the balance. Why'd the Lord give him that? Makes no sense.'

51

'An imponderable for many believers, I'm sure,' I said. 'This horse.'

'Next one,' said Cam. 'Must be.' He was rough trade today—unshaven, old corduroys, scuffed boots, a quilted jerkin. His usual out-of-town wear was a dark suit worn with a waistcoat.

We slowed, rounded another tight bend, didn't pick up speed. Cam was looking right, found what he was seeking. We turned right, no mailboxes to mark this intersection, took a downhill track, grass on the hump, grass growing in the ruts, weeds invading from both sides.

A few hundred metres from the road, the track reached a gate, an agricultural affair made of gum saplings in a bolted frame. I got out, the cold a shock, raw in the nose and mouth. The gate had a homemade latch, a sensible one, not the usual rural skinbreaker.

'Good with a farm gate, Jack,' said Harry when I was back in the warmth. 'Never touch the bloody things myself.'

'Damn right,' said Cam, expressionless. 'Got somebody does gates.'

It was a long way to the farmhouse, a steep, winding descent through dense bush and then, suddenly, you were on level cleared land, a broad terrace, two or three small paddocks hacked from the forest. The homestead you saw from afar: a slab hut with a lean-to, a big corrugated-iron shed, half open. Closer, you saw the split firewood stacked to the shed roof, five or six years of firewood, a horse yard with a rabbit-fenced enclosure beside it, possibly a vegetable garden. They also grew more exotic things in these misty hills.

In the near paddock, two rugged-up horses had heard the

vehicle from a long way away and were waiting to greet us. With them—a friend but standing apart—was a patrician Anglo-Nubian goat. Cam parked outside the shed, beside an old Dodge horse truck, red once, now the colour of rust, dents inside bigger dents. Apart from the firewood and half-a-dozen galvanised feed bins, the open shed had a rack with four saddles riding single file. They were as old as the truck but gleaming. Horse tackle and coiled ropes hung from wire strung across the space above head height, and against the side wall stood a rugged workbench with a blacksmith's leg vice. Tools were laid out on the bench like a museum display.

'The animal's here?' I said.

No reply. They got out, I got out. A keen wind was coming from far away, crossing Ninety Mile Beach from Bass Strait, coming from Antarctica. Harry made himself comfortable in his garments, adjusted them, a herringbone tweed jacket, thick grey flannels. 'Tidy,' he said. 'Man keeps a grip on things.'

A door in the shed opened and a cattledog came out, behind him a man in moleskins and a checked shirt. The dog stood still, eyes fixed on us.

The man walked over to Cam, some stiffness in a leg, and punched him under the collarbone, a medium-hard hit. 'Mongrel,' he said. He was tall and stooped, any age from fifty, boxer's shoulders, long nose, self-administered haircut.

They shook hands. The dog relaxed, embarked on a sniffing spree.

'Hurts,' said Cam, rubbing his chest. 'Harry, this's Chink.'

They shook hands.

'Know ya,' said Chink. 'That Derby, read that.'

He was talking about Harry winning the English Derby in

53

the late 1950s, a famous ride, Harry seeming to lift Ceasefire's head with both hands to edge out Pride of Shannon by nostrils. The photograph was on the wall in Harry's study, not big, not in pride of place. The first time I saw it, I was struck by Harry's hands—his long, powerful fingers.

Cam waved at me. 'Jack, Chink.'

We shook hands. Chink didn't have the air of someone who wanted to hurt but he could have clamped two leaf springs flat.

'Want some tea?' said Chink. He was looking at Harry.

Harry shook his head. 'Need to keep this short,' he said. 'How far?'

'Just down the track. Forty.'

'Before we go,' said Harry, looking around, scratching the cleft in his chin, 'seen the papers?'

'Nah.'

'Could be bullshit?'

'Bloke at the pub's seen the papers.'

Harry didn't seem impressed by this authentication. 'The bloke at the pub told you,' he said.

Chink understood Harry. 'Know him,' he said. He waited, then pointed a thumb at Cam. He seemed to be saying he trusted the man as he trusted Cam.

Harry nodded, satisfied. 'Spotted the animal in the paddock, did you?'

Chink took the weight off his lesser leg. 'Come by there one day,' he said. 'He took a run, rug rottin on him. Knew him for a thorough.'

'How's that?' said Harry.

Chink looked at Harry for a while, unblinking. 'Bit to

do with horses,' he said. 'Fifty year.'

'No offence,' said Harry. 'And then?'

'Asked around. Got the name.'

Harry nodded. 'Lost Legion.'

'Yeah. Membered it. Funny old world.'

'This bloke, he's the owner?'

'Reckon. He got left the property, everything. More brains in a tinny.'

'We'll follow you,' said Harry.

We remounted and watched Chink and the dog walk towards the paddock gate. The horses and the goat moved to meet them. Chink opened the gate a crack, the goat shot through. Chink found something in his shirt pocket for the horses, they put their noses in his big hand. The trio came back, the goat walking behind Chink, butting him, the dog third, nipping at the goat.

'Like one of them kids' stories,' said Harry.

Chink opened the back of the truck. The goat was waiting like someone in a bank queue. Chink picked it up as if it were weightless and loaded it, closed the door, latched it.

We followed the Dodge back to the road. The dog's head poked out of the window, barking at the world. Its colour matched the truck's bodywork. We turned right and, after a while, took a side road to the right, going downhill again, the country opening up.

Harry and Cam had an exchange, incomprehensible to me.

'Can I join this universe of knowledge?' I said. 'Who's Chink?'

'Hardest man alive, Chink,' said Cam.

'The goat likes him,' I said.

'Hunted brumbies with Chink,' said Cam. 'In the Snowies, Tumut, up around there. All uphill, cold as buggery, snows any time, snows at Christmas.'

'And now?'

'No Chink, no horse. The thing's a killer.'

'Say no more. I understand perfectly. We've driven hundreds of kilometres into the wilderness for you to buy a killer horse.'

'You, Jack,' said Harry.

'Me?'

'I want you to buy it. Supposin we do.'

I studied the big, lumpy piece of Gippsland that had come into view, more settled here, the odd weatherboard farmhouse smoking under a low, troubled sky, eroded creeks, leaning sheds, rugged-up horses, some signs of agriculture.

When the land was almost flat, the Dodge, dog riding shotgun for the left flank, turned right. We followed, went through a belt of trees, down a back road for a kilometre or two. The truck pulled into a driveway. We stopped behind it. All humans got out.

A horse was in the paddock, in the middle, twenty metres away, a tatter of a rug on its back. It looked at us, a glance, put its head down. If this was the horse, I could not see how the animal could be indentified as a thoroughbred.

We walked to join Chink. He was standing at the fence, hands in his pockets.

'Small,' said Harry.

Chink didn't say anything. He made a clicking noise. The horse raised its head. Chink clicked again. The horse looked at us, moved its head as if easing a strain, looked away in a deliberate manner.

We waited. The horse shifted, one eye looked at us.

'Thin,' said Cam.

Chink turned his back on the horse, looked down the valley. Cam and Harry turned. Not be outdone, I turned.

'Earnin a quid around here,' said Harry. 'What's the secret?'

'They don't tell me,' said Chink.

A sound behind us, the horse. He was three metres away, looking at us: eyes interested but not sharp, small movements of his head.

'No mongrel,' said Harry. 'Bit of wear on the legs.'

Now I noticed the scar tissue on the horse's forelegs.

Harry looked at Chink. 'Let's see him move,' he said.

Chink depressed the top strand of the fence by half a metre and made to swing a leg over. The horse took off over the wet, pitted paddock, rug flapping, ran twenty or thirty metres, stopped and looked backed at us, breathing hard.

'Nothing,' said Cam. 'Chink?'

'Sound,' said Chink. 'Decent tucker, bit of work.'

'Okay,' said Harry, 'where's this bloke?'

At the pub, a peeling single-storey structure at a T-junction, two utes and three dogs outside, we pulled up beside Chink. Cam got out, lit a Gitane, went around the bonnet and spoke to Chink, foot on the running board, looking up, wind erasing the smoke from his lips. He came back, flicked the cigarette, got in.

Harry looked at him.

'The bloke's a bit bombed, apparently,' said Cam. 'Also even bombed these woops can see keen coming in the dark.'

Harry turned and looked at me, the dry eyes, no lack of alertness here. He gave me an envelope. 'Here's the form,' he said. 'And Jack, the point's not the stiff paper. I just don't want any talk.'

I sighed and left the warm container. Chink got out of the truck, fell in with me, pushed in the dirty door. The room was overheated, cruel fluorescent light, smelling of cigarette smoke, beer-sogged carpet, old frying oil. Two men were playing pool, the one on strike showing us a deep cleft between pimply buttocks. Another man was talking to the woman behind the bar. We went over to customer number four, in the corner, a fat bearded man wearing a filthy, sagging jumper and a baseball cap. He appeared to be impaled on his stool.

'Den, this's Jack,' said Chink. 'It's about the horse.'

Chink left, moved down the bar.

Den looked at me, the turn of head took effort, screwed-up red eyes. His nose had sores on it and it was running. He didn't move to shake hands. I looked at his hand on a beer glass and I was glad that he didn't.

He drank. 'Bloody racehorse, mate,' he said. 'Not your bloody…' He didn't finish, put a hand up his fetid jumper, hand-knitted if I was any judge, and scratched himself, a task for which one hand was clearly inadequate. Then he reached down to the floor, groaned at the effort, and produced a plastic bag.

I put my back against the bar.

Den looked into the bag, dug out a small plastic-covered brown book with a window on the cover.

'Lookit this,' he said, opening it.

I took it gingerly and looked. It was Lost Legion's official history. The most recent owner was given as Dennis James Chaffee. The writing was legible although a fluid had stained the pages. Some things are best left unspeculated upon.

'Dennis James Chaffee is you?'

'Yup. Me uncle. Left it to me. My bloody horse.'

'Very nice,' I said. 'How much?'

'Well,' Den said, his face concertinaed. 'Bloody up to you, mate. Gimme'n offer. Fuckin racehorse. Class, not your…'

'A hundred,' I said.

Den pushed back the baseball cap. Grey scalp and sparse spiral strands of greasy hair came into view. 'Stickit up ya arse, mate,' he said. 'Fuckin hundred, thing's worth…fuckin six hundred.'

I put the horse's book on the counter. 'Just an idea I had,' I said. 'I can buy the kid a well-trained old horse for three. Nice to meet you.'

I was near the door when Den shouted, hoarse voice, 'Did I fuckin say no?'

I turned. A beckoning movement from Den, an awful hand urging me back. I returned.

'Four,' he said. His eyes were sliding around the room. 'Fuckin bargain. Lucky I need the money.'

'Take a cheque?'

Now he looked at me. 'Fuuuck,' he said, shaking his head. 'No?'

'Fuckin no's right.'

'Know how to transfer ownership?'

He shook his head. 'Me old lady done that.'

I got out Harry's envelope. Den winced, for a moment he thought something police-related was happening to him. Lost Legion's new owner was going to be A. J. Aldridge. Mrs Aldridge, cook extraordinaire, Harry's English housekeeper of forty-odd years.

I took the book and filled out the transfer of ownership form. Then I wrote out a receipt.

'A receipt for two hundred,' I said. 'Chink'll deliver the other two when they send the book.'

I went out to the brute vehicle. Harry's window descended as I approached. 'Two hundred now, two more when it's registered,' I said.

Harry nodded, not unhappy, looked at Cam. Cam found an envelope in some dashboard cavity, removed notes, passed the envelope to me.

I went back. Den had new drinks—another beer and a shot glass of something dark. Rum it would be.

'Two hundred cash,' I said. 'Sign here.'

Den signed the form and the receipt. He might just as well have made crosses: Den, His Mark. 'Listen,' he said, uneasy, eyes floating, 'I'm not helpin you load the thing. Don't go near it, fuckin thing's lucky I don't drill it.'

'Chink will load it. When the time comes.'

I caught Chink's eye. He came over.

'I'm buying this horse,' I said. 'Should be able to pick it up inside a week.'

Chink nodded. To Den he said, 'I'm puttin a goat in with it. Don't let anythin happen to that goat.'

'Don't need no fuckin goat.' said Den. 'Got me own root.' He laughed, the sound wild pigs make.

On the way back, in a Latrobe Valley coal town waiting in the drive-through lane to buy Harry's snacks, I said, 'Good day's work. Rose early. Travelled for hours. Enjoyed hand-combat with the man they call Mr Talkative. Then I met Gippsland's most wanted sperm donor and snapped up a gentle riding pony for Mrs Aldridge. Bargain price, too.'

'Well,' said Harry, leaning across Cam to study the menu, 'the Lord could smile on us for savin the beast. Run two thousand faster than nature intended.'

'No one mentioned speed,' I said.

'Outback Burger?' said Harry. 'New that. Whaddya reckon?'

'Roadkills,' said Cam. 'Find flattened kangaroos, wombats, grind em up, add sixteen secret bush spices…'

'Two Big Macs,' said Harry. 'Jack?'

I was thinking of home, of a quiet whisky and soda, followed by beef and pork sausages, cooked in the oven in red wine, accompanied by mustard mash and glazed carrots.

'No thanks,' I said. 'I'm on a food diet.'

Sarah Longmore lived on the top floor of a grand building in St Kilda, three storeys of redbrick Victorian, bay windows at each end, long balconies with cast-iron lacework, six chimneys in sight from where I stood at the ornate gate.

I pressed button number five, felt the camera on me and looked: it was behind a thin strip of plateglass set in stainless steel in the wall to the right of the gate.

The gate unlocked, two clicks, the kind you hear in prisons when you visit clients. I went down a wide chequerboard path bordered by box hedges. Beyond them were long and narrow lawns, ironing-board flat, edged with beds of lavender. In the centre of each lawn stood an old oak, still green. The broad front door had another board of five buttons.

I pressed.

'Come in, Jack.' Sarah Longmore's voice, excellent quality, her real voice.

More prison clicks.

I pushed at the intimidating door, put my hand on the wood above the shining brass plate, reluctant to mark a surface polished by hand, not sealed with some toxic chemical. The door swung as if weightless. I went into the building's hallway, fully six metres square with a tiled floor, an ornate pattern, vaguely Arabic. It was lit from above, natural light from landing windows and a skylight two floors up.

I went up four flights of stairs wide enough for women wearing hoops to pass. At the second floor's tall window, I paused to get my breath. A gardener appeared below, a man in a uniform with an electric mower. Nothing so raucous as a Briggs & Stratton two-stroke was allowed to bother the inhabitants of this building.

There were two doors leading off, solid cedar six-paners. I moved aside a brass cover on the one nearest. It hid modern locks, two of them.

The door opened.

'Jack.' Sarah Longmore in dark grey trousers, a loose poloneck top, soft-looking garments, no make-up that I could see. It was hard to believe that she was the dirty-faced metal-grinder in overalls.

I followed her down a short, wide passage into a sitting room full of light from three sets of french doors that opened onto a balcony. The furniture was old, expensive, and the back wall was crammed with pictures, dozens of them, almost butted against one another, every shape and size, frames fancy and plain. I recognised Williams, Blackman, Tucker, the Boyds, Olsen, Dobell, Perceval. It was an expensive way to cover a wall.

'Nice collection,' I said.

'They belong to my father,' she said. 'He lets me live here. Reluctantly. Coffee?'

I said no. The morning coffee had been taken. She fetched a big shallow cup from another room. We sat in armchairs.

'We were talking about the break-in,' I said.

'Yes. My car was being serviced, about a month ago. I went to the gym but when I got there I was feeling terrible. I had flu coming on. So I took a cab home and fell asleep on the sofa. It was early, before six. When I woke up, the place was in darkness. Then I heard voices.'

I looked at her neck, as perfect as that of the dancer Marietta di Rigardo in the painting. Marietta with bruise.

'A man came in,' she said. 'I could see his shape in the doorway. I shouted. He vanished but I heard him bump into someone and say, "Fuck, get out".'

'Not a break-in?'

'They came up the fire escape and in the kitchen door. Probably climbed the back wall from the lane. Otherwise you have to get through the street gate and the front door.'

'The kitchen door was locked?'

'Deadlocks and an alarm. Nothing damaged, the alarm didn't go off.'

'What time was it?'

'Just before seven.'

'When would you usually get back from the gym?'

'Around eight. I eat somewhere afterwards. Anyway, I had a few moments of panic and I rang Mickey.'

'You'd broken up with him, he was seeing your sister. Why him?'

64

'There wasn't any bad feeling. That's why this is so fucking ridiculous. I often spoke to him. He was an interesting man. An arsehole and an interesting person and someone you could rely on. For some things. Is that incomprehensible?'

'Not to me. You didn't think of the police?'

'There wasn't anything taken, they hadn't broken in. Can you imagine the look a woman gets from the cops when she calls them over and tells them that?'

'I can. Go on.'

'I rang Mickey and twenty minutes later Rick arrived with the gun.'

'Rick?'

'His driver.'

'Did it surprise you that Mickey would send someone around with a pistol?'

Sarah shook her head. 'No. Mickey is…he was the kind of person who had guns.'

I didn't pursue the matter. 'You were happy to take it?'

'Not at all. I told Rick I didn't want it but he had his instructions, he was embarrassed, I had to take the damn thing. I put it in the linen cupboard but it haunted me.'

'When last did you see it?'

'Every time I opened the linen cupboard. Well, not the gun, the box. It was in a box, like a chocolate box. I put it under the towels.'

'Anything else?'

She rose, the graceful rise on muscled thighs, and went to a table behind a sofa, lit a cigarette with a slim metal lighter, looking at me.

'Two Sundays ago, I came in, I'd been in the country, and

I opened the bathroom cabinet and someone had moved things. Someone had been in the place.'

'The home help? Moved the aspirin.'

Sarah smiled, the half-furtive smile. She shook her head. 'It's not silly. I have a thing about order. Not all of me, one side doesn't care. But where I live I know when something's moved. And there's no home help.'

I wished that I knew when things had been moved. I wished that I knew where things should be so that I could know if they'd been moved.

'You say you were at home on the night Mickey was killed?'

She gave me her headlights, trapped me in the highbeam. 'I say that because I was. Nobody can prove otherwise.'

'Ring anyone?'

'Just Sophie. She was in one of her down moods, everything's a total fuckup.'

'Where was she?'

'At home. In Richmond. It was early, sevenish.'

'She wasn't seeing Mickey that night?'

'No. She was going to a party.'

'You established that?'

She wasn't happy. She touched the cup to her lips, put it down, drew on the cigarette. Its tip glowed steel-burning bright.

She waited and I waited. She knew what I meant but she didn't want to answer. A stillness in her. Without looking, she ground the cigarette to death in an ashtray the size of a dinner plate.

'I didn't seek to establish that,' she said. 'She told me. It would have been very odd indeed if she hadn't told me. Sophie tells you everything.'

I wished I'd accepted coffee. Something to do with my hands.

She put her cup to her lips, put it down, stood up. 'Second chance. I can warm the coffee without ruining it. It's filter.'

'Please. Black.'

She left. I rose and paced the painting wall, slowly. Paintings are strange things. Some affect you directly, they connect with something in the brain, unprotected contact. But seeing paintings so different in kind and quality so close together had a disorienting effect, and standing back didn't help. I was only halfway, at the first woman, a Grace Cossington Smith, when Sarah returned, no fear of spillage in her walk, my coffee in a heavy cafe cup. It was unharmed by reheating, dark and oily and Jamaican.

'This isn't meant to be an interrogation,' I said. 'I'm assuming you didn't kill him. I'm asking the questions other people will ask.'

'I understand that,' she said. 'Do you know what it's like to feel guilty even when you aren't? My father has the capacity to do that to me.'

I got on with it. 'What was the state of Sophie's relationship with Mickey?'

'Not wonderful. She said he was manic one minute, everything coming good, then he'd go black and the next thing he was talking about suicide. Violent swings, you'd say. Sophie should know. Christ knows what it was like when their downers coincided.'

'Did you know him to be like that?'

'Not the suicide end of the pendulum. The highs, absolutely, that was Mickey. But I think things were going well in business when we…were together.'

'And his wife. Do you know her?'

'Wife isn't the term that comes to mind, it wasn't exactly a suburban marriage. But, yes. Corin Sleeman. She's an architect, she commissioned a piece from me for a building.'

'Something I could stop by and have a look at?'

Sarah lit a cigarette, eyes on me. 'It may not astonish you to hear that the developer rejected it,' she said.

'Unequal to the challenge,' I said. 'Did she know about you and Mickey?'

'When she commissioned the piece? I didn't think so then, like a fool.'

'So she wasn't necessarily indifferent?'

Sarah tilted her head. 'You're knowledgeable in the areas of betrayal and revenge?'

'An academic interest. Everything's in books.'

She touched her lips with a finger, the nail unvarnished. 'Yes,' she said, a nod and a smile. We sat, cups in hand, the scent of coffee, gossamer smoke in the sunlight.

'Who found him?' I said.

'Apparently he didn't ring Rick to be picked up. His mobile was on and he wasn't answering, so Rick rang security at the building and they went in.'

'The weapon,' I said. 'Did you tell anyone you had it?'

'No. Just Sophie.'

'Which leaves Mickey and Rick and whoever they told.'

'I suppose so. I can't imagine Mickey telling the world.'

'What do you know about Rick?'

She hung her head, closed her eyes in mock contrition. 'I don't even know his surname. He's big, going bald, he's polite.'

'And now he's an unemployed vegetarian, I presume.'

Sarah shrugged.

'The cops. When did they arrive? I haven't been told that.'

Only because I hadn't asked.

'Sunday morning,' she said. 'Just before nine. They asked me to come to the station. When we got there, they left me alone for about half an hour and then they came in with the gun. I told them about it and while I was doing that I realised I needed a lawyer.'

'Many people don't have that reaction.'

Sarah gave me the child's direct look. 'I've seen the movies, mate. It's not just the guilty who need a lawyer.'

I nodded. 'Sound attitude. Everyone needs a lawyer. And a couple in reserve.'

'So I rang my father and Andrew came to the station. I thought I'd be leaving with him. The movies didn't prepare me for a week in remand.'

'Nothing in life would. What does Sophie do?'

'As in, for a living?'

I nodded.

'Nothing. Cursed with artistic leanings, the Longmores. I was trying to paint so she wanted to be a painter. She fucked a lot of artists but that didn't help with the actual painting.'

She fetched another cigarette.

'Pottery was next,' she said, 'but potters were too boring to fuck, plus she hated the feel of clay. Computer-generated crap, that went on for a while. Soph quite liked it but the men were worse than potters. Then she met Ernst, a photographer, a man who carried his telephoto lens in his underpants. That was my impression, anyway.' She blew smoke. 'She had a little falling out with Ernst and he took his long lens elsewhere. But she still takes photographs.

69

Compulsively. Terrible photographs.'

We sat silent for a while.

'Will she be a prosecution witness?' I said.

'Against me?' She closed her eyes and shook her head. 'No, for Christ's sake, she knows I didn't do it, couldn't do it, wouldn't have any fucking reason for doing it, how can I get this over…'

'Having a key to Mickey's place? How does that work?'

'I had it, I never gave it back, he never asked, I forgot I had it. I told the police that. Now that may be fucking dumb but it's not exactly the act of a guilty person. Telling the police about your key to the victim's apartment.'

I didn't comment. Guilty people had done stranger things. Time to go away and think of questions I should have asked. I finished the coffee.

At the door, she touched my arm. I turned. No direct childlike look now, her gaze averted, her shoulders lowered.

'Jack,' she said, 'I'm not a great client, but thanks.'

I found myself awkward.

'I'm trying to be tough,' she said, still not looking at me. 'Someone who can handle this kind of nightmare.'

Resist the urge to offer comfort. I had learned that the painful way. In my time, they didn't give you that advice at law school. Or perhaps they did, and on that day I woke with a gully-trap mouth, rose to fall again, buried guilt in sleep, missed the tutorial.

'I think you are that someone,' I said. 'In a word or two, what was Mickey's charm?'

'He was funny, clever. And a dangerous feel. I'd never met anyone like him. He sparked you.'

'That'll do,' I said.

I drove back to Fitzroy in a mood not far from gloomy. Federation Square didn't help. It had an innocent awfulness, like the results of allowing small children to play at cooking. In Brunswick Street, luck delivered to me a space not too far from what would soon be the fashionable street's newest eatery. On opening day, anyway. New cafes, bars, bistros opened regularly—places to hang out and exchange hilarious one-liners with your friends while sitting on old sofas and 1950s chairs. And they closed. This had started in the 1980s. For a long time before that little changed in the long shabby street of clanging trams, dangerous pubs, ethnic clubs, marginal shops, murky pool cafes, the offices of minor trade unions.

Then young people began to appear. At first alone and shy as urban foxes, they grew in numbers, became bolder. Soon they were loitering in the laundromat, venturing into the pubs, daring to claim a table in the snooker dens. Places catering for their special needs—breakfast in mid-afternoon, for example—opened. Affiliation clusters developed, here dud musicians, here talentless artists, here the illiterate writers, here those who combined all these qualities in spades—the film people.

The old inhabitants, like many original owners, thought the newcomers were simpletons but harmless. So when the speculators arrived and offered to buy their once unsaleable properties, they hid their smiles, took the money and ran for a new brick-veneer in the west.

In the mid-1980s, on a spring Sunday morning, a Volvo stationwagon parked in Brunswick Street. A young couple got out. She was trim, blonded, tanned. He was already broadening in the midsection, sockless, short and hairy legs ending in boatshoes. From a restraining chair in the back seat, he unloaded a child, complaining, flailing. They took it into a cafe.

They were going to have brunch.

The old Brunswick Street was dead, Brunchwick Street born. There was no turning back.

I thought about these things sitting in my car watching a signwriter at work on the window of Morris's two-down, two-up building. It had once been the premises of C. K. Dovey, printer of personal and business stationery, advertising material, invitations to occasions of all kinds, calling cards. People passing would see Ken standing at the cabinet, selecting each letter from its tray, placing it in the stick in his left hand, inserting spaces—en spaces, em spaces, line spaces. He put the metal down on his steel stone in a frame, a chase, cut decorative borders, mitred their corners, locked the assemblage up tight with quoins. Then he transferred it to the press bed and inked it with a roller.

On Ken Dovey's window, the painter had outlined the word *Enzio's* in a fat italic hand and was working on the E in gold paint.

I got out and crossed the street, made my way in the late-morning throng, young and youngish people mostly, modish, long-haired, hairless, the odd balding man with a small tuft sticking out of the back of his head like a vestige of tail, people in Melbourne black, people in Gold Coast white, people in saris, sarongs, the odd suit, the odd secondhand pink tracksuit, many naked midriffs, some not much wider than a greyhound's, some not much narrower than a 44-gallon drum but the colour of lard.

'Going where I'm going?' said a woman behind me.

'In principle, I'm willing.'

She came up beside me, brushed against me, you could feel the solidness of her arm, the muscle, not an unpleasant feeling.

I didn't have to look down to meet her eyes, slate eyes. She was letting her hair grow; it was almost army bootcamp height.

'How's business?' I said.

Her name was Boz. I'd done the work when she gave up being a film grip to buy a two-truck inner-city removal business with a line in carting works of art. The seller was an apparently exhausted man ready for a long rest. When I tried to ensure that he didn't start up a week later under another name and pinch the goodwill he claimed to be selling, he had to be wrestled to the ground and sat on.

'Excellent,' she said. She licked her lower lip, showing a

viper of pink tongue. 'I may have to get another truck.'

'Wait a while,' I said. 'Till you see it's all flow and no ebb.'

We walked. The oncomings seemed to part for us—well, for a six-feet-two woman, with a broken nose, in overalls.

'Fussy bastard, this Enzio,' she said. 'We go to collect the gas stove he's bought, it's disgusting. It looks like it's been in shearers' quarters for fifty years, they fire up all eight burners and chuck on a dead sheep, turn it over at half-time in the footy. Just looking at the fucking thing makes you itch. Enzio makes me get the blankets and wrap it up like it's a French antique.' She shook her head. 'Had to throw away the blankets. Good blankets.'

'Well,' I said, 'he tells me it *is* a French antique. Chucked out in some refurbishment of the Melbourne Club.'

We entered the stove's new home. Enzio, scowling, his expression of choice, was on a ladder, painting a wall. He was wearing tracksuit pants and a singlet and he had sprinkled paint on his thinly covered scalp, his stubbled face, the exposed hairy parts of his body, on his garments.

'Jack, Boz,' he said. He pronounced her name Boss.

'Good colour,' I said. 'Ancient nicotine. When's opening day?'

It couldn't be soon enough for me. I'd had no home in Brunswick Street for months, not since Neil Willis, absentee owner, wedding-reception gouger, sold Meaker's, my hangout of too many years, to some jewellery-hung wise boys looking for a place to run drug money through. They'd sacked the staff and accused Enzio, the cook, of stealing from the kitchen. It had taken some doing but I'd managed to wring the workers' entitlements out of Willis, including Enzio's superannuation, fourteen unpaid years of it.

Meaker's was now called Peccadillo. My hope was that when they nailed the new owners, it would be for some offence to which that term did not apply.

'So?' said Enzio to Boz. 'Where my furniture?'

I could see that being able to look down at her for once had empowered him.

Boz gripped the stepladder with a big hand, gave it a little shake, an exploration. Enzio cried out. The balance of power had been redressed.

'Waiting down the street, mate,' she said. 'You're going to have to make room out front. Two spaces.'

'I got a plan for that,' said Enzio. 'Carmel!'

Carmel the waif waitress sacked from Meaker's appeared in the kitchen door, paintbrush in hand. She was wearing a skullcap and looked about twelve. She was thirty and knew much of men and the world.

'Move the cars,' said Enzio. 'The furniture's coming.'

'Listen,' she said, 'I'm not being paid for my time here.'

'Please,' said Enzio.

'That's a first,' Carmel said. 'That's a personal best for you. Move them where?'

'The lane. Two minutes.'

'Keys?'

'On the counter.'

She went out.

'Here's your lease,' I said. 'You are now legally occupying this building. Rent's due the last Friday of every month, paid straight into the bank. The account number's written on the first page.'

Enzio came down the ladder. He took the envelope, held it in both hands. He went over and put it on the counter, patted it. 'Never thought,' he said, shaking his head. 'Never thought.'

'Yes, well. When?'

He looked at me. I thought I saw a glint in the black eyes. He cleared his throat. 'Monday,' he said. 'Monday we open. Six o'clock, we have a little drink, champagne. Okay?'

'Okay. See you on Monday.'

He followed me to the door, took my sleeve. 'Jack,' he said, barely audible, 'listen, I want to say to you, I want to…'

I said, 'Enzio, don't say anything. Monday, I'm having poached eggs with the lot. Soft. I've had it with hard poached eggs.'

'I hold them in the boiling water,' he said, showing me a cupped hand.

'Ordinary cooking methods will be fine,' I said. 'It's just a matter of the timing.'

At the office, my two rooms, tailor's table, two chairs and a framed degree certificate, I made a pot of tea and sat behind the tailor's table to read the three-page report on Mickey Franklin.

The work was by Simone Bendsten Associates, specialists in due diligence and the lice-combing of candidates for jobs with share options and performance bonuses and a company jet. Once the firm was just Simone, a Scandinavian-Australian refugee from the finance world working from home. Now it was three people in an office off Brunswick Street.

'Jack,' she'd written on a card, 'the press clippings are attached. We haven't been able to add much.'

I read, marking bits, sat in thought for a while, trying to see Michael Franklin—funny, clever, dangerous-feeling

Mickey Franklin. The report said he'd worked for MassiBild, the Massiani family construction company, for six years before going out on his own in 1995. It listed more than twenty inner-city residential developments he had been involved in, including the Serena apartment block in South Melbourne where he was murdered. Franklin's most recent project, the $250 million Seaton Square complex in Brunswick, had been stalled for more than eighteen months. The tangled history of the project took up a page and a half, a case study in how not to deal with the neighbours' concerns. There was a list of creditors, including a company called Glendarual Holdings. 'Glendarual is Sir Colin Longmore's investment vehicle,' noted Simone.

The report ended:

> Franklin had a reputation in the property and invest-ment sectors as someone who did not linger in projects, accepting lower than possible returns in order to move on. Descriptions of him include: 'tightrope act'; 'not a person we'd want to be involved with'; 'high-pain, low-gain operator'; 'much too hurried for us'; 'one-man bobsled team, no thanks'.

Between them the *Age* and the *Herald Sun* had found four photographs. Two gave a good idea of what Mickey looked like. In one, he was in a dinner jacket, bow tie, in profile bending forward to kiss a much younger woman, a piece of hair falling. She was offering her mouth, no cheek kiss here, she wanted to kiss him. A birthday, perhaps a twenty-first, the woman had that shining look. The second was taken at the opening of a gallery in the Serena building. He was photographed with his wife, Corin Sleeman, a slim woman with short fair hair that looked as if she'd finger-combed it straight out of the shower.

I read the report again and then I set out for the city centre, walked up to Brunswick Street to catch a tram. Once tram rides from Fitzroy to the city were more or less free, it was only a few blocks, the connies knew you, looked the other way. That had come to an end too.

Drew waved at me from a table to the left of the door of a cavernous faux-Milano place on Little Collins Street where the staff fawned on regulars and made others feel like they'd gatecrashed a private function.

I went over and sat on an uncomfortable chair. 'Not proving easy,' I said.

'Nothing of worth in life is easy,' said Drew. 'Why is that, do you think?'

'I don't think.' I looked around at the lunchtimers, mostly men in dark suits, hard voices, eyes that darted. 'I'll give you a why. This place?'

'Convenience. I'm making a house call nearby on a colleague who finds himself in an awkward position. Drug-wise.'

'Not the colleague seen after midnight helping the staff of McDonald's? Using the fat straws to vacuum a tabletop?'

Drew ran a fingertip over his upper lip, appraised me. 'Becoming more in touch with the world,' he said. 'I'm not sure that's a good thing.'

'I agree. I liked the old naive me more. I plan to revert.'

'Unfortunately,' said Drew, 'naivete never comes back. Like virginity and that feeling of your first tongue kiss.'

He caught a waiter's eye before the man could look away and pointed at the menu. Insulted, the balded one slid over and took out his pad. We ordered from the fixed-price menu, two courses and a glass of wine. The man's demeanour suggested that we were cheating, like rich tourists lining up with the homeless at a soup kitchen.

'And the red,' said Drew. 'Recommend it?'

The waiter shrugged. 'It's red, it's wine,' he said. His eyes were elsewhere.

'That good? My. Two glasses, please.'

We watched him go. He was pear-shaped, a big backside, something unobjectionable in people who hadn't given offence but capable of arousing a violent urge.

'Once the aim was to earn a lavish tip by grovelling,' said Drew. 'Now they want you to grovel. You saw her?'

'What do the jacks say about the gun?'

'Found in the course of a routine search of the area around Mickey's building.'

'Following a tip-off is what I'm told.'

Drew cocked his long head. 'That's good for a fit-up yarn.'

'If admitted. Also good for a dobbed-in-by-unknown-accomplice, unfortunately.'

'Someone betting she's willing to go down alone? No. Accords better with weapon planted by the person who shot

Mick five times through two folds of towel.'

'Thick Egyptian cotton towel, no doubt. If there was a tip, it makes this very difficult.'

The waiter arrived, clicked down two glasses of red wine. He was leaving when Drew said, crisply, 'Waiter.'

Pearbum stopped, turned like someone with a bad back.

'I haven't accepted this wine,' said Drew.

Pearbum took in air, you could see the inflation of the midsection.

Drew sniffed his glass, one deep sniff, and put it down. 'Oxidised,' he said, his eyes on Pearbum. 'Wine from a new bottle, please.'

Pearbum's chin and eyebrows went up. Drew gave him the stare, the unblinking, sceptical look used for cross-examining hard-arsed police witnesses.

Pearbum looked back, but he was basically soft-arsed and looking into Drew's eyes reminded him of this. He lowered chin and eyebrows. 'Certainly, sir,' he said. He gathered the glasses.

'Masterly,' I said. 'Now we get the eyedrops in the food.'

'If they dare,' said Drew. 'They dare only against the weak. What else?'

'Not much. It seems the feds were asked but they were busy.'

'Asked what?'

I shrugged. 'Sarah thinks she was being watched.'

'I'm not surprised. I'd watch her. What's *thinks* mean?'

'She kept seeing the same woman in the street.'

Drew shook his head. 'Anyone to back that up?'

'Only her sister and the deceased. Then there's the actual property invasion and the suspected one.'

'I know about them,' said Drew. 'Unreported is the problem.'

'What about Rick the driver?'

'I was going to ask about Rick.'

Pearbum's replacement arrived, a slim youth carrying a bottle and new glasses. He uncorked the bottle and poured a splash for Drew, who gave it a cursory sniff and nodded.

'As two blokes having lunch,' said Drew. 'What?'

'She probably did it,' I said, 'but she presents well. No visible twitches, engaging candour, scorns angry jilted lover angle, says little sister Sophie was always saying give me your toy.'

I tried the wine. Pearbum had captured its essence: wine, red. 'Sophie's a hope. She may be able to point the finger somewhere else, vaguely point, there's a chance.'

'We'll have to talk to her,' said Drew. 'Our mutual friend say anything about her?'

'No. I don't think she's on their team.'

'We'll find out in due course. The old boy says she's staying with friends.'

'Mickey worked for the Massianis for six years,' I said. 'I read they're on this building royal commission's playlist.'

Drew put a finger to the outer corner of an eye, took on a strange Asian-Caucasian look. 'My instinctive reaction,' he said, 'is that if Mickey could've hurt the Massianis, he'd have long been part of the structural underpinning of a prestigious office tower.'

'I'll ask him about that,' I said.

'Do that,' said Drew. 'Ask him. He went to Monash, Steven Massiani, tell him you went to Melbourne. He's probably haunted by feelings of inferiority like all Monash graduates. Law and engineering, first-class honours. For what that's worth.'

Drew looked up at the painted ceiling, at the badly painted fat nudes and cherubs and bowls of fruit. 'I wonder why they don't combine law and transgender studies,' he said. 'What about law and hairdressing. Law and podiatry. Law and Hopi Indian ear candle therapy, law and…'

The youth arrived with our first course: slices of chicken breast stacked with things in between. Standing in a puddle of balsamic vinegar sauce.

'They used to fan the food around the plate,' Drew said. 'Now they give you mounds, you have no idea what to do.'

'Wreck it,' I said.

We wrecked, we ate.

'Plus,' said Drew, 'I've never seen the point of pine nuts.'

'It's about texture,' I said. 'Get you to the footy this week?'

He put his head to one side, gave me the sympathy look designed to lull prosecution witnesses. 'Saints play Carlton,' he said. 'For the Saints, I have nothing but contempt. For Carlton, I reserve a special loathing.'

'You wouldn't care to umpire the game?' I said.

Walking up Collins Street to a tramstop, a cab pulled in ahead of me to discharge a passenger. A business lunch, I thought. Transport to and from would be billable.

'Smith Street, Collingwood,' I said to the driver, whose hairs were arranged across his scalp like swimming lanes. He was writing something on a pad. 'Know where that is?' I said, gently.

'Think I'm off the fuckin boat, mate?'

'I assume nothing,' I said.

'Fuckin Smith Street,' he said. 'Talkin to an Abbotsford boy, mate. Born and bred.'

'Good,' I said. 'So you'll have a rough idea.'

The driver sulked until the Spring Street lights, when he said, 'So. What's your team?'

'Saints,' I said.

'You poor cunt,' he said, immensely cheered. 'Still, Carlton on Satdee, even your girls got a chance. Poofs Carlton.'

'Carlton,' I said. 'Possibly.'

I passed the leaden afternoon in paperwork, attending to legal matters, writing letters of inquiry and impotent threat, itemising bills for small services performed. In the dusk, the air cold and damp, I walked to the post office, a place now without a hint of gravitas, and consigned my missives to the steel bin, no doubt the only lawyer in the country who posted his own letters.

On the way back, I passed a woman retching dryly, and, in the alley, two boys grabbing and snarling, both pale and pinched, chapped lips and flaking skin, noses leaking.

It was after eight, I was home, behind the label of the Maglieri, deep in a melancholy reverie, not listening to Abdullah Ibrahim, once Dollar Brand, when the bell rang. I went down the narrow and dangerous staircase, more perilous now, and opened the door with caution.

A big man in dirty jeans and T-shirt, no hair to speak of, a beard or a painful shave coming on.

'G'day, mate,' he said.

'Len,' I said. We shook hands. I always expected to come away with splinters in my fingers.

'Time again,' he said. 'Christ knows why you buggers need fires.'

Melbourne cold was a joke to Len. He was from beyond Avoca, Melbourne was like Bali to people from beyond Avoca.

The old Ford truck was backed in, wheels against the kerb, ready to unload the last two cubes of redgum, dry, split small. It came in autumn and in mid-winter, heavily discounted courtesy of a horse owner for whom Harry Strang had managed a sizeable coup.

I sat on the stairs and watched Len and his offsider, a silent ginger youth, unload and stack in the recess beneath me. We talked football. There was no point in trying to help. These were pros, you got in their way. When they were finished, Len said, 'The boss says thirty bucks will be fine.'

Money paid, thanks said, hands shaken, I was halfway up the stairs when the phone began to ring. I made haste.

'A shortness of breath?' said Drew. 'Is this a bad time? Or is awkward the word?'

'Just getting wood,' I said. 'Downstairs.'

'My instinct confirmed. I'll be brief. The party's father wants words, contacted me directly. From my position, that's…what is the word?'

'Awkward,' I said.

'Exactly. Ever the slotter of the black ball. I'd prefer to take instructions from the client. Perhaps my associate could call on him.'

'In the billable universe, anything is possible,' I said. 'Is this part of my Cyril employment?'

'It is. There's no reason to speak of that to the client. Ten tomorrow at the Macedon estate?'

I thought of humming up the Calder Highway in the Alfa. Perhaps the day would be sunny. 'Directions? Or will any forelock-tugging rustic in the vicinity be able to direct me?'

I went back to the kitchen. More wine needed. What to eat was also a question becoming urgent. Left over was a complete sausage and another biggish bit, just under half. Also a lot of mustard mash. How can you eat the same food two nights running? I tried a spoonful of the mash. How can you not?

I put the mash on to warm up, plus a bit of milk, sliced the cold sausage into thick coins and added them. Peas wouldn't hurt. I microwaved the last of the tiny frozen peas with some butter, leant against the sink, rolling the Maglieri in the mouth. A balanced meal coming up, all major food groups represented: the dead animal group, the lumpish underground vegetable group, the things hiding in pods group, pungent seeds group, fat cows group. Preceded and accompanied by the fermented grapes group.

I ate while watching television and reading the *Age*. The eating was the best part. Bed and book. To hell with Instanbul and knowing too much, I attempted something else, bought on the title, *Greek Kissing*. It was about two English families holidaying together on the island of Leros. An Australian artist was introduced at the end of the first chapter. Soon after, I slipped back into my gloomy trance, sightless eyes on the ceiling, endless running of negative thoughts, just registering the sound of the city, a low wet thunder spiked with shriek and squeal and shot and slam.

Sir Colin Longmore came out of the rose garden, tall and gaunt, big-nosed, like General de Gaulle in stooped old age at Colombey-les-deux-Eglises. A dog, a spaniel, sagging like a sofa, followed.

'Jack Irish,' I said.

He walked across the terrace, pulling off a gardening glove finger by finger, and put out a hand.

'Longmore,' he said. 'Good of you to come.'

'My pleasure.' I said. His hand felt more like that of a brickie than of the man who owned the brickworks, passed down the generations from Ronald Calway Longmore, mine-owner, grazier, land speculator, founder of Longmore Brick and Tile, whose products built a lot of nineteenth-century Melbourne.

'Irish,' he said. 'Not a name you hear a lot. Had an Irish work here before the war.'

I felt a stiffening in the neck and shoulders, deliberately turned to look at the massive house with its turreted roofs, gables and battlements, mullioned windows, rusticated brickwork and stone quoins. 'I imagine you had most of Melbourne work here at one time or another,' I said.

He studied me, old bird eyes under sloping grey thatch, he'd taken my meaning. 'I'll show you,' he said.

I followed him across the rose-brick terrace, down three steps and through an archway of entwined creepers. A gravel path at least a hundred and fifty metres long stretched out between close-planted poplars, yellow leaves hanging on. The eye went to the end, to a stone archway with two iron gates.

We walked side by side, crunching the gravel. His brogues needed polishing, they were cracked over the little toes.

'I remember these poplars going in,' he said. 'We grew them in the tree nursery. We had that then. Associate. What's that mean?'

It took a second to adjust. 'I used to be Andrew Greer's partner. Now we sometimes work together.'

Longmore didn't respond, a raised eyebrow. I offered nothing.

'What's your role in this?' he said.

'To help prepare Sarah's defence.'

'Defence? Had the gun, she tells me.'

'Gave it back, I understand.'

He sniffed. 'Defence'll need a QC. Team of QCs.'

'Andrew impressed that upon her. She doesn't want one.'

Behind us, the spaniel farted, a drawn-out emission.

'Fire in your own time,' said Longmore.

We walked.

'Bad business,' he said.

'Yes.'

The poplars' branches were woven. We were in a sky-roofed tunnel. Colin Longmore stopped. I stopped. He dipped into his jerkin pocket, came out with a stubby pipe, a short-stemmed piece of plumbing for burning tobacco outdoors, a decent hat brim would shelter it from the rain.

I couldn't remember when last I'd seen anyone smoke a pipe.

Longmore found a lighter, a Dunhill, flared on the sides like a Chevrolet of the 1950s, an item from the golden age of smoking. The lighter flamed. He applied the flame to the bowl, sucking like a calf on a teat.

We walked down the crackling path. A cold day, autumn on the north slope of the hill of Macedon. The hill had early provided Melbourne's rich with relief from the town in its septic delta, the rivers fouled with tallow and tannin and excrement, the air sallow from the smoke of mills and foundries and smelling of the steam of tanneries and tobacco factories. The Dandenongs, the other hills, the hillocks, were an alternative but the properly rich favoured Macedon. England was home and every kind of European tree their gardeners planted thrived at Macedon—oak, elm, plane, ash, chestnut, holly, medlar, quince, crab apple, linden, hornbeam, hazel, birch, beech, box—box clipped into hedges and box allowed to be trees. It was also the case that you couldn't get trees to produce their best autumn display in the Dandenongs, the sea was too close, there was a humidity. You needed a crueller climate, one that would make the sugar in the maple and liquidambar leaves turn to fire, convert it to blood in the perfectly heart-shaped leaves of the katsura.

'A difficult woman, Sarah,' said Longmore. 'She was an impossible girl. Nothing like it in her mother. Sweetest nature, her mother.'

'Impossible how?' I said.

He seemed not to hear me, walked shaking his head. Then he said, 'She's been in trouble. I suppose she's told you that.'

'Not the details.'

'Terrible temper, even when she was little, nine, ten. Then one day she had this…well, not a temper, it's a madness, a fit. We had her seen by the psychiatrists. Professor Whatsisname, Bently, Benleigh, something like that, at the university, supposed to be an expert—they're all supposed to be experts, charlatans, wouldn't have a clue. Dreams, bloody nonsense, looking for something to blame. Bred in the marrow, that's what it is. Her mother's brother had it too.'

The spaniel came between us, speeding, galvanised for a few dozen paces. Then it stopped and started again, plodding.

'What happened?' I said.

Longmore looked at me.

'When she was in trouble.'

Silence. There was something calming about being confined by tall trees, walking down a narrow path towards a gateway that could be an exit or an entrance to some other confinement.

'Well, they were living like pigs,' said Longmore. 'Take that back, I've got some regard for pigs. We had pigs here once, my father thought it would be nice to grow your own bacon, ham, that sort of thing. Not at all dirty, pigs. Humans make them dirty. Bugger up everything, humans, a disgrace, don't deserve the planet.'

We were nearing the end of the allée. A building could now be seen through the wrought-iron gates, a small two-storey stone building with its steep roof sheathed in copper that was green with verdigris. It stood at the centre of a brick-paved square, perhaps an acre in area, bordered by high clipped hedges. Around it was a narrow moat, stone-edged, brimming with dark water.

'Lovely little thing, isn't it?' said Longmore. 'Come down here every day, twice in summer.' He coughed. 'Just as well, given the limited number of summers left.'

It was a lovely thing, not little but small, perfectly proportioned, with bluestone foundations, walls of dressed sandstone, and sills and arches of granite. It would stand unchanged and beautiful when everyone now alive was dead and forgotten.

We crossed the moat by a short iron bridge. Longmore opened the front door and saw me in: one big square room, the floor of polished pink stone, the slabs butted so tight, the cutting so clean that in places no edges could be seen. In the centre of the room, surrounded on three sides by a horse-shoe-shaped bench, a mahogany staircase rose in a tight spiral. I walked to one of the narrow gothic-arched windows on the west wall. A shallow alcove between the windows held a stone cup full of wax. A wick had burnt to the bottom and died.

'Peaceful place,' said Longmore. He was standing at the single back window, hands in his pockets.

I joined him. We were looking directly at a long stone rill that fed the moat, a dark line drawn across the paving to the hedge.

'My mother designed this,' he said. 'When she was little,

Sarah used to sit upstairs for hours reading. You never think at that age they'll ever bring you pain.'

'The trouble Sarah was in,' I said.

'They had to take the chap to hospital. Head injuries, collarbone broken, they said he was like someone who'd been in a motor accident.'

'Who was he?'

'Damn near killed him. They'd been taking drugs. He said she gave him no warning. Broke a bottle over his head. Full bottle of wine. Hit him with other things.'

Longmore had a coughing bout, recovered. 'Her mother was always nervous after that if the phone rang, couldn't answer the telephone.'

I gave up on the victim's identity. 'How old was Sarah then?'

He eyed his pipe bowl without pleasure. 'About eighteen,' he said. 'Walked out on school when she was sixteen. We were in the Toorak house. The school was delighted, I can tell you.'

'She was living at home when it happened?'

'No. She'd cleared off, met this crowd in Fitzroy, they called themselves artists, just smeared paint around like babies, took drugs. Of course, the public galleries bought the rubbish, they weren't actually after paintings. Young bum, that's what they were buying. Taxpayer-subsidised sodomites.'

The spaniel plodded around the corner. It walked to the rill, looked at it hopelessly, turned and looked at us, head on one side, sad. Then it sat down, a slow going down, always looking at us, a sinking of an old bum.

'Won't cross the bridge,' said Longmore. 'Doesn't like bridges. A bit like me.'

'He was one of the artists?' I said.

'Who?'

'The man Sarah attacked.'

'Oh. Hopeless bugger, not an ounce of talent. Gary Webber. I could have understood beating him up on aesthetic grounds.'

He got out the lighter and applied it to the pipe, sucking, sucking, his eyes on the bowl. Then they turned on me, thoughtful.

'Ah,' he said, 'yes, the point of this.'

I followed him out of the front door, the only door. He turned right and we went around the building, inside the moat. On the north flank, the dog side, he stopped and pointed at the wall below the window.

'There,' he said, 'that's the point.'

He moved on, gave me room. I bent and looked. On a bluestone foundation block, a thin strip was polished to tombstone smoothness. Letters and numbers were chiselled into it. Unless pointed out, you would not notice the inscription. It said:

J. I. Irish. AD 1936.

'Built this,' said Longmore. 'Six of them on the job for the masonry, he was the master. I came here every day, got here early, before them most days, stayed all day. I brought my own sandwiches, tried to help. Got in the way, I suppose. They were rough the young ones, said things I didn't understand until years later. Still, they tolerated me.'

'The employer's son,' I said and regretted it.

He didn't look at me, chewed his pipe stem. 'Yes,' he said. 'Be a fool not to consider that. Anyway, they were kind to me and I was happy.'

The spaniel barked at us, aggrieved, cut off from his friend by a border he could not cross.

We walked around the building.

'Always happiest here,' said Longmore. 'We had all the summer holidays here, my mother and I. My father came up sometimes. She didn't like the sea, not a sea person. Nor am I.'

'Do you remember him?' I said.

'My father?'

'No. The stonemason.'

Longmore took the blunt elbow joint out of his mouth. 'There's a photograph my mother took,' he said. 'A big man. Big shoulders, big hands.'

We left the beautiful building anchored in its calm quadrangle and walked back down the avenue of trees, the spaniel holding station behind us. A breeze had come up, it was worrying the poplars, challenging the tenacity of the last leaves.

'Was Sarah charged for the assault?' I said.

He took the pipe out of his mouth and spat sideways, not successfully. He wiped a sleeve with the side of a hand. 'It didn't come to that. Things you can do.'

Twenty metres on, he said, 'I married late, y'know. Well beyond forty when we had Sophie.' Pause. 'Seems young enough from here, though. Got any yourself?'

'A daughter.'

'Rather had a boy?'

I was unprepared. 'I don't know,' I said. 'I don't feel I've had anything. I didn't bring her up. Her mother left me when she was tiny.'

'Yes,' he said. 'I didn't feel I'd had anything till their

mother died. Always too busy. And she took care of everything. When I had to deal with them they were almost grown up. Then I wished they were boys.'

He blinked rapidly, seemed to be trying to expel something from his eyes. 'Never was any good with girls,' he said, 'I suppose that's why I married so late.'

'Do your daughters depend on you for money?'

'They didn't for a while after their mother died. She had her own money and she left it to them. They spent it at speed, of course, both of them. Profligate is the term.'

We walked in silence, just the chewing sound of our feet on the gravel, the scrabbling noise of the dog behind us. Near the house, I said, 'I'm told you're on the list of creditors for the Seaton Square project.'

He didn't reply, his eyes on the gravel. After a while, I tried again.

'I heard you,' he said. 'The backers were calling in six mill. He was battling with objections, the usual mess. I said no but Sophie pestered me.'

'How long ago was that?'

Longmore raised his eyebrows. 'Three or four months, I suppose.'

We walked up the steps to the terrace. On the level, he stopped, gave me a quick look. 'You've seen those metal things she makes?'

I nodded.

'Clue to her mind there, don't you think?' he said. 'To what's wrong with her.'

'Apart from the desirability of a QC, is there something else you'd like me to convey to Andrew Greer?'

He was patting the dog. 'Get her to plead guilty to

manslaughter. She's not a murderer, she's not well. She doesn't remember these episodes. To this day she denies what she did to Gary Webber.'

The wind was moving the ivy on the facade, the red and yellow leaves trembling, the wall seemed to be alive.

'I'll pass that on,' I said. 'My understanding is that she won't. I'd like to talk to Sophie. It's important.'

'I'll tell her. She's gone off somewhere.'

'Thank you for showing me the building,' I said.

Longmore nodded. 'Anything to tell me, Greer's got the number. No, you've got it, you rang. Or come out, I'm always here, pretty much. Redundant now.'

'The stonemason,' I said. 'J. I. Irish. That's my grandfather.'

As I said it, I felt that I should not have completed the circuit to join us across the years.

'Yes,' he said, not looking at me, no expression in his voice, 'I knew that when I saw you.'

'Well, goodbye,' I said. We shook hands.

I was walking away when he said, 'What school'd you go to, Jack?'

I turned, reluctant. 'Melbourne Grammar,' I said, resenting having to say it.

He was looking at the bowl of his pipe, raised his arm and wrist-flicked. A yellow stream of tobacco juice caught the light as it laid a stripe in front of the prone spaniel's nose.

'Happy there?'

'No,' I said. 'I don't blame the school for that.'

'Loathed it, myself,' said Longmore. 'Still, funny old world. Not as random as it seems, eh?'

I nodded, carried on down the path and I felt his eyes on me even after I'd turned the corner.

Steven Massiani was thin, ascetic-looking, premature lines bracketing his mouth, seated behind an almost bare desktop in a corner office on the sixteenth floor of the old Isaacs Building. He was on the telephone and he waved me to sit with a hand that would be of little use on a MassiBild building site.

It was a big room, big windows on two walls, panelled in wood painted a warm mustard colour. On the back wall were photographs of sod-turnings, deep pits, concrete pours, groups of men in hardhats celebrating tree-raisings on tower buildings. The right-hand wall held family photographs: weddings, a degree ceremony, parties, many photographs of a big, dark man with two boys, toddlers in some pictures, getting bigger. I could identify Steven Massiani, the smaller of the boys, always a serious face. His brother, David, was plump to begin with, a big open face. In the later pictures, he was his father's height, the same jaw, the same eyes, the same stance.

Massiani said goodbye and put down the phone. 'Mr Irish.'

We shook. 'Thank you for seeing me,' I said.

He opened his hands, made a small movement of his head, gestures that said: it costs me nothing to see you.

'I like your office,' I said.

'It was my father's,' said Massiani. 'I haven't changed anything.' He had a soft voice, a priest's voice, a voice for the confessional. 'It'll always be his office, I'm afraid.'

'I thought you'd be in one of the towers,' I said. 'High up.'

He shook his head. 'This is the first building Dad owned. Bought in 1959. People always expected him to knock it down but he loved this building. All he did was fix it up and put in a new lift, that was just before he died. He liked fast lifts. It's much too fast for the height.'

'He didn't change the name,' I said. 'Call it the Massiani Building.'

'It's the Isaacs Building while we own it. My dad said people who changed the names of buildings would also desecrate tombstones.'

'Is there a Massiani Building?'

He smiled. 'He didn't like memorials. You wanted to talk about Mickey. We had very little to do with him after he left us.'

'I'm just scratching around,' I said. 'Our problem is that Andrew Greer's client didn't kill Mickey, so we are forced to ask who did.'

'Of course, that's your job. He worked for the company for five or six years, we gave him opportunities. Then he left to follow his own course. My father encouraged him in that. Mickey wasn't a corporate person. Do you know what I mean?'

'I think I do.'

'Yes. We invested in his early projects as a sign of support for him. He had no standing in the financial community.'

Massiani steepled his hands, pale fingers, small nails, nibbled at.

'You have no investment in Seaton Square?'

'No. We've learned our lesson in the suburbs.'

'It seems to have been a disastrous exercise.'

He unsteepled, steepled again. 'Scaled down, less ambitious, it may still be viable. Mickey was always shooting for the moon.'

'Always?'

'Well, he was an ambitious person.'

'May I ask you a hypothetical question?'

A shake of the head. 'About Mickey's death, I'm not the person to ask, Mr Irish.'

'It's not about what you know,' I said. 'Before this, if someone suggested that Mickey was in danger, would you have guessed personal or business reasons?'

'An impossible question,' he said.

Behind his head, a helicopter appeared, a long way away, coming from the northwest, moving like a black insect crawling on dirty water. The windows were double-glazed, no sound reached us.

'I understand he was a close friend of your brother,' I said.

'Close?' A small frown. 'I don't know about close. They went to the races, the beach house, a drink after work, that kind of thing. It was before David was married.' He scratched a cheek. 'A long time ago.'

The small telephone on the desk buzzed. 'Excuse me,' he said. He picked it up. 'Yes.'

He swivelled his chair. I looked at him in profile, a neat face.

'Bruce,' he said. 'Thanks for calling. Yes. Sometime soon, can you do that? Monday would be excellent, fine. Yes, it is that matter. And there's another small thing. Good. Yes. Wait to hear from you. Thank you, Bruce, I appreciate this.'

He turned back to me.

'The impossible question,' I said. 'It would help our thinking.'

'This is a headkicking industry, Mr Irish,' he said, 'but I haven't heard of many developers murdered just for being developers. Is that an answer?'

'Thank you,' I said. 'What kind of work did Mickey do when he was with you?'

'Anything my father gave him to do. For a year or so. Then it was dealing with the contractors, mostly. That's more than a full-time job, it's actually more than a job, it's a preparation for hell. That can lead people into doing silly things.'

'Such as?'

He was looking at his fingernails. 'Well, I suppose you know this royal commission into the building industry has heard some allegations about cash payments, that sort of thing, that go back to Mickey's day.'

'Mickey was involved?'

'Involved? If he was involved, we were involved. And we weren't. No, I'm saying it's possible he knew more about what the contractors were doing than he ever told us. Told my dad, that is. I had nothing to do with Mickey, he didn't report to me.'

His phone rang. He said a few polite words, replaced the tiny handset.

'Anyway,' he said, 'I'm sorry Mickey's not available to tell the commission what he knew about those days. Needless to say, the contractors won't share that view.'

'The commission was going to call Mickey?'

A shrug. 'No idea. Probably not. I'm just saying that we'd have been happy to have Mickey alive to testify if required. Anyway, I'm not bagging Mickey. He could get things done. He was good with people then.'

'He lost that gift?'

'Some people are good intermediaries, good at negotiating on behalf of others. When they represent themselves, they're less good.'

'Have you heard anything about his behaviour in the weeks before his death?'

'Only that he'd been acting…erratically.'

'Why would that be?'

A shrug. 'The problems with the project, I suppose. Possibly added to by a bit of chemical dependence. That's what I heard.'

'Before he joined you, what did he do?'

A look of thought. 'I don't know. My father took him on, someone recommended him. He had part of an engineering degree, he dropped out of uni. Queensland. He came from Brisbane.'

'The crown's case is that Mickey owned the weapon that killed him,' I said. 'Does it surprise you that he would have a gun?'

Massiani waved a hand. 'People have guns,' he said. 'Some people feel a need to have something to protect themselves with.'

'Did he marry Corin Sleeman while he was working for MassiBild?'

'After he left.'

I had run out of questions. I got up. 'I'm grateful for your time.'

'I hope the Longmore woman gets off,' he said. 'If she didn't do it. One of Australia's finest families.'

An edge revealed, the micro-bevel on a blade.

Without consideration I said, 'Mickey's talent with people, that seems to have extended to his sex life.'

I thought I saw something in Massiani's eyes, as one registers the faintest cloud shadow on a bright day. He rose, shorter than I'd expected, and came around the desk.

'My father had a saying,' he said, 'to the effect that when it comes to men, some women have a connection missing between the head and the body.'

'That sounds like a piece of ancient wisdom,' I said. 'Where did the Massianis come from?'

He offered his thin, unworked hand. 'Corsica. We're wogs. You'll know the term.'

Steve Massiani opened the door for me. I said goodbye and walked down the corridor. The woman behind the desk said, Goodbye, Mr Irish. The lift slid me to the ground floor, a slick, silent, hurtling passage.

I put on my raincoat and went into Collins Street, thought about how to get to the office. I'd take a cab, this was business. But first, coffee. In a slanting rain, I walked down to Exhibition Street and along to Bourke and up to

Pellegrini's, where nothing changes and the staff appear to know several hundred people by name and preference.

'Hey, Jack, where you been?' said the man making coffee. 'Short, right? My mum saw Andrew on television. Tell him I want him when I murder this bastard here.'

'When you *kill* him,' I said. 'The jury will decide whether it's murder.'

I drank my coffee and thought about Mickey Franklin and the Massianis. Not much warmth there. Why then had they backed him when he started out as a developer? Was there a falling-out later? Business or personal? There was something personal if I read Steve correctly. Did it matter? All I was doing was trying to justify whatever horrendous daily rate Wootton was charging Drew for my services.

Wootton. The prelim scan in forty-eight. Whatever that was, he hadn't received it. I waved to the men behind the counter and left, caught a cab with a taciturn driver.

At the office, I rang the last number I had for D. J. Olivier in Sydney. He was capable of reaching the places Simone Bendsten couldn't reach. A voice said, 'You have called a number that is no longer connected.'

I sat in the chair and did some drowsing, looking at the ceiling. No cobwebs. In a room dusted once in six years? I got up and inspected the room. Nothing. Spiders hung out their nets in air currents, they fished where there was life, where the air moved, where there were living things. In this room, there were no flows, nothing could live here except me.

The phone rang. It was D. J.'s assistant with the ruling-class voice. I wished I could think of a way to get her to say *fuck*, she gave the word an extra vowel. She put me onto the man.

'Jack,' he said. 'Turning into a regular.'

'Given the last bill,' I said, 'you don't need many regulars to keep afloat.'

D. J. Olivier laughed, a man comfortable in the knowledge that he owned the only pub in town. 'The labourer is worthy of his hire,' he said. 'My late dad used to say that.'

'Your late dad and the late St Luke. I've got a name.'

'Spell.'

I gave him Mickey.

'And ramifications?'

'Ramify,' I said. 'Ramify to buggery.'

I shut up shop and walked around to Taub's Joinery, let myself in with my key and felt, as I had from the beginning, that this was my proper place of work.

Charlie was at one of the massive redgum benches, his back to me.

'So, Mr Busy,' he said, not looking around. He claimed that his hearing was bad. If this was true, another sense, unknown to medical science, had developed to compensate.

I walked across and stood beside him. 'Just mucking around?' I said. 'No work to do?'

He said nothing, chiselled with precision and economy, a thumb the size of a doorknob guiding the blade. I knew what he was doing. He was making dovetail blocks to attach the big desk's top to its frame.

'No one will see those, you know,' I said. 'And if they do, they won't understand. And if they do understand, they won't care.'

How best to attach tops to bottoms. The crude use screws. But wood moves—it shrinks as it dries, and it also moves with the humidity levels. The wider the surface, the bigger the movement. Something has to give. Since the screws won't, the tabletop cracks. Less crude woodworkers use metal fasteners that allow for movement. Not Charlie. Charlie scorned metal. He solved the problem in the most difficult way: dovetail-shaped pieces attached to the top slid into dovetail blocks on the rails.

Charlie pushed half-a-dozen blocks my way, a sweep of a hand. 'I can hear on the wireless nonsense,' he said. 'You want to be useful or talk rubbish?'

'Oh, all right,' I said. 'You should be a talkback host on the ABC, drawing things out of people, sympathetic.'

I went to the chisel cupboard and chose one. All the tools were sharp. In this workshop, following some ancient European work discipline, blades were sharpened after use, wiped with oil and put away. Those chisels prone to rust had their little oily socks to wear.

At the bench, I held a male piece against a block and marked the angles with a knife. 'A router,' I said. 'This is what routers were invented for. We're like printers rejecting the Linotype machine.'

Charlie finished a block, removed the dead cheroot from his mouth and blew down the precise channel in the wood. 'You can teach an idiot,' he said, 'but you cannot make him learn. Grosskopf said that.'

'And we're all indebted to him. On the money every time was Grosskopf. Didn't go to his head either. What's the bowls news? Still thrashing the pishers?'

'Four on the ladder,' said Charlie, holding up massive fingers. 'Good thing for them I don't start earlier. Before they were born. The fathers, some of them.'

We worked side by side, finished the blocks, testing the slide of each one, they couldn't be too tight. Then we set about fixing them to the short rails of the desk, gluing them into housings Charlie had chiselled out. After that we made buttons for the long rails.

When I looked up, the light was almost gone from the high and dusty northern windows. 'That's it,' I said. 'Beer time.'

We sharpened chisels, burnishing on leather strops. I swept, coaxed Charlie out of the front door, slightly easier this evening because there was nothing being glued, no clamps to fiddle with.

On the way to the Prince, walking down wet streets lined with Golfs and Civics, here and there a bump in the line made by a four-wheel-drive, Charlie said, 'They want me to give it up.'

'Give what up?'

He waved a hand. 'The work.'

The early autumn evening colder now, felt on the face. 'Who wants?'

'The family.'

We parted around a puddle, came back together, touched for an instant, my twenty-year-old raincoat from Henry Buck's brushing an overcoat that John Curtin might have worn.

'All of them?' I said.

Charlie had three children, all female, and six grand-children.

We turned the corner, the pub was in sight, a lick of light on the pavement, two people leaving, parting, heads together for a few seconds, more than just friends.

'Most,' Charlie said.

'And Gus?'

Gus was a grand-daughter, a trade union executive. Charlie thought she was the brains of the family, his true heir.

'No, not Gus.'

'I'm glad to hear that.' I was partial to Gus. 'So what do you tell them?'

Charlie looked at me. 'What do you think? I tell them, they find me not breathing, they can know I've given it up.'

'Sensible retirement plan,' I said, returning to breathing.

The pub was busy, Stan's scalp glistening. Charlie headed for the bowls cabal. The Youth Club was in its corner, animated, an argument in progress, situation normal. Wilbur Ong, sitting against the wall, saw me coming in the dim, freckled mirror that had seen my father and my grandfather coming.

'Jack,' said Wilbur, 'listen, they're offerin $3.25 on the Sainters tomorrow. These blokes don't want to be in it.'

'Is that so?' I said, trying to catch Stan's eye. 'Not a vote of no confidence in the team on the eve of the first game, is it?'

Norm O'Neill shook his head, raised his eyes to the ceiling, shifted his glasses with a thumb, adding another smudge. 'Sometimes I wonder,' he said.

We waited. Stan looked my way. I signalled a round.

'Some people,' said Norm, looking at Wilbur, 'you ask yourself how they get through the day, don't walk in front of a bloody tram, think the drain cleaner's the bicarb.'

'Sometimes you wonder why some people got a team at all,' said Wilbur.

'There's your team,' said Norm. 'You stand by em, thick and thin, team's like family, can't walk away from the family.

Course there's always the odd few mongrels in a family, more in some than others I can reliably say. Yes, indeed, lend em a quid, you can bloody write that off, then there's...'

'Goin somewhere?' said Wilbur. 'Or just rantin about the brother-in-law, what's his name? The fat one. Dropped off in Coles, lookin at the meat.'

Norm lowered his chin, looked at Wilbur, at me, at Eric Tanner. 'The point is,' he said, 'you don't go bettin on the buggers just cause they're your own buggers. You wait till they've got some form. Common bloody sense'll tell you that. Had any.'

Things went on like this for a good while, broadening to take in such issues as disloyal remarks allegedly made before a Fitzroy–Richmond game in 1973, the relative merits of Kevin Murray and Ragsy Goold as defenders, and the fact that Wilbur's nephew had once stood for the Melbourne Football Club committee.

Through the thicket of pub noise, I heard the dot-dot-dash hoots. I collected Charlie and we went into the vaporous night, mist around the streetlights.

Gus was double-parked in a new car, a smallish four-wheel-drive. When Charlie was in, I said, 'Paid for by the sweat of the workers, this stylish machine?'

She leaned forward to look at me, a face of planes and angles under a sharp haircut. 'Bestowed upon me by the oppressed in gratitude for my sleepless vigilance on their behalf,' she said.

'Need any help with a vigil,' I said, 'come around. My door is always unlocked.'

'I'd have thought all the sawing would have seen you nodding off by 9 pm,' she said.

'I can find strength when the need arises.'

'You'd be horrified if I took you up on that.'

'An assertion that should be tested,' I said.

'Enough talk,' said Charlie. 'Take me home, I'm hungry.'

We looked at each other for an instant longer than we ever had, his grand-daughter and I. Then they were off, turned the corner, huge indicator flashing.

Home in Linda's car, along slick streets, cushioned from cold and noise, thinking about her in London. I missed being with her, hearing her warm, quizzical, sceptical voice on the radio. I missed knowing that she might ring late at night to talk, might arrive on my doorstep at any time with a bottle of Bollinger and make unambiguous suggestions while I was opening it.

I parked under the first tree, leaves still holding, there was a pocket of warmth around the gardens in autumn, we had our own climate here. Home. Sit for a while in front of the old brick building, the streetlight catching drops rolling off the leaves, turning them to silver tears.

A car drew up beside me, only centimetres away. Its passenger window came down. A big pale face looked at me. I pressed the button and my window descended.

'Mr Irish.'

He was middle-aged, lined brow, moustache, probably grown in youth to look an age he had now long passed.

'The Red Shield Appeal night campaign,' I said. 'I never refuse the Salvos. I'll need a receipt for tax purposes.'

'Mickey Franklin,' he said.

'Yes?'

'I'll give you a name.'

'A name?'

110

'Janene Ballich.'

'How do you spell that?'

He spelled Ballich.

'Names are useful,' I said. 'Come in and see my collected phone books.'

He ran a lingering finger over his top lip. 'Jack,' he said, 'this is serious shit, mate. Goodnight.'

The car reversed and was gone in seconds.

I was in the bath on Sunday morning, drinking tea, soaking away the aches and pains that an afternoon at the football can cause, when the cordless phone rang.

'Youth Club survive the excitement?' said Linda.

'It was they who supported me from the arena,' I said. 'One under each arm, one prodding me from behind. How do you know anyway?'

'I am in the communication hub of the world,' she said. 'We know everything, even the results of football matches at the far end of one of our spokes. Lesser spokes.'

'You can't have lesser spokes. All spokes are equal.'

'Believe me, we have lesser spokes. And lesser spokes-people.'

'We is it? Five minutes and it's we. Attack dog to corgi. What took you so long to call?'

'Things to do,' said Linda. 'Settle into my Thames-side

apartment, stock up at Harrods, testdrive a few rentboys, that sort of thing. I've missed you a bit.'

'You too have been in my thoughts whenever I get behind the wheel of your car. Don't hurry back. How long is this nonsense going to last anyhow?'

I was turning the hot water tap with a big toe. It gushed.

'What's that sound?' said Linda.

'Just a friend in the shower. Came by needing a shower.'

'You bastard. Hold on a sec. Nigel, open another bottle, darling.'

'So. How long?'

'It's going well,' she said. 'As far as I can tell. Management's happy, they say they're happy. Full board of callers. Hard work though. Umpteen bloody papers to read, magazines, trying to crack the code. There's too much fucking nuance in this country, I can tell you.'

'The men like to be spanked, the women are happy to oblige. They both like uniforms. How hard can that be to grasp?'

Linda laughed. 'Maybe you could come over and produce me.'

'Come over and do something for you. I'm not too hot at production.'

We talked, the autumn sunlight moved across the room, it was almost midnight in London when we said goodbye. I dressed and made breakfast but even Angel Cardoso's sublime jambon from Geelong and thoughts of the Saints' seven-goal last quarter couldn't cancel the sense of loss. I walked to Gorb's and bought the papers, read them sitting on a bench in the park, starting with the sports section.

SAINTS OVERPOWER CARLTON. That made me feel better.

It was a beginning, a clean start to the season.

At home, a message from my sister on the machine. I rang.

'Jesus,' said Rosa. 'What's happening? Is this a time warp? The response time just shortened by twelve days.'

'We are constantly tuning our operating procedures,' I said.

I crossed the Yarra in Linda's Alfa and we ate in a place that was uncertain whether it wanted to be a restaurant or a house party that charged. Then we toured the art galleries of South Yarra, the soft-shirted owners treating Rosa the way casinos treat highrollers. In the last one, I left her talking to the smooth young art pimp and wandered around. The smallest chamber was given over to four large canvases dotted with crude animals and symbols that appeared to be lifted directly from the art of the Nupe in northern Nigeria.

Rosa and the gallerista came up behind me.

'Excellent investments,' said the man. 'I'm afraid Gary's got a terminal smack habit. This's the work of two years. Could be the last.'

I looked at a signature. Gary Webber. I thought of the walk at Macedon. Sir Colin had spat the name. People the Longmores touched didn't seem to lead lucky lives.

'Well,' said Cyril Wootton, 'that's not very good, is it? Have to do better than that, won't you? Clients on premium rates expect premium results, don't they?'

Replete after the long-awaited breakfast of soft-poached eggs with the lot at Enzio's, I was sitting in a client's chair in Wootton's office, a chamber appointed like the Writing Room on the first-class deck of a P & O liner. Cyril was behind his large desk, small, plump hands folded on the leather inlay, his head cocked, very much the bank manager with a defaulting borrower, say, a farmer whose livestock, crops and homestead had been destroyed by a freak hailstorm.

'Cyril,' I said, 'I suggest you go easy on the terminal interrogative phrases.'

'What?' he said, coming upright in his chair, alarm in his eyes, eyebrows risen. 'What's that mean?'

'Interrogatives again,' I said. 'To business. The person's

phone calls for a month or so.'

Wootton sat back, adjusted his tie, smoothed his oiled hair, sniffed. 'Sometimes,' he said, 'I think you forget who is employer and whom is employed.'

'Always uppermost in my mind, Cyril,' I said. 'That and grammar.'

'It'll take a day or two,' he said. 'It's become more diffi-cult. Apparently every Tom, Dick and Harry wants this sensitive information now.'

'It is annoying when the agencies of law enforcement jump the queue,' I said. 'Speaking of which, is that records clerk dog of yours still in place?'

Wootton had suborned a civilian in the police force, a grudge-bearer of some kind, the public service was full of them—evolutionary losers in the Darwinian in-fights, politi-cal suck-ups beached a mile inland by the tsunamis of change in government, ordinary incompetents embittered by being ignored for promotion. These people needed little encouragement to defame their superiors. A few long lunches, a day at the races, dinner with a prepaid harlot or two, and they were groomed and ready for service.

'I assume so,' said Wootton.

I reached across for one of his pads and wrote the name Janene Ballich.

Cyril put on his new glasses, round and gold-rimmed. 'What's this?' he said.

'Some connection with the deceased. She may be in the jacks' database.'

Cyril gave me his banker's look again. 'One conserves one's resources for the truly important,' he said. 'One begins with the newspaper files.'

I'd had enough prudent bank manager. 'Really? One could also easily find oneself bereft of one's only employee remotely capable of dealing with one's titled clientele. With me, sunshine?'

'I'll make the request,' he said, not happy.

'An answer today would be nice.'

'That is not within my control.'

'Pull on the chokechain,' I said. 'What's the point of having dogs if you can't command them?'

A knock on the door.

'Enter,' said Cyril.

I turned. It was Mrs Davenport, Wootton's receptionist. In the innocent pre-AIDS days, she had been the front-of-house person for a specialist in social complaints who ministered to the big end of town. It was perfect training for her job with Cyril. Through his parlour too passed people burdened with painful and embarrassing afflictions which they did not wish to become common knowledge. Mrs Davenport treated these clients as she had her earlier ones—with an air of frigid disdain.

'Your next appointee will be here in fifteen minutes, Mr Wootton,' she said. 'As you know, the person does not wish to be kept waiting.'

'Thank you,' said Wootton.

She withdrew.

'If I get anything, I'll send it around,' said Wootton. 'To which of the places you flit among?'

'Between, Cyril. I flit between. It's thieves I'm among.'

His eyebrows rose again.

'Charlie's,' I said. 'Put it in the box at Charlie's.'

In the reception room, I said goodbye to Mrs Davenport.

'I can't promise when I'll be back,' I said. 'Can you endure that uncertainty?'

She gazed at me, unblinking, no emotion disturbing her white marble countenance. I longed to reach out and touch her hair, disturb its frozen waves like an icebreaker piercing the Arctic sea.

'In future, please ring before seeking to see Mr Wootton,' she said.

'But it's really you, you, you I want to see.'

'Good-day, Mr Irish.'

At the door, I turned and said, 'Mrs Davenport, have you any idea of the effect your icy demeanour has on men?'

She didn't look at me. 'I understand there are telephone counselling services for those unable to seek professional help in the normal way,' she said. 'Good-day again.'

'God,' I said, 'you just keep tightening the screw, don't you?'

I went down to the street with birdsong in my heart.

'In your hands, Mr Irish,' he said, a plump face under slick hair, a brisk voice. I knew him, he'd delivered before.

I said thank you. There was no signing for envelopes from D. J. Olivier. I went back to my table and opened this one with a sharpened bicycle spoke I'd found in the alley and sterilised. A wad of A4 sheets of paper, some photographs, laser-printed. A sticky yellow square was attached to the first page. One handwritten sentence: 'Care might be in order.'

A stranger to care, I returned to my chair behind the tailor's table. I read:

MICHAEL RAIMOND FRANKLIN

Born 1962, Brisbane. Father Gianfranco Francesca, labourer, mother Alessandra Francesca, nee Cometti, household duties. Only child. St Patrick's

College, graduated 1979. Engineering University of Queensland 1980–81. First-class honours, passes all subjects.

Passport information: First use, 1982. Stamps, in sequence, for United Kingdom, France, Spain, Italy, France, Italy, Switzerland, Austria, Switzerland, Italy, France, United Kingdom, Australia, September 1986.

Registered as employee of Casterton Construction, Brisbane [see below for Casterton] in December 1986. Position: supervisor.

I skimmed pages about apartment rentals, two property purchases, car leases, a boat purchase, air travel, hotel and restaurant bills, traffic fines.

Employed by MassiBild, Melbourne, 1989–1995. Occupation given as 'executive'.

Tax details followed. Mickey had done well in Brisbane; Melbourne was also good to him. D. J. Olivier had seen the tax returns Alexander Marti Partners of Brisbane filed for Mickey.

Married Corin Grace Sleeman 1996. Sleeman is an architect whose firm, French, Marconi & Kinane, has worked on many MassiBild projects. She was photographed with Steven Massiani at the Melbourne Cup in 1995.

Director Yardlive Pty Ltd, registered 1992. Other director is Bernard Karl Paech [see below]. Six properties registered in company name. Yardlive, trading as Joinville Developments, has put up two medium-size apartment blocks, one built by MassiBild, and been engaged in a number of inner-city redevelopment projects.

Credit card and customs information followed, six pages. I was too weak to read it.

> Nothing else known. Subject mentioned in document leaked to *Sydney Morning Herald* in July 1999 but not published. Source unknown, possibly National Crime Authority. (Part of document attached.) The document refers to Casterton Construction as a company with links to Anthony Kendall Haig and gives details about Haig.

RELEVANT PART OF LEAKED DOCUMENT

Anthony Kendall Haig. Born 1952, Sydney. Mother Felicity Lorraine Kendall Haig, no father recorded. Haig has married twice. Divorced Catherine Jean Kelly, 1989, son by her lives in US. Seeks company of much younger women.

First income tax paid in 1985–86, occupation given as 'investor'. Gross income $78,472, taxable $32,863. Return filed by Alexander Marti Partners, Brisbane, filed all subsequent returns. [For Marti, see AI/674/87 continuing.] Huge income growth since, presented as commissions and trading in commercial and residential property. For 2000, gross of Saint Charles Holdings was $17,783,000.

Audited by Tax in 1996, 1998. No action. File note 1998 says: 'Transactions continue to be complex in the extreme and, as repeatedly noted, worthy of full-scale investigation.' (This officer, shifted from Audit in August 1998, will not co-operate.)

Subject's company Saint Charles involved in hundreds of property dealings, usually arranger of loan finance but often buyer and seller. Deals with dozens of developers, construction companies and private companies all over country. Finance generally offshore. Frequent provider is First Crusader Finance, Monaco. This entity run by Charles Robert Hartfield, once partner in Melbourne solicitors Alan Duchard, Gaitelband, legal advisor to property developer Tendram, part owned by Hartfield's wife's cousin, Selwyn Howard Cornell. Tendram into receivership in 1990, debts of $260 million. Estimate is upwards $30 million sent offshore in 18 months before collapse. Hartfield now has Polish passport, resident of Monaco. [Wife, now of Noosa, is attempting to sue Hartfield.] Haig is close to Hartfield and spends time in Monaco. [See Attachment 3B.]

Subject's connections make action difficult. He is a donor to both parties through Saint Charles. Large circle of associates includes former federal cabinet minister Michael Londregan, now in business as investment advisor in Sydney.

Two investigations discontinued under pressure. February 1995, death of employee James Gavin Medlicott, 36, found to be suicide. Medlicott twice arrested for sex offences, charges dropped. Present offsider Bernard Karl Paech, 44, accountant, worked for Massiani family company MassiBild 1991–97. [For Paech, see AI/ 857/86/89/94-98 continuing. For Massianis see AI/992/83-4/92-6 continuing.]

Massibild and associated companies involved in many deals with Saint Charles. Paech operates from office in Little Collins Street, Melbourne. Michael Raimond Franklin, mentioned earlier, worked for

Casterton Construction of Brisbane (a company with links to Haig and Paech) from 1986 before moving to Massibild in Melbourne in 1989. Informant W3 identifies Franklin as key player until he left Massiani in 1995 to start property development firm Joinville Development. Paech was for a time co-director of the parent company, Yardlive. [See Attachment 3A.]

That was the end of the fragment. The report said more would follow. I looked at the photographs. Two men on a city street, the blurred foreground suggesting that the photographer was across the road. 3A was written in a corner. The taller man was Mickey Franklin looking sideways at his companion, questioning, two fingers holding his dark glasses up on his forehead.

The other man was broad, pudgy, balding, round glasses, scratching his head. Was this Bernie Paech?

The second photograph, labelled 3B, showed the deck of what was probably a big motor yacht seen through a thicket of masts and rigging. A man in a T-shirt was talking to a young woman in a bikini, a girl with short wet-looking blonde hair. Anthony Haig?

Seeks company of much younger women.

When did he start doing that? How old did you have to be to be accused of this offence?

Another woman had her naked back to the camera. To her right, a fat man with a shaven head, dark glasses, was looking into the camera, pointing. He had a cigarette in his mouth.

This would then be Charles Hartfield, solicitor, once of Melbourne, now of Monaco. He didn't look too happy at the instant of being snapped but he would probably look content on other occasions. But perhaps not. Pinching $30 million, dumping the wife and kids, becoming a Pole, that could carry a price. In the long run, it might have been easier to do honest work in William Street, drive home to Kew or Glen Iris in the BMW, go to the place at the beach in the Merc wagon on weekends.

I looked at the first photograph again, Mickey Franklin and Bernie Paech in the street. Now I saw that Bernie wasn't scratching his head, he was on the phone. Mickey was wearing a well-cut piece of cloth—it lay on him like oil on a dead penguin.

Too late to ease my way out of this? It was a job for a team and a team might not get anywhere either. Mickey had no doubt done naughty things, that was the norm in his line of work. But you didn't get knocked for it. Apart from which, he'd been on his own for years, a corner-shop operator, no threat to the Massianis or any other giant. Sarah Longmore might or might not have killed Mickey but I was highly unlikely to find any other firm suspects.

An involuntary groan, a sound born of impotence and anxiety. It was followed by thoughts of coffee. I set out for Brunswick Street. The street was abuzz, teeming with people talking on their mobiles about their fantastic new jobs/projects/relationships. Until recently, I would have had a quick browse in the bookshop where the gun shop used to be, but it too was gone. A business called Twicks in its place, and, in due course, Twicks, a purveyor of tastefully arranged homewares made by slave labour somewhere, would be another stratum in the ghostly midden of departed businesses.

Enzio's was having a successful opening day. It too was trilling with mobiles and alive with the sound of happy banter. I found a seat against the wall for the second time that day and spotted a few Meaker's regulars who'd transferred: the pharmacist who'd quit pill-dispensing to write terrible plays; the publisher with the drinking problem who'd once stuck her tongue into the tight cleavage of a cabinet minister's wife at a book launch; the haggard maker of documentary films known to have tried to fake his own kidnapping to extort money from his rich father.

I thought about Mickey Franklin. He was starting to look like someone with a fair bit of unexposed form. A key player, said the document leaked from somewhere, no doubt a government agency. Player in what?

Olivier's fragment didn't have the sound of yet another investigation into rigged tenders, union pay-offs, cash and kind bribes, safety trade-offs, sweeteners for inspectors, over-invoicing, under-invoicing, insurance rip-offs, off-site beatings, severe discomfort caused by poisoned fast food, tragic accidents in freeway traffic put down to the inexplicable failure of vital bits of brakes and steerings. It had the ring of crime intelligence-gathering, the sort of stuff passed around meetings in Canberra.

This stuff wasn't going to help me. I had a name, that was the way to go. My coffee arrived. The taste of it improved my mood greatly.

After lunch, I went around to Charlie's and spent the afternoon assembling drawers, each one subjected to rigorous quality inspection.

'I can do this, you know,' I said after a while. 'It doesn't require a twelve-year apprenticeship under a sadistic *Tischlermeister*.'

'Just looking,' said Charlie.

Wootton rang while we were cleaning up. 'That name,' he said. 'I've tracked down the mother.'

Into Tingaboora under steady rain, just before 11 am, passing rotting wooden houses, listing hay shelters, paddocks growing crops of old car bodies and their innards—seats, engine blocks, gearboxes, radiators, drive shafts, axles. Erosion rivulets ran down the slopes, fence pickets hung in space over gullies, and, on the flatter bits of ground, a few sheep stood, sad prisoners in their massive growths of dirty wool.

There were four streets in the town, two running parallel each way, a noughts and crosses grid. I drove up and down them, all gravel except for the main one, looking for the name and number. The two running east–west turned to mud beyond the last unstable broken-guttered weatherboard houses. A hundred metres away, across a bumpy moss-green floodplain strewn with rubbish and engraved with the deep doughnuts made by drunken hoons, a line of willows marked a creek. Two cows were tethered at the end of one street, heads together. They looked at me, gentle eyes, creatures spared the pain of wanting something else. At the end of the other street, a goat was chewing a beer carton, absorbed in the task.

No street names, no numbers I could see. I gave up and parked the Stud in the main street, a few doors down from the pub, the Balmoral, beyond the hairdressing salon and the milkbar.

I sat, tired, the back, in the neck, not keen to do anything, easy to rest my head against the door jamb, have a little sleep. A car, a swish. Minutes passed. I sat up, wiped the windscreen. A man wearing a Collingwood beanie on top of a pulled-down balaclava was approaching. Sinister, helmeted, an impoverished knight reduced to pushing a bicycle with a flat back tyre. The eyes in their apertures looked at me, the man veered from his path to get a closer look. Our eyes met. He looked away, looked again, moved along, looked back, stopped. I thought he was going to come back, knock on the window, ask me a question. He wouldn't want anything, people didn't beg in these towns. But he didn't. He made a head and shoulder movement suggesting some inner shiver. Then two women came out of the pub, perhaps mother and daughter, both grown up too quickly, both in lurid pink tracksuits. The younger one was carrying a child on her hip, her arm hooked around its midriff. It screamed, drummed heels. She stuck her cigarette in her mouth, smacked the child's face with a fluid forehand, said something to her companion, a slew of words.

I waited until they passed before getting out. It was a raw day, icy air smelling of wood fires and damp and turned earth. In the Balmoral bar, a sad place of fake wood, formica, split plastic seats extruding yellow foam, the smell was of fried onions, cigarette smoke and something chemical, carpet cleaner perhaps, sickly. There were five customers, an old woman at a table by herself, two wizened men at the bar, a man and a woman playing pool. She was shooting, leaning over the table and showing a roll of naked fat the colour of porridge above huge buttocks sausaged inside stretch pants.

I went to the bar. The barman was side-on to me, head tilted, listening to a small radio on the bottle shelf. I looked at my watch: the first race at Moe, first of four maidens, all hope and no pedigree. I didn't bother him, turned my back and looked around, stopped short of the buttocks and came back along the photographs on the wall. Football teams.

'Fuckin nag,' said the barman.

The race was over. He had the long, choleric, dog-jowled face of an eighteenth-century hanging judge, all he needed was the horsehair wig to cover his moulted scalp.

'Good-day,' I said. 'I'm having trouble finding street signs.'

'Yeah?' Eyes just red slits, weeping.

'I'm looking for Eales Street.'

'Yeah? Drinkin?'

'No thanks. Just looking for help.'

'Not the fuckin tourist bureau here, mate. Fuckin pub.'

He went off down the counter, turned right through a doorway. He had a limp.

'Eales,' said the nearest of the wizened men. 'Say Eales?'

'Yes. Eales.'

He gave me a good examination. 'Bank,' he said. He looked vaguely fishy, head rising to a point, no dip between forehead and broad nose, mouth lipless.

I registered. 'No. It's a family matter. No trouble involved.'

The man beyond him was leaning forward to look at me, alert eyes in a face like a thrashed golf ball. 'Ballick, right?' he said.

'Right. Mrs Ballich.' I said the name as he had.

The men looked at each other, nodded, pleased.

'How did you know?' I said.

They turned to me, Fish and Golfball.

'The girls, not so?' said Fish.

'Janene,' I said.

Golfball made a whistling sound. 'Janene,' he said. 'She come in here one day, back from Melbin with this other sheila, this bloke, flash car. Big bloke, mind you. Like that Rocca.'

'Soft,' said Fish. 'Soft. Wog. Had the wog look. Pissweak wogs. Wogs and Abos. No guts.'

'Well, the wogs run, din they?' said Golfball, eyes on me, waiting. 'In the war.'

'That's possible,' I said.

'Like dogs,' said Fish. 'Bloody pathetic. Our fellas coulda shot em up the arseholes. Showed mercy they did. Up the arseholes, crawlin. Like dogs.'

'So,' I said, 'Eales Street. Which one is that?'

Golfball waved to his left. 'Last one,' he said. 'Last on the right. The young bitch gone off too now. Darwin, they say.'

'Bloody good riddance,' said Fish. 'She's a lowie, deadset. Pulled fellas like a bitch on heat, they come from bloody miles around, lizards damn near pokin out.'

'All Abos and chinks,' said Golfball. 'Darwin. Me Uncle Ross was up there once. White man's grave he used to say.'

'Piss artist, your Uncle Ross,' said Fish. 'Still, hadda beat his liver to death with a stick.' He eyed me. 'Door open and engine goin, mate. Mary Ballick's run outta roots in this town. She'd be hungry.'

The barman appeared, he'd had another drink in the back. 'Still here?' he said. 'Still not fuckin drinkin?'

I took out a fifty-dollar note and put it on the counter. 'These helpful gentlemen are a credit to your lovely town,' I said.

He looked at the money, frowned.

I beckoned. He hesitated, came closer. I looked into his eyes of red. 'Give them whatever they're drinking, judge,' I said. 'And don't keep the change. Clear to you?'

'Okay,' he said. 'Okay.'

It took me two minutes to get to Mary Ballich's house, a weatherboard standing behind a wire fence on a bare block, nothing growing except couch grass and weeds and moss and fuzzy grey mould on hundreds of dog turds. The house's white paint was almost gone, the naked wood turned grey. Smoke lisped from a brick chimney that had lost most of its mortar and would fall down in a high wind one day soon, some soot-blackened bricks would go through the rusted corrugated iron, through the lath and plaster ceiling.

An old orange Corolla with a savage list to starboard stood in front of a fibreboard garage it had never called home.

I parked outside the front gate, half open, leaning, its hinge post broken at the base, and got out.

The rain had stopped but the wind had picked up, coming over the featureless green undulations with a whooing sound that acted on the brain the way organ dirges did. I went up the cracked concrete, stepped up to the verandah, avoiding a collapsed plank. The verandah felt unsteady, nails loose in rain-eroded boards. I stood before a screen door with holes in the flywire of the upper panels. They had the look of holes punched—drink and testosterone holes. I opened the door and the dents in the front door said mine was not an unreasonable assumption.

I could hear the television inside. I knocked, knocked again, less politely. After a while, I hit the door a few times with four knuckles and waited. It opened.

'Yeah?' A woman, short, plump, face pink with new make-up.

'Mrs Ballich?'

'Yeah?'

'Jack Irish. I spoke to you…'

'Oh yeah,' she said. 'Didn't think you'd be early.'

In the passage, we shook hands. She was in the last phase of pretty, doll-like, a small nose, rosebud lips.

'Pleased to meet you,' she said, smoke and alcohol and mint toothpaste on her breath. 'Back room's warm, almost bloody warm, this fucking place.'

I followed her, walking on nylon carpet, feeling the sag of the floorboards. Down there in the underfloor, the stumps would be rotten, the air would smell of decaying wood, damp earth, of fluids leached through carpet and underfelt, there would be chewed bones and the skeletons of small creatures. It would be icy cold, cold a hundred sunless years in the making.

The back room had been two rooms once, the kitchen and something else, floors not level. Knocking out a wall left gaps, patched with whatever came to hand. A fire was

133

burning in the kitchen hearth, logs smouldering, more smoke than heat. The curtains were drawn, two overhead lights on, one a pink plastic chandelier.

'Whole fucking day to warm up,' said Mary Ballich. She picked up a remote control from a chair, pressed several buttons before the television died. 'Fire goes out, place's a fucking freezer inside ten minutes. Start again next day. Sit down, have a seat.'

I had the choice of a squat leather chair, its arms folded and held down with buckles, and an old office chair. I sat on the office chair. Mary went to a counter, a two-litre cask of wine on it, wet circle on the carpet below the nozzle. She showed me a glass, half full, yellow liquid in a Vegemite container given a second life.

'Little heartstarter,' she said. 'Shit, I slept so fucking bad, I can't tell you. Take a wine?'

'A small one,' I said. 'Thank you.'

She found another Vegemite glass for me, filled it from the tap. I got up to take it from her.

'Cheers,' she said and went back to get hers, lit a cigarette, offered me the pack. I shook my head. She sat down on the yellow leather couch. It sighed.

'A lawyer,' she said. 'Didn't get the other bit.'

'I'm acting for someone in a criminal matter. Janene's name came up as a possible witness. I found out she was a missing person, so I rang all the Ballichs in the book.'

'Witness?'

'She might know something that would help our client.'

'Can't help if she's missin, can she?'

'No. But we might be able to help look for her. That would be up to you.'

'Well, the cops done fuck-all. Not interested, don't give a shit.'

'You reported her missing in January 1995,' I said. 'That's a long time ago.'

'Yeah. Look around, another bloody year's gone.'

'How did you know she was missing?'

'Didn't answer the phone. Got a bit toey. Then I get a call from the real estate agency, they reckon she's done a runner, left all her stuff behind.'

I tried the wine, wet my lips with it. Sweet, a strong smell of acetone. 'Runner from what?'

'This unit in St Kilda. We went up to Melbin, got the stuff.'

'Janene was in touch regularly?'

'Well, nah. I used to ring her. Sometimes ya need a talk.' She inhaled deeply, blew smoke out of the corner of her small mouth. 'Sometimes ya need a few bucks too. What's the good of bloody kids they can't help ya out, that's what I say. Things I bloody went through for em, you don't want to know. Don't want to know.'

'Janene had a job?'

'Model,' she said. 'She was a model.' She drank half her glass of sweet yellow wine. 'There's a photo over there.' She pointed.

I crossed to the back wall, to two photographs hanging between the curtains.

'Top one,' said Mary. 'That's her. Other one's Marie, my little one.'

They were both studio portraits, full length. I could see nothing of Mary Ballich in either of them. At about eighteen, Janene Ballich had a waif look, long fair hair, big eyes, long legs made longer in a little black dress by the photographer's upward angle. Her sister was about fifteen when the picture was taken, dark, big-mouthed, a look in her eyes that said she would only be a certain kind of teacher's pet.

I went back to my chair. 'Tough business, modelling,' I said, looking at Mary.

She looked back, pulled a face. Deep lines appeared between her eyes. 'Yeah, well, she done a bit of escort on the side. Like between modellin jobs, y'know.' She finished her wine and got up for more. 'How's ya glass?'

'Fine, thanks.'

She filled hers to the brim, spilled a little on the carpet, drank some before journeying back to the sighing couch.

'So, did she have an agency for bookings?' I said.

'Nah, Wayne done that. He was like her agent.'

'Wayne?'

'Wayne Dilthey. He come here with her once. Stuck on her, I reckon, the cuntstruck look, pardon me. They come in his Porsche. Grey one. Whole fucking street come out.'

I took out my notebook and guessed at the spelling, there wasn't any point in asking. 'Any idea of when you last spoke to Janene?'

Mary had a sip, blinked at me. Now I noticed the marks on either side of her nose. She was short-sighted and she didn't want to be seen in glasses. 'November,' she said. 'My birthday's the twelfth of November. I was really pissed off, no fucking prezzie, not even a call. I give her a ring, get the message fucking thing. Next morning she rings, all sorry, sorry, sorry. Some crap about her friend in hospital, always a bullshit story to give you, Jan. From when she was little. Jay Bailey, she used to call herself. Didn't like her name.'

'November 13, 1994, that's the last time she was on the phone?'

'To me. The other time, I was at the pub with my fren. The bloke livin here, he was here, pissed half off his brain as per usual, she give him a message.'

'Saying what?'

'Fuck knows,' she said. 'The turkey tole me the next day, he can't remember nothin. Reckons she was upset, that's all, the fucking spagbrain.'

The smoke was getting to my throat. I had some wine— alcohol, sugar, acetone—the stuff could knock out any complaint. 'Any idea when that was?'

'Yeah. December 4.'

My throat felt better. The stomach would be the next problem. 'You remember that?'

'Nah. The cop said.'

'What cop was that?'

'Cop come here. He had the calls she made.'

'That was after you reported Janene missing?'

She was lighting another cigarette. 'Nah. Just before Christmas. Didn't know she was missin then, thought she was just bein her usual mongrel. He come about her mobile, reckoned someone pinched it, he was checkin the calls.'

Her glass was empty. She showed it to me, I shook my head. She got a refill, spilled more from the tap this time, spilled some on her front when she sat down. It was going to be a short day indoors. Short out and much shorter in.

'Married?' she said.

'I've been married.'

'Kids?'

'One.'

137

She looked at me, nodding.

'Give you his name, the cop?' I said.

She frowned, waved her cigarette. 'Well, it's gone. Ugly bloke, tell you that, the dark glasses, these big bumps over his eyes. How's ya drink?'

I finished my glass. 'Driving,' I said. 'Can't take a chance.'

She gave me a good stare, blinking, pulled at her top between the breasts with her cigarette hand, pulled it away from her body. 'Could stay over,' she said. 'Get an early start in the mornin.'

'That's tempting,' I said. 'Would you have a picture of Janene I could borrow? I'll copy it, send it back.'

'Got a photo of Jan and Wayne and the other little bitch,' she said. 'The time they come here. In the Porsche.'

She got up and left the room, not unsteady in her walk on the long legs she'd passed on to Janene. She was back in seconds, stood beside me, touched my arm with a hip, held the photograph for me to see, bent over, head close to mine, leaning on me.

'Lovely girl,' she said.

Janene was thinner in this picture, even more like a starveling now, but she looked groomed, expensive short haircut, well-cut pants, a silver bracelet wristwatch. She also had bigger breasts, hard-looking, pushing against a tight shirt. She was posing against a grey car. Beside her, an arm draped over her, was a big man, bony face, short dark hair, black glasses, a bodybuilder. He had two rings on the visible hand: pinky and index fingers, one ring bigger than the other. His other arm was around a small, dark young woman, also well dressed, scarf, dark aviator glasses. She could have been a rich Year 12 student at the polo.

'The other one's Katelyn Feehan,' said Mary, unasked. 'Up herself little bitch.'

'Also a model?'

'Yeah, that kinda thing.'

I stood. It was not easy, I feared that I would unbalance Mary Ballich, dislodge her. But she was not without experience in remaining on her feet.

'I'd like to copy this picture,' I said.

'Got the neg,' she said. 'Give you that.'

'No,' I said. 'You should keep the neg, that's precious. I'll take this one and I'll pay for you to get copies made for yourself.'

'Yeah, okay,' she said, had some wine. 'Jack's a nice name. Sure you're a lawyer? More like a human.'

I got out my wallet, put two fifties on the table. Mary picked them up.

'Settle down, mate,' she said. 'Only a photo.' She offered them back to me.

'It's also for your time,' I said. 'In my business, you charge for your time and you pay for other people's time.'

'Bit like escortin then,' she said and she smiled, the small mouth, it had its own erotic charm. I realised I had not seen her teeth.

'I'll probably have to call you again,' I said. 'Ask more questions.'

'You can call any time,' she said. 'Jack.'

At the front door, I said thank you and put out a hand.

She took it, raised it and gently bit the flesh behind the thumb. 'Any time,' she said.

'Dilthey,' said Cameron Delray. 'Never heard of him. Where are you?'

'Drouin,' I said.

'That voluntary?'

'A tidy town. I'm passing through.'

'Give me a bit.'

I was approaching Dandenong before he rang back. I pulled over, watching a storm sky building over Melbourne, coming from the west, blue-black rolling clouds.

'Got him,' he said. 'Want to do something today?'

'Might as well.'

'King Street. It's called the Officers' Club.'

I groaned.

'You'll fit in with the public-service crowd. Crack a fat on the way to the station, twenty bucks. Juices em up for the wife in Camberwell, they come in holdin the briefcase in front.'

'What those women have to endure. After a long day driving the kids. Where in King Street?'

He told me how to find the place.

'Tell em Mr Costello's expectin you. Popeye. He's a nice bloke, could've been a judge, just got off on the wrong foot.'

'And who am I?'

'Say Cam rang.'

In the city, the storm broke as I was leaving the parking garage in Little Collins. I retreated and watched the deluge. It lightened after a few minutes and I set off. In time for the sleet and then the hailstones, small marbles skittering in the street, bouncing off the cars, just too small to dent.

The man ahead of me at the Officers' Club counter was wearing a fawn raincoat and carrying an umbrella and a briefcase. He put his change in a side pocket, didn't bother about his wallet.

'Mr Costello's expecting me,' I said to the receptionist.

She might have been Mr Costello's mother, still helping at the school canteen after all these years. The man leaning against the wall could have been the school bully, still waiting to take half or more of whatever you bought.

'And it's who?' said Popeye Costello's mum, friendly.

'The person Cam rang about,' I said.

She picked up a telephone, pressed a button. 'The person Cam rang about,' she said. 'Yes, right.'

'He's got someone with him,' she said. 'Through the portrait room and into the club room. You'll see a door in the right corner, it's got two green lights over it. Have a seat outside. Michael won't keep you waiting.'

I passed through the portrait room, a characterful chamber, panelled, lit by brass picture lights above paintings of several centuries of British soldiers, mostly in dress uniform. The frames were gilt, broad, carved. Everything was fake.

The club room was large, dim, a bar on the left, not busy. The officers, not many of them, were standing around two small podiums upon which women were performing. The women were fully dressed and their behaviour suggested that they were uncomfortable in their garments. There was tugging, rubbing and long-nailed groin-scratching of a languorous heat-affected kind.

The officers, all in civilian dress, were offering helpful suggestions.

'Show us yer pussy,' said one.

The woman pulled up her skirt. Beneath it she was naked and shaven. The officers made approving noises.

As I crossed the room, I had a view through a door into a corridor lined with booths curtained with semi-transparent material. A young man came out of one, followed by a big-breasted pale woman in a bikini and high heels. She was adjusting the top. The man looked as a first-time parachutist might upon landing.

I took a seat on a slippery banquette in the corner. The door with the green lights opened and a long-haired man in a leather jacket came out. His face was mostly nose, spread over it like a frog.

'He's only fucking human, Pop,' he said over his shoulder.

The man in the fine-striped shirt and stockbroker braces behind him said, 'Nobody's proved that to my fucking satisfaction. Just do it.' He came into the doorway. 'Cam's mate? Come in.'

He waited for me to go in and closed the door, went

around a glass-topped table covered in papers, some in piles clamped by bulldog clips. Two three-drawer filing cabinets stood together against a wall with four small security monitors on them. That was it for furnishings.

'So what's your name?' he said.

'Jack Irish. I'm a solicitor.'

Popeye Costello had a round face and round glasses and a big grey-flecked moustache. He scratched it, scratched his bald head. 'You the one knocked that fucking Marty Scullin?'

'Yes.'

'Goodonya. The cunt. You could've sold tickets, got a full fucking house at the MCG. What can I tell you about the Dill.'

'The Dill?'

'Wayne Dilthey.'

'I'm interested in a woman called Janene Ballich. His name came up.'

'She worked here a coupla months. JJ she called herself. Nice kid, country kid, bit raw, the punters like that. Bit thin too. Not the needle though. Show one fucking track here, they get the arse, that's what I call human resources management, i.e. junkies are more trouble than they're fucking worth.'

'And Dilthey?'

'Yeah, the Dill. Worked for me, '92–93. Came from Brisbane, bloke I know up there gave me a ring.'

You never know what you can ask. 'What was his job?'

Costello shrugged, held up big hands. 'This and that, y'know.'

I waited but I knew there wasn't any point. 'Janene disappeared in 1994,' I said.

Costello tapped his fingernails on the glass tabletop. 'Didn't know that,' he said, 'but they do, they do. The kid was no Einfuckingstein, that can be a major risk factor. They get taken in by these cunts, the talkers.'

'Like Wayne?'

'As a for example?'

'Her mother says Wayne was Janene's agent, so to speak.'

Costello laughed, a good laugh, showed his lower gold fillings, you wanted to laugh with him. 'So to fucking speak,' he said. 'The prick.'

I had to feel my way here. 'Taken in and they disappear?'

He tapped nails again, still amused, but I was on borrowed time. 'Well, disappear,' he said, 'what's that mean?'

'Possibly dead,' I said.

More tapping. 'Or possibly just fucked off. Check Kalgoorlie, check Darwin, check fucking Port Hedland. Thousands of fucking disappeared kids, mate, can't all be dead.'

His telephone rang. He listened, grunted, found a remote. Out of the corner of my left eye, I registered the monitors come on. I looked: reception, bar, overheads of the big room, two people on the floor, a woman, flashes of naked flesh.

'Fuck,' said Costello, weary. 'Another fucking idiot. I shouldn't have to do this anymore. Excuse me.'

He got up, not hurried, left the room. I watched the grey murky screen. A man was on top of the woman, the officers didn't seem to be coming to her aid. Then someone appeared and kicked the man in the head, it jerked him sideways. It was Costello. He kicked the man again, grabbed him by the collar and the seat of his pants, lifted him bodily, ran him headfirst into the bar counter, stepped back, did it again, carried him off-screen.

A minute or two went by, watching the screens. The wrestler wasn't leaving by the front entrance, nothing happened there, just the tuckshop lady talking to someone in uniform, a security guard. No, it was a cop. Not urgent talk, the cop was laughing. She gave him something. It looked like a Freddo. It was. He opened it and ate it.

Costello came through the door. 'Shit,' he said, on his way back to his chair. 'Always when the fucking gymrat's on his smoko. Doesn't fucking smoke either. Naturally.'

I said, 'I don't want to waste any more of your time. Wayne and Janene.'

He was pulling at his cuffs, getting comfortable again, not a sign of exertion or unease on the round face, a man in round glasses who had just kicked another man in the head twice, lifted him clear of the victim, run him into the bar twice. Then he had possibly taken him down a fire escape and thrown him into the alley.

Costello was pensive. 'The Dill,' he said, 'he had this idea, he thought he could run a high-class catering business.'

'Not just a pimp?' I said.

Costello was looking at the screens. Nothing was happening, the place was almost empty, most of the officers had gone on to do their duty in Camberwell, the cop downstairs was gone, gone to patrol the lawless mid-afternoon streets, the taste of a free Freddo chocolate frog in his teeth.

'The cunt thought aiming high was the ticket,' he said. 'Looking for the geese with the golden eggs.'

'Aiming high?'

'Ambition's not a bad thing in a young bloke,' said Costello, not looking at me. 'But the Dill, he had no fucking idea. He wanted everything at once, like the world owed it to him. Brisbane, can't take it out of them. You can put a Buck's suit on the pricks but they're always fucking Brissie, big time's the Breakfast Creek Hotel, have steak and beer for every meal.'

'I'm not quite with you,' I said.

Costello took off his glasses and closed his eyes, pinched his nose. 'The Dill reckoned he could milk the big end of town. Follow the money, he says, you can't go wrong. Provide a complete service. They want it, they get it.'

'It didn't work?'

'Seemed to go all right.' He opened his eyes, put on his glasses. 'Bought the suits, the Porsche. Came in here one day, looking nice, he's got a deal for me, a big favour, cut me in cause he's grateful to me. Two hundred grand up, hundred per cent interest inside four months.'

'Hard to refuse,' I said.

'Know what I'm talking about?'

I nodded.

'I told him, thanks very much, kindly fuck off. Big mistake, Wayne says, he's tight with blokes reading the drug squad's mail, nothing can go wrong. I said, you ignorant prick, don't ever come back here, fuck off back to Queensland before you get grill marks on your balls.'

'When was this?'

He scratched his moustache. 'Early winter '94, I remember the fucking heating was playing up, girls bitching, nipples like corks. Not many complaints from the punters, mark you. May, June '94, that would be right.'

I said, 'This was part of Wayne's complete service? Women, the stuff?'

'Women?' A lift of the chin, glasses catching the overhead light. 'Menu, mate,' he said. 'Girls, boys, micks, dicks, cockfrocks, fladgers, bondies, whatever. Customer-driven, that's the ticket.'

'And Janene? On the menu?'

Costello shrugged. 'I suppose,' he said.

'Then there's someone called Katelyn Feehan.'

'No. Doesn't mean I don't know her. Cash-in-hand business this, mostly. Call yourself Eva Braun if you like.'

I took out the photograph Mary Ballich had given me. 'Janene and Wayne and Katelyn, I'm told,' I said.

'Well, the cunt,' he said, a note of admiration. 'Pinched her, little bastard.'

'Known to you?'

'My word. Mandy Randy the schoolgirl. Three or four shifts a week for a while, two, three months. I wanted her in every day. Fighting off the pricks for personals. That went down big with the other girls, I can tell you.'

'Personals?'

He said, 'Sorry, Jack, didn't know you'd been in the seminary. In the booths you get a close-up. See the business, bit of touch, depends on the girl.'

He looked at the photograph again, whistled, shook his head. 'The cunt. Pinched her off me. Probably snaffled fucking Donna now that I think of it.'

I took back the picture. 'Cash in hand,' I said. 'So you'd have no details?'

A pitying look. 'Mate. Like the French Foreign Legion here.'

A buzzer.

Costello leant down to a speaker box. 'What?'

'A Mr Brown,' said the voice of the tuckshop lady.

'Send him,' said Costello. He stood up, offered me his right hand. 'Business,' he said. 'Nice to meet you, Jack.'

I stood up. 'Thanks for talking to me,' I said. 'I appreciate it.'

'Thank Cam, just don't quote me,' he said, smiling. 'To anyone.'

I thought that it would be bad to meet him when he had a reason not to smile at you. 'Take that for granted,' I said. 'How do you think I could get in touch with Wayne?'

Costello blinked twice, shook his head. 'Well, there's that shit where you all put your hands on the glass. What's it called?'

'A seance.' How had I missed the signals? The tenses?

'Two in the head in a motel up there near the SA border,' he said. 'Some nothing shithole. Early '95, February, I think. No one charged to the moment, far as I hear.'

Last port of call, he was seeing me to the door. 'Any idea?' I said.

'Mate, stuff like that I've got no ideas. That's the reason I'm still here.'

In the street, the storm was over, clouds blown away, the light neon blue and dying. I walked up King Street against the ebbing tide of sombre-suited workers, people waiting at home for the lucky ones, people to kiss at the front door, small ones to pick up and hug, smell the clean and innocent skin and hair of the newly bathed and be for an instant clean and innocent too.

No chance of that for me.

At length, I came to Carrigan's Lane and parked across from the office, beside the clothing factory. It had a soul once—the women and girls who worked in it and came out on smoko and at lunch to stand on the pavement, lean against the brick wall, suck on cigarettes. There was always giggling, they laughed a lot and did quick mocking pieces of theatre that were obviously imitations of people in authority. They sang snatches of pop songs, sometimes short solos, often operatic. The young women gave the older ones cheek, lots of cheek, in return they got gestures of disdain, hand and head and whole upper body eloquent, and joking threats of violence. Sometimes there would be real aggression between the younger ones, some grudge taking fire, but older peace-makers stepped in, quick to pour scorn on both parties.

In the first years across the street, in the tailor's shop, I could stand at the window and watch all that. I was watching on the last day. They came out with their final paypackets, stood around, young, old, no laughing, no singing. They touched, there was hugging, quick kisses, they told each other it wasn't goodbye. Some came out of the door and could not bear it, walked, just a hand raised and a *ciao*.

These thoughts were in my mind when someone knocked on the car window next to my head.

I started, heart jumping, looked up, bade the window come down.

'Where'd you get this car?' said Kelvin McCoy. 'Property of some poor bastard gone to jail because of your incompetence?'

'Good afternoon,' I said. 'I'm not averse to being paid in kind. You once offered me one of your creations. A steam-rollered bunny pasted on a field of used condoms. I recall it vividly. In nightmares.'

'Big mistake, knocking that back, Jack,' he said. 'Typical misjudgment. Fifty-eight grand at auction last year.'

I motioned for him to move away from the door and got out, got a full view of the man. McCoy's postbox-like upper body was draped in layers of textiles, four or five of them, including what appeared to be a sleeping bag and an old fishing net.

'Any pleasure at profiting from the sale of the disgusting object,' I said, 'would have been offset by the disgrace of being known to own it.'

McCoy looked me up and down in a theatrical way. 'In the suits a lot these days. I'd stick to the carpentry, mate. Never were can't make a comeback.'

'Speaking of style,' I said, sniffing, 'is that Trawlerman's Armpit aftershave? If not, I suggest you check the net you're wearing for overlooked catch. Fish dead for a month or so, possibly longer.'

We thrust, no parrying, and parted. I was at my door, when McCoy shouted, 'I'm having a party Friday night. Don't come.'

I went inside and, in the back room, the nominal kitchen, made a pot with loose tea bought from a terrifyingly correct shop in Brunswick Street. The bleached-looking owners wore loose garments that were probably made from pulped *Age* Culture sections.

I waited for a decent time, and, from a height, filled the lovely china cup given to me by Isobel. I had brought it here from my old office, a relic of the time when I was a respectable person. If the roof fell in now, if some disaster pulverised the place, chips of this cup would quite wrongly tell an archaeologist that on this site there was once civilised life.

Precious vessel in hand, I went to the front window, sipped, looked at the wet tarmac, the shining cobbles, at the two lines of swooping writing on the wall above the front door of McCoy's atelier.

> *Guy de Paris*
> *Garments of Distinction*

The lettering was so faded that you had to know what it said to read it. In the last light, I thought about what to make of Janene Ballich and the ripples from her. The man who'd parked beside me was saying that she was connected with Mickey Franklin in a way that mattered.

A hooker and her ambitious pimp—she was missing so long she had to be dead, he was dead. And Katelyn Feehan aka Mandy Randy? Where was she? Like Janene, she was recruited from the Officers' Club by Wayne Dilthey to join his catering corps ministering to the needs of the rich.

The rich. Mickey Franklin and the rich, Mickey and the Massianis, Mickey and Anthony Kendall Haig and Charles Hartfield and Bernard Paech.

Did Sophie Longmore, Mickey's last screw, know anything about these people? Not likely. They went back too far and Mickey wouldn't have talked about them. Where was Sophie? Gone somewhere. I'd probably been told, hadn't paid attention.

I went to the table and rang Sarah Longmore's mobile.

'Yes,' she said, more command than greeting.

'Jack Irish.'

'The journos have got this number,' she said. 'It's supposed to be silent, I've had two slimes, they start out trying to ingratiate…'

'Where are you?' I said.

'At work. At what I choose to call work. I'm about to leave.'

'I'd like to have some of your time.'

'You can have all my time if you're prepared to be hounded by fucking tabloid scumbags and television thugs. They followed me into the police station today when I went to sign the bail book. The cops had to kick them out.'

'That's trying,' I said. 'They don't have work staked out?'

'Not yet. I'm taking considerable pains to see that they don't.'

'There tomorrow? I could come around.'

'All day. From around ten.'

A silence and then she said, 'Or we could do it today.

Have a drink somewhere. Whatever.'

The ethics of an after-hours drink with a client. What ethics? I'd had a during-hours beer with her. Anyway, she wasn't my client, I was Cyril Wootton's hireling. And even if she were, some lawyers spent large parts of their after-hours drinking with their clients, the bigger the client, the more after-hours drinking.

'That would be helpful,' I said. 'Save time.'

'I'm a bit wary of public places,' she said.

I hesitated only for a moment. 'We could meet at my place,' I said. 'It's not far out of your way.'

Sarah didn't hesitate at all. 'Fine. Where is it?'

I gave her directions, then made haste to get home and inflict some order on the place. At least it was clean, courtesy of a recent purge. The bell rang when I'd got the fire going well and was stuffing old newspapers into the box seat under the sitting-room window. I went down and opened the door.

She was in jeans and a short leather jacket, tiny drops of water in her finger-combed hair. A sexy look, it made me nervous.

'Hi,' she said. 'I'm feeling awkward. I haven't pushed you into this, have I?'

'I thought it was my suggestion?' Behind her, I could see the rain drifting like net curtain across the streetlight on the edge of the park.

'Made under duress.'

'Come in. I haven't got any German beer, just Cooper's.'

'Cooper's is not just.'

When I came in with the beer, she was standing in front of the fire. 'A very welcoming room, Mr Irish. Is there what would once have been a Mrs Irish? Or similar?'

I shook my head, gave her a big glass, a bottle of beer in it. 'Neither. I've got names I need to ask you about.'

'Ask.'

I didn't know whether to stand or sit. I stood on the other side of the fire. 'David Massiani.'

'Met once. All smiles and arm-punching. When David'd gone, Mickey said, you'll never meet a more insanely treacherous cunt. Mickey worked for the Massianis once, you know that?'

'I do. That's all?'

'Yes. May I smoke?'

'This room's no stranger to smoke.' That was putting it mildly.

She took the Camel packet from an inside pocket, plucked one. I pulled a splinter from a piece of firewood, lit it and offered. She put the cigarette in her mouth, came closer, tilted her head back, looked at me though the flame, close, drew.

'Thank you,' she said. 'You know how to live off the land here.'

'We get by,' I said. 'Subsistence living. Grow our own truffles, force-feed the geese. In the evenings, we make our own amusement.'

She laughed, a laugh seen in her eyes. How was it that you always knew whether people were really amused? Why was I so pleased to have made her laugh?

I drank a good bit of the Cooper's and wiped my lips. 'Anthony Kendall Haig,' I said.

'Yes.'

There was something more than affirmation in her voice. She smoked, blew the grey stream at the fire, it was claimed by the updraught. This fireplace sucked like no other fire chamber I had known. It was one of the most important survivors of the explosion that sent the building's roof into the North Fitzroy sky, tiny pieces falling on the football oval, on St George's Road, on the bowling greens. Pieces of my dwelling fell on the tennis court where I once played Drew Greer for almost three hours, and lost.

'Yes?' I said.

'Mickey once worked for him too. In Brisbane. He's an interesting man. Sophie said he was the money behind Seaton Square. There was some argument going on between him and Mickey, I think. You'll have to ask her.'

'I'd like to ask her lots of things. Your father promised to arrange it. Can you put me in touch?'

'I'll ring her.'

'Why's Haig interesting?'

She had some beer, smoked, looking at the fire. 'He's got this rough exterior, left school at fourteen, a self-made man. Then you find out he can talk about art, history, music. Unusual person.'

I waited, admiring her cheekbones. 'And?'

'I slept with him,' she said.

'During the Mickey affair?'

'Yes. Just a fling.'

'Did Mickey know?'

'No. We were on the rocks, it was right at the end. The night I had the fight over the parking space, that's the night I met him. He came to dinner at Mickey's.'

I tried the names Charles Hartfield and Bernard Paech. No, she said.

'Gary Webber. An artist. I understand you attacked him.'

Sarah closed her eyes. 'Oh fuck,' she said, calm voice, 'that's from my father, isn't it?'

'We don't want it going off in our face in court,' I said.

She drank. 'I was about sixteen, trying to hang out with this bunch of painters. I thought they were so cool, they had this outlaw artist air, they were all drop-outs from something, school, art school. And Gary Webber, he was the coolest. One night, I went to the studio, upstairs in Smith Street, it was late, and three of them started pushing me around, they were off their brains. I thought it was a joke. You play along. I played along.'

Sarah threw her cigarette into the fire. 'Anyway,' she said, she sounded as if she wanted to end the story, 'I was just a silly kid trying to pass myself off as street smart. I'd only had sex once before that night. I should still have been at school.'

'What?' I said.

Something between smiling and showing pain, dentists would know the facial movement.

'They raped me,' she said. 'It went on and on and when I thought it was over, I was lying there, Gary Webber came in. He was totally bombed and he wanted his turn. I tried to fight him and he punched me in the chest a few times, hard, in my stomach too, he was dancing around like a boxer, he had his hands up, and then he was going to hit me in the face. I was against this counter thing and he took a step back, ready to hit me. There was a full wine bottle and I got my hands on it and I hit him first. I kept hitting him with it until it broke.'

Her voice, the small sag of her shoulders, touched me. I believed her and I felt an urge to put out a hand and say that. Instead I said, 'I understood that you claimed to have

156

no memory of what happened. Is this the newly recovered version?'

She looked at me, not the child eyes I'd seen at our first meeting: sad, grown-up. She put her glass on the mantelpiece.

'Goodnight, Mr Irish,' she said. 'Thanks for the beer.'

She walked for the door. I said nothing, felt a clenched fist in my stomach. This had been a bad idea, I had made it worse.

The door was difficult to open from the inside, there was play in the doorknob, the small screws worked themselves loose, they needed tightening from time to time. She twisted the knob, and, without turning her head, anxiety in her voice, said, 'Can you let me out?'

I crossed the room, reached around her, put my hand on the doorknob, pushed, turned, the tongue moved enough. I pulled the door open a crack.

'I keep meaning to fix the damn thing,' I said. 'I'll see you down the stairs.'

She was still, we were close, I could feel the electricity in her. She pushed the door closed, spoke without turning.

'I wanted to die after that night,' she said, voice thin. 'Three men treated me like a toy. They did anything they wanted to. Then I almost killed someone. I would have killed him, I didn't care. So if I'd been offered surgery to take that night out of my brain, I would have said yes, yes, yes. Yes, please.'

Her forehead was against the door. I was looking at the nape of her neck, the clean dark hairs in the soft and pale hollow.

'I couldn't speak about what had happened,' she said.

'Not to anyone. I didn't have the words for it. So if I said I didn't remember, then I didn't have to speak about it.'

A silence, the crackling of the fire, the wash of rain on the roof, the swallowings in the downpipes.

'I was just a young girl,' she said. 'Can you understand, Jack?'

'Yes,' I said, and I did touch her. I reached out and put my right hand on her shoulder.

Sarah turned and looked up at me, a sheen on her eyes. I took my hand away but I could not take back the touch. She moved closer and I drew her to me, no urgency in the embrace, just the desire to touch.

But she raised her face and we kissed. It was just a gentle pressure of lips, I tasted beer and nicotine and salt, and I knew that could not be the end of it. I put a hand on her neck, felt the taut muscles, she put both hands behind my head, pulled me with strong hands, strong arms, our lips opened.

There was a moment when we came apart and I said, gruffly, 'Sarah, I don't think…'

'Think,' she said, as throaty, 'Don't think. I want to lie down. Is that possible?'

'Possible?' I said. 'It's probably compulsory.'

I rose in the dark, pulled on the ancient garments and set out on my route. Punishment for the body in a cold, moist dawn. I ran over surfaces glistening, slippery, treacherous for ankles. In the parade, I saw the night's sad survivors limping towards home. I saw the pioneers of the opening day, going to some dull task with narrow eyes and thin lips.

As I shambled along, I thought about sex and remorse. I always felt regret after the first sex with anyone. Something in my history triggered a feeling of wrongdoing. Enthusiastic consent wasn't ever enough for me to look back with pleasure. I shook my head, ran the moisture off my hair with a hand. Never mind the past, this time I had other good reasons for feeling guilty. Linda had been gone not much more than a week. Sarah was almost a client, she had been in an emotional state. There could be no excuse for having sex with her.

'Listen, Jack,' she'd said, standing at her car in the small hours, not the old ute, a VW, 'I was going to make a pass the first chance I got. But I didn't mean it to be teary. I'm sorry about that.'

She took a fistful of my old T-shirt, pulled me close and we kissed goodbye, not a short kiss. I went back to bed, tingling, her scent on the pillows, dropped in and out of sleep.

I turned right off Brunswick Street to run through the gardens, the tree trunks black, still holding the night, the lamps of the park making rough wickerwork of the bare lower branches. Just ahead was the place where a man had tried to shoot me. For months afterwards, I avoided coming this way, and then one morning, running on automatic, mind on something, I found myself approaching the near-fatal spot. The taboo was broken, it never bothered me again.

Sarah couldn't exonerate me by saying she was primed for action. She would say whatever was needed to prevent the thought entering her mind that she had been a victim again.

But she was not my client. I was just a researcher. Doing the academic work, the oral history. Vansina, was that his name? The oral historian. Vansina. Could be a soccer player. Did they still call themselves oral historians? It could mislead.

Nonsense. I was trying to save Sarah from going to prison for murder. Drew and I stood between her and the years of nothing, the evening meal at 5 pm. She knew that, she knew how important I was to her future.

That was why it was my duty to avoid personal involvement.

Still, as personal involvement went, it had been intensely pleasurable. She was strong and erotic. Also clever and funny and self-mocking afterwards, easy to be with.

Ah, lust. Guilty of lust, it had ever been so. Lust had often overruled what passed for my common sense, my principles. And would again, given the chance.

I looked across at the tennis courts that had been the scene of the Greer–Irish marathon. No more could I play Drew Greer at tennis for three hours. Play and lose to him. He never spoke of that late summer afternoon that became a summer evening. I didn't speak of it either but the loss still rankled with me. I should have won, I was cruising to victory and then I let him back in and my nerve went.

To win and not to gloat. Drew was good at that. Still, he'd had a lot more experience of winning. Had a lot more backbone too. *Backbone*. I hated the expression, my grandfather used it, he was a backbone expert, X-ray eyes for backbone, could spot backbone in toddlers. I hated it yet I thought it.

Home in sight, feeling weak in character, in body, in mind, my legs full of lead sinkers.

I had a long shower, thinking about whether to tell Drew. Of course I should, he was entitled to know. Why? It was a private matter, it wouldn't change anything. Indeed, it was better that he didn't know. She was his client, nothing should cloud his judgment. The prosecution could at any time offer a deal and he would have to put it to her, offer advice. Cop manslaughter, you'll get the minimum, that's the best we can hope for. I don't think we want to fall for this, they know how shaky their case is, we've got an excellent chance of an acquittal.

Drew didn't want to be offering advice to a client in the knowledge that his friend was her lover.

I wasn't her lover. One night, that would be it. Yes? I

didn't like the chances if she kissed me again. She knew a bit about kissing, knew a bit about things beside kissing too...

Oh, shit.

I dressed formally, my defence on days of uncertainty, made tea, sat at the kitchen table and tried to read my book for an hour, mind wandering like a goat on a hillside. Then I put on a tie, red silk, English, hardly worn, no knot wrinkles, went downstairs and fired up the neglected Stud, listened to the animal-enclosure sound of eight cylinders for a while, aimed the beast towards breakfast.

Sex and Principle, Body and Mind, torn between. And hungry. Nothing less than a repeat of the Cholesterol DynaHit at Enzio's would be of any use at a time like this.

Just me, an office cleaner called Vern who drank at the Prince, and a couple, women. Carmel, the waif who knew all the midnight things, took the order. 'I advise you that there is a new first-shift cook,' she said. 'As owner, Enzio wants to sleep in. We are encouraging that.'

'Properly trained, the person?' I said. 'Well-briefed?'

'Smartarse little turd,' she said.

A message. I'd read the first five pages of the *Age* before the food came. Eggs hard, bacon burnt, sausages charred and split, tomatoes raw, ditto the mushrooms, toast cut too thin and barely exposed to heat.

I ate what was edible, a picky affair, read the sports pages, the horse stories, thought about how much I missed Les Carlyon. Where was he? Why didn't he write for the paper anymore? No one wrote better about the people who lived on dreams, didn't whinge unduly about the hip-and-shoulders of disappointment, went to bed and got up with trouble and debt, carried on anyway, prisoners of love and habit and not knowing what else to do.

Nearing the end of the food, I found the eyes of Bruno the Silent, a Lygon Street legend Enzio had plucked from vegetating in outer Reservoir and rechained to the coffee wheel. Bruno was sitting on a cushioned high stool with a back, giving him some ease from the leg pains caused by forty years of standing.

I nodded, he nodded. Bruno had first exchanged nods with me deep into my second year at law school, after I'd been ordering the same thing three or four times a week for more than eighteen months. One morning, as I came through the door, he looked at me, not an inquiring look, just a look one might give a known dog entering your premises.

I'd nodded. Bruno nodded. I sat down, opened the newspaper. Soon a short black arrived.

Now Carmel picked up my half-eaten remains. 'I have nothing to say,' she said, eyes down. 'I merely wait upon table.'

'It's not easy to get the timing right,' I said. 'He may get better at it and become a Brunswick Street breakfast legend.'

'Possibly,' she said and gave me a look that brooked no misinterpretation. I watched her go, always a pleasure. A minute later she came back with the small glass of tar-black liquid. Looking out of the window at the life in the street, I sipped the dark bullet, felt the small surge of optimism kick in.

Time to go. A man in a good suit, judgment impaired by sex and red wine. I went to the counter, nodded to Bruno the Silent, paid Carmel, caught a glimpse of the cook, his hair, peaked and golden-tipped, his plump mouth. Outside, in the awakening street, standing beside the Stud, I switched on the small telephone. It rang immediately.

'Jack?'

Sarah. I felt a little tightness in the throat. 'Yes.'

'Sarah. I tried you at home, left a message. I've had a call from someone, a man.'

'Television jackal?'

She laughed. 'No. He says he can help us. Help me. He's coming at 9.30. He wants you here. Can you make it?'

'You're at work already?'

'Couldn't sleep when I got home. I should have stayed. It was all too brief.'

'Passed in a flash. Telling this person about your place of work, I don't know about the wisdom of that.'

'He knew. Will you come?'

'Yes,' I said, 'I'll be there. Did he give a name?'

'No. He said it was dangerous for him to talk to us but he would.'

'I'll see you in half an hour.'

'Good,' she said. A few seconds. 'Jack.'

'Yes?'

'Regrets?'

'No,' I said, no trouble lying. 'You?'

'Not a single one.'

I said goodbye, got into the Lark, sat and thought about why I was in the beginning-of-the-affair state, thought about Linda in London, watched a woman in overalls washing a window. A small brown dog sat behind her, head up, inspecting her work. Then I drove to Kensington.

Sarah's old yellow ute was alone in the parking area, right-angled to the patchwork building. I considered waiting for the visitor to arrive. No, it might spook him. I got out. The wind was keen here, coming off the bay not far away, carrying the sounds of the railyards and docklands, clanking, roaring, groaning. Underfoot, the damp gravel made a squealing noise.

I slid open the door. The big space was gloomy, as before, the human-like metal forms somehow even more menacing at second meeting. I walked past the witches, paused to look again at what I'd at first thought to be two boxers, touched the stainless steel. It was icy, like having local anaesthetic on the fingertips. I went across to the pack of humanoid dogs attacking something, mounting each other in their fever, walked around it. These creations were all saying something about humans, about the world they made. I needed to know their titles.

I would ask the creator. I walked down the shed, around the scrapmetal pile, the car bodies, car doors, the assorted steel junk.

Sarah was where she had been the first time, in the open space. She was on one knee, wearing a full black mask, welding something onto the metal figure. A stream of sparks was erupting from the seam she was creating.

I stopped and watched her, her deftness. She must have felt my presence, she could see nothing but the glow of the weld through the helmet window. She stood up, raised the torch, turned her back on me, doing something, I saw the flame diminish, die. She put the torch on the stand, turned.

Sarah pushed up the helmet and looked at me, took off a glove, ran fingers through her hair, smiled the half-furtive smile.

She was lovely. My throat felt dry.

The world behind her went white, then bright orange.

The floor between us erupted.

In the air, backwards. A knife of pain. Darkness, I couldn't see, pain in my side, something inside me.

I could see flames, hear a terrible roaring sound. Get to the door. I crawled. More explosions. A blow to my back.

The door, open, blown off, I felt a wind on my face.

Get there, just get there.

Black.

Nothing.

They let me out on a Friday in early May, round 6 of the football, damp, a wind shaking the bare trees. Drew carried my bag to his car. It wasn't necessary, but I didn't want to argue about it.

We drove in silence. He was going the wrong way.

'What route is this?' I said. 'Have they reconfigured the city while I wasn't looking?'

'My place,' said Drew.

'Mine, I think,' I said. 'I have a need for home.'

'You can't come out of hospital after umpteen weeks and go back to an empty house,' he said.

'Bullshit. Anyway, what do you mean *empty*? Furniture gone? Haven't you noticed it's been empty for fucking years? No one there except me. Take me home.'

I heard the harsh tone of my voice.

We stopped at lights. Drew turned his long face. 'Jack,' he

said, 'don't spoil my plans. Tonight, we have a beer or two. Then we eat these steaks from the main man. With them, a red I've been saving for fifteen years. Then we sit in front of the fire with a drop of Rutherglen nectar and watch the footy.'

He coughed. 'Unfortunately,' he said, 'we then see the Saints get their scrawny arses kicked to buggery.'

I looked away, willed myself to be a normal person.

'Steak?' I said. 'Just steak? Is that all?'

'Good boy,' said Drew.

I saw relief on his face.

'With home-cooked thick-cut chips,' he said.

'Yes?'

'Well. Heated at home in the home oven. Defrosted. That's close, isn't it?'

'And the wine? What's that?'

We pulled away, he jerked his head at me. 'I can just as easily drop you off at home,' he said. 'You appear to me to be fully recovered.'

'Drive,' I said. 'Just drive. It's what you're not good at.'

Taken home on a Saturday of fleeting sunshine. At the boot factory, at my downstairs door, I said thank you to Drew.

'Well,' he said, 'I'll come up and see if you've got everything you need.'

'If I need anything, I'll go out and get it,' I said.

I set off up the stairs, stopped after the first few, shocked by my weakness, the heaviness of my legs. I looked down. Drew was rubbing his unshaven jaw. I thought I could hear the sawing sound.

'What?' I said.

'You know what,' he said.

'Fuck off,' I said. 'That's not going to happen again.'

'You're too quiet for my liking.'

'Well, it's a good thing I'm not dependent for my state of mind on your liking.'

He shook his head. 'You and explosions,' he said. 'There's

a fearful fucking symmetry.'

'Thank you for that perceptive observation and goodbye.' I set off upwards again.

At the top, I had to stand for a minute to recover before I unlocked the door and went in. Everything was as I'd left it on the morning: on the kitchen sink, the glasses, the teapot and cup. The novel was on the kitchen table, place marked with an old window envelope, a bill-carrier.

I washed up, put the spoiled cheese, fruit and vegetables in the bin, switched on the heating, walked around—sitting room, study, spare bedroom, kitchen, sitting room. I looked out of the window at the trees, the park beyond, there were children playing, splodges of colour. I sat down, got up, went back to the window, put my forehead against a cold pane.

I didn't want to go into the bedroom. I'd left the bed unmade that morning. Her perfume would be on the pillows, the sheets.

Drew offered to get cleaners in, I said no. Why? What stopped me?

A drink, a drink, and then I'd do it. I felt a strong desire for a drink, went to the kitchen and looked in the cabinet. Whisky, a Glenlivet, an unopened bottle. Just the ticket, a whisky, neat. I took down the bottle, found a cut-glass tumbler, also an explosion survivor, now we were both explosion survivors, I didn't want to think about explosions, poured two fingers, added another two.

I had the glass to my mouth, I had the peaty smell in my nose.

That's not going to happen again.

Explosions.

You and explosions. There's a fearful fucking symmetry.

I poured the liquid back into the bottle, spilled a lot, put it away. I went into the bedroom, pulled the sheets off the bed, pulled off the pillowcases, didn't breathe, stuffed everything into the laundry bag, half full already. I lugged the bag downstairs. But then my energy was spent. I left the bag at the front door, went slowly upstairs, each step an act of will, and I lay down on the sofa and closed my eyes.

When the telephone woke me, it was dark, I had no idea where I was, panic.

'Are you all right? You sound awful?'

Rosa, the baby my father never saw, named for a Communist heroine.

'A nap,' I said. 'I was asleep.'

'How could you leave the hospital without telling me? I ring the hospital only to find that you've been discharged.'

'I didn't know they needed your permission.'

A deep sniff.

'I trust you're not doing a line while talking to me,' I said.

'I resent that,' Rosa said. 'I assumed that, being your sister, I assumed I would be the one.'

'Which one?'

'The one to take you home.'

'It's just driving, Rosa, it doesn't have any significance.'

'Who took you home?'

'Drew.'

'I think I might have been told. I wanted you to come here.'

'Why?'

'Why? So that I could look after you, that's why. Is that a bad instinct?'

Standing in the dark, only the weak light from the street-lamp in the window.

'It's a good instinct,' I said. 'Thank you for having it. Only I don't need looking after. I'll be paying for the looking after I've had until I die. After I die. So now I'll just get on with what remains of life. What about lunch, you could shout me lunch? Name the place.'

The silence.

'Jack,' she said, 'I tried to pay the hospital bills. They'd been paid. You owe nothing.'

Tiny branch shadows moved in the corner of the window, twitches of dark little fingers.

'Some clerical error,' I said. 'I appreciate you trying to pay. If you'd succeeded, I'd have repaid you.'

'What do I have to do to be your sister?' she said. 'I think I'll stop worrying about it.'

'You don't have to do anything and you don't have to worry about it. I'll drive over your way tomorrow for brunch. You'll know the top brunch spot, where the Nokia elite gather to chatter. To people elsewhere.'

'You shouldn't be driving,' she said. 'You've had head injuries.'

'I'm better than before, they say. Reflexes of a teenage Afghani warlord. You should see me collect bananas in Super Monkey Ball.'

'Bananas?' A note of caution in her voice. 'Jack, do you have pills you should take?'

'These monkeys are inside bubbles and you have to…'

'So,' she said. 'Elevenish. I'll pick you up. There must be a place over there with edible food.'

Food. I hadn't eaten since breakfast.

I wanted someone to bring me food.

No one was going to bring me food. I put on lights and

went in search. The pantry needed to take a good hard look at itself, it was a museum of preserved foodstuffs. I found a can of mushroom and leek soup, made in Scotland some time after the union with England.

The freezer too was overdue. Unidentifiable objects. I pulled something from under an ice overhang. Turkish bread. How long did frozen bread remain edible? Halfway edible. We would see.

I started the warming processes, opened a 1989 bottle of Elizabeth semillon, found hiding in the pantry in its grey papier-mâché sleeve, the last of a case. I took it to the sitting room. A fire, I needed a fire.

Tomorrow. Do some shopping. Go to Piedemonte. Just buy the necessaries. Then take a walk, there wasn't anything wrong with my legs. After that, make a fire.

Why did I always say at least one wrong thing to Rosa? She brought out something in me, she turned me into a version of my grandfather, my mother's father. For him, unqualified approval did not exist, he was unreserved about nothing. I learned early that, even when he smiled at me, I should brace myself. That's a nice report, John. But I see here…

When I was older, it became clear that he hated the fact that his daughter had married a stonemason, worse, one who belonged to the Communist Party. And I was the result of that union. *Ergo.*

There was no photograph of my father in the Toorak house until the day of my grandfather's funeral. After the cemetery, mourners came back and tea and fruitcake and sherry were served, people patted me, kissed my cheek, shook my hand. When everyone had gone, we went into the smaller sitting room. My mother sent me to find a bottle of whisky, that was something new. My mother and grandmother drank a few glasses. I could sense something in the way they talked about the funeral, how well it had gone. They were relieved.

My grandmother left the room and came back with a picture in a silver frame. She put it on the mantelpiece. It was the photograph taken after the civil marriage of William John Irish and my mother. He was in a dark suit, a handsome man and large, black hair disciplined with oil, a head and more taller than my pale and lovely mother, in a cream suit herself, a neckline hinting at bosom.

Where had it been? Had my grandmother kept it hidden, in a drawer?

For Rosa, born after her Commie father was dead, her grandfather was the first male of importance. The infant knew only the Toorak house, sleeping in her mother's nursery, in her mother's cot, with her mother's stuffed animals, cared for eight hours a day by her mother's nanny. When she was a baby, the old man took her out in the grand pram on Saturdays and Sundays. I had a clear memory of him, in a tweed jacket, leaning into the big-wheeled carriage, his nose pointing, his hand causing chuckling sounds.

'Gramps was lovely,' Rosa once said. 'I miss him so much. Perhaps he never had the chance to bond with you.'

I said, '*Bond?* What do you understand by *bond*?'

And in asking this, I knew the rich, thin-lipped old bastard lived on: my mother had bequeathed me his genes. And I knew also that my unease about that fact matched exactly my grandfather's feelings about the genes of a Communist stonemason in his grandson.

I fetched my supper and sat in the most uncomfortable chair because I wanted to punish myself. I drank a glass of wine, had half a bowl of soup. The soup had aged well, the bread was edible. Had the Turks ever mounted any polar expeditions?

Tired in the moving parts. Inside too, in the core. I'd stripped the bed, I would have to make it. Not tonight. The spare room, I would sleep in my own spare room, the bed was made. A mug of Milo. No milk, no Milo. Shit.

I brushed my teeth, avoided looking in the mirror, not wanting to see myself. I switched off the heating, the lights, stood at the front window and looked out at the visible universe. Bare branches moving, headlights on the street beyond the parkland.

I was turning back the covers when I thought about putting on the answering machine. It was 9.15 pm. Someone might ring, adults weren't supposed to be horizontal at 9.15 with the intention of sleeping.

To the sitting room, press the button on the machine, back to the bedroom. A good mattress on the bed, hard. I opened my book, got comfortable on the pillows, drowsy immediately, fought it, a few paragraphs, put the book down, switched off the light, half turned. The blessing of sleep, the laying on of oblivion.

I woke in sweat, heart thudding, dreams vivid, incoherent—fleeing in terror, heavy crippled legs, climbing sheer surfaces that crumbled, ladders with missing rungs, rungs that broke underfoot, the abyss below, pursuers close, gaining.

It was a long time before I fell asleep again, lying in the dark, needles of pain when I moved, feeling sad in the way

I'd felt since waking up in hospital, a chronic sadness.

In the morning, I found the keys to the Lark and to Linda's Alfa inside the front door, pushed through the letter slot. The cars were outside. Cam. The Cam taketh and the Cam returneth. The one person who didn't come to see me in hospital. Instead, he sent a parcel with half a bottle of Grange Hermitage 1983 in a flat silver flask.

I liked him even more for that.

Time passed, a chain of forgettable and forgotten days, weeks. I fended off almost everyone who inquired, didn't reply to most telephone messages, extinguished them. People became exasperated.

'If you don't get back to some semblance of your former self,' Linda said from London one morning, 'I'm coming back and I'm taking stern measures. Arse-kicking I'm talking about.'

I had no rejoinder.

I went to Charlie's on most days, made myself do that. With no heart in it, I worked at tasks he gave me to do. He didn't say anything about my absence, carried on as always, lectured me on accurate measuring, the need to tune tools after every use, the virtues of a slow and humiliating apprenticeship in the trade, the wisdom of certain European thinkers. Sometimes after my run I went back to bed, sleeping fitfully, not getting up until midday, sleeping badly that night, the old dreams back, the unconnected images: my father coming towards me down a passage, picking me up, raising me above his head, my mother crying, holding me tightly to her in a doorway, car lights gleaming on wet bluestone gutters.

I woke earlier and earlier and, as the body pains lessened, the runs got longer and longer. I didn't go to the Prince much. I caught people frowning at me, exchanging glances. People told me jokes. Everyone seemed to want to cheer me up.

In mid-June, I read a bank statement, the first time in months. There was a deposit of $50,000 about which I knew nothing. I rang the bank. The money was an electronic transfer from a Luxembourg bank called CreditInternat.

The hospital bill? It had been paid, said Rosa. I hadn't thought about it again. I rang the hospital accounts department. Paid by electronic deposit from CreditInternat.

The next day, I ran through the dawn streets as far as once-lovely Royal Park, ran down to the tramlines, turned and angled across the expanse, through the clumps of grass and the scrubby native trees. The splendid parkland was now ruined, courtesy of a government falling for some vague pencil sketches produced by mystical landscape designers in the 1980s. Soon they would find bodies here.

I ran home, showered, dressed, and, without calling, drove up to Macedon. When I'd parked outside the garages and got out, I stood on the raked gravel for a few moments. A day in its final quarter, winter stillness. Clean, cold air, the perfume of woodsmoke and leafmould and regret.

I was on the second terrace of the stone path when the

front door opened, inhabitants warned by a sensor at the gates, no doubt. A woman in jeans and a poloneck sweater. She had blondish hair to just below her ears, parted at the left. I didn't need to be told who she was. Sophie. I could see Sir Colin Longmore in her—the chin, the forehead. But she had Sarah's build, tall and whip-thin, the long neck.

'Jack,' she said.

'How do you know?'

She pointed at the forecourt. 'My father. You've been on the security camera.'

We shook hands.

'Leaving messages on your machine doesn't work,' she said. A direct gaze, disconcerting, no automatic smile.

'I've gone off answering machines for the moment,' I said.

'I can understand that,' she said. 'Come in.'

She led me down a long, broad, unadorned passage, through a room with no clear function, into a sitting room, not large, a sisal carpet, rugs on it. Sir Colin got up from a severe wooden chair. He was in an old grey jumper and corduroys, shoeless, long blue bootsocks pulled up over his trousers. It gave him a pixie-like look.

'Jack,' he said, his hand out. 'Bit thin but you're vertical, that's the ticket.'

'I wanted to ask about the paying of my hospital bill and a deposit in my bank account,' I said.

Sir Colin looked at his daughter, a sliver of a look, looked back at me.

'I'm sorry?' he said, his eyebrows now not on the same plane, the left higher than the right. 'Are you demanding money?'

I turned and left the grand house, found my own way out.

No one came after me. The front door closed with the sound I remembered from the second-last door at Pentridge Prison, the Stone College, in the old days, when I had a respectable job, did what I could for people who generally found themselves where they were because life hadn't opened up before them like a flower. Early on, it hit them in the face like a big fist.

I liked those people more, a lot more.

'Funny business,' said Harry Strang. 'Travellin well, good Lord's givin all the other bastards the rough end. Smack. Holy boot up ya own bum.'

Beyond Camperdown in the mist, three of us in the big BMW, Harry at the wheel. I was in the back, reading the *Age*. Cam was doing something on his laptop.

'Ireland,' said Harry. 'Never should've bin there. Two meetins to go, championship in my pocket. Get a call from this trainer, done me a couple of good ones when I first come out. So I go up on the Wednesday, get on this nice little grey for him.'

He took a large hand off the wheel to reach for the winegum ashtray while overtaking a milk tanker. A truck was coming at us. Its airhorn brayed. I groaned with fear. Cam looked up, went back to his screen.

We escaped annihilation by a short half-boot.

'Panicky, your average truckie,' said Harry. 'No bloody judgment. Where was I? Yes, the finger. There I am, a perfect sit, we're goin to street the cattle. Come round the bend, straighten up, the pony in front throws a shoe, I never see it, hits my bloke between the eyes, I'm airborne, crossin the rail at altitude.'

Harry looked back at me, sharp brown eyes, a look longer than I liked. He snapped fingers. 'Broken leg,' he said. Another snap. 'Bloody collarbone too.'

'Unfortunate,' I said.

'The championship it cost me,' he said. 'Plus a swag of bickies, needless to say. Didn't need the bickies that much, would've liked the championship, my word.'

'And the moral of the story?' I said, looking at the land, dark-green, waterlogged, like Ireland with added extinct volcanoes.

'Avoid Ireland,' said Cam. 'And don't return favours.'

Harry shook his head, pained. 'Don't ya listen?' he said. 'Life, I'm talkin about life.'

'Oh, that,' said Cam.

'Any life in mind?' I said. 'Any particular wimpy, self-pitying existence in mind?'

Harry waved his left hand in dismissal. 'Gettin up and goin,' he said, 'that's the important thing. Not so, Cam?'

'The goin part,' said Cam, not looking up. 'I'm the goin expert. Left with the best of them.'

Harry sighed, sought comfort in winegums. 'Near here. Getting close, as I remember.'

'Over the hill and about two ks,' said Cam. 'There's a shed fallin down. Just after.'

Harry looked at his watch. 'Give her a ring. Did it quicker

last time as I recall,' he said, putting his foot down.

I breathed again when we left the main road, turned inland. We travelled through a bumpy landscape, winter creeks running, sheep in clumps and strung up slopes like woolly beads. I got out for the gate at Middle Hill, Breeding and Training, W. & L. Halsey. It was a good gate, well hung, over a grid too, no easy escape from Middle Hill. The mist was gone now, sky full of fast-running cloud, blue holes coming and going.

'You only bring me for the gates,' I said when I was back in the warmth, rubbing my hands.

Black Angus cattle on both sides ignored us as we went up the gentle rise, over the crest.

'Nice things, cattle,' said Cam. 'Shame to eat them.'

At the homestead, we parked on dry gravel in front of a big steel shed. The earth beneath us had been ripped and veined with drainage pipes, there was no other way to provide such a surface.

A door in a door opened and a woman stepped out. She was wearing what had been closest to hand in the icy dawn: a jumper at the point of fibre collapse, a short Drizabone, a tracksuit bottom possibly from the 1956 Melbourne Olympics, elastic-sided Blundstones. As she came, she had a hand on the knitted headgear, the beanie.

We got out. I thought it was the sight of Cam putting on his dark-grey Italian overcoat that decided her against the beanie. She ripped it off, stuffed it in a pocket, pulled up her saggy pants.

'Mr Strang, Cam,' she said. 'Freeze your bum off today. Yesterday, like Bali.'

'Bracin,' said Harry. 'Don't think you've met Jack. Jack

Irish, Lorna Halsey. Jack's my legal fella.'

We shook hands.

'How's he doin?' said Harry.

'Good,' she said. 'Like a dog with Chink, never seen a horse so rapt. Can't believe he's supposed to be a killer. My girl's ridin him.'

'Chink settle him?' said Cam. He wasn't looking at her, gazing around like an inspector. 'Stay over?'

'Three days,' she said. 'Slept in the barn, in his swag. Couldn't get him no further than the kitchen. Not house-trained, he reckons.'

'Tells the truth,' said Cam.

Lorna was looking at Cam, a look you recognised after you were eighteen.

'This way,' she said.

We crossed the shed towards an open door, across the concrete floor of a tidy room for farm equipment, horse tack, feed, entered a big gravelled courtyard with horse boxes on each side. Two long heads stabled next to each other looked at us. The fourth side of the yard was an open-sided shed.

Crossing the yard, Lorna said, 'Chink's something, makes you feel like a beginner. Got a mongrel here, supposed to be broken, won't let anyone on him. It took about fifteen minutes, Chink's riding him like he's the clerk of the course's pony.'

'Keepin this beast outside?' said Harry.

'Chink's advice. In the near paddock.'

It was even colder on the other side of the buildings, the wind up the slope bringing tears. A teenage girl in rain-gear was riding a horse in a paddock with a good surface, not too wet. She saw us. Lorna made a signal, a circle with an index finger.

The rider took the horse around on an oval course, canter, brief gallop, canter, came to us, reined in near the gate and sat patting her mount.

Lorna opened the gate and went in a few steps. The rider brought the horse up to her. She rubbed its nose and its neck, talked to it, led it over.

'Sure that's the animal?' said Harry.

The horse was not recognisable as the one we'd seen in the paddock in Gippsland. This Lost Legion's coat had sheen, its head was up, you could see the alertness in its eyes.

'Good, not so?' said Lorna, stroking the animal. 'This is my girl, Terry.'

We said hello to Terry. She was around fourteen, had red hair, bits sticking out under her riding hat, a few big ginger freckles.

Harry went into the paddock, put a slow hand on Lost Legion's nose. He found something in a side pocket of his corduroy jacket, fed it to the horse, its big mouth in his hand.

'Got a bit of condition,' said Cam.

'Chink reckons he wouldn't eat for days at the start,' Lorna said. 'Then he comes around, pigs in, puts on the kilos like a new bride.'

Cam went in, walked around the horse, not close, approached it from the front, showed it his hand, rubbed at the base of a relaxed ear.

'Looking good,' he said. 'Sounds like you heard more from Chink in three days than I heard in two years. Fed him what?'

'Tea,' Lorna said. 'Drinks whisky in tea.'

'Used to be the reverse,' said Cam.

'How long before we'll know somethin?' said Harry.

'He's keen enough,' Lorna said. 'You want to be careful, though, he's been out so long. And the legs, who knows? I'd like to take him over a lot of ground.'

'No hurry,' said Harry. 'We'll do it right.' He looked up at the girl on the horse. 'Like the way you ride,' he said. 'Your mum probably had you up when you were little.'

Terry blushed, looked away. 'That's right,' she said.

We walked back, turned right into the house, sat in a big room and had tea and biscuits. They talked bloodlines and distances and times, Harry gave the horse diet lecture. I looked out of a big window, watched the clouds scud, saw a hawk drop from the sky like the angel of death.

In the car, on the main road, Cam driving, I said, 'I'm not suggesting that you'd need a reason to take your high-powered legal representative into the frozen wastes with you.'

Harry's profile appeared around the headrest for an instant. 'Get a bit of country air in the lungs, Jack,' he said. 'Livin in Fitzroy, thereabouts, all that factory smoke, tannin the hides, not healthy.'

'Getting worse all the time,' I said. 'Now it's also pollution from Cohibas and the PNG Gold. Plus the crack smoke, that can be really bad in the early evening.'

'Lunch,' said Cam. 'There's a place up the track here does a good steak roll. Local beef.'

'Get there,' said Harry. 'Step on it.'

'Shame to eat them,' I said. 'They're so nice.'

'Jack, listen,' said Harry, 'this horse, I want to set up a little arrangement, five shares, that's us three, the lovely wife, Mrs A. Arrange that, can you?'

'I can arrange that,' I said, 'but why?'

'Bit of fun. Nothin down, nothin to pay. Win anythin, we

take off expenses incurred, split the balance five ways. Cam'll cook the books.'

'What exactly do you have in mind for this horse?' I said.

'Early days. Get him up and runnin, that's the first thing. Do the arrangement thing then?'

'What happens if he doesn't win anything?'

A hand came up, wagged. 'That's a little punt I'm havin,' Harry said. 'No burden on the rest of you. Where's this food place? Gettin the weak feelin.'

'Hang on,' said Cam. 'Want to keep you goin till you make us rich.'

I was at Taub's most days through the heart of winter, getting there early, putting on the radio, firing up the stove, making tea, drinking a mug sitting in the sagging armchair with my back to the light from the dusty high windows.

Charlie grew to expect to find me there, the place warming up. He complained when I wasn't. One day, he showed me his drawings of a bookcase, a huge break-fronted thing, two metres tall, as wide, twelve drawers, four glazed doors. The drawing was done in an old business ledger, in pencil, hand-drawn lines ruler-straight, isometric views, oblique views, all elevations, annotated with measurements.

I flipped back through the pages: dozens of pieces of furniture drawn in the same detail.

'You've never told me about this book,' I said. 'You give me drawings on bits of paper torn off the edge of the *Age*.'

Charlie was sunk in his chair, drinking two-teabag tea out

of a mug made for him by one of his grandchildren. It was a misshapen vessel that spilled liquid if filled beyond a certain level.

'That's all you need,' he said. 'What, a child doesn't know the alphabet, you give him that Chomsky?'

'What Chomsky?' I said.

He waved the mug. 'An idiot,' he said.

'Right, that Chomsky. Why are you showing this to me?'

'Make it,' he said. '*Swietenia mahagoni*. Get it down.' He pointed skywards, at the Bank, the priceless collection of wood in the rafters at the back of the building.

'Make it?'

'They say I should drink green tea,' said Charlie, looking into the horrible mug. 'The girls. So tell me. Green tea.'

'Forget green tea,' I said. 'They're selfish, they want you to live forever. What do you mean, make it?'

He raised the unholy grail, studied me over its rumpled rim. 'Jack,' he said, 'I wait until you want to take responsibility, I have to live forever. Green tea. What is it?'

'Hang on here,' I said, alarmed now. 'I can't do this. Not the whole thing. No. I can do bits, yes.'

Charlie drank tea, lowered the container. 'The glazing bars, that you can't do. I'll show you.'

I said, 'As I see it, this job would need a router. I'll buy a router.'

Charlie got himself upright, walked towards the back, towards the sink. 'So,' he said. 'You think a person learns something, a little bit. But no. Everything wasted on them, all the time still a puppy dog.'

I said, 'I suppose it could be done without a router. Improvisation. I could make do.'

'They didn't give me lunch,' said Charlie. 'The little one's got a temperature.'

'I can probably find something for you to eat,' I said. 'They do a decent porridge sandwich down the road. Porridge on TipTop white.'

It was going to be a clear morning. The daylight through the high windows was strengthening.

'The drawings,' said Charlie. 'Can't understand, ask me.'

'I can understand,' I said. 'Pictures I can understand.'

'So,' he said. 'Green tea.'

'It's the just the raw material of tea,' I said. 'Until you make something nice out of it, it's just a piece raw tea.'

And so it began, with Charlie standing on the ladder pointing out pieces of dusty grey timber. When we'd got them down, he said, 'From Cuba. 1901.'

'As old as the Commonwealth of Australia,' I said. 'The Boer War, death of Queen Victoria.'

'Bruckner Symphony No. 6,' said Charlie. 'That was the year.' He began to hum and conduct with both massive hands.

Weeks later, I was dry-fitting the many pieces of the front assembly on one of the low benches when Cam arrived to fetch me. He was in corduroys and a tweed jacket, smoking a Gitane. 'Jesus, boss,' he said to Charlie, 'sure the boy knows which bit goes where?'

Charlie sucked on his dead cheroot, took it out and looked at it, shaking his head. 'No,' he said. 'With some people, you can only hope.'

In Elgin Street, on the way to Parkville in a refurbished Kingswood, soft Dolly Parton on eight speakers, I said, 'What's this about?'

'Lost Legion,' he said. 'Looks like we're goin racin. How you been?'

'Good,' I said. 'Did I ever say thanks for the Grange?'

'Goin bad in the cupboard. You or the Salvos.'

'Do they accept gifts of alcohol?'

'Not any old piss. They'll take the Grange. Saints in the deepest, I notice.'

'I don't want to notice. I have enough pain.'

Harry's garden was a pleasing sight in any season. Now it was stark, bare of greenery except for the old box hedges. The oaks stood in their decaying leaves, sparrows jostled on the two feeder tables, the cold sky was reflected in the stone-rimmed oval pond.

Mrs Aldridge answered the knocker, took my overcoat. 'Mr Strang's in the viewing room,' she said. 'Watching cartoons.'

She led us to the small cinema, opened the door on near-dark and the smell of a Cuban cigar, it entered the head like a sweet poison.

'Jack, Cam,' said Harry. The screen went blank. We were behind him, he was in his seat, the middle armchair. ' "The Simpsons", that Homer. You watch that, Jack?'

'On too early for me,' I said.

'That's why the good Lord's given us the VCR. Sit.'

I walked the three or four steps and sank into the chair beside him. Cam went to the bank of electronic equipment.

'Never filled you in on this Legion,' said Harry. 'That's remiss. Shareholder should know what's goin on. Full disclosure. Now this nag, the breedin's bugger-all to speak of, he comes a bit good at three. Six starts, clocks a win, second, two thirds.'

'This is where?' I said.

'Over there in the west. It's all sand and cowboys, all low grade, the ore's all low grade, everythin's a notch or two down from the rest of the world. Anyway, this Legion, nothin over 1600 metres, only win's at 1400.'

'Ready,' said Cam.

'These WA palookas, Jack,' said Harry, waving his Havana, 'these sandbiters, they give him a long holiday, then they put the little thing in a 2400. Why you would you do that? First up and 800 extra? Only the good Lord knows. That or the pricks thought they were havin a laugh.'

The aromatic cigar smoke was inducing a terrible craving in me. The denial of the pleasure of a good cigar. I needed to rethink that.

'Go,' said Harry.

We saw Lost Legion miss the start by about five lengths—horses leapt and then there was daylight and then he appeared.

'Now note, Jack, the jock reckons he's blown it,' said Harry. 'He's buggered, he decides to take the animal on a little walk.'

We watched Lost Legion ambling along, getting further behind, for the first 350-odd metres. By then the field of twelve was strung out, at least twenty lengths from first tail to last nose.

'Now the best you would think the fella would do is just catch up, show the stewards he's tryin,' said Harry. 'Trainer's not goin to thank him for thrashin the horse from there. But no, not this turkey, he gets the blood rush. Watch.'

Just before the 2000-metre mark, Lost Legion's jockey was galvanised, suddenly took to the stick, manic riding. The horse responded as if a brake had been released. By the time he ran out of legs, Lost Legion was in front, fifty metres from the post. He finished fifth, lathered.

'Now when you put the clock on the last two thou,' said Harry, 'bloody thing could near enough've won the '79 Australian Cup from Dulcify. Tell him what happened after, Cam.'

'They give him a rest,' said Cam. 'Come back in the autumn, somethin in him's gone. He runs fourths and fifths. Give him another rest. In the spring, first up, he runs seventh. Second was worse. Sack the jock. He runs tenth, big field. Try someone else on him: six of eight, hangin in all the way. They try blinkers, he beats one home. Off to the paddock again, comes back, two stone motherless lasts. Vets can't find anythin. This's the last outin of his career.'

On the big screen, horses going into the starting gate somewhere.

'Bunbury,' said Cam. 'Where that little Hobby jumps off the horse, he's so keen not to win.'

The light was flashing. The gates opened and the field went away in its bumping, jostling urgency.

Except for Lost Legion. He would not leave the gate, stood head down and still. His small rider urged him repeatedly, gave up, climbed off, climbed out of the cramped stall, walked away, his head down, whipping himself with his stick—not hard, reflectively.

'After that, he starts to act up till they can't come near him,' said Cam. 'Breaks a stablehand's leg, kicks a float to bits, bites someone. They give up, get rid of him.'

Harry switched the lights on from the console on the arm

of his chair. 'Let's bite somethin ourselves, have a drop of the dark fluid,' he said.

We returned to the study. Harry sat behind the desk made for him by Charlie Taub. Cam and I sat in the green leather armchairs beneath the cliffs of racing books. Mrs Aldridge came in with coffee in a silver pot and a choice of small steaming raisin scones and chocolate-dipped meringues.

'One each for you, Mr Strang,' she said, brisk English voice, pouring coffee.

'I keep tellin you, Mrs A., I've given away the ridin,' said Harry. His powerful hands were on the desk, I thought I saw twitching.

When she was gone, he put four of each on his plate.

I took my coffee and a scone, yellow Normandy butter leaking from the line of division. Blue Mountain and homemade scones with Normandy butter, this was what the gods on Mount Olympus commanded their Mrs Aldridges to feed them at mid-morning.

Harry's jaw was moving, eyes thin with taste appreciation. 'Lorna, she reckons he's nearly ready. Down for a barrier trial next week. After that, it's when we want to go.'

'Go?' I said. 'As in unknown horse found in Gippsland with sores and wearing rotten old rug wins comeback race? Or what?'

'That is pretty much the question,' said Harry. 'Cam?'

'Well,' Cam said. He pointed at the last meringue.

'Go for your life, son,' said Harry. 'Could save mine accordin to what passes for wisdom around here.'

I saw the dark object disappear into Cam, ingested. He was a neat eater, like a fish.

'Have a try or two in the country,' Cam said. 'Stay away

from the books and get a proper look, don't push him. We could take a long-term view.'

Harry drank from the white china cup, looking over our heads, his eyes on his Charlie Taub bookshelves, on his books. He was in some of them, just a mention, the horses were what mattered, you didn't try to breed jockeys.

'Feel myself movin away from the long-term view these days,' he said. 'But I can hear sense. Jack?'

'What about the other shareholders?' I said. 'Don't they get a say?'

'Got the proxies,' said Harry. 'More or less. Yes or no?'

I said, 'What does saying yes entail?'

'Go for a win first up. Bugger the long-term view.'

Rain smudges on the tall window behind Harry. We'd probably passed the day's top temperature.

'Yes,' I said. 'I've had it with the long term. I'm a short-term man now.'

'Go it is,' said Harry. 'Cam, tell Lorna we're lookin for the right race. It'll be soon.'

Breakfast at Enzio's, just coffee and sourdough toast with Vegemite. When she brought the ingredients, Carmel said, 'I should have mentioned before, the boy wonder's gone.'

'Better offer?' I said.

'Bruno decked him. The boy told the silent one to get away from the machine so that he could, I quote, make myself a fucking decent cup of coffee.'

'An inflammatory speech.'

'On the floor and out the door. Whingeing all the way. We had to ring Enzio. He's doing the whole day now.'

When she brought the coffee, Carmel said, 'He wants me to be the manager, sort of. He says he's not having any more little pricks in his kitchen. What would your view be of that?'

'I applaud the absence of little pricks everywhere.'

'No, me and the manager thing.'

'You'd be the public face of Enzio's?'

She shrugged, the bird shoulders. 'I'd be clean-shaven, that might be a plus. Perhaps my body language would be seen as less threatening. And no cigarette stub behind the ear.'

'I like the smoking-ear look,' I said, 'but for what it's worth I think you'd be an ornament to the position.'

'Thank you. I'll give it some thought.'

She was leaving when I said, 'Ahem, we won't be going down the skinny soy decaf latte and organic prunes poached in goat's milk route, will we?'

Over her shoulder, Carmel said, 'I'm too young to die violently.'

I had just started my coffee, when Sophie Longmore came in, a short camel jacket over jeans, carrying a bag like a slim briefcase. She looked around, I looked away but I could see her coming.

'The man from across the road suggested you might be here,' she said. 'He came out while I was knocking at your door.'

That would be McCoy, ever eager to make the acquaintance of attractive women.

'I'm just leaving,' I said.

She sat down, bag on the other chair.

'Why don't you sit down,' I said.

'I'm sorry. Are you angry with us, Jack?'

I didn't want to have this discussion. 'I'm just finished with you,' I said. 'Also, I don't like being asked whether I'm angry. It's either unnecessary or it's provocative.'

Head down. 'I'm doing this badly.'

Carmel arrived.

Sophie said, 'Could I have a short black?'

I drank half of my thimble. 'Well, I have to be somewhere else. Goodbye.'

She put a hand on my elbow. 'I came to say how sorry I am about everything. About what happened to you and about the other day. That's all.'

I shrugged.

'I wasn't sure what you were saying and my father jumped to a conclusion,' she said.

'It didn't take him long either.'

She moved her shoulders. 'Jack, he's nearly eighty, it's his first instinct, he thinks the whole world's trying to take his money away from him. Sometimes he's right too.'

There was a silence. It occurred to me that it had been possible to misunderstand what I'd said.

'I found that my hospital bill had been paid and some money paid into my bank,' I said. 'If it was your father, I wanted to give it back.'

'That's what I thought you were saying,' she said. 'He'll want to apologise to you himself. I wanted to come after you but I was too ashamed by what he'd said.'

She had the Longmore frankness. There wasn't any rage to maintain. 'Forget it,' I said. 'I should have been unambiguous.'

Sophie's coffee arrived.

'She was the last person who'd have a gas accident,' she said. 'You do know that?'

'I'm ignorant about gas accidents,' I said. 'They said it wasn't unusual.'

Two homicide cops had taken a statement from me when it was deemed that I was out of danger. Then two fire people came, a severe-looking woman in her forties and a younger man with thick glasses. They had my statement to homicide. The woman had questions about the position of the gas cylinders, about what Sarah had done in the seconds before, what I'd smelled, the number of explosions.

When Drew came a few days later, he said, 'They say they think the first explosion was in the store, an LPG cylinder. Apparently there was an old inspection pit and that went up too, full of gas. Plus other cylinders about the place. Not unusual, the woman says. Only the scale. Generally, it just destroys lone amateurs, your backyard self-taught welders and artists who like buggering around with steel and fire. Should happen to McCoy.'

Sophie Longmore shook her head. 'She wasn't a beginner, she'd done welding courses, she checked everything three times.'

She drank coffee, touched her lips with a paper napkin. Short nails. She bit her nails.

'The inquest will tell us,' I said. I didn't say it with conviction.

'I think people who can get an innocent person charged with murder can get an explosion past an inquest,' she said.

Her eyes didn't leave me, she had the look of someone leading up to something. Practising the law teaches you to recognise the expression. 'That's possible,' I said. 'We'll have to wait.'

Sophie took her bag off the chair, opened it and took out an A4 envelope. 'I think she was being watched,' she said. 'Why would she be watched?'

I wanted to be away, into the cold morning, a top of fourteen, said the radio, that would only be few hours away, then the slide into the serious cold. Rain expected, showers in the city, gale-force winds for the bay and strong winds inland, ice, frost, snow for the alpine areas. A sheep alert for country Victoria. How did they respond to sheep alerts in the country? Wrestle the jumbucks into thermal longjohns?

'I don't know,' I said. 'People have been known to think they're being watched when they're not.'

Sophie looked at me without blinking for longer than necessary. 'Not unusual,' she said. 'Is that the expression?'

I felt tired. So early in the day. Excusable perhaps on these short days. The circadian rhythms interrupted, a form of jetlag. 'I have to go,' I said. 'Work.'

'I took these pictures,' she said, offering the envelope. 'They're actually very bad. The negs are in here too, it might be the printing.'

'Pictures of what?'

'Sarah was getting out of the car and said, that's her again. I saw the woman and I took a few shots, she turned her back and walked away. She was talking to someone in a car.'

'Why do you want to give me these pictures?'

Sophie didn't look at me, eyes down, drank coffee, looked up, her father's pale eyes, down again.

'I don't want her remembered this way,' she said. 'I worshipped her. She was everything to me.'

'Are you asking me to do something?'

'I wouldn't dream of asking you to do anything yourself. You've gone through enough. I hoped you'd know someone who could…help.'

I looked out of the window. The wind was disturbing hairstyles, pushing open unbuttoned black overcoats.

Just say no.

'What was Mickey's relationship with Anthony Haig?' I said without looking at her.

Sophie sighed. 'He had money in Seaton Square. Most of the money, I think. When it stalled, he wanted to get out.'

'I thought the money came from a finance company?'

'The way Mickey talked,' she said, 'Haig and the company, well, they're the same thing. He was ballistic about Haig.'

'Haig's got an employee called Bernard Paech.'

She nodded. 'Bern, they call him Bern.'

'He was also once a director of Mickey's company. If Haig was calling in the money, how did that work?'

'I don't know. Mickey didn't explain a lot, Jack.'

'But you went to your father to bail him out?'

'In love,' she said. She finished her coffee. 'But I'm not stupid. I wouldn't have asked my father if I thought Mickey was a loser. Mickey'd made a lot of money out of development. And Seaton Square, well, it's such an incredible opportunity.'

An incredible opportunity. An opportunity to change the character of part of the city. People like Mickey were social planners, they decided the future by deciding where they could make money. Was this the genius of capitalism? How did Venice get the way it was? What about Florence? Paris? Vienna?

'I need to think about this,' I said. 'Give me a number.'

Sophie took her case off the chair, snapped it open and found a pad and a pen. She was writing when I said, 'When did you decide that Sarah didn't kill Mickey?'

She didn't look up. 'The idea never crossed my mind.'

The pictures in hand, I said goodbye, went into the windy street.

'Leave it, Jack,' said Drew. 'It's finished.'

'Money in my account, hospital paid. Leave it?'

He moved his chair, left, right, not far. 'It probably is Longmore, pre-empting a damages claim.'

'No. He looked at me as if I were a blackmailer. Contempt.'

Shifting the chair, movements of the head and the mouth. 'Well, you've had a bad time, I wouldn't discount the possibility that you might have misread that.'

'Well, fuck bad time, I know contempt, I'm not that scrambled.'

'He didn't treat me like the papal envoy either,' he said, 'but he's a hirer, he hires, he fires, we're just service providers in his life, fence-builders on the fucking estate. Dig holes, line the fucking poles up, string the wire, fuck off, we're nothing. And offshore accounts, he wouldn't want to shout about them.'

'So I just declare it as income?'

'Consultancy fee. Tax don't care. Grateful that you told them.'

I said, 'I don't think she killed Mickey.'

His phone rang. 'Put him on, thanks. Laurie. Yes, yes, sorry. I am guilty, mate, guilty as charged. The same to you in spades. Listen, can I ring you back, five minutes? Thanks.'

Drew looked at me as he spoke. Sad brown eyes. I'd never noticed sadness in his eyes. Had it always been there? How did you recognise sadness in eyes? Was I seeing my own stupid sadness in him?

He put down the phone. 'Free for a drink later?'

I said, 'I don't think she killed Mickey.'

'Jack, Jack, it doesn't matter who killed Mickey. We'll never know, we don't care, we had a client who may or may not have killed Mickey but we don't have her anymore and so it's over.'

I got up.

'Not rushing you,' he said. 'Hang around here all day. Come back and work here, the offer always stands.'

I said, 'Kind of you, it could become some sort of legal rehab centre, there's probably a grant available. I'd like to tell you that I'm no more brain-damaged than I was before. Can I see Sarah's file?'

Drew sighed, looked down. Then he picked up his phone. 'Karen, give Jack the Longmore file, will you?'

'Thank you,' I said.

He opened his hands. 'Ring me if you want to have a drink later.'

I collected the file and walked down the elegant street to the Lark, admired it as I came. I loved the car and it was nothing but trouble. A metaphor for something, the Lark.

The office was cold, air stale. I left the front door open, opened the back one, and a gale went through. When the air was changed, I closed the doors, put on the heater, made tea, sat down in the client's chair with Sarah's file. It didn't take long to read. The prosecution case was that she'd had an affair with Mickey, been replaced by her sister, was known to have the weapon that killed him, was seen near his apartment building on the night of 16 March, at around the time of his murder. Prosecutions had proceeded on much less.

I read bits again, mulled. The gun part was bad. She'd admitted once having it. Being near the scene, that was terrible.

The witness was a woman called Donna Filipovic. Her statement said she'd heard about Mickey's murder on the radio and contacted the police. She lived in an apartment block near Mickey's. She'd noticed a woman about six months earlier when there was an argument about a parking space. The woman was about to reverse into it when another driver pulled in. The woman got out of her car and wouldn't let the man open his door. He eventually reversed out and drove off.

Ms Filipovic told the police that on the previous night, just before midnight, she was walking her dog when she saw a woman come out of the side entrance of Mickey's apartment block. The woman came towards her, walking quickly, passed her, and got into a car.

From a large number of photographs of different women shown to her by the police, she'd identified Sarah Longmore as the woman she'd seen before and saw the night before. She said that she was not in any way prompted by the police officers but had been left alone with the photographs.

A heatless lemon-yellow rectangle of sunlight had fallen across me. Dust motes moved in it, not in any hurry, presumably some of them skin and dandruff, tiny bits of me that had abandoned ship, floating about, carrying my DNA.

Nothing gained from reading the file except bad feelings. Did it matter if Sarah had killed Mickey?

I had no wish to pursue that line.

The witness on the night, near the time, that would have tested Drew, shown whether he was the equal of those in the bar's murder squad, the criminal silks, men and women steeped in violence who could convince juries to give psychopaths the benefit of the doubt.

I drank the cold remains, flicked back through the pages, looked up at the piece of sky, torn clouds, ragged, all the shades of grey.

Something flickered in the mind.

The witness. Her name was Donna Filipovic.

I sat, uncrossed my legs, crossed them again. The name. I thought about talking to Popeye Costello. *Probably snaffled fucking Donna now that I think of it.*

I went to the table, found the number, I gave the receptionist my name.

'Please hold on while I see if he's available,' she said, a concerned help-line voice. She was back in seconds. 'If you'll leave a number,' she said.

I went back to the client's chair and sat in the gathering gloom, sunlight gone, almost falling asleep, jerked awake by the phone.

'Yes,' said Popeye Costello.

'When we were talking, you said a name,' I said. 'You said the name Donna.'

'Yes?'

'Is that also a Foreign Legion name?'

'No, that's the bitch's name.'

'And the surname?'

He hesitated.

In the west, the sky showing streaks of orange, an unhealthy colour, like the flames of a burning tip.

'Filipovic,' he said. 'Donna Filipovic.'

The address the homicide squad had for Donna Filipovic was an apartment on the fifth floor of a building called Bolzano, about two blocks from Mickey Franklin's dwelling. She wasn't in the phone book.

Admission was by key or concierge, a man in a dark suit who came out of a door in the marble lobby, adjusting a striped tie.

'May I be of assistance?' he said through the intercom system, from inside the glass doors. He had the perfectly groomed grey hair and voice of an assistant from the men's department of the long-gone George's department store in Collins Street.

'I'm a lawyer,' I said. I took out my Law Institute card and held it to the glass. 'I'm trying to get in touch with one of your tenants on behalf of a client.'

He raised his chin and his nostril crimped. 'I'm afraid we

admit no one without the tenant's permission. May I have a name?'

'Filipovic,' I said, 'Donna Filipovic.'

'Could you spell the surname?'

I did. They didn't require him to call people 'Sir' here, that would be a relief.

'I'll make inquiries,' he said.

It was early afternoon, the street quiet by inner-city standards, the temperature falling. A door in the foyer opened and a woman with pink-purple hair came in carrying a shopping bag from David Jones. She went to the lifts. Only visitors would come through the front door of this building, the residents would park in the basement, come up the stairs to the foyer or take the lift.

Mr George's came back. The shiny black tips of his shoes caught the downlights.

'We have no one of that name,' he said, a small, pleased smile.

I took out my notebook, found a page, any page, looked at it. 'You certainly did in March,' I said. 'Have you lost your records?'

He put his head to one side, shrugged the tiniest shrug. There was uncertainty in him.

I said, 'I don't normally do this kind of thing myself but it's important to a valued client. May I have your name?'

He licked a lip. 'Ashton, Morris Ashton.'

'Mr Ashton, I'm saying to you as a matter of fact, I repeat, as a matter of fact, that Ms Filipovic had an apartment in this building in March this year. If you don't want to be helpful, I'll get a court order today to see your register of owners and tenants.'

While I looked into his eyes, he considered this statement. No more than three or four seconds went by.

He pressed a button. The doors parted. 'If you'd care to come to the office with me,' he said.

I followed him. The office was neat, no security screens, two desks, a computer on each, a bank of filing cabinets, a copier.

'May I copy your card?' he said.

I took it out. He put it on the copier surface, closed the top, punched the button. The light moved.

'Thank you,' he said, opened the machine, gave me the card. 'Please sit down, this won't take a moment.'

'I've been sitting all day,' I said.

He sat down, clicked at a keyboard, waited, clicked, put his head closer, he was short-sighted.

'No,' he said. 'I'm afraid there's no record of that name. Do you have the apartment number?'

I gave it.

He clicked. 'Ah, there's no registered occupier. It's a corporate apartment. The person may have been a guest. Is that possible?'

'I suppose I'll have to ask the owners,' I said. 'Who are they?'

He looked at me, uneasy. 'We're not at liberty to disclose that information,' he said.

'Mr Ashton,' I said. 'I'm sure I don't have to tell you that this information isn't secret, it's on the public record. Are you trying to be obstructive?'

Flutter of eyelids. He didn't have much experience in dealing with this kind of bluster.

'That apartment is owned by Amaryllo Holdings,' he said.

'One of three.' He gave me the spelling, the details.

'So anyone could claim to have been staying in the apartment and you wouldn't be able to confirm or deny that?' I said.

'It isn't any of my business,' Ashton said. 'The owners are free to have anyone they like stay in their apartments. We require only that they tell us when the premises are occupied.'

I gave him the date of Mickey's death, 16 March. 'Was the apartment occupied then?'

He was even unhappier now but it was too late. He looked it up. 'Yes, it was.'

'And when did that cease?'

'Um, about two weeks after that date.'

'When did that period of occupancy begin?'

'A week before that. It had been unoccupied for about three months.'

As I walked back to the car, it was on my mind that I should have done this first. I should have gone for the only important witness, not buggered around with the victim. We hadn't really believed Sarah, that's why we'd gone for Mickey. Not we. It was me. I'd put off looking at the witness.

In the car, I rang Simone Bendsten and gave her the company name. She rang back as I pulled up down the street from the office.

'Owned by another company, Vindolanda No. 3, registered in Monaco,' said Simone. 'That will almost certainly be a dead end. Amaryllo's local address is Alan Duchard, Gaitelband, barristers and solicitors, in Prahran.'

A firm I'd heard of before. I said thanks, went inside and looked at Sophie Longmore's photographs. Four prints, ordinary snapshot 10 x 15s, seriously bad black-and-white photographs, taken from inside a car. Sophie had drawn arrows on them pointing at the subject, a youngish woman in black, but glare all but ruined two. The third was better but the woman was half-obscured by a car, looking away. The fourth was the least bad, the subject was in the street talking to the driver of a car. Unfortunately, her head was down and her straight hair fallen forward, curtaining her profile. There was a front-seat passenger in the car, a head could be made out, but that was all.

All too hard, all too pointless. Sarah was dead and the rest didn't matter much now. Sophie could choose the ways she wanted to remember her sister.

I knew what nonsense that was as I said it to myself. There was no choice in these things, the memories came anywhere: in the shower, at the traffic lights, studying cans in the supermarket, anywhere you were alone. And, worst of all, they came in dreams, in the mind's mysterious cinema. There they were real, the past was undone, you felt the touch of those you had loved, the happiness was restored. That was the worst, the cruellest.

I rang Sophie Longmore's mobile number. She answered after two rings.

'Jack Irish,' I said. 'I have to say I can't do anything more in this matter and I don't know anyone who can. I'm sorry.'

Twittering on the line, she was far away or some obstacle stood between us.

'I'm sorry,' I said, again, she might not have heard me.

The sounds stopped. 'Jack, please,' she said, 'you're the last person who has to say sorry.'

I wanted to end the conversation at the point, but I didn't want to be the one to do it.

'Well,' she said, 'thanks again, Jack, I didn't tell you, that morning, Sarah left a message on my voicemail.'

The sounds again, the pre-electronic sound of cat's whisker scraping on crystal. It began to rain, I was looking at big tropical drops hitting a car outside, wet explosions, watched them become freezing spaghettini.

Across the way, a light came on upstairs in McCoy's premises. I said nothing, felt the cold in the room, in the heart, in the stomach, in the bone.

'Jack?' she said.

'Yes, I'm here.'

'She said she was feeling cheerful for the first time in weeks and it was because of a man.'

'Sorry,' I said, 'didn't hear that, you're breaking up. So I'll say goodbye.'

I sat in the gloom, my mind wandering around in the tall maze that was the whole business. I didn't intend to. I didn't want to think about it at all, but that wasn't possible. I had to accept that I couldn't leave it alone.

Janene Ballich, table dancer. Why had the man in the car given me her name that night? Who was he? What part did Janene Ballich play in the story of Mickey Franklin? I'd been to Gippsland, I'd talked to Popeye Costello, all I got were more names: Wayne Dilthey, Katelyn Feehan aka Mandy Randy, Donna Filipovic. Janene was missing, probably dead. Wayne was definitely dead, shot in some country town. Where was Katelyn?

Time for a beer. No Charlie tonight, he was playing bowls, handing out another thrashing to the youngsters in Brunswick.

It couldn't be coincidence that I'd hear Donna's name in

Popeye's office and then find that she was the witness against Sarah who could place her near the scene of the crime. I remembered Popeye's whistle when he saw Katelyn Feehan in the photograph with Wayne Dilthey.

The cunt. Pinched her off me. *Probably snaffled fucking Donna*…Snaffled Donna from table dancing and giving personals? To join Wayne's pleasure-service business? Donna, who just happened to be spending three weeks in a corporate apartment owned by a company in Monaco when she saw Sarah. Where had she been living when she first saw Sarah, during the altercation with the parking-space thief?

Was Donna lying, prepared to commit perjury in a murder trial? What could induce her to do that? How could she know about the argument with the driver unless she'd seen it?

I got up, stretched, put on my overcoat. I was at the front door when I remembered. That was the night Sarah said she'd met Anthony Haig. She was on her way to dinner with Mickey and Anthony Haig on the night of the parking fight.

You'd talk about something like that. You left your car standing in the street and held a driver captive in his own car. You'd still be full of adrenalin and indignation when you arrived at your destination, the story would spill out, it would be remarkable if it didn't.

So Donna could have been given the story by someone Sarah had told it to. Or by someone who heard it from that person. Sarah might have told the story to dozens of people. She would certainly have told it to Sophie, and Sophie…make that hundreds of people.

Monaco? A company in Monaco. I went back to the

table, found my file, the stuff from D. J. Olivier, skimmed down the pages.

> Subject's company Saint Charles involved in hundreds of property dealings. Finance generally offshore. Frequent provider is First Crusader Finance, Monaco. This entity run by Charles Robert Hartfield, once partner in Melbourne solicitors Alan Duchard, Gaitelband...

The Melbourne address of the company that owned the apartment Donna stayed in was Alan Duchard, Gaitelband, barristers and solicitors of Prahran.

I rang Telstra inquiries, was rejected as incomprehensible by the voice recognition software, gave the name Saint Charles to a grumpy human, got a number, declined the exorbitantly priced direct connection.

It was picked up on the third ring. 'Saint Charles.' A man.

'I'd like to speak to Anthony Haig.'

'I can try to raise him. Your name?'

'Jack Irish. I'm a solicitor.'

'Hold on.'

Silence. I held, looking at the bare walls, just the framed professional certificates. A painting or two would be nice. Why had I never done that? Why had I kept this place looking like the abode of a lawyer monk?

'Mr Irish. Tony Haig.' A rough voice.

'Mr Haig, I'd like to talk to you about matters concerning Mickey Franklin,' I said. 'Is that possible?'

'Of course,' he said, no hesitation. 'I'm edge-to-fucking-edge this week though...listen, why don't you come around to my place tomorrow night, evening, it's early, a little gathering, we'll go off and have a chat? How does that fit?'

'Fine,' I said, not showing my surprise.

'It's a building called Marengo in…'

'I know it.' Everyone knew the Marengo, designed by an architect with popstar status.

'Around six, they'll have your name at the desk. See you.'

I drove to the Prince, squeezed the Stud into a half-occupied loading zone. The men were at battle stations, bickering.

'Well, you're a bloody stranger,' said Norm O'Neill. 'Put us into these Sainters, bloody poisoned chalice, then we never see hide nor hair of ya.'

'I was thinking we might go on Sunday,' I said. 'Carlton again, at Docklands.'

'The tent,' said Eric Tanner. 'Bloody disgrace a great outdoor game now gets played in a circus tent.'

'Tell you what,' said Norm O'Neill, 'no shortage of clowns in the tent when the Saints play. Young and old, the big fella can't clap hands, misses. Needs a damn good lookin over by the eye, feet and hand specialist.'

'Eye, feet and hand?' said Wilbur. 'What kind of specialist is that?'

'Jesus, I don't know,' said Norm. 'Ever heard of co-ordination? Sometimes I wonder about the ignorance in the world.'

On the twenty-fifth floor, the lift stopped and allowed me into a room in the building's core, a box of reinforced concrete, but not claustrophobic, lights in four deep alcoves and spots in the ceiling. The effect was of a small Moorish courtyard.

I crossed to a steel door pretending to be made of wood. An electronic keypad glowed. Above it was a button with the camera symbol. I knew about this. The entrant was required to put in a code number, press the button that switched on the video cameras to give security a full view of the lift and the anteroom. If this didn't happen quickly, it triggered a security alert. Inserting or adding a number was an alarm signal and armed people would arrive inside a minute.

I pressed the button marked Ring. The electronic sentry went green with approval, I was being watched from the foyer, where I'd given my name.

The door slid open, revealing a short passage. I went down it into a double-height panelled foyer with a staircase rising to a landing. At left and right were sets of double doors, eight panels each, no doubt salvaged from some nineteenth-century boom-time building long fallen to the breaker's ball.

A man appeared on the landing. Medium height, medium age, full head of crisp greying hair, medium length, brushed back and to the side with a parting.

'Jack,' he said, warmth in the single word, and started down the stairs, treading lightly.

I waited.

'Tony Haig,' he said. 'I told them to ring me when you got here.'

A perfect dark suit, white shirt, grey tie, regular features, the nose a trifle truncated—he could have been the life model for a dummy in Myer's window in 1965.

We shook hands. He showed the strength in his hand but he didn't overdo it. 'Come up,' he said. 'I'm glad you rang, thought about ringing you. More than once.'

We climbed the staircase side by side. I felt his arm behind me, just touching my jacket, as one might escort an elderly relative up a staircase, taking care but not wishing to suggest the need for it.

'There's a bit of symmetry about you being here tonight,' he said.

You and explosions. There's a fearful fucking symmetry.

'Yes?'

'We're celebrating the resurrection of Seaton Square, Mickey's Brunswick project. That closes a chapter, not so?'

'I don't know,' I said. 'I'm never sure whether anything's finished or just lying in wait.'

Haig laughed, it was a genuine sound, good-humoured. 'Spoken like an old-world pessimist,' he said.

The hand behind me touched me in the small of the back, a gesture of intimacy and affection. It was a European touch, not what someone did casually to another man going into the pub in Tingaboora or Rainbow.

'Glad you could come, Jack,' he said.

I reached the landing and he opened a door and ushered me through. We stood above a big room, longer that it was wide. Two or three dozen people were standing with drinks, a small bar set up in a corner, white-shirted waiters with trays moving in the crowd.

Beyond a wall of glass lay a vast scape of lights, horizontal and vertical, moving and still, pinpricks, strings, clusters, pillars, silver, pinks, yellows, blues, reds. At this height, everything was calmed by distance and rain.

'I don't know who you'll know,' said Haig.

I saw Steven Massiani near the window with two men and a woman.

'Probably no one,' I said.

We went down the two steps to the room. A waiter offered champagne in expensive flutes, the wine with a minute silver bead.

'The Billecart Salmon,' said Haig. 'Know the stuff?'

'Only by name,' I said, drinking some.

'Good fizz,' he said. 'Too good for some of this lot.'

He took me around, introduced me to people. He didn't say what I did for a living and he didn't say what they did. Most of them were youngish, in black or grey, jackets worn over collarless shirts, the full range of hair, from nothing to plenty. Many of the men needed a shave, some could have done with a swift kick up the arse. One woman had hair like a monk's cap and wore a silken sleeveless top slit to the belly, olive-skinned bulges showing. I knew the names of a few of them: restaurant owners, fashionable architects, a gallery owner, a photographer, two artists. We stopped briefly at the small court of an ageing film director—two women and a youth I thought I'd seen on television, mostly cheekbones and big brown eyes, all absorbing cinematic genius through their pores. The director paid close attention to Tony Haig, ignoring his own acolytes while we were there. It was a food chain.

Haig left me with two men who soon returned to talking money. I thought it was money, I registered only the term 'capacity to service'. They could well have been talking about stud horses.

I walked across to the window, uneasy, knowing that I shouldn't have accepted the invitation, should have met Haig at another time, perhaps not at all. There was no reason to be in this place, with these people.

The view was dazzling but the canvas was too big. Like all views, it needed to be painted to be appreciated properly. When I turned, I saw the paintings on the long gallery wall, well spaced, all sizes. I went up the stairs and had a look. Modern paintings, no artist I recognised, all oils, lots of landscapes and seascapes—cliffs, promontories, bays, coves, water, light. There was also a sequence of dark paintings by the same artist, views of snow-topped peaks, icy lakes, forests and plunging rivers that conveyed a loneliness and a sadness.

And there were portraits, marked differences in style but all striking because the subjects, men and women, had faces of character. At the end of the line was one of Tony Haig. He was in a collarless white shirt, tanned face half in shadow. Behind him was a blank wall, white, rough-plastered, with a single aperture, like a gun-slit. One tendril of a creeping plant was stealing through the slit, invading, a thin green snake, a leaf at its tip.

It was a fine painting, the Haig portrait. They were all worth looking at, paintings of merit as far as I could judge. There was not one that you would pass by with a single glance.

A man of taste and means, Anthony Haig. Or possibly just of means—taste was something the rich could buy.

'Interesting, aren't they?'

I turned. Behind me was the woman I'd seen across the room in the group with Steven Massiani.

'You're Jack,' she said. 'Tony pointed you out. I'm Corin Sleeman. I was married to Mickey.'

She had her hand out, close to her body. I took it. It was small, a child's hand, my hand felt inflated, I felt like an enfolder.

'It's been horrible,' she said. 'A really bad dream.'

She had the face of a girl in a pre-Raphaelite painting, not the hair, which was blonded and careless, but the nose, the brow, the poreless skin, the innocent and expectant mouth. The pre-Raphaelite child in middle age, a face no less arresting for the signs of time.

'At least we've woken up,' I said. 'Who are these painters?'

'Corsicans,' she said. 'Tony collects Corsican art.'

'He would have a corner on the market then,' I said.

'I liked Sarah's work,' she said. 'I had her do a piece for a building in South Melbourne. The client's wife hated it, loathed it, a Frankston girl, her father was a smash repairer.'

'She'd know crumpled metal,' I said. 'It might have brought back memories of the days when her father started work by hosing off the blood.'

She started to smile, had pause. 'Come and join us. You know Steven, I understand.'

'We've met,' I said.

We went down and to Steven Massiani, Haig and another man, his back to us. As we approached, he turned. He was overweight, balding, with round glasses on a small nose. I'd seen him before, in a photograph, walking down a street with Mickey Franklin. Bernard Paech, once a director of Mickey's company, Yardlive.

'Hello, Jack,' said Massiani, hand out. 'Good to see you looking well.'

'You don't know Bern,' said Haig, 'Bernard Paech. He works with me. With me but not always for me.'

I shook hands with Paech. He was smoking a cigar. 'The co-director of Yardlive,' I said.

'Briefly,' Paech said.

A waiter appeared. Everyone except Massiani took new glasses of champagne.

Haig raised his flute. 'Health and happiness,' he said.

We drank.

'Steven's joined me in the Seaton Square project,' said Haig. 'Corin's done the redesign.'

I looked at Massiani. 'Do I remember you saying you'd learned your lesson in the suburbs?'

He smiled, a shrug. I now saw in his face someone who had known unhappiness early, perhaps beginning in the preschool playground. 'A good memory,' he said. 'Tony's the great persuader. Plus we've saddled him with the risk.'

'I'm not the great persuader,' said Haig. 'Bern's the persuader.'

'What happened to the objectors?' I said.

'Allayer of concerns,' said Paech. 'That's what I am.'

'Was that easy for Seaton Square?' I said.

'No more difficult than putting condoms on a bucketful of snakes,' said Paech. 'Well, marginally easier. New proposal. Scaled down. A good package. Subsidised childcare centre, public park, that sort of thing.'

He drew on his cigar, blew smoke at the ceiling. 'Also the three main objectors changed their minds, a big help that was.'

Haig laughed. Corin Sleeman didn't laugh, looked away. Massiani didn't laugh either. He was looking down, holding his empty glass by the base and running his flat hand, the fingers, around the rim. Through the noise of talk, the soft music playing, I heard the thin, hollow high sound he was creating.

'The important thing,' he said, looking up, at Paech, 'is that it'll get built.'

Paech was about to speak but he didn't.

'And if it's well done,' said Massiani, 'in a few years no one will remember the objections.'

'That's right,' said Paech. 'Exactly.'

He'd received the message.

Haig scratched his head. He had an amused look. 'Jack,' he said, 'you haven't had the tour.'

He took my arm and we crossed the room, went through a door into a passage. There was a glimpse of a kitchen on the left, three men and a woman standing at a counter, one man's head down, close to the granite countertop.

'The idiots,' said Haig. 'Like movies? I love movies. I watch one every day, that's the minimum, I've watched five in a day, what kind of habit is that?'

He showed me into the first room off the passage to the right. It had two couches and a soft armchair facing a huge television screen, two smaller ones beside it. There seemed to be a dozen speakers on the electronic wall, and hundreds of tapes and CDs in racks.

'I'm an insomniac,' he said. 'Also I can't fucking get to sleep. I wake up on this couch, clothes on, the first thing I see is Grace Kelly kissing Cary Grant, the lucky bastard.'

We left the room, went down the corridor, Haig in front. He opened a door, found a switch, lights came on, not bright.

'This is my special room,' he said. 'My special interest.'

It was a large space, a combination of library and museum, with tall bookshelves, glass cases, paintings and other framed objects in alcoves. There was a devotional feeling, the shadows, the way the light lay in soft pools and skewed rectangles, hung down the walls, the glow of colour in the paintings, the lustrous gilt of the frames.

'My collection,' he said.

I looked around the room. It was a museum and a shrine to Napoleon Bonaparte and it spoke of obsession and deep pockets.

'You didn't put this together by getting to French flea-markets before the crowds,' I said.

Haig smiled, pleased, a boy's smile. 'You won't believe the junk. After they brought his bits back from St Helena in 1840, Napoleonic memorabilia became an industry. Nothing like it again until Elvis.'

We toured, Haig pointing and explaining, not lecturing. There were hundreds of books on Bonaparte and his times, dozens of oil paintings and drawings of Bonaparte, five or six busts, bas-relief profiles and figures, statuettes, battlefield maps, a pistol, a sword, signed notes, letters and documents, a silver cup in a leather holder, a horse's hoof on an ebony base, a lock of hair, a pair of boots, a telescope with gold inlay, a quill pen beside a silver inkpot, an ivory letter-opener, an ebony and silver baton, a fragment of a flag.

'Why Napoleon?' I said. We were looking at a single patent-leather shoe with a buckle of gold.

'My father. He was a Corsican. Stefanu Leca. Steve Leca.'

He went to a bookshelf and took down a small, battered, cloth-covered book. '*The Life of Napoleon*, by A. J. Danville,' he said. 'My dad bought this and a little English dictionary at a secondhand bookshop in Brisbane. He didn't have any English. He got it from this book. At night, cutting cane all day.'

Haig showed me the edge of the book, dark marks.

'Blood from his hand, the first few days. He'd never done any manual work. His father was a tailor.'

'Where does Haig come from?' I said.

'My mother. My father was working on her father's property near Bundaberg. He'd taught himself engines, bricklaying, plumbing, he could do anything, fix anything.'

He put the book away and stood with his back to the shelf, his face half in shadow as it was in the portrait. 'My father put the daughter of the house up the pole. They chased him off the property like a fucking dog, threatened to kill him. She went to Sydney to have the baby, stayed there with her aunt, didn't go back to Queensland till I was three.'

'So you were raised as Haig.'

'Yes, didn't know anything about my father till just before my mother died. I was always told I was adopted. Then my mother told me. She was ill and she told me.'

I went to the exhibits in the middle of the room, two death masks of Napoleon, one plaster, one bronze, on a slender plinth under glass and spotlit from above.

'The jewels,' said Haig. 'Found them in Cuba. His doctors on St Helena made a gypsum cast of the emperor's head after he died. One of them, his name's Antommarchi, he sold copies and then he went to live in Cuba. It's more than possible that the plaster one is an original, from St Helena.'

'Did you ever meet your father?' I said.

'I tracked him down in Broken Hill. Buggered by work but happy. Brought up two kids after his wife died. He wouldn't take anything from me, I had to force money on him, then he gave it to his kids. His other kids.'

'And he gave you the book?'

Haig was on the other side of the plinth, looking at the masks. 'The book was special for him. He knew every word in it. He told me that in the beginning he had to look up all the conjunctions and the prepositions. I wish I had his little dictionary but he'd lost it.'

I said, 'Someone paid my hospital bill and put fifty grand in my bank account.'

He looked up. 'That was me,' he said. 'If it bothers you, please give it away.'

Disarmed, unhorsed.

'Why?'

'An impulse, a whim. I liked Sarah very much. You got hurt trying to help her.'

226

'You'd do that on a whim? That much money?'

Haig laughed. 'I'm a rich man, you won't believe what I've done on a whim.'

'Do you know someone called Donna Filipovic?' I said.

No furrow in the brow. 'No.'

I took a chance. 'A company called Amaryllo, registered in Monaco, I understand you're connected with it.'

Haig smiled. 'Connected?'

'Through Charles Hartfield.'

Haig raised both hands, wide, blunt-fingered, passed them across his temples, smoothed hair needing no grooming, lowered his hands, held them palm up.

'Jack,' he said, 'What's this? Sarah's dead. You don't have to find a defence for her anymore.'

'Did you remember Sarah telling a story about an argument with a driver near Mickey's apartment? It was the night you met, dinner with Mickey.'

'No.'

Looking at him over the emperor's death masks. 'The witness Donna Filipovic,' I said. 'She's lying, she wasn't there, she never saw Sarah that night. Someone fed her that story.'

'The family, they're paying you to go on with this?'

'No,' I said.

He stared at me. 'Let's say for argument's sake Sarah didn't kill Mickey,' he said. 'Then you ask, who would take the trouble to kill him and set her up?'

I didn't reply.

Haig exhaled loudly, a sad shake of the head. 'Why would anyone bother?' he said. 'Given the fuck's mood swings, all-round mental state, the drink, the drugs, Mickey was going to do the job himself. Just a matter of how long.'

'You provided the finance for Seaton Square and then you wanted to pull the plug on him,' I said. 'He was enraged with you. That's right, isn't it?'

'Jack, Jack,' he said, 'Mickey fucked up Seaton Square almost from the kick-off. All he got right was getting hold of the property. And that's another story. After that, it was like the Cresta fucking Run in a shitstorm. Everything was a stuff-up—everything. He wound the thing up and up. I'll tell you I'm no stranger to ambitious development but this was insane. And he wouldn't listen to anyone. Well, he'd listen, sit there nodding his fucking coked-up head, yes, yes. Then he'd go off and do the opposite.'

He paused, shaking his head again. 'Mickey enraged with *me*? I can tell you, many times I'd have shot the cunt if I'd had a gun. And fuck the consequences.'

Silence in the museum of Bonaparte, no sound except the stern ticking of the brass clock, said to come from the emperor's first place of exile, Elba.

'But while you're looking for people to blame, Jack,' said Haig, 'try the people the stupid prick bribed over Brunswick. In his worst moments, he was going to take them down with him.'

'I need a piss,' I said.

'This way.'

We left the room. He opened another door.

'Through the dressing room. You'll find your way back. Straight down the passage.'

A four-poster uncanopied bed was tightly made, the dark wooden floor shone, the curtains were open. I could see across the wet smudged city to Williamstown.

I went into the dressing room. It held the stock of a small, expensive men's outfitters. On the shelves to the left were laundered shirts. Socks and underwear and sweaters were in glass-fronted drawers. Two racks held shoes, twenty pairs at least. On the right hung suits, sportsjackets, trousers, casual jackets, overcoats, raincoats. A regiment of ties was draped over rods on either side of the long mirror at the end of the room.

The door to the bathroom was open. It was big and plain, not a bathroom the interior decor crowd would create. Someone wanted this chamber to be a place for ablutions only: two small basins, a glass shower stall the size of a small room, a toilet, no bath.

I had my pee and went back to the party, found Haig. 'I have to go,' I said. 'I'll send you the tax receipt from the Salvos. Thank you for the thought.'

He walked me to the landing, touched me again in the affectionate way. 'We've got a lot in common, Jack,' he said. 'Working-class fathers, rich mothers. How'd you like her father?'

'Not much,' I said. 'Not a great deal.'

'Even more in common than I thought.'

A hand offered, we shook.

'You've got to look after yourself,' he said. 'Life's full of bullshit. Full of Mickeys. The trick is to walk away from them. I'm learning that, I'm nearly there.'

I was halfway down the staircase when he said, 'Jack.'

I stopped, looked back. He was standing with his hands clasped in front of his chest. 'I'm going to my house in Corsica next month,' he said. 'Private flight. Why don't you come? Good this time of year, hot, dry, it smells like nowhere else on earth. The maquis, the sea. Sweetness and salt.

Napoleon said it was the only place he would recognise blindfold.'

'Thanks,' I said. 'Can I let you know?'

'Ring Bern,' he said. 'We'll have a good time.'

I departed Marengo. A block away, I eased the Stud from between German bookends, an Audi and a Mercedes, and set out for Fitzroy. A wet night was on the city, the towers glowing in the damp air that softened everything, carried a smell of burnt fossil fuel.

Home, the place where they have to take you in. There weren't any of them left but I could still be sure of admittance because I had the key.

I parked outside the boot factory and went upstairs to the cold rooms.

Four men in an old Studebaker Lark, on a Sunday afternoon, we went to the football in the indoor stadium. At the first change, St Kilda leading by eight goals, I brought out the samosas I'd smuggled through security, concealed on my body. We ate in silence for a while, then Norm wiped his lips of flakes, held out his hand for another one, and said, 'Jack, bin sayin the team's on the edge of a big one.'

Eric coughed. 'Scuse me,' he said. 'Scuse me, what you bin sayin is the team's full of duds and the coach shoulda stayed in Warrnambool,' he said. 'I'm the one's bin predictin this.'

'You idiots,' said Wilbur. 'Saints bin twelve-odd goals in front and the Hawks come back and win. Idiots.'

'Not today,' said Norm. 'That was another bunch. This lot puts me in mind of the Lions in '48.'

'Jeez,' said Wilbur, 'I reckon yer short-thingy memory's

goin. Round 11 in '48, Lions play the Saints, Lions top of the ladder, Saints got one draw from thirty-one games, one draw from thirty-one games, that's sparklin form, not so? Who'd yer reckon wins?'

Norm finished chewing, put up a hand and added smudges to his glasses. 'Don't do to dwell on the past,' he said. 'Unhealthy.'

At the halfway mark, St Kilda's lead was all but vanished. I went off and got the pies. When they too were almost gone, Norm said, 'Big worry, this lot. Puts me in mind of the day the bloody Hawks come from twelve-odd goals behind…'

'Shut up,' said Wilbur. 'Just shut up and eat.'

In the last quarter, matters improved. The Saints stood up. So did we, often, as we watched our team humiliate Carlton. The arrogant Blues, the benchmark for football arrogance, they were run off their legs.

On the way to the Prince, the Youth Club agreed that they had all predicted the famous victory, seen it coming from a long way, always been on the cards, matter of time.

Serving the beer, Stan said, 'Well, looks like your team could miss the wooden spoon this year. Not coming last, that's like winning a grand final for the Saints.'

Norm looked at him, adjusted his thumb-blurred monster glasses for a clearer view. 'The problem with you, Stanley,' he said, 'is you don't have yer dad's judgment. Now yer father, had he not bin dragged screamin from this place by wife number two, Morrie'd be shoutin us a round.'

'Have I taken any money?' said Stan, chin up, skewered through the heart. 'Have I asked for money?'

I was home by seven, lighting a fire on a winter's night, filled with the sweet humming happiness of having seen my team win. Did people who often saw their teams win lose this feeling? That was so far beyond my experience as to be unthinkable.

I stood in front of the fireplace, watching the Avoca kindling flare on top of the grey, powdered and weightless remains of an Avoca tree, hands deep in the pockets of the old footy coat. It was a terrible garment, elbows and cuffs threadbare, lining torn. The pockets held tickets, bits of biscuit, matchsticks, keys to forgotten doors, coins no longer current, a plastic lighter, coughdrops coated with fluff and crumbs. On the front were stains: beer, tomato sauce, the brown fluid that leaked from pies, champagne from a bottle uncorked in the parking lot after a Fitzroy win.

I was thinking about uncorking a bottle, about what to eat later, when the phone rang.

'Comin your way,' said Barry Tregear. 'Only got a minute.'

'Time for a drink?'

'No, mate. Just a word.'

'Hoot,' I said.

I was unwinding the cork from the screw when I heard the horn. Opening the front door of my building, feeling the shock of cold, seeing the wind shaking the bare oak branches, I regretted not putting on the footy coat.

The passenger door of the dark Falcon was unlocked. I got in, grateful for the warmth of the cabin.

'You'd be a happy man,' said Barry. 'Sticking it to the blue boys like that.'

'My word,' I said.

He was studying me. 'Christ, you're thin,' he said. 'Eating?'

'I'm eating.'

'Yeah? The salad sambo? Get into the junk, mate. Build you up quick. Now, this stuff. First, the girl. Feehan. Hooker. Reported missing 15 February 1995. No trace. Then there's Dilthey. What I read says he's got a couple of tickets in Queensland, small stuff. Local, there's nothing. He had a job in the table-dancing business for a while. Someone says he was running a few girls and boys but they couldn't find them. Then he's in a motel in Kaniva. Tied to a chair, mouth taped up, hands broken, smashed, face the same. And shot up the nose with a .22. Twice.'

Barry's window slid down. He lit a cigarette with a lighter.

'Clearly person or persons didn't like the boy,' he said. 'The file's open, empty basically, no one saw anything, one other customer that night, it's a Sunday, he heard nothin. The bloke who runs the place, he's asleep. More asleep than is usual as I read the document. Medication.'

He scratched his head. 'That's it.'

'What was Dilthey doing out there?' I said.

'There's a map in the car, he's written down mileages to buggery in South Australia.'

He lit a cigarette, slit eyes on me over the flame. 'Read your statement,' he said.

'Like the way I express myself?'

'Pure fucken poetry,' he said. 'You get there, it's an appointment, in the door. But you don't go down to the business end, you fuck around for a bit, lookin at the art shit. Then when you're what, ten metres away, the bang?'

I didn't like what was coming. I didn't want to hear it. 'More or less the way I phrased it,' I said, 'but I put lots of work into the rhythm.'

Sucking on the filter cigarette, eyes on me. 'Behaved the way you should've, you're not sittin here thin but nevertheless fucken alive.'

'The bang gang couldn't find anything.'

'No,' he said. 'Possibly cause they're not dealin with a cunt tries to send the Frankston falafel shop to kingdom come with the barbie gas his cousin's husband cleverly took the trailer to Geelong to buy.'

The gloss off the evening.

'Well,' I said, 'you'd like to know for certain, wouldn't you?'

Barry shook his head, eyes closed. 'Christ, Jack,' he said, 'you don't need to know anything for certain. I go into that fucken hospital, you're lying there looking dead, white like a tissue, stuck full of tubes, fucken wired for ten speakers.'

The wind had strengthened, it was whip-cracking the thin oak branches outlined against the streetlight. At the light's faint edge, I could see two figures on the open ground: a man being pulled home by a large dog.

'You don't need to know,' Barry said, looking ahead, into the dead glass. 'Never mind fucken certain, you don't need to know anything.'

'Yes, well, I've got something on the stove,' I said. 'Thanks, mate.'

He looked at me, I couldn't bear the gaze, nodded, said goodbye, left the car.

The quick, neat swing of the vehicle, red tail-lights burning for a few seconds, gone. I went upstairs, poured wine, sat in front of the fire, uneasy now.

When I came back from hospital to the long-empty house, there were no messages on the machine; no blinking red light greeted me. The thought came from nowhere, released by Barry Tregear's words.

In all that time, not a single message? Had I forgotten to switch on the machine that morning? Pushing the button was part of the ritual of leaving, but sometimes, distracted, I forgot.

I was pouring another glass of wine when I remembered Sarah on the mobile, I was outside Enzio's: *I tried you at home, left a message. I've had a call from someone, a man.*

That message at least should have been waiting for me. My machine had been wiped.

I couldn't push it away anymore. Whoever murdered Mickey murdered Sarah. And I was supposed to die there too, in the brick and tin shed, blown to pieces, just collateral damage.

I rang the most recent number I had for Cam, left a message. He rang back in seconds. When I told him what I was after, he said, 'Jesus. Well, I can ask around in the hospitality industry. Don't hold your breath.'

'She's upmarket,' said Cam. 'My bloke says they must be paying top dollar, she only goes out once or twice a night.'

We were in South Melbourne, in the area behind the Arts Centre, parked down from a new six-storey apartment block faced with a marble-looking material.

Cam was behind the wheel. I hadn't seen the car before, an HSV, a Holden given performance-enhancing substances so that it growled like a refined cousin to the Lark. 'Goes out alone?' I said.

'The boyfriend, he fetches and carries.'

'Boyfriend?'

'The pimp.'

'And now?'

'She'll come out with the dog in a minute or two,' he said. 'I'll see if she'll have a word.'

'Beware of the dog.'

'That's her.'

A tall woman in a raincoat over black pants and wearing a headscarf was crossing the narrow forecourt leading a dog the size and shape of a football. She turned to come our way, down the wet pavement.

'Vicious-looking brute,' I said.

'There's a gun in the glovebox,' said Cam. 'Shoot the thing if it goes for me.'

'Just pick it up, drop-punt,' I said. 'See if you can hit that Merc on the other side.'

When she was ten metres away, Cam got out. He was in a charcoal suit, a decent bit of white cuff showing. He walked around the car. I could see that she'd seen him, a flick of a glance. She was a handsome woman, long nose, full lips.

Cam stepped onto the kerb. He said something. She stopped, the dog stopped. Cam went up to her, not too close. The dog strained at its leash. I could see her face while he talked. She wasn't happy but she wasn't alarmed.

Cam turned and she followed him, reeling in the dog and picking it up, hand under its body. They came up to the car. Cam opened the back door for her. I turned my head. She was holding the dog on her lap, a hand under its mouth, stroking. It had an amiable expression, bright brown eyes, little ears like furred seashells. It didn't mind being in the car.

'Someone's given Sarah Longmore an alibi for that night,' I said. 'For the time when you said you saw her.'

'Alibi?'

'The person lives across the road from her place. He's a peeping Tom. He was watching her windows that night.'

'You're fucking joking,' she said. 'Got a smoke? Don't take mine on a walk.'

'French,' said Cam, taking out a packet. 'They're strong.'

'I can smoke fucking rope,' she said.

Cam offered her the packet, lit her cigarette with a lighter. The car was suddenly full of pungent Gitane smoke, Donna's perfume still there, like ermine edging on a goatskin cloak.

She coughed once, smothered another. 'Fucking perve? Believe him? What took him so fucking long?'

'Scared,' I said. 'Very scared. He's got a conviction for it. Thought he might go inside, they like perves inside.'

I could hear her breathing.

'You were the prosecution's key witness, Donna. And you were committing perjury. Making a false statement, that's always bad. But this, this could've led to wrongful conviction for murder. That's terrible. Eight years a bloke got for that, minimum six to serve.'

Just the sound of Donna's breathing, quick and deep. The dog made a yawning sound, its small jaw cracked. I looked around again. She released the dog and it walked up and down the seat, neat turns, sniffed the crack, something down there?

'What do you want?' said Donna. 'I'm going to fucking confess to something? You think that? Think a-fucking-gain, that's all I'm saying.'

'That's a nice building you live in,' I said. 'Unit's in your name, is it? Got a vote on the body corporate?'

'Where's the fucking ashtray?' Voice harsh now, not hoarse.

Cam put a hand back, took the butt from her, opened his window and shot out the stub, sent it a long way, despoiled the street.

'We would think,' I said, 'that only a mad person would just come out and tell a lie like this. So that rules you out. Then we have to ask why you did. What's in it for you? Do it for someone? Do eight years inside for someone?'

Silence.

'Do it for someone?' I said. 'We're giving you a chance, it won't come twice, believe me. This is your chance, Donna.'

'Eight years?' she said. 'Eight years? Well, eight years is a whole lot better than fucking dead, so why don't you get out your fucking perve and charge me and go for your fucking lives.'

Donna had some trouble opening the door but she did it, tried to slam it behind her but it just thunked. She dropped the dog on the pavement, from too great a height, I thought. It looked up, offended. She walked, jerked the animal with her.

I brought down my window and shouted after her, 'What happened to Janene, Donna? And Wayne?'

Donna stopped, turned, came back, pulling the dog. She wore a golden crucifix on a golden chain. The little cross was in the hollow of her throat. 'What's that mean?' she said.

I said, 'You know what it means. Want to reconsider your position?'

'You're no fucking cops,' she said. 'Piss off.'

She went. We sat. Cam looked at me.

'I liked that dog,' I said. 'I never thought I'd say that about a small dog.'

'You change,' Cam said. 'I never liked small women.'

He started the car. 'Coffee, feel the need?'

'Serious need.'

Cam dropped me in Brunswick Street to get my mail and I walked back to the office, sat at my desk, opened the letters, got out the files. I had been a neglectful solicitor and that was unforgivable. It would cease now. Wallowing in self-pity, the curse of the single male. Single male with interruptions, in my case. But single was the steady state: I always reverted to being alone, seldom of my own volition.

I didn't get much done, thinking about Donna. Eight years in jail was better than dead, she said. The suggestion was that whoever got her to lie about seeing Sarah would have no qualms about killing her. I had no difficulty understanding why she thought that.

A knock on the door.

I got up and went to open it. Once I'd left it off the latch.

A big man in a suit, black-framed dark glasses, big bulges over his eyes, nose large and spread out.

'Mr Irish?' he said. His hands were on his hips.

'Yes?'

'Have a word?'

'Come in.'

I stood back.

He took a step in, his left leg, and he hit me off his right leg, in the chest, just under the collarbone, my hands came up and he hit me again, in the chest again, his fist went between my forearms. He tried to hit me in the throat but my chin was down, then he hit me in the stomach, left hand, right hand. I was going down in a mist of pain.

He kicked me in the chest, I felt my head hit the desk behind me, bounce forward, I was on my knees, I was fainting, the light was dim, a terrible pain in my chest.

He gripped my head by my hair, held my head up by my hair in one hand.

He slapped my face. Over and over again. His palm and his knuckles. 'Smart boy,' he said. 'Clever fucken boy.'

He let me go and I fell forward, lay in my pain and tears, my face on the old rug. I felt something warm on my head, in my ear, running down my face. The smell came to me, feral, salty.

He was pissing on me.

'Don't mess with this business anymore,' he said. 'Hear me, Irish? Next time I'll bring someone round, and, when I'm finished, he'll fuck you, okay?'

I heard his zip and I heard the door open and close. I heard a car rev and pull away. After a while, I got up and went home, stood under the shower for a long time, washed my hair three times. I dressed, found a plastic bag and put the clothes I had been wearing into it, tied the

242

top, took it down to the big bin.

Upstairs, I poured a neat single malt, took the near-full bottle and sat in my chair. My hands were shaking, just a tremor, barely detectable. My face hurt, I could feel the puffiness, but I didn't want to look in the mirror. I drank steadily, it grew dark. I didn't put on the lights, sat in the dark drinking, and, at some point near the bottom of the bottle, I fell asleep.

I woke in my bed, clothed, shoes on, face stiff, hurting everywhere, dehydrated, the shame undiminished, the soiled feeling still upon me.

I showered until the hot water ran out, dressed, stood in the kitchen. It was past 10 am. I wasn't hungry, I was still more than a quarter drunk.

A drink would take away the pains. Medicinal drink. Vodka. Linda liked vodka and orange juice sometimes. Vodka and vitamin C. The old VC, did more good than harm, a health drink.

I touched the tabletop, steadied myself, closed my eyes and said the mantra, not said even after the hospital. Then I drank a glass of milk, put on the heating, lay on the couch, arms folded across my chest. Hugging myself. Weak sunlight crossed the floor and lay upon me. We had often shared our couch, Isabel and I, lying as if in a bath, facing each other, feet in socks, legs enclosing legs, legs passing between legs, reading the papers, reading books, tweaking toes, tickling insteps, one thing leading to another, hands invading pants.

I drifted off and when I woke it was afternoon, the light thin, the day sliding away, most of a day gone, a day subtracted from the total, the wounded creature's cave would soon be darkening again.

No.

I got up, unsteady, almost fell over, went to the bathroom. Now I looked in the mirror. There were welts on the bridge of my nose, on my cheekbones, down my face, dried blood in places.

He didn't mind that I saw his face. He didn't care or he wanted me to see his face.

Next time I'll bring someone round, and, when I'm finished, he'll fuck you, okay?

No.

No. No next time.

I took the toilet disinfectant, the chlorine, drove to the office, took the carpet by a corner, his piss was in it, my tears of humiliation. I dragged it across the street and threw it into McCoy's skip, came back, sprayed the floor with chlorine, threw buckets of water over it, brushed it, brushed the water out of the front door. I was standing with the broom in my hand, feeling weak, eyes down, the door open.

'I pay for that fucking skip,' said McCoy. 'Not a public facility for anybody to dump their junk.'

'Sorry,' I said. 'Send me the bill.' I turned my back on him but I wasn't quick enough.

'What's wrong with you?'

'Accident,' I said.

McCoy blocked the door, the light. 'Bullshit,' he said, offended. 'I know fucking fighting. You're supposed to be a lawyer, what are you doing fighting?'

'It wasn't exactly a fight,' I said. 'I got king hit and the rest followed.'

'Client?'

'No. A bloke who knocked on the door. Never seen him

before. Now, if you'll excuse me, I have work to do.'

McCoy gave me a good staring. 'For Christ's sake, check who's outside before you open the door,' he said. 'Give me a buzz, I'll give them a fucking checking over.'

He left. From the window, I saw him remove my rug from the skip and take it inside. No doubt he would be wearing it when next I saw him.

Action. No more moping. I took Sophie's photographs and the negatives to Vizionbanc in South Melbourne, parked the Stud outside in the loading zone. The woman looked at my face in a clinical way, not disguising her interest.

'I'm hoping your magic will help with these,' I said.

She looked at them. 'Fucking awful. In a hurry?'

'I cannot begin to tell you,' I said.

Her plastic surgeon's gaze played over my face. 'Yes,' she said. 'Have a seat, Jack.'

She went into the back. They didn't keep office hours, these picture people.

I flipped a few photography magazines, including a big one full of nudes, women and men, some bound, some oiled, many cut off at the head. There was a picture of a man in a suit with what looked like a sea creature hanging out of his fly, the sort of blind pointed thing I imagined to be found at great depths, living off sulphur bubbles in the eternal dark.

I was at the window, hangover not abating, watching well-dressed people go into the pub across the street. It had been a bloodhouse in recent memory, scene of a famous fight between factions of the Painters & Dockers Union. I'd appeared for one of the accused, a near-homicidal man called Tully with fists the size of small cauliflowers. Thinking about his hands brought other hands into my mind, the

245

rings on his fingers, seen through blood as he backhanded me, the…

No.

I thought about photographs, the number of photographs I'd peered at since I started taking assignments from Wootton, pictures of missing people, their wives, lovers, friends and relatives, their dogs, their cars, photographs taken outside courts, in clubs, on the beach, barbecueing meat, in pools, at weddings and twenty-first birthday parties, kissing people, even a homemade porn video featuring a man and two women, one dressed as an Ansett air hostess, complete with little hat and name tag. It occurred to me for the first time that she might have been a real Ansett hostess.

'He says it's the best he can do,' said the woman.

I turned. She was holding up an A3 envelope.

'The neg's a bit better than the print,' she said. 'Want a look?'

I shook my head, gave her my business credit card, said my thanks for the service.

It was the wrong time to be on the streets, drizzle, evening peak hour, drive time. The woman with the Italian name was on the radio. She had a way with her, clever, bursting with cheek, a naughty laugh that could blow away the rain. I went up Lygon Street to King & Godfree. Thirsty, I needed two bottles of beer. Carlsberg, no other beer would do. I bought six bottles.

Behind the stripped oaks lay a warm dwelling. I'd forgotten to switch off the heating and I was glad of the oversight. I drew curtains, put on lights, put on music, didn't agonise over the choice, put on Elvis, the greatest hits, he always made me feel better. In the kitchen, I removed the cap from a Carlsberg and drank three-quarters of the bottle straight off, flooded myself with Danish hangover medication, tears coming to my eyes.

To the sitting room with the bottle and another one.

I sat in my chair and took the four big laser prints out of the envelope. In the top two, the woman's face was much clearer, a snub nose, but the angle was bad. I turned to the third picture.

The woman standing at the car. The car's number plate was readable now.

You could also see the lower half of the face of the woman in the passenger seat. You could see the crucifix in the hollow of her throat.

I knew that crucifix.

And you could see the driver's hands on the steering wheel.

You could see the rings on his fingers, big rings on big fingers.

I touched my face.

I knew the rings. I felt a joy.

Eric the Cybergoth rang back when I was halfway through the second bottle of beer. He coughed for a while, the man who put the hack into hacker.

'Redmile Solutions, four vehicles, want them?' he said, nasal and throaty and apparently speaking from beneath an eiderdown.

'Might as well.' I wrote down details of four vehicles, the address in Abbotsford. It was just off Johnston Street, in the dip, not a great distance from where I sat. I said goodbye, reached for my book, found a number.

'No, we never sleep,' said Simone Bendsten. 'We can't afford to now that we are in fact we and not lonesome me calling myself we like Queen Victoria.'

I went to the kitchen and rinsed an arbitrary quantity of rice, put it in the rice pot, covered it with a certain amount of water, threw in two cubes of frozen chicken stock, put the container into the microwave and punched in an arbitrary cooking time.

It would turn out soggy, it would turn out as a hard rice cake. Or each grain would be perfect, moist, independent of its neighbours. There was no knowing.

And I didn't care. I opened a can of tuna and went to the cupboard for the plum sauce from the Adelaide Hills. There could not possibly be enough tuna swimming around Thailand to supply every supermarket in the world with as much tuna as they needed. What was this stuff? Patagonian toothfish?

Capers, gherkins, where? The phone.

'Jack,' she said, 'The *Age* carried a report on 12 June 1995 of two men accused of assaulting a building contractor called Darren Kluske in a parking lot in Melton. Kluske said he was working on a MassiBild site at the time and he'd seen the men on building sites before. He believed they worked for a company called Redmile that, quote, does Massi's dirty work, unquote.'

'Names?'

'Brian Robert Grayling and Reece Stedman. Twenty-two June, charges withdrawn. A prosecution witness declined to testify. The name also shows up in the building industry royal commission a week ago.'

'Yes?'

'In Perth, a witness told the commission his job in 1998 was to distribute cash payments to workers on five sites. The money was given to him in plastic bags by, quote, different blokes from Redmile, unquote. He was asked about Redmile but he said all he knew was the name and that they were, quote, heavies, dangerous people, unquote.'

'Can you run the two men?'

'We're ahead of you, Jack. Grayling's dead, there's a death notice in 1998. Stedman was a detective sergeant in the Victoria Police. On 17 May 1993, he was named in an internal affairs report on the drug squad leaked to the *Herald Sun*. He is known to, quote, associate with drug dealers, pimps and prostitutes, unquote. Two days later, 20 May, the paper carried a story saying the three drug-squad members named in the document had resigned from the force.'

'Well done,' I said. 'You are as a dutiful child to a blind man.'

'If I don't get some exercise soon,' she said, 'only the less sighted will go out with me.'

'My sight is reasonable and I will always go out with you.'

'Starting when?'

'Well, how does damn soon sound?'

'Sounds fine, if vague. But you have my number.'

I ate my simple meal watching television and reading a two-day-old newspaper. In a report on the royal commission, a MassiBild employee denied any knowledge of the practice of contractors supplying subcontractors with cash to pay workers.

All too complicated. Too many names, brain of dough. The bones of my face ached, my chest and stomach hurt where I'd been punched. I was also badly hungover.

I switched on the answering machine, turned the volume to nothing, kicked the wedges under the doors, went to bed. While I was trying to keep from thinking, sleep claimed me like quicksand.

I woke late, it was after nine, eastern sunlight on the curtains. In the bathroom, I looked. The swelling had almost gone from my cheeks, welts less livid, a few thin scabs formed.

Under the falling water, I thought about near-death experiences, people trying to kill me, beating me up, threatening me. Not what I'd had in mind when I took the decision to give up practising criminal law.

Dressing, I thought that, when this was over, I would tell Wootton I didn't want any more jobs. Between leases and contracts and a bit of luck with the horses, I could get by. Selling the Stud would help. It was like owning a yacht, the cost per hour of use was shocking.

When this was over. When would that be? When I found out what had happened to Janene and Katelyn, the missing women? Dead women? My thoughts kept coming back to them. This matter began to take on its strange shape the night the car pulled up next to me outside the boot factory.

Mickey Franklin.

Yes?

I'll give you a name.

A name?

Janene Ballich.

How do you spell that?

B-A-L-L-I-C-H.

Names are useful. Come in and see my collected phone books.

Jack, this is serious shit, mate. Goodnight.

Serious, indeed. Janene and Wayne. Dead Wayne, entrepreneur of the senses, one-stop Wayne. I put bread in the toaster, old but good bread in an old toaster with sides that opened, sat at the kitchen table in the sunlight, and remembered Popeye Costello's words.

Girls, boys, micks, dicks, cockfrocks, fladgers, bondies, whatever. Customer-driven, that's the ticket.

And Janene? On the menu?

I suppose.

Tea. I emptied the kettle, refilled, put a teabag into the teapot, empty and clean. When did I do that? Thinking about Wayne Dilthey, cocky Wayne standing between Janene and Katelyn in the photograph. That would have been close to the highwater mark, lovely young spunks on either side, his bottom touching the Porsche.

Wayne Dilthey. Like a sex-and-drugs supermarket that did home deliveries. Was that how it worked? Where was Wayne going when fate caught up with him in Kaniva? Mileages to buggery in South Australia written on his road map, said Barry Tregear.

The toast was smouldering. I turned it over. At the time,

you often failed to understand the significance of what people were telling you. Your mind was usually ahead, thinking of the next question. What set great cross-examiners apart was that they listened to witnesses' answers, never got ahead of themselves, stayed with a topic until it was flat as a bunny ironed by several roadtrains. That was the way you nudged the witness beyond the rehearsed answers, edged them into the ad-lib zone, Drew's term.

Wayne was on the run, clearly. Something happened and he ran. Did something happen to Wayne and Janene and Katelyn at the same time? A merchant and his stock. Merchants didn't get attached to their stock, they didn't collect it, they dealt in it, that was what trade was about.

Smoke of toast. Caught just in time, a little scraping would remove the toxic black bits. I put on the second round, spread butter and the mysterious black substance, Australia's soy sauce. Since when were malt and yeast vegetables? Why wasn't it called Maltemite? Yeastamite?

Kettle boiling. I poured water into the teapot and grated parmesan onto the Vegemite. Very good with parmesan was the mite. Bugger cheese and onion, they should make parmesan and Vegemite potato chips, now that would be fusion cuisine: Parmemite.

Detective Sergeant Reece Stedman, disgraced cop, worked for Redmile in 1994. The man in the Redmile car to whom the woman watching Sarah reported was the man who attacked me. Was that Reece Stedman sitting in the car with Donna Filipovic?

Why should it be?

Toast-turning time. Perhaps marmalade with this round? There was also a good French blueberry jam. The marmalade

253

came from somewhere rural, bought by Linda. Tooling around the countryside in her Alfa, stopping to buy produce from desperate roadside rustics.

Tooling alone? I had done no rural tooling with her. City tooling, yes.

How could these things come into my mind? In the midst of very serious shit, body hurting, face battered, I felt a flicker, no, a flame, of sexual suspicion and resentment involving someone who was probably gone for good.

Going to South Australia. Wayne.

He had no reason to go. He could have been going further, to Western Australia, you had to get over South Australia to get there. It stood in the way, a hot and waterless piece of ground in the main, an obstacle.

Why would Wayne be going to WA? Because it was a long, long way from Melbourne?

He wouldn't have known the way. You'd pull up at some place on the highway that offered food, go inside, you'd be eating a fat-saturated piece of fried something and looking at the map. Christ, it's a long way, you'd say to yourself, and the stomach acid would burn in the oesophagus even before you'd finished eating.

Take out a pen, write down the distances in the map's margin, add them up, estimate how far you could get that day. Write down the mileages from where you were to buggery in South Australia.

It wasn't that your destination was buggery in South Australia, it was because that was the end of a stage. Because the map stopped there.

I left the table and went to the sitting room and rang Bendsten Associates, gave my name to the brisk person, Simone came on.

'Don't tell me this is the damn-soon call?' she said.

'Not just yet.'

I gave the name Dilthey in Brisbane. It took very little time.

'Just the one,' she said. 'K. J. Dilthey. You do know that you can find out this kind of information yourself by asking directory inquiries? I have to charge you.'

'I prefer your voice recognition software,' I said. 'Number?'

I rang it. A woman answered. I asked for Mr Dilthey.

'He's not really up to it,' she said. 'I'm the day nurse.'

'I'm ringing from the probate office of the Supreme Court in Melbourne,' I said, lying without effort. 'It's about his son's estate. Our understanding is that Mr Dilthey is Wayne's sole heir but we've had an inquiry from someone else. You don't happen to know whether there are other relatives, do you?'

'No,' she said, 'but hang on, I'll ask the lady next door, she knows everything, been there for yonks.'

'I'll hold,' I said.

I drank the last of the tea. There was a sparrow on the windowsill, pecking hopefully. I should put out crumbs. Isabel always emptied the breadboard tray onto the windowsill. Surely this bird could not remember that?

'You there?'

'I am.'

'She says there's a daughter. Teresa. She's Wayne's twin. She got pregnant and had a big fight with her dad and she left. She says she thinks she married him, he was a local bloke, a brickie. They left Brissie.'

'Did she say his name?'

'Hang on, I'll ask.'

The sky was clouding over, platoons of puffs moving north.

'There?'

'Yes.'

'His name's Paul Milder,' the nurse said.

I went back to Bendsten Research. 'Paul and Teresa Milder in South Australia and WA,' I said.

'Hold on.'

It took Simone about two minutes. 'There's a P. and T. Milder in Dunsborough, Western Australia,' she said. 'Nothing in SA.'

I wrote down the number and the address, said thank you again. The sunlight was gone, the puff-clouds banked up, the room darker. My feeling of recovery was waning.

You don't need to know, Barry Tregear had said. *Never mind fucken certain, you don't need to know anything.*

He was right. Of course, he was right. The man slapped me at will, then he pissed on me. His piss ran through my hair, down my cheeks. I tasted it.

I couldn't live with that. That couldn't be the end of something.

Flying over land, the Bight behind us, dark blue and sullen from our great height, whitecaps like tiny teeth, I hired a car.

The doll-lipped, petulant cabin steward left off his hissing conversation with his colleague to become attentive and obliging, succeeded in cranking me up a vehicle notch, some kickback involved no doubt. I didn't care, the whole venture was brainless enough already. What did fifty dollars matter?

The feeling of doing something stupid became stronger as I lost my way soon after leaving the Perth airport, got off the freeway and drove through endless suburbs, rows of termite-proof brick houses built on sand, all with their straggly, sagging trees, solar panels, stained concrete driveways, basketball hoops. I cursed not bringing sunglasses. The light was too bright for winter, it wasn't really winter here, they had nothing that resembled winter, no dormant season, no time when moss grew, no dark decaying worm season when humans could stay indoors, sit before dying fires feeling cheated by fate, bad luck, bad character, bad blood, my grandfather had no doubt about the influence of bad blood. How could anyone in this climate gain a proper understanding of melancholy?

On the other hand, the locals probably didn't miss melancholy much, enjoyed themselves outdoors all year round, wore short pants, towelling hats, sported in the warm pale-blue waters, ignored the threat of stinging creatures, shark nibbles. A lifetime of surfing was less dangerous than a single 3 am walk down King Street, Melbourne.

Eventually, and by accident, I found myself on the highway going south-west. The road was dominated by four-wheel-drives, mostly driven by impatient, angry-looking freckled men. It was a boring journey, flat landscape, sparse vegetation, turnoffs to Coolup, Wagerup, Cookernup, Wokalup, Burekup, Dardanup, Boyanup. Up, Up and Away.

Busselton was reached across what pretended to be a river, dammed near its mouth, stagnant, a suspicious green. I drove around. There was little to the town, all of it seemingly built since the 1970s: a few business streets of surf shops, two newsagents, hotels, hardware places, chemists. The seafront was largely given over to parking, tennis courts, an amusement park, a big grassed area where a man was training an alsatian to sit and stay. In the seafront cafe, I ordered a long black from a young woman with tanned pimples, streaked hair.

What to do? Knock on Teresa Dilthey Milder's door? Ask her if she knew what had happened to Janene Ballich and Katelyn Feehan, her brother's hookers? Why should she know?

Twins were closer than other siblings.

Stuck on her, I reckon, the cuntstruck look, pardon me.

Janene's mother, Mary Ballich, the freezing Gippsland day, the leaky weatherboard house that was a machine for consuming fuels. The sentence that came back to me, wrapping paper floating in the wind. It had no importance, not then, not now.

'Can I get you something else?' The waiter.

'Where would you stay if you were a tourist?' I said.

'Not worryin about money, y'mean?'

I found the recommended hostelry a few kilometres out of town, although it was impossible to know where the town ended. It was mock-Polynesian, thatched with nylon fibre, built on the narrow strip of sand between the road and the sea.

I took my leave, went down the herringbone brick path to my tropical room. I poured half a tooth glass of Glenmorangie from Cam's silver flask and went to bed. After I put out the light, I lay on my back and listened to the sluicing of the sea. Perhaps it was the book, perhaps it was just my cast of mind, but it was a dolorous sound, small comings and goings. I drifted away sad and uneasy.

Early in the morning, showered, I walked on the empty strip of beach left by the high tide. The day was grey, sea and sky joined seamlessly at the horizon. Away to the right, I could see the dark line of the pier. To the left, a long way away, a low blue cape came out from the land. I went that way, as far as the mouth of a narrow creek, possibly tidal, possibly some kind of drain. A man wearing a baseball cap was fishing in the creek, casting a spinner, a gleam of silver in the yellow water. He looked at me. I said good morning. He grunted.

I went back to the hotel and had breakfast in the restaurant, a meal that would not linger in my mind.

Dunsborough wasn't far away, the road straight and flat, scrub vegetation on either side, Christian fundamentalist holiday camps, extravagant houses inside walled compounds. One monstrosity was called The Shack.

The town was brand new, built on sand, the houses on tiny plots shouting speculation. Paul Milder had presumably done well here. I found the tourist information centre and a map, found Blue Cape Crescent, six houses around a loop of tarmac a block from the sea. The houses were all built of unrendered brick and timber, angular, sharp roof lines, gardens of drab native plants and listless trees.

Number 14 had a green Forester in the driveway. The path from the street curved around a pond, nothing in it, a shallow concrete cone, and led to a big front door of jarrah, old timber, resawn, marked with bolt or spike holes. There was a bell, a small brass ship's bell. I tolled it and didn't have to wait long before the door opened, opened fully, the people who lived in this place were not suspicious or fearful.

'Yes?'

Teresa Dilthey Milder was a big woman, handsome, long black hair pulled back loosely, she could be a native of a Mediterranean country. She looked like her co-tenant of the womb. I had his photograph in my jacket pocket, standing between Janene Ballich and Katelyn Feehan.

'Mrs Milder?'

'Yes?'

Her T-shirt said CAPE ESCAPE, the letters undulating on the hills of her breasts.

'My name's Jack Irish. I'm a lawyer from Melbourne.'

I gave her my Law Institute card.

'Yes?' She gave back the card.

'It's about Wayne's death.'

'What about it?'

'It appears to be connected to another murder. Can we talk for a minute?'

She led the way into a big living room-kitchen with a glass wall. In summer, it would be shaded by a creeper-covered pergola, now bare.

'I've just made tea,' she said. 'Would you like a cup?'

'Please.'

She crossed the room to the kitchen. In the garden, I could see a sandpit and a swing. On the counter that divided the room were crayons and paintbrushes in a pot.

'Milk, sugar?'

'No milk, one spoon, please,' I said.

Teresa came back with two mugs. 'Sit down,' she said.

We sat in leather chairs that hissed under us. 'Nice house,' I said. 'Did you have it built?'

'Paul built it, yes.'

'So much light.'

'Yes. The architect's really good. She lives down the road.'

'I see in the paper that you have to be a millionaire to live here.'

'They can't be talking about us,' she said.

We looked at each other. She was less tense now.

'Did you know what Wayne did for a living?' I said.

'Security. Clubs, that sort of thing.'

'The last time you spoke to him,' I said. 'Was he worried about anything?'

Teresa hesitated. 'No. It was about a month before his

murder. We talked about the kids, my dad. Paul spoke to him for a bit, coming for a holiday, fishing, bloke stuff.'

'They got on?'

'Oh yes, always got on. He knew Paul and…anyway.'

'Were you close, the way twins often are?'

She raised her eyebrows. 'Dunno. Not always when we were kids. A bit, I suppose.'

'Twins get feelings about each other, don't they?'

A shrug. 'I get feelings all the time. The kids. Usually wrong, thank Christ.'

I drank some tea, didn't say anything, looked at her. Teresa was uneasy, uncrossed her legs, re-crossed them, wasn't keen to look at me, looked at the garden, a coastal garden, not much colour.

'Wayne was on his way here when he was murdered,' I said.

Her head jerked my way. 'How do you know that?'

'I know.'

'Well,' she said, 'what the hell does it matter? What does it matter where he was going? What's the point of this?'

She got up. 'I've actually got things to do,' she said. 'So if…'

'He didn't ring you before he left Melbourne?'

'No. I said so.'

'Has anyone been in touch with you about Wayne, anything to do with him?'

'No. No one.' She turned, taking her mug to the kitchen.

I said, 'Janene Ballich.'

A movement of the shoulderblades, I thought. Teresa turned, but not quickly.

'What?' she said.

'Janene Ballich.'

'I'm sorry?'

'The name doesn't mean anything?'

'No.' Clipped.

'Katelyn Feehan? Did he mention her?'

'No.' Just as quick. I couldn't read her black eyes.

I got up, offered my mug. 'Thanks for talking to me. And for the tea. If you want to find out whether I'm trustworthy, I'll give you the name of a judge of the Victorian Supreme Court. You can ring him.'

Mr Justice Loder wouldn't be happy about giving me a character reference but he wouldn't say no.

She took the mug, held the two in front of her.

'I don't think Wayne's murder is a simple story,' I said. 'But I hope the story's over. Hope. We can only hope. Goodbye.'

'Bye.'

I was a few paces down the path when Teresa said, 'Sorry, your number. In case. You know.'

'Of course.'

I went back and gave her my business card. 'I should have given it to you at the beginning. You might need a lawyer one day.'

When I looked back, she was still in the doorway, watching me go. She raised a hand. I raised a hand back.

Home. Time to go home. Declare an end to foreign ventures. I had seen the unexciting country, tasted the food. I had wasted time and money, mine, there was no one paying for this.

On the highway, humming with traffic both ways, new houses crammed into developments on the right. I saw a sign on a building site, Milders' Homes. Would it be better if the apostrophe were simply abandoned? I was approaching a T-junction, some shops ahead, when the thought came to me. *He knew Paul and…anyway.* Teresa had been about to say something about Paul and Wayne. She hadn't finished the sentence.

I pulled off the road, borrowed the local phone book from the man in the office at the supermarket. There it was. I'd never looked in the directory. Simone Bendsten had used the white pages on the web.

It took less than ten minutes to get back to Dunsborough. In the town, I stopped to look at the map, find Powlett Street. It was near Blue Cape Crescent, I'd driven down it. The green Forester was parked outside number 8, a private house, a city house, unseen behind a terracotta wall with a wooden gate and double garage doors.

I parked and went to the gate, tried the handle. It was open, a brick path went directly to the front door, the twin of the one made by Paul Milder. There was a brass knocker in the shape of a dolphin. I raised its head and let it fall, twice.

The wait was short. The door opened, neither fully nor fearlessly.

A woman, late twenties, tall, with short hair. Her face had filled out, but she still had the waif's cheekbones.

'You're looking well, Janene,' I said.

We went down a passage into a sunroom, north-facing, long and narrow, its floor tiled, cane furniture. French doors were open to a terrace, there were internal wooden shutters to close in summer against the West Australian sun.

I nodded at Teresa Milder, standing at a small bar.

'How did you know?' she said.

'Just a guess,' I said. 'I'd like a talk with Janene.'

The women looked at each other.

'I'll be fine,' said Janene.

Teresa looked at me.

'She's got nothing to fear from me,' I said.

They went out together and I could hear the low sibilance of their speech.

Janene came back, elegant in her white T-shirt and khaki pants, the long legs I remembered from the photograph. She went to the bar and took a cigarette from a packet, didn't offer, lit it with a kitchen match from an oversize box, that would be for the barbecue I could see outside, a brick structure, neat, the Milder brothers' trademark no doubt, two brickie brothers made good in the west.

'Well,' she said, deep draw, violent expulsion of smoke. 'Terry says you're a lawyer. I've been waiting for some cunt with a gun or a knife. Sit down.'

I sat. She didn't, she leant against the bar, standing between two stools.

'What?' she said. 'Just tell me.'

'I've got questions,' I said. 'But to begin, Wayne was on his way here when he was murdered. He'd sent you here, to his sister. Is that right?'

She looked away, drew on the cigarette. 'What do you want?'

'Since Wayne,' I said, 'other people have been murdered. One of them was a client of mine, a person I liked. I want to find out who killed these people.'

'Fucking cops' job,' she said, moving her shoulders, restive in her skin.

'It should be.'

A bird walked into view on the terrace, a rock parrot perhaps, olive and yellow and blue, pecking with its tiny beak. Another followed, soon there were many, all pecking. Fights broke out.

'Your mum misses you,' I said. 'All these years.'

Janene looked at me, away, hugged herself, put her hands inside her short sleeves, massaged her arms, shivered in the warm day. 'What do you want? What do you fucking want?'

'Tell me what happened,' I said. 'How you come to be here. Tell me about Wayne and Mandy Randy.'

She drew on the cigarette, smoke plumed from her nostrils, she went to the door, disturbed the birds, drew again, threw the stub away, a graceful movement, like tossing a dart.

'I'll have to go out and get that,' she said. 'He can't bear to see a fucking breadcrumb, hair in the shower, a bit of grass, weed, whatever, it comes through a crack, he kills it with this fucking spray.'

'My plane's at 4.30,' I said.

'Go,' she said. 'I've been scared so long, this doesn't mean a shit. Go. Goodbye.'

'Sorry to have bothered you,' I said, getting up. 'I'll tell your mum you're alive, living in a nice warm house near the beach. She'll be happy. She could fly over and stay for a while, get the cold out of her bones.'

I left the room, walked towards the big front door. I could feel her behind me.

'What can I tell you?' she said.

'Good luck, Janene,' I said, not looking back. 'I'm finished with dead pimps and whores and their clients. If I can find you, anyone can. And will.'

She made a soulful sound, a groan and a sigh.

'Wait,' she said. 'Wait.'

I turned. She was showing me her palms.

'Come and sit down,' she said. 'I'll tell you.'

I followed her back to the sunroom. She sat. I sat opposite her.

'I was working for Wayne, doing escort jobs,' she said.

'Let me be clear,' I said. 'You were a call-girl.'

'If you like. But it was all upmarket, businessmen, professionals.'

'And Katelyn worked for Wayne too?'

'Yeah.'

'Donna Filopovic?'

'Yeah, Donna too. Anyway, on the night, Wayne had a call from someone and he picked up me and Katelyn, it was dress-up, little black dress, we went to the River Plaza. It was about midnight. This bloke, black tie, was waiting for us, took us through the foyer. Wayne came up, that was for show, they took us to the suite.'

Janene got up and lit another cigarette, came back with a saucer for an ashtray. 'I'm not supposed to smoke,' she said. 'He's turned into a health nut.'

I waited.

'Well, there's four people there, three blokes and a girl, a woman.'

'Did you know them?'

'No. Well, I thought I'd seen one bloke before, the big one. But no, I didn't know them.'

'What happened?'

'We stood around the bar and had some champagne. The big bloke, he's pretty much off his face. There's music, he wants to dance. Not interested in me, just Katelyn. I danced with the nerdy guy. We did a couple of lines, Wayne brought the stuff.'

'Wayne was there?'

'No. He just took us, came up in the lift and went down. The other bloke too, the one who met us.'

'And then?'

'Well, it went on for a while, The big guy's lifting Katelyn up like a doll, his hands can meet around her waist. Then he wants an act, y'know.'

'Act?'

'He wants an act. I said no, that's not in the deal. I mean, if he wanted an act he should have ordered one. I didn't do acts, wanted to do acts for fuckheads I'd've stayed at the club. Anyway, he gets really pissed off, red face, pulls out money, like hundreds, throws it on the floor. The spunky guy calmed him down. So the prick does some more C, he vacuums it up, and he takes Katelyn off. I thought, shit, girl, sooner you than me.'

'What happened to you?'

She gave me a direct look. 'You want to know this stuff?'

'Yes.'

She shrugged. 'The spunky guy went off somewhere and I'm dancing with the nerd and the woman comes up close behind me and she lifts up my dress, so I reckon it's a threeway. That's okay, not the end of the world, and we go to the other bedroom and she wants to know my name, she's really friendly. Anyway, it turns out they both like to watch, so it's first her and then it's him. She's like a movie director, when she's watching, she gives orders—do this, do that.'

It was warm in the room, sunlight on the carpet, outside, the exotic birds feeding. Janene put a hand under her T-shirt and scratched her stomach while she drew on the cigarette. She didn't mind talking about sexual matters.

'Also she liked the stick,' she said. 'She's on me, he's giving it to her. Christ, she made a noise. Then there's a knock on the door, I thought it was someone to say turn it down. He goes to the door and there's a bit of whispering. Then he comes back and he tells me to get dressed in the bathroom. So I get my stuff and go in and when I come out, they're gone and the fucking door's locked.'

269

Janene got up and sent out another cigarette end. The birds thought it was food and rushed.

'Christ,' she said, 'I'll have to run the air-conditioning for an hour.'

She lit another cigarette, leaned against the bar. 'I knock and I wait, knock again, after a while I'm a bit panicky and I give the door a fucking good hammering. I'm thinking about ringing reception, only it's going to be a bit hard to explain. Anyway, the door opens and there's this guy, he's very calm, he says there's been a bit of a problem, nothing to worry about, Wayne's on his way to pick me up. I calmed down. It was a few minutes, the door opens and it's Wayne. Let's go, he says.'

'What about Katelyn?' I said.

'That's what I asked. He said there's been an accident. Then he grabs me and we're out of there, no one to be seen. He took me back to my place. I was really fucking shaken up, I can tell you. I wasn't tough, I'd never been on the streets, just clubs and escort, upmarket escort, nothing ever happened to me. Then he says, you've got to go somewhere safe for a while, these people are dangerous. I said, fuck, the cops, that's where I'm going. He says, listen to me girl, you talk to the cops, we will both have to go and live down a hole in the fucking desert for the rest of our lives. You can't help Katelyn, you've got to help yourself, help me.'

There was a faint sheen of sweat on Janene's face. She hadn't thought about the night for a while, had presumably never spoken about it.

'Then he says, we're sitting in the car, he won't look at me, he says, they want me to kill you. Give you a hot shot. That or they kill both of us. I knew he was telling the truth. I knew

270

we were in bad trouble. I said, Jesus Christ, who are these people? He says, they're rich people, they're powerful people, we're fucking bugs.'

She sighed, closed her eyes, shook her head. 'I said, Wayne, did you tell them you'd kill me? He says, yes, so for fuck's sake, just do what I tell you or I will. I went upstairs and threw some stuff in a bag. We went to an ATM, I took out what I could and I gave Wayne the card and the PIN. That's the last time I was Janene Ballich.'

She got up, left the room, came back, slid open the glass door. The birds backed off but they knew what was coming. She threw a handful of seeds onto the paving, closed the door.

I watched the birds pecking, waited for her to sit down.

'How did you get here?' I said.

'We drove to Adelaide. I got on a plane.'

'In what name?'

'Jean Quinlan. Wayne got a Queensland licence for me in that name. He sent it with the rest of my money.'

'That night, the date?'

'December the third, 1994.'

'So you flew from Adelaide on December 4?'

'That's right, yeah. Tried to ring my mum from the airport, got some pissed dickhead.'

'And at this end, what happened?'

'I waited at the airport for Teresa.'

'What did she know?'

'Wayne said I was his fiancée and my family were nutters, my brother wanted to kill me.'

'She knows the truth now?'

Janene nodded. 'When they killed Wayne, I told her. I

thought she'd tell me to piss off but I had to tell her. She's a good person, she didn't owe me a fucking thing, but she just gave me a hug. She's my friend. Lots in common now, both married to arsehole Milders, except she's got the kids and I'm the infertile bitch.'

'And your husbands, they know?'

'Jesus, no. No.'

'How old were you then?'

'Nineteen. And a half.'

'Katelyn?'

A shrug. 'Looked fifteen, I don't know.'

'Someone must have tried to find out what happened to her.'

'She said all she had was a half-brother but she hadn't seen him since she was little, ten, something like that. These foster people had her, they ran a roadhouse in the back of buggery, then the man left and another one came on the scene, he was on her like a rash. She was thirteen. The mum kicked her out. That's all I know. She told me that once.'

Katelyn Feehan, looking fifteen, dead in a five-star hotel, next-of-kin someone she hadn't seen since she was ten. I looked at the birds, the pickings were slimmer now, they were jostling like footballers, a lot of use of the body.

'Being scared, it's always there, every day,' said Janene. 'They killed Wayne, he was fucking right about them, they'll kill me.'

'You can only stop being scared,' I said, 'when they can't touch you.'

'Who?' she said, her right hand sprang out, fingers spread, sharp gesture. 'Fucking who?'

272

'If it came to it,' I said, 'could you identify the people you saw that night?'

'Yeah,' she said. 'The big one, I'd know him, I would definitely positively know him. And the nerd, probably. I don't know, I'd have to see him.'

'The spunk and the woman?'

'Yeah, him. I'd know him. If she looked the same, I'd say yes. But if she'd changed her hair and stuff, well, maybe.'

'The man who came to the bedroom door. Would you recognise him?'

'Don't know. Maybe.'

'Janene,' I said. 'I'll need your help. Will you look at some pictures?'

She raised both hands, automatic, ran middle fingers outwards along the tops of her eye sockets, under the unplucked brows. 'Jesus,' she said. 'What kind of pictures?'

'Just people in the street, ordinary pictures.'

'Yeah, okay.' She fetched another cigarette, sat down.

I opened the folder and took out the photographs of Mickey Franklin. 'Just say if you recognise anyone and where you've seen them.'

I gave them all to her and I didn't breathe.

She looked at the top one. 'Fuck,' she said, 'that's him. He's the one came to the bedroom door, said Wayne was on his way.' She looked at the others. 'Yeah, that's him. The others I don't know.'

'There's a chance of settling this business once and for all,' I said. 'You wouldn't have to be scared anymore.'

'Well, that would be nice,' she said, 'but I'm not putting myself on the line. I mean, they think I'm dead, don't they? They don't know I'm alive.'

'They may know you're alive. They may have thought you'd be too scared ever to put your head up.'

'They'd have fucking thought right,' she said.

'Things have changed. Now they may want to be sure.'

'Jesus,' she said. 'It's just me, it's just my word against them.'

'I don't think they'll see it like that,' I said. 'They won't want your word heard at all.' I got up. 'You can be kept out of this, Janene. With luck. But I might need you to look at other pictures.'

'Okay,' she said, 'but I'm not coming to Melbourne, right?'

'Can you go to Perth?'

'Yeah, I suppose.'

'If I need to, I'll send the pictures over the net to someone I can trust in Perth. You can look at them there.'

'You can send them to Teresa at home, she can do that scanning stuff. She sends progress pictures of houses all over the place. I'll give you the e-mail address.'

Janene went away and came back with a card.

We went to the door. 'Goodbye,' I said. 'I'll be in touch.'

We stood awkwardly. She puffed out her cheeks, nodded. Then, on impulse, she kissed my cheek. 'I feel better,' she said. 'Like there's some way this can end. I'm trusting you, Jack. You won't let me down?'

'No,' I said. 'I won't let you down.'

At the airport, I rang Wootton, told him what I wanted to know about the River Plaza. Then I flew home, sitting beside an elderly woman in the window seat who was going to see her grandson play football in an under-15 grand final in Dandenong.

'Hate flying,' she said as the take-off engine noise rose. 'Be a dear and hold my hand, will you?'

I held out my right hand. She put her small palm on it, threaded her fingers through mine, closed her eyes. The noise increased, we were running, I could feel the tension in her fingers. I gave a little squeeze. We broke free of earth and rose into the blank white West Australian sky, lorded it over the thousands of brick bungalows, the shining solar collectors, banked over the small hills, turned in the direction of the world.

'I think we're up,' I said. 'Safe, for the moment.'

'Thank you, dear,' she said and let go of me. I missed her hand, I didn't hold many hands, couldn't remember the last hand held.

I read the *Australian*. The lead story on page three was the building industry royal commission. Counsel assisting the commissioner put it to the MassiBild representative, Dennis Cambanis, that until recent times the company's building sites were 'dirty money laundries'.

'I mean by that there was and may still be a widespread system of paying workers cash top-ups and the cash is dirty money. It comes out of the drug trade, it is discounted money.'

'I've never heard of anything like that, your honour,' said Mr Cambanis. 'This is just rubbish. With respect, your honour, I think counsel has been watching too much television.'

'Like a banana?' said my sidekick. 'I've got a spare. One's plenty for me.'

'Thank you,' I said. 'My name's Jack.'

'I'm Nola.'

We peeled our bananas. Nola put the peels into the banana bag. It was a good banana. I should eat bananas, a source of potassium, Isabel had always put a banana peel under her tomato seedlings.

'Both the girls went east,' Nola said, chewing thoughtfully. 'Couldn't wait. Don't know why. Only place east I ever wanted to go was Tasmania. Saw this thing on the telly. All that water, so green. Like England. Mind you, never been to England either. My late hubby was English, he never wanted to go back. I used to say, when you retire, we'll have a trip to England. Over my dead body, he always said. Would've had to have been, died a week after his retirement do, they gave him a clock. Came home, he'd had a few, he says, last bloody thing I need from now on's a clock.'

I smiled and nodded. I didn't want to be trusted with Janene's life. I didn't want to be trusted with anything heavier than a lease. Isabel died because my client Wayne Waylon Milovich thought I'd done a bad job when entrusted with his future. My life since then had been guided by the principle of taking care but not responsibility. But not over this business. I'd drifted away from my beacon, I'd lost sight of the flashing light. Now I was giving assurances.

My last session with Milovich was brief, I had four people to see and an appearance that morning. While maintaining his innocence, the creep now wanted to plead guilty. I told him the prosecution's case was shaky, I thought I could take it apart, he had a good chance of walking. 'Well, I'm in your fucken hands,' he said. On our day in court, everything went wrong, we struck a mago in a bad mood, and Milovich got twice what a guilty plea and a bit of contrition would have earned.

So I could put my finger on the day, on the precise moment in the battered room in Pentridge, when the only part of my life in which I was unreservedly happy had its date for expiry set. But that was with hindsight. In the course of this business I'd had at least two signals that only a potato could miss. I hadn't missed them. I'd ignored them.

A prostitute who looked fifteen killed by a big man in a suite in the city's most expensive hotel. Who was he? Who were the others? People who knew Mickey Franklin, who knew him well enough, trusted him enough, to call him in to take care of things.

Did they send for Mickey? Was he the fixer? Did Mickey make the problem with the dead girl disappear? In December 1994, Mickey still worked for MassiBild. He was a fixer for MassiBild. He dealt with the contractors, a preparation for hell, said Steven Massiani.

'From the eastern states, are you, Jack?' said Nola.

'Just the one,' I said. 'I'm from Melbourne.'

The refreshment trolley was approaching.

'What about a little drink?' I said.

She patted my arm. ' Well, Jack, it's naughty but I don't mind half a glass of beer around this time of day.'

It was raining on Melbourne, no wind, just water falling through air pollution. A dented bus from security parking collected me, a reckless youth with a bad mullet driving. 'Col sends his regards,' he said. 'He says, let me get this right, he says to say you're a person of interest to someone and you're not due back till next week. Make sense?'

I looked at the darkening world pinstriped with grey. 'Tell him I said thanks,' I said.

After the awful tollway, the jammed streets, I parked where I could look across the open space and see the old boot factory, my place of residence.

Early evening in the expensive inner city, a woman getting home, claiming a park, taking her briefcase out of the Volvo, the bag heavy with paper brought from the paperless office, bleeping the car, flashes of light, yellow.

I sat. I wished I could smoke. I saw my new neighbour come home. After a while, her lights went on upstairs, the two street windows. The curtains closed and the building was dark again.

A tired man sitting in his old Studebaker watching his own house, burdened with knowledge he'd sought and now didn't want. My mobile rang. I'd only just remembered to switch it on.

'Back from the state of sand, are we?' Wootton.

'I'm no stranger to sand,' I said. 'My life's built on it.'

'Detect a note of melancholy, old sausage? Bit liverish? Hit the organ with a couple of decent scotches. Cheers it up no end.'

From the boyish yelps in the background, I gathered that he was at the Windsor, administering the liver tonic to himself.

'Any luck with that stuff?' I said.

'My helpful concierge has prised open the lips of his counterpart at the establishment. Using a rolled-up three-figure note, I'll ask you to remember.'

'It's indelible. What?'

'Booked for that night by a company called Barras Holdings. The occupants aren't recorded.'

'Don't people have to sign the register?' I said.

'Not in the case of corporate bookings.'

'So the Bersaglieri Running Band could have stayed up there that night?'

'In theory.'

'And black-tie functions?'

'Hold on, I've got it here.'

I listened to the younger stockmarket advisors having a laugh, that would be about the shittiness of dealing with the gripes of people you'd put into shares you wouldn't personally touch wearing a cast-iron condom.

'As one might expect,' said Wootton, 'the place doesn't record the dress required of guests. But my person suggests that black tie would be the Conrad Spratt Youth Foundation dinner in the Flinders Room and the Concrete Association dinner in the River Room.'

The windows were fogged. I found the handle and wound.

Steel cogs meshed. You felt that the Stud's winders could raise and lower a drawbridge. Cold, damp air came in, carrying the seductive chemical smell of the city.

'No,' I said, 'not those.'

I was looking at the boot factory, not seeing anything.

My scalp tightened.

A lighter had flared in a window, someone lighting a cigarette.

Someone was standing in the dark at one of my front windows. Waiting for me, for the Stud, to come into view.

'Still there, sport?'

'Yes.'

'There were other small things on at the hotel that night but we won't have a list for a while. I'll bear the cost of this exercise as a mark of something or other.'

'Mark of Cain would be about right,' I said, eyes on my upstairs window. 'Thanks, Cyril.'

What to do? Someone waiting for me to come home, sitting, standing, walking around in my house, opening drawers, looking in cupboards, opening my fridge, taking a piss, pissing in my bathroom.

Not pissing. I didn't like that thought.

By the dim streetlight, I found the latest number in my little book.

'Home invasion,' said Cam. 'Taking up your personal space. You could send the jacks in. You're a citizen. You're entitled.'

I could hear a piano in the room with him, slow, deliberate notes, repeated, then a quick passage, lovely, nothing I knew. 'I've had it with this stuff,' I said. 'I live there.'

'I remember that,' he said.

In his silence, the piano, talented hands. Why was it that he always seemed to have a musical person in his life?

'Lighting up in the window is smart,' said Cam. 'He thought he was in a movie. This is presumably just a fuckhead sent to hurt you. We can kick his arse but maybe you need to think about kicking some heads. That way they don't send anyone else.'

Where to start kicking heads? Who sent the man to my office to bash me? The people who killed Mickey and Sarah, that was all I knew.

Around the corner from the factory, a grey four-wheel-drive pulled into a space. Someone got out.

'I think the shift's changing,' I said.

At the corner, the person turned left, went directly to my front door.

'Shift change or someone visiting me,' I said.

The door opened, someone came out, the newcomer went in, the door closed.

'New shift,' I said.

The man walked around the corner. He was going to his replacement's car...no, he walked past it, I lost sight of him, he had his own car, probably in the next street.

'The new one's parked just around the corner,' I said.

'Cheeky,' said Cam. 'That's not acceptable. Got anything to mark it?'

I opened the glovebox, rummaged around, found a roll of masking tape. I told Cam. He gave instructions.

'Is this wise?' I said.

'Beats me,' said Cam.

I was back in the same parking place inside ten minutes, got out my little silver flask, watched, had a few sips, the lovely burn of neat single malt, a kind of smoking. An occasional car, the odd person crossing the park in the drizzle, men, young, in a hurry, late for the children's bathtime at home perhaps. They would die regretting every chance missed to nuzzle a plump, powdered tummy.

Fifteen minutes went by. The mobile rang.

'Any minute,' said Cam. 'Probably best you don't go home tonight. I can fix you up.'

'I'll be fine,' I said. 'But thanks.'

A single light coming down the street where the vehicle was parked. It stopped. Near the car?

'There's a motorbike,' I said.

'Yeah. Tell me what happens.'

Headlights came on, the bike was moving, the grey four-wheel-drive came out from the kerb behind it, followed it to the corner, the bike turned left, the vehicle followed.

'They're there,' I said.

The bike went beyond the boot factory. The big, shiny vehicle stopped in front of it, on the wrong side of the road, on the park side. The driver opened the door, got out, in dark clothing, leaned back inside, doing something.

I heard Cam say, speaking to someone else on another phone, 'Mate, I'm from the council. You're parked in a residents' zone, so we want to ask you politely not to do it again. But there's a small penalty this time. Look out the window.'

Across the park, the man had left the driver's door of the four-wheel-drive open, he was walking to the motorbike, not hurrying. He got there, got onto the pillion.

A yellow light inside the four-wheel-drive, a puff of yellow. It turned orange, then red.

The motorbike jumped away, turned right, mounted the kerb, violated a public park, travelled across country.

'Any action there?' said Cam.

'The Toyota thing is burning,' I said. 'Outside my house.'

My front door opened, a man came out, stood, his hands raised in horror.

'Good,' said Cam. 'Well, you might piss off now before the crowds arrive.'

The four-wheel-drive was burning inside, sucking in air through the open driver's door. There was a small explosion in the vehicle, a thump.

'Sure you don't need a bed?' said Cam.

'Sure,' I said.

The Stud started without demur and we left, my heartrate up but I was feeling better about the world. There is nothing like an act of meaningful violence to restore one's belief in the possibility of some control over life.

I went to the office. It seemed undisturbed, the Mickey Franklin document box was in the new hidey hole under the fridge. Outside, in the wet, I paused to listen to the music from McCoy's atelier-seductorium. Vivaldi. In a perfect world, these hackneyed sounds would justify a Special Operations Group raid on the premises to save some barely nubile art student from the advances of the priapic carpet-clad poseur.

To South Melbourne, to Vizionbanc, keeping an eye on the cars behind me. I gave the woman the file of photographs and Teresa Dilthey Milder's e-mail address. She gave the pictures back to me in five minutes. Finally, to Carlton, to Linda's apartment, a tired man, a man without a home.

Linda's apartment was a nice substitute for a home. It had no food but it had sofas and a flat-screen television and a turbo-charged heating system. And it had drink. I took a bottle of Carlsberg from the pantry shelf and half lay on the sofa in the sitting room, feeling the room warming, my blood movement slowing.

What was the man waiting for me going to do when I walked in the door?

Next time I'll bring someone round, and, when I'm finished, he'll fuck you, okay?

I didn't want to think about that. I was now in serious trouble. I had probably been in serious trouble for a while. Anyway, there wasn't any going back. The problem was how to go forward.

The man who parked next to me under the bare oaks and gave me Janene Ballich's name, that person knew about the night at the River Plaza, knew that at some point Mickey was there.

Was he saying that Mickey's death was related to him being there?

Who could know these things and want to tell me?

Someone unhappy about Mickey's death. Someone close to Mickey. Someone wanting the truth to come out but afraid to talk to the police. How could this person know about Janene Ballich? Told by Mickey? Why?

I didn't know anything. I didn't even know how to back off now that I'd shown signs of fight by having the Toyota torched.

I was too tired to go out in search of food, had a look around the kitchen, opened the fridge. Empty. Oh Lord, at the airport Linda had asked me to switch off the fridge and freezer. Just another thing left undone. I looked for the freezer. Where was it? Cleverly concealed in a cupboard.

Paydirt. Thank God I hadn't switched it off. It held a loaf of bread and a round tin-foil container labelled chicken and mushroom pie. So what if the pie's use-by date was long passed? Frozen was frozen, frozen was like death, there was no use-by in frozen. We could eat woolly mammoths found in glaciers if we chose to. I took the pie to the stainless steel oven.

Smeg is not a good name for a cooking appliance. The resonances of the word Smeg are not good. I opened a bottle of Spanish red, Marqués de Murrieta, 1994. Linda had never got over Spain, she'd been there with her rock star. People should get over Spain, move on.

I took my glass back to the couch, got the television's remote control to work. 'Nightcall' with Barry Daly, an earnest-looking ABC man, strange hair, eyebrows in a chevron, his whole being oppressed by the news of the day. Barras Holdings. The name kept coming back. The hirers of the penthouse suite, what kind of company was that? I didn't have to look up Simone Bendsten's number, my index finger danced over the buttons.

'We are indeed still active,' said Simone. 'A rush job for counsel assisting the building royal commission.'

'When it comes to totting up the bill,' I said, 'do unto counsel what counsel will be doing to the taxpayer. Can you squeeze in a tiny inquiry?'

'When did I say no to you, Jack?'

'I cannot tell you how singular you are in that respect,' I said. 'Something called Barras Holdings.'

A second or two of hearing distant voices, bantering, and music, a laugh, the sounds of a good place to work.

'That's B-A-R-R-A-S, is it?' said Simone, something more in her voice than an inquiry about spelling.

'Yes.'

'Not doing any work for the commission, are you?'

'No.'

She coughed, small Melbourne winter coughs, brought on by cold and damp and melancholy.

'Jack,' she said, 'I shouldn't say this and it's obviously pure coincidence but the commission is interested in Barras Holdings. It's an investment company. On the public record, just in the last three years we can find nearly two hundred properties Barras bought, either off the plan or on completion. Apartments, houses, commercial properties. Barras usually sells them within months. For rather modest gains, as far as we can see.'

'So counsel thinks Barras is dodgy?'

'Our job here is research, if you take my meaning.'

'I do. And who owns the company?'

'Sole director is K. M. Etzdorf of an address in Monaco. He signs all company documents. The registered address is Marti Partners, Brisbane.'

Monaco, home of Charles Robert Hartfield, late of Melbourne, and Tony Haig's boating companion. Alexander Marti Partners, accountants to both Mickey Franklin and Haig.

'One last thing,' I said. 'Does Barras deal with MassiBild and a company called Saint Charles?'

I could hear Simone breathe out. 'Very much so. Directly with Saint Charles. And with companies associated with MassiBild. It's complicated, to put it mildly.'

'Far too complicated for me,' I said. 'I hope my next call is of a social nature.'

'Calls of any nature welcome,' she said.

I said goodbye and checked on the pie, poured some more of the Marqués, an exceptional drop. When I came back, Barry Daly, sad as ever, was speaking against a scene of men in suits entering a building: '...sitting in Melbourne today heard an allegation that former federal cabinet minister Michael Londregan used his influence to get planning approval for three sixteen-storey towers to be built in a twelve-storey zone in Melbourne's CBD. The proposal had been rejected four times by various authorities.'

There was a still of ex-senator Londregan, a tall man in a dark suit, florid, jowly, thinning curly hair. He was shaking hands with someone, it looked like a reception line.

Bradley Davis, an accountant, a former employee of

MassiBild, told the inquiry that he attended a meeting of MassiBild executives where the then head of the firm, Mr Vince Massiani, said the Concerto development would go ahead, the government would approve the extra four storeys the next day.

Daly's eyebrows spoke of his pain at having to relay such information. 'Four storeys in three towers meant twelve extra storeys,' he said. 'Counsel assisting the royal commission, Kevin Carstairs QC, asked Mr Davis what the permission meant in financial terms. Mr Davis said upwards of $40 million.'

There was a shot of the buildings. I knew them by sight, characterless and intrusive constructions, fortunately impermanent, they would be gone within fifty years. I also knew Kevin Carstairs from his golden youth, when he was an earnest Balwyn boy, couldn't catch a joke in a laundry basket, so eager to answer questions in class that he squirmed in his seat, moved his bum like someone with a terrible itch.

'What was the date of this meeting, Mr Davis?'

'December 2, 1994.'

'And the decision on the building was announced the next day? That would be December 3.'

'That's correct, December 3.'

'Did Mr Massiani say how Michael Londregan influenced the government, Mr Davis?'

'Well, he said the election was coming up and Londregan could do the government a favour.'

'A favour. Did he say what kind of favour?'

'No. I was surprised he said anything. Mr Massiani didn't often often say anything that wasn't strictly business. Practical stuff. Housekeeping.'

'Your impression then was that Mr Londregan had secured this outcome for MassiBild?'

'Oh yes, definitely. It had been chucked out so many times.'

Pie time. I was in the kitchen taking it out when my mobile rang.

'Jack? Sophie Longmore.'

'Good evening.' I felt awkward.

'Jack, I know this doesn't concern you anymore but something odd came by courier today.'

'Odd how?'

'It's a bill and a card and keys from something called Galvin Security Storage in Tullamarine. The bill's for six months advance payment on a storage unit. Whatever that is.'

'Haven't rented any storage?'

'No, never. But the letter's addressed to me. I had to sign for it. It says that to ensure maximum security the locks have just been changed.'

Something flitted through my mind. 'I might have a look,' I said. 'Can you drop off the keys?'

'I've got them with me,' she said. 'I'm in the car, on Punt Road, I'm going to Macedon. My father's complaining about his health.'

'You'll pass close by. I'll meet you.'

I gave her directions, looking at the pie with lust. I put it back in the switched-off oven, watched sad Barry for a few more minutes. He was interviewing the federal industrial relations minister, until recently a big undisciplined dog easily teased into outbursts of barking. Now he'd been to obedience school, bribed media turncoats had drilled him, and he uttered the same affable low-key bark over and over.

I went downstairs, jacketless, to the corner, stood in the light and shivered. A car came down the street inside thirty seconds, the driver waved, so precise was my estimate of the time it would take to drive from Punt Road to Linda's corner.

The car pulled up in front of me. I went to the driver's side.

'It's a bit spooky,' said Sophie. She gave me an envelope. 'It's been hired in my name for six months.'

'I'll have a look and give you a ring.'

'Thanks, Jack. I didn't know who else to tell.'

I went back to Linda's apartment and opened the envelope. Galvin Security Storage, 112 Rigoni Street, Tullamarine. A swipe card, two keys, and a PIN number for unit 164, entrance J, an account for $300 for six months rental.

I put my head back against the sofa, closed my eyes. Tomorrow. In the morning, early.

I was running out of tomorrow mornings. I groaned, rose and found keys, left without thinking about a coat.

Tullamarine was no lovelier by night, high fences, ugly buildings, glaring security lights, oil rainbows lying in the pitted
streets.

Galvin's sign said the premises were guarded by twenty-
four-hour video-monitored security. The swipe card got me
through the boom gate, into a floodlit compound with a huge,
low, windowless single-storeyed building of cinderblocks.
Roll-up garage doors A, B and C faced us. I went right,
foolishly, had to drive around the building to get to door J.

I got out, cold, moist air, shivered in my shirt, and
approached the door. An electronic keypad was under a light
to the right. I put in the card, tapped in the PIN and the
door rose, a low clanking noise, dark inside except for the
glow of a small console with a single fat button. The instruction said: PRESS FOR 20 MINUTES LIGHT. DOOR WILL CLOSE IN
TWO MINUTES.

I pressed. Tube lights flickered, stabilised, showing a corridor, roll-up doors on both sides, big numbers spray-painted on them. I walked down the internal road under the white lights and, before I reached storage unit 164, the entry door behind me clanked down.

J 164 was on the right, halfway to the end. Another light button. A key unlocked the door, you had to raise it by hand.

A cinderblock box, a bit bigger than a single-car garage. In the middle stood a red Maserati, from the 1960s, I thought. Framed artworks leaning against the walls, perhaps a dozen, a few pieces of furniture at the back.

I looked at the works along the nearest wall. All the artists were dead except for one and he was a day-to-day proposition: blue-chip art, investment art. Was this Mickey's small cashable stash, put here in Sophie's name in case he went under because of Seaton Square and people wanted to seize his assets?

I walked to the back of the chamber. A glazed colonial bookcase, it would buy two Mercedes. A commode, Egyptian Revival, if genuine worth a bit. A small desk, Georgian.

I looked in the car, opened the glovebox: a manual and a logbook. The boot opened—empty. I checked the bookcase, the desk drawers.

Cabinetmakers of old often amused themselves with their work, Charlie taught me that, and I always groped fancy antique furniture, even in public places.

I removed the four top desk drawers and felt around above them, stuck my arm in and felt the back, looked in a few other places. I studied the commode, touched the ram's broad head on the right, ran my fingers down its sides, feeling the smooth curled horns, finding the small buttons at their centres.

I pressed one. It didn't yield. Neither did the other. I pressed them simultaneously and they went in. My pulse quickened. I pulled at the ram's head.

It slid forward.

A secret drawer, narrow and deep. In it a notebook, long and slim, two videotapes. I flipped the notebook: names, dates, amounts, page upon page. I looked at the tapes. One had no label, the other said COPY.

I pushed the ram's head back and tried the one on the left. No luck. He didn't repeat himself, your ancient craftsman.

I took the items and left the building, the enclosure, drove back along the tollway-avoidance route. It was busy, the city never seemed to quieten, people's nightlife now began when it used to end. In Linda's parking bay, I sat for a moment, feeling the tiredness of too much sitting.

Time to watch a video.

My door opened.

'Get out, cunt.'

A body, an arm. A knife pointing at my throat, a wide blade, held on its side.

I dropped a video and the notebook between the seats, got out with the other tape.

He was standing back, squat and pale, football head, a leather jacket. 'Walk,' he said.

I walked out to the street.

'Stop.'

A dark vehicle pulled forward, a stationwagon, the man's hand gripped my belt, pulled me back into the knife. It pressed against me at a point beside my spine where a thrust would penetrate some vital organ quietly pulsing in the body's inner dark.

'Hands back or die, cunt.'

I obeyed, felt the handcuffs. The back door opened. He walked me across the pavement, into the car, powerful hands inside dragged me, pushed me down, down, between the seats, my face down, something thrown over me, a foot on my neck, the vehicle moving.

The chicken pie in the cool oven. It would be wasted.

I thought of that, how irrational is the mind.

'Hear me, Jack?'

We'd been driving for a long time, irregular stops, starts, slowdowns, then acceleration, a feeling of cruising at speed, we had to be on a freeway.

'Yes,' I said, eyes closed, thinking about my breathing, about keeping it regular and deep, moving the diaphragm, trying to flex my muscles to fight off cramp in my arms and legs.

'You're a stupid cunt, Jack. I don't understand that, it makes no fucking sense to me.'

Even through the blanket over me, I thought I knew the voice.

'Get him up, let him sit.'

The foot came off me, the blanket was pulled back. I tried to raise my upper body, couldn't, you needed hands. I got a hand, it gripped my shirt collar, pulled me up, choking me. I squirmed, got to my knees, got a foot to work, to push, managed to twist and get onto the seat. The pain in my legs as I half straightened them made me close my eyes.

We were on a highway, four of us, men, in a big station-wagon, my arms aching from being behind my back. Something wrong with my eyes, I blinked a few times. Dark tinted windows. You had to get used to them. I looked at the man beside me, he wasn't looking at me, a big, fat man, no hair. I couldn't see the people in front because of the headrests, then the driver looked back at me—potato nose, glasses, big lower lip.

I knew him well and the fear I felt dried my mouth and my eye sockets.

You are likely to remember someone who held you by the hair like a trophy, slapped your cheeks repeatedly, jerking your head back and forth. You will certainly remember the intense, stinging pain, the taste of your tears as they ran down into your open mouth. And if the person then ground your head into the floor and pissed on you, full recall is guaranteed.

'Call me Reece,' he said. 'Should make you call me fucking Mister.'

Reece Stedman, formerly of the Victoria Police.

We drove in silence down the Western Highway, the new outer-urban awfulness to the right, we passed Melton, went into the valley of Bacchus Marsh. On the slope going out, the driver spoke.

'Fucking bang takes out a whole fucking building,' he said, flat, nasal voice. 'Got to be the luckiest cunt on earth to come out of that. Like a second fucking life. You'd go and comb fucking beaches, wouldn't you?'

I felt something close to relief. They didn't plan to kill me. They could have killed me where I stood on the pavement in Carlton. This was going to be another punishment. I could survive this.

'But fucking no,' he said. 'So I take the fucking trouble. I drive through the fucking traffic to your fucking shithole to give you a personal message. I tell you very nicely to fucking cease and desist in your fucking annoying behaviour.'

Stedman wound down his window, sent his cigarette butt out, raised the glass. He held up his left hand and I saw the rings.

'Why, Jack?' he said. 'The woman's dead, you don't owe anybody a shit, you've got the money, we gave you a nice present, what the fuck can you hope to achieve by going on with this?'

'Just curious,' I said. 'I wanted to know what happened to the women. And Wayne.'

He looked back at me. 'That is so fucking smart, I can't fucking believe it. Listen, I'll tell you what happened. Then you promise me, you'll fucking forget everything, never speak of it again, enjoy the money? How's that?'

'I accept,' I said.

He hacked to clear his throat. 'You'll let this business go? Forever and a fucking day?'

'Yes,' I said. 'It's over. Forever.'

'What kind of records you kept?'

'Just some stuff in a file. Not much.'

'Notes, that kind of thing?'

'No, I don't keep many notes.'

'Where's the file?'

'Where I was staying.' I said Linda's address. 'The key's in my pocket. You can go back and get it.'

'And this tape?'

'It's from Mickey's lock-up.'

'Huh?'

'Mickey's lock-up. Near the airport.'

'How'd you know about that?'

'Found out today. It was in Sophie Longmore's name.'

A whistle. 'Well, fuck. How'd we miss that? You're a clever boy, Jack. Watched this tape?'

'No, haven't had a chance.'

'That's good, that's good. What else you find?'

'Nothing. There's a Maserati, some paintings, few pieces of furniture.'

'Right. So you'll draw a line under this now?'

'Yes. I will.'

'You see, Jack,' he said, 'that's how easy it could have been.'

'It would be nice to have the handcuffs off.'

'Jeez, sorry, forgot. Happy, get the cuffs off Jack.'

The fat man beside me pushed me forward, stuck a hand in, cursed, pulled at my right arm. My right hand came free, I brought my arms around my body, blissful relief.

'What happened to Katelyn Feehan?' I said, straightening my arms, elbows cracking, the cuffs dangling from my left hand.

'An accident,' Stedman said. 'Bloke got carried away, hurt her. Tiny little whore, too small to be a whore, could pass for thirteen.'

'The body was never found.'

'Funny that,' he said.

'And Wayne?'

'Gimme a smoke,' Stedman said to the man beside him. A hand offered a cigarette, lit it with a lighter.

'The fucking Dilthey,' he said around the cigarette, oozing smoke. 'Unreliable prick. Can't have a cunt like that knowing anything you want quiet. Just outlived his usefulness.'

'And he killed Janene?'

'Put her in a hole, the dumb fuck said. Some fucking dog will go in and find her one day. Should've taken care of it myself but, busy night, can't do everything.'

He didn't know about Janene. She was safe.

'I don't understand about Mickey,' I said.

'Out of hand. Blow for breakfast, lunch and dinner but he wants in, he wants to play with the big boys. Then he threatens he's got the goods. Exit visa that second. Date stamped. But not a bad bloke, Mickey, good head on him when he was straight, talk sense into arseholes. As at the fucking River Plaza that night. One minute the pricks are knocking back the Dom and sniffing the happy snow, then they've got a fucked-up whore problem, freeze like bunnies in the light.'

I had a clear picture of the whore, Katelyn Feehan, in the photograph Janene's mother gave me, taken on the day of the excursion to Gippsland. I saw Wayne and Janene and Katelyn, the three of them, going down the highway in the Porsche. It must have been a good outing, an agent and his models, all doing nicely.

'Why not just knock him?' I said. 'Why set Sarah Longmore up for it?'

'Can't just knock the cunt. Too many fucking questions, you just knock him.'

'But Sarah's trial was going to raise a lot of questions.'

300

Stedman glanced back at me. Even in the dim light I could see the contempt. 'Mate, mate,' he said, 'you know fuck-all, don't you? The bitch wasn't ever going to trial.'

How stupid I'd been. Sarah was always doomed, we could never have saved her. The point of the whole business was to provide an explanation for Mickey's death that could never be disproved.

We were slowing, Stedman turned off the highway, climbed a hill on a dirt road. My feeling of relief was gone.

'So, can we do a deal?' I said, trying to keep a whine out of my voice.

'Deal's done, mate,' he said. 'Just dropping in here to see about some business, take you home.'

We went up and down hills under a near-full moon, the road got worse, corrugations gave way to bumps and potholes that were too much even for the expensive vehicle's suspension. The headlights gleamed on water in the holes, lit up the stringy trees on both sides.

A sick feeling was growing in me, acid rising. We rounded a corner.

'Look for a fucking skull and crossbones,' Stedman said. 'From now. On the left.'

Inside a few hundred metres, the man next to him said, 'There.'

I saw it in the lights as we turned, a tin sign nailed to a tree, crudely painted, white on black. It said: NO ENTRANS KEEP OUT TRESPASERS DIE. We drove along a pitted, wandering track, downhill for three or four kilometres, climbing for a few minutes, going to the right, then over a ridge and down steeply.

'Here fucking somewhere,' said Stedman, and the

headlights picked up a parked vehicle, an old Dodge truck. There was also a white Valiant, rust patches on the boot. Stedman parked between them, lights on a corrugated iron building. He hooted, two sharp blasts.

Two men appeared, one short and broad, wearing a beanie, the other tall and thin, stooped, hair to his shoulders. The short one had a full beard.

'Chokka and Jimbo,' said Stedman. 'Ferals. Fucking animals. Jimbo's the proof that fathers shouldn't root their daughters.'

He got out, stood with the door open, cold coming in, the sound of dogs barking. 'Where's the fucking stuff?' he said, no greeting.

Jimbo turned and went from sight. Chokka walked over. He was wearing denims near-black with dirt, a filthy upper garment. Bits of dried food were stuck to his beard.

'G'day,' he said. He smiled. Tooth stumps.

Stedman closed the door. He walked away with Chokka, around the Dodge, out of view. I breathed out. This was just business, dodgy business, drug business almost certainly, but it didn't involve me. The three of us sat in silence.

Jimbo appeared in the lights, carrying a bag, half-full, yellow, an agricultural-looking bag, fertiliser, poultry feed. He looked around. Stedman and Chokka came out from behind the truck. The threesome walked towards us, went behind the vehicle. The rear door opened, I heard the bag going in, the door thunked down.

Stedman got back in. 'Totally scrambled, Jack,' he said. 'Apes would be fucking insulted to be related to these idiots.'

He engaged reverse. 'Let's go home,' he said.

I breathed out, a full breath. It was going to be all right, there was going to be a way out of this.

My door opened, two hands grabbed my head, pulled me, I had no resistance, went sideways, fell to the ground, hands dragged me away from the vehicle, I felt a huge weight on my chest, someone sitting on me.

'This is the end of this crap,' said Stedman. 'Fucking circle closed. Look in his pockets, Chokka. Keys.'

Hands groped me, found Linda's keys.

I couldn't breathe, I tried to fight, the weight was overwhelming, schoolyard bully weight.

'Cheers, Jack,' said Stedman. 'The boys'll look after you. Great tradition of hospitality out here, not so, boys?'

The men made spitty, guttural noises.

'Don't fuck him without foreplay,' said Stedman. 'Grease him up with the WD40.'

'Bagga fucker,' said Chokka.

They pulled a bag over my head, my shoulders, dragged me by my feet, twenty, thirty metres over hard-packed dirt, through a doorway, handcuffed me to something.

'Have a sleep,' said Chokka. He pulled the bag off me. 'Getting up fuckin early, right, Jimbo?'

Jimbo laughed, a high-pitched nasal sound, somehow both childlike and chilling.

They left, slammed a tin door. Jimbo was still laughing and the dogs were still barking. I didn't move for a while, lying on my back, hands held behind my head, elbows at eye level, fear and self-pity pushing everything out of mind, shutting down my brain. Then I began to feel the cold— fierce cold, the ground beneath me, the air.

Suit pants and a cotton shirt, thin socks. I would die of cold before any other fate could befall me.

I could see my breath. There was light from a small

window, just four panes, smeared, cobwebs moving.

Light from where?

Moonlight, it was just off full moon. You didn't always notice the moon in the city, it wasn't a city thing, the moon, superfluous to city requirements.

What were they going to do to me?

Kill me.

I felt the thing I was handcuffed to. The leg of something, I could make it out, a bench of some kind, steel pipe legs. I wriggled away until I could slide the cuffs down to the ground. If I could lift the bench…

The leg didn't terminate. It curved. The legs were one length of pipe, bent upwards to meet the top. I wriggled back and ran my hands up. There was a flange: the pipe was bolted to the top, two bolt heads.

I wasn't going to escape. I was going to freeze to death or I was going to live until they came for me and killed me.

No.

I got my palms under the benchtop, pushed, I didn't know what I was trying to do, I was trying, that was all that mattered.

I could not move the benchtop a single millimetre.

What else?

I squirmed around and tried to get my legs under the bench, use the strength of my legs to do I knew not what. I couldn't. There was something in the way.

Think.

I thought.

I tried things, hopeless, pointless, stupid things, my wrists were painful, I thought I could see blood staining my shirt-sleeves. I ached everywhere.

At length, I stopped trying to free myself, lay, shivering,

teeth clicking. A kind of numb peace came upon me and I slept, dreamed I was lying on the ground and someone was kicking me in the side. I tried to sit up and couldn't.

I opened my eyes, felt another kick, higher, in the ribs.

'Fuckin wakie wakie,' said Chokka. 'Bag him.'

Jimbo lifted my head by the hair, pulled a plastic bag down to my shoulders. I panicked, shouted, inhaled, exhaled, smelled my stale breath.

The handcuff was off my right hand.

'Geddup, fucker,' said Chokka. 'Gotta shotgun here, any shit I blow your fuckin balls off.'

I stood up, my hands were cuffed again, behind me, someone pushed me. I walked, collided with something, the door probably, trying to breathe as shallowly as possible, feeling the plastic being sucked in, moist air in the bag, something jammed against my spine, a gun muzzle. I walked, stumbled on something, a hand pushed me sideways, changed my direction, no idea of distance covered.

My collar was gripped from behind, stopping me, the bag pulled off my head.

Air. So sweet, so clean.

Dogs barking, close, metres away.

The muzzle in my back.

'Said to just fuckin shoot ya, bleed ya, crush ya in the stampmill, chuck ya bits in the acid,' said Chokka. 'Gotta acid bath here.'

'How much,' I said, 'to let me go?'

He laughed, a choking sound, ending in coughing, hawking, spitting. 'Howsabout fifty?' he said.

'Fifty's fine,' I said. 'I'll go to fifty grand.'

The terrible ruined laugh again. 'Nah, mate,' he said.

'Fifty fuckin million, mate, how's that? Go to that, fucker?'

I was seeing now, the moon, cloudless sky, was it near dawn? It was freezing, my whole body seemed to be shaking. We were on a level surface, concrete, between sheds, a dark hill opposite. The ground sloped away sharply. A machine to the right, the height of a truck. This was a mine perhaps, long ago.

Jimbo came around the corner to my left, two dogs on short leashes. One was big, white, it could eat from a kitchen counter, the other was below knee-height, brindle, broad, round head, low centre of gravity, some kind of pitbull cross. The dogs pulled away from Jimbo, came back, collided, the big one snarled, I saw teeth.

'Big boy's not blooded proper,' said Chokka. 'Just roos. Little fucker's the killer. Bought him off a fuckin slope, killed so many dogs the other slopes won't let him fight anymore. Turns out he's also a fuckin tracker, gets a scent, nose fuckin down, he's off. Go anywhere too. Run up a tree after a possum, straight fuckin up like he's goin up stairs, the fuckin poss looks back, big fuckin eyes. Bang. They fall out of the tree, he's got it.'

Jimbo brought the dogs up, let the small one sniff my legs, held the big one back. It bared its teeth at me, widely spaced fangs like a fish trap. I stepped back, felt the muzzle press.

Jimbo laughed, the deranged child sound.

'Happy, boy?' said Chokka, the voice of a father. 'More fun than the girl he brung, hey? Whadya reckon, Jimbo?'

Jimbo dropped his head shyly, long strands of filthy hair covered his face. When he raised his chin, threw back his hair, he was looking sideways, embarrassed. Snot was running from his nostrils and he put out a long reptilian tongue and licked it into his mouth.

I felt cold in a way that had nothing to do with the temperature, cold in the core of my body.

'Was the girl still alive when he brought her?' I said.

Jimbo looked at me, head tilted. I could see the whites of his eyes.

He was smiling. He nodded. 'Smelt nice,' he said.

My arms were pulled back by the handcuffs. I heard the snick, they were free.

'Run, fucker,' said Chokka.

I didn't know what to do.

'Five minutes start,' he said. 'Howzat? See if you kin run faster'n these fuckin dogs. Fair go, hey, mate?'

Jimbo squealed with sexual pleasure.

Chokka kicked me in the base of my spine. The shock went into my skull. I stumbled a few paces, fell to my knees.

'Go, fucker!' Jimbo screamed. 'Go! Go!'

I got up and ran into the dark, downhill, down the bare slope, there was a path, slippery, leather-soled shoes, I fell, got up, slipped, fell, rose, ran, got off the path, there was grass beside it, it was less slippery, a terrible pain in my left knee, it was of no consequence whatsoever.

The dogs wouldn't kill me. They would maul me. I would be alive when Chokka and Jimbo arrived.

So it wouldn't be over.

Only that part of the entertainment would be over. I would be alive.

Like Katelyn.

Get off the path, idiot.

I veered right, into the scrub, the moon was gone, ran

over roots, ran into something, a tree, stunted thing, hit it with my right shoulder, spun around, fell over, got up.

Run.

Chokka wouldn't wait five minutes, this wasn't a sport with rules. He wanted to see if the small killer dog could track me.

Just run.

I ran, stumbling, falling, face whipped by low branches, I could see things, the moon was out, a sharp dip, going down, I kicked something, arrow of pain, broken big toe. I fell, knees in water.

A creek.

Go up the creek, stay in the water, dogs can't smell you in water.

Hollywood. I knew that from films. Would the films save me? Would *Cool Hand Luke* save me? Water didn't save Cool Hand Luke. No, that wasn't Cool Hand Luke, that was Sidney Poitier handcuffed to a redneck.

How long? How far had I run?

I walked in the water, wobbly walking, no firm footing, feet freezing, slipped on a rock, fell awkwardly, my right knee meeting something hard.

Fuck the creek.

I got out of it, uphill now, some strength in my legs, surprising, a small hit of optimism moved through me.

I could get away from these mad ferals and their killer dogs. They were not very smart.

I was smart.

Smart enough.

Apes would be fucking insulted to be related to these idiots. Exactly. Stedman told them to kill me. But they wanted some fun.

I could come out of this.

A branch caught my nose, blood in my mouth, lots of it. I swallowed blood, blood was probably good for you, drinking your own piss was said to be good for you. Gandhi drank his own piss. A pioneer recycler.

The scrub was denser here, the ground riven with erosion furrows. I kept falling. Once I thought I'd sprained an ankle but the pain subsided.

Top of the hill. A stitch, pain in my side.

Barking.

Oh Christ, they were coming.

Keep going. Just keep going.

Downhill, steep, I tripped over something and rolled four or five metres. Felt no pain, just exhaustion.

Get up. Run. I couldn't, I walked.

Barking. Much closer.

Run.

I stumbled down the slope, sweat in my eyes, mouth open gasping, trying to get air, legs like stumps, dead things, weights I was dragging.

I didn't see the dense bush until I hit it. It seemed to grab me. I fought it, wrestled my way into it…

Oh Christ, trapped in a thicket like Brer Rabbit, the savage creatures would tear me apart at their leisure.

Barking, loud, maddened barking, not twenty metres away.

No. No.

I threw myself forward, dragged at the branches.

Ground crumbling under my feet. A precipice.

Jesus. Falling.

I tumbled down a slope, grabbing at stones, saplings,

nothing holding. I hit water, rolled into it, got water in my mouth, swallowed it, mud-tasting water, ice-cold water, in my nose. I got up. I was up to my waist in a dam, a few metres from shore.

Howling dogs. Somewhere above me. Close.

I turned, tried to see the bank I'd fallen down, just a dark mass.

A blur. The smaller dog, coming down.

It landed on the narrow muddy bank on four paws, bounced, did not hesitate.

It leapt for me, straight for my chest, my throat.

In the second it was in the air, the moon came out and I saw its fierce cannonball head clearly, the whites of its wide-spaced eyes, the open jaws, the spiky teeth, the tongue.

Then the animal was on me.

Our heads collided. Blackness, pain.

I went over backwards, fierce pain in my left shoulder now, the dog's teeth in me, both my hands on its broad collar, trying to pull it away.

We were underwater, its weight on my chest.

Something said: Don't push. Pull.

Stay down.

I pulled the dog to me, felt its jaws moving in my flesh, intense pain in my whole shoulder, up my neck.

Stay down.

I needed to breathe. I hadn't prepared myself, hadn't drawn a deep breath.

Hold on.

The animal's body was thrashing, paws scrambling against me, trying to get purchase. I could feel its strength, totally out of proportion to its size. My grip on its collar was weakening, I had to let go, get my head out of water. Breathe.

Stay down.

I felt the teeth come out of me. It did nothing for the pain. The dog's head was pulling backwards, astonishing strength in the neck. I couldn't hold it.

Hold on. Just hold on.

No, I couldn't.

I felt the dog's strength go, I felt it as intimately as if it were my own.

It stopped thrashing, the neck was not fighting me.

I rose to the surface, breathed in the cold night air, smelling of stagnant water and mud. The dog was on my chest. I let it go, it floated away.

Baying from the shore. The huge white dog was a few metres away, looking at me, the hayfork teeth.

Christ, this would never be over.

I backed away, across the dam, it wasn't wide, ten metres perhaps. It was deep in the middle, I turned, swam the five or six strokes needed, started to walk out, mud holding my shoes, looked back.

The big dog was gone.

It was coming around the dam. How long would that take? From which side? I couldn't see the end of the dam, it tapered at both ends, that was all I could see.

I could hear shouting, then a whistle, not a human whistle. A beam of light touched the top of the vegetation across the dam.

Chokka and Jimbo were on their way.

On the bank, I stood in complete exhaustion, nowhere to go, I couldn't run anymore. I touched my shoulder, looked at my hand. It was black with my blood.

I turned and walked a few paces, kicked something, almost fell over. It was an old truck door lying on the mud. I stood and looked down at it in a stupid, fuddled way, shook myself, looked up.

The white dog was twenty metres away, in full stride, all legs off the ground, coming for me, silent, huge, powerful, head the size of a giant marrow.

Fuck you.

I bent and grasped the ancient door by its top, pulled it up, heard the glup sound as I broke the bond between metal and mud, it wasn't heavy, just a sheet of rusted tin.

The dog was two cars' length away, the awful teeth biting air.

I turned like a hammerthrower, turned to my right, arms at full stretch, swinging the door parallel to the ground, reversed direction, came back with the door, released it, threw it at the dog, he was about to spring, melon head up.

The door's rusted bottom edge severed the massive Baskerville head. The head went up, the torso kept coming, ran into me, hit me like a motorbike, knocked me flat, lay on me, covered me.

Hot blood in my mouth, in my eyes, up my nose, I breathed in the blood, felt the warm weight of the headless creature on me, its final jerks.

The whistle, three or four blasts, sharp, imperious. The light coming around the other side of the dam.

Chokka and Jimbo. No more dogs.

Just me and the boys left.

I was filled with a maniacal joy, a fifty short-blacks hit, anything was possible, I didn't much care about anything. I got out from under the dog, spat the blood, walked the way it had come, walked, to fucking hell with running, I'd done the running.

Jesus, Chokka would shoot me. He was always going to shoot me when the dogs had finished.

Run.

Still able to run, my legs moved, how amazing, no, not amazing, running on terror-produced chemicals flooding through me, why doesn't matter, just run.

I ran, clockwise, around the dam, crawled up a bank, away from the flashlight, away from the boys, I had a start. There was a passage through the scrub here, once a path perhaps, running again, this wasn't bad, settle down to a pace, I could keep going like this…

'Freeze fucker!'

Light in my eyes, close up.

Jimbo.

I kept going, dived at the light, didn't care, heard the crack, felt something brush my face, hot, I had him by the hair, long hair, he fell backwards, I went with him, on top of him, got him by the throat, squeezed, sat on him, bashed his head against the ground. He offered almost no fight.

After a while, too tired to go on, I stopped, reached for the torch, found the rifle, bolt action. I worked the bolt, pressed the muzzle against his throat.

Jimbo lay with his eyes closed, playing dead.

I got up, stood back. 'Get up,' I said, 'or I'll shoot you.'

I wanted to shoot him but he got up instantly.

'Run, you bastard,' I said.

He ran.

I ran the other way, switching off the torch, carrying it in my left hand, the rifle in the other. Where was I going? Go back to the mine, open ground, it would be light soon, surely? I could find a position, see them coming.

The overgrown path ended at a wider track. My sense of direction was gone. I turned right, tried to run, couldn't. Never mind, I had the rifle. I walked in the right-hand wheel furrow. The moon seemed to be down but the sky was lightening, just a shade. The track went uphill then down. If I was going towards the mine, the creek I'd crossed would be down there.

Would they go directly back to the mine? They'd know the quickest way, they'd be there before me.

Panic. I started to run again, got my legs moving, it wasn't too bad, it was downhill. My left shoulder was now a steady ache. Tetanus. I needed an injection. The least of my worries. Water. I was in water, the creek, I was going the right way. No, only the right way if Chokka wasn't there first.

Uphill from the creek. How far had it been? Not far. A minute or two of petrified running. I stopped, walked fifty or sixty metres, the track was steep, the rifle heavier with every step.

A building against the sky ahead, to the right. I kept going. The track intersected with another one running towards the mine. This was the way we'd driven in. I turned right, walked beside the track.

The old truck and the Valiant came into sight. I crossed the track, put the truck between me and the buildings.

Was he waiting for me? Coming back was a stupid idea, I should be in the bush, they didn't have dogs now, they couldn't track me.

The vehicles. The Dodge truck and the rusty Valiant. Would they leave the keys in them?

I went between the truck and a row of steel drums, stooping, reached up and opened the passenger door. It was heavy and it squeaked. Too hell with caution, I got in, reached across the steering column to feel for keys.

Nothing.

I was withdrawing my arm when I touched a projection.

Key in the dashboard.

I pulled myself into the driver's seat. The gear lever was on the floor. I put my foot on the clutch, moved the lever. It was heavy. Where was first?

Never mind. Put it into neutral. See if it starts. It probably won't, it probably hasn't run in years. I turned the key.

A whine, a whine that died.

Light, a torch switched on. Chokka, fifty metres away.

Another starter whine, another fade-out.

Something hit the windscreen, slapped against it, a short shriek. Bullet glancing off.

Oh, God. Out. Take cover.

The engine fired.

I got it into gear, let in the clutch. Shit, first gear, going forward. I was scrabbling around, pulled the stick towards me and down, clutch in. Yes. Jerking backwards. I couldn't see anything, right hand down, into a roaring turn, smack on my door, another bullet, find another gear, lurching forward, not first gear, sluggish but moving.

Swinging the huge beast left, I put my foot flat, a long travel, Christ, no lights, looking for the headlights switch, pulling knobs on the dashboard, lights on, off the track, flattening bushes, hitting a rock, bumping back onto the road.

No more shots.

The truck picked up speed, reached the right gear speed. I changed up, flying high as a hawk on adrenalin and relief. The speedo was pre-metric, we were doing forty-five miles an hour and it felt like a hundred, everything vibrating, slack steering, total concentration required to keep the truck on the track. Top speed was close, probably fifty. Road twistier than I remembered, that wasn't surprising: I'd been cold with dread in the back seat, not paying attention to the road.

They would come after me in the Valiant. They couldn't let me go, I was supposed to have been killed, bled, stamped, bits put in the acid bath, those were their instructions from someone who would do exactly that to them.

The day was dawning, grey in the sky now, an end to hideous night, there was a sharp drop to the right.

Lights behind me. Close.

There would never be an end to this night.

The back window exploded, I ducked, broken glass hit the back of my head, stung my neck, bounced off the windscreen.

Without thinking, I took my foot off the accelerator, slowed, obeyed an imperative from the cluster of brain cells that handled survival, the survival control centre.

I coasted, slowing, head to the right, foot on the brake, eyes on the mirror.

The Valiant slowed with me. I could make out two shapes in the front.

I stopped, changed gear, I knew the gears now.

The Valiant stopped, well back from me.

I didn't move. They didn't move.

Waiting. Did they think I was hit? I had Jimbo's rifle. They weren't brave people, they weren't going to rush me.

Waiting, engine running. I liked the thumping sound of the old Dodge.

No more waiting. Punched, slapped, pissed on, home invaded, handcuffed, kicked, attacked by killer dogs, shot at.

An end to the night.

I let in the clutch and went backwards, foot flat, engine screaming, hit the Valiant with a bang, the impact jerked my head. I braked, got into first, pulled forward ten metres, braked, gear change, back again, foot down, engine howling in pain.

A solid, jarring crunch as I made contact with the car.

I braked, opened the door, took the rifle. It would be an interesting murder trial. I looked forward to it, Drew could defend me, try the battered solicitor defence.

Perhaps not.

The Valiant was twenty or more metres down, in a ravine, upside down. A wisp of red light near the sump, a flame.

The occupants might survive. Or they might not.

I went back to the Dodge, gave it a pat, hoisted myself into the cab, got going. I liked this truck. Perhaps I could buy it from Chokka's estate, stable it with the Stud. We could grow old together.

The day had dawned by the time I reached the highway, joined the early commuters. At the first traffic lights, a man in a Range Rover looked up at me, looked away quickly, didn't look again.

What he could see was a vintage truck driven by a man with matted hair and an unshaven face smeared with blood and dirt.

He couldn't see the handcuffs hanging from one hand, couldn't see much of the wet, filthy, torn, bloodstained cotton business shirt.

He couldn't see anything of the grey flannels, now black, ripped at both knees and caked with mud.

He couldn't see the soaked shoes, ruined, bought in William Street from Mr Conroy, kept in shape with shoetrees, regularly polished.

He probably thought I was just another suburban solicitor on his way to work.

The lights changed, we proceeded. By some miracle, I drove unchallenged all the way home.

I didn't care much about Stedman coming for me, I'd kill him, find a way. I parked the Dodge truck outside the boot factory, got the spare keys from their hiding place under the stairs, went up to my violated home and showered for a long time, examining the tooth wounds in my shoulder, the bruises everywhere. Out, I made plunger coffee, added cognac, the very superior old pale, a lot of cognac.

Hunger. It came upon me suddenly.

Nothing since the banana on the plane.

I ate Norwegian sardines on toast, two tins, four slices of bread, drank two cups of coffee.

When had I last slept? Busselton. When was that?

I drove to George's corner shop in the Stud and rang Cam. It was a long ring, a woman answered. I said it was Jack for Cam.

'He's around here somewhere,' she said.

A wait.

'Choppin wood,' Cam said. 'Swore I'd never chop wood again.'

'Small dogs, small women, wood,' I said. 'You can change.'

'I knew I shouldn't have said that. Find somewhere to sleep?'

'Not exactly,' I said. 'Got a boltcutter?'

'Don't go anywhere without one.'

He picked me up in the HSV. The boltcutter couldn't fit between my wrist and the handcuff. With a hard click, Cam sliced through the chain joining the handcuffs. 'Have to wear that one for a while,' he said. 'There's a bloke in Brunswick can take it off.'

'Don't you want to know?'

'Never talk about sex.'

Cam listened to the story on the way to Linda's, driving with his fingertips, blank face like a careful judge.

'Jesus,' he said when I'd finished, 'you really know who to fuck with. Is there a course you can do?'

'Some things you can't teach,' I said.

At Linda's building, Cam parked illegally. The Alfa was where I'd left it. I went over. Unlocked. My mobile was on the passenger seat. I held my breath, leaned over, put my left hand between the seats, pain from the bites.

Tape. Notebook. I breathed again. We went upstairs. At the apartment door, Cam opened his corduroy jacket and took the big Ruger out of his waistband.

'I don't think you've got any warnings left,' he said. He knocked loudly. 'Federal Police,' he said. 'Open the door.'

We waited.

'Reckon they think you're in the acid,' Cam said. 'Boys and the dogs watching the bubbles.'

I opened the door. Cam went first. The file was gone but nothing else touched. I fetched two Carlsbergs from the pantry, uncapped them, and we sat in chairs and watched the video on the big flat screen.

A hotel security surveillance film, poor quality, date and time shown along the bottom: *03.12.94 23.14.*

It was a compilation tape, people coming and going in a hotel foyer, eight scenes, not long, the last one at 2.36 am on 4 December 1994.

The tape ended.

Cam drank beer. 'Have meaning?' he said.

I was looking at my mobile. A message. 'It has meaning,' I said. I pressed the numbers.

'Hello.' Quick.

'Jack Irish.'

'The pictures,' said Janene. 'It's them.'

'Will you give evidence?' I said.

A long silence.

'Without you, Janene,' I said, 'they'll go free and they'll know money can buy anything and that you were just bugs to be squashed.'

She made a sniffing noise, I thought I heard her swallow.

'Will you look after me?' she said.

I touched my shoulder with fingertips. 'I'll look after you,' I said.

'Promise?'

'Promise.'

We waited on the winter evening pavement, rocks in the city stream, trams squealing behind us, leaning against a car not our own, Cam smoking a Gitane, the pungent blue smoke drifting to me, wrapping around my face, making me eighteen again.

They came out, dark overcoats, handsome, she wore a scarlet scarf, long, not wound around her neck, just a loose knot on the chestbone.

I took two paces across the space. They saw me.

'Jack,' said Tony Haig. He had perfect teeth, a wry, welcoming smile. 'Coming to Corsica?'

I was obstructing the pedestrian traffic, people had to walk around me. I didn't care. 'The River Plaza,' I said. 'The dead girl.'

Dogteeth holes in my shoulder, the three good-looking people, rich people, they owned the world, *we were just bugs,*

Wayne said that, we looked at one another, a metre separating us.

'Come inside and talk,' said Steven Massiani. 'This is solvable.'

I looked at Corin Sleeman. There were thin lines running down beside her mouth.

'She wasn't dead, Corin,' I said. 'Did they tell you she was dead? Did they tell you Senator Londregan killed her? She was alive. Katelyn was alive. They took her away and gave her to crazies to kill. Did they tell you that?'

She looked at me and I knew who had sent the man to give me Janene's name. 'What about Janene Ballich, Corin?' I said. 'She had to die too, didn't she?'

Corin was looking down, her eyes closed.

'And then there was Mickey,' I said. 'And Sarah Longmore.'

'Jack, Jack,' said Tony Haig, 'you're not well, you need a rest.'

'Can't live with something like this, can you, Corin?' I said. 'Do you dream about it?'

'No,' she said. 'I can't live with it anymore.'

She did not raise her head, crossed the space and came to me, put her hands out to me like a child seeking comfort.

I put out my hands, my sleeves pulled back, the handcuff showing.

'For Christ's sake, Corin, shut up,' said Massiani. 'Just shut fucking up.'

'Let's go,' I said.

We walked down the street, Cam behind us. At the corner, I looked back. Haig and Massiani hadn't moved, eyes on us.

In the car, I rang Barry Tregear.

'It's about some murders,' I said. 'I'm bringing someone to make a statement. There'll be another witness arriving tonight. They'll both need protection.'

He coughed, a cigarette cough. 'What about you?'

'No,' I said, 'not now. I know for certain now.'

Hands on the mounting yard rail at Flemington, windy day, I looked at Lost Legion. He was sweating a little, a gloss on his neck, on his chest, moving his feet as if finding the soft surface painful.

The jockey came out, Danny DiPiero, an apprentice, nine wins, first ride in the city, claiming three kilograms. Just a boy, he'd probably had the treatment in the room from the veterans, small men whose bodies were contour maps of vein and muscle and sinew, no subcutaneous fat, young men with faces aged by too little sleep, no food, too much food, induced expulsion of food, cooking in steam. And the drugs, some taken for their designed purposes, others not.

Danny stood earnestly before Lorna Halsey, silken arms folded, looking up at her, nodding. Harry Strang had chosen him, he had seen something in the boy at his fifth ride as he piloted a hopeless nag through a pile-up in a maiden in

Murtoa to steal third place. 'Little bugger can ride,' he'd said. 'Learns the game, he could be useful.'

I hadn't seen Harry. You sometimes glimpsed him in the crowd, the sharp face under a hat and above a buttoned-up raincoat bought in England when Harold Wilson was prime minister. By now, he'd be somewhere on the public stand with his equally old binoculars.

I looked around for Cam. He would be taking the decision. The sweating would be worrying him, it could get worse, the horse wasn't happy, sometimes they ran their race in the mounting yard.

Down the rail, I saw forearms, snowy cuffs, long sallow hands with fingertips touching. I leaned forward and I saw the profile. Cam felt my eyes, looked my way briefly.

I stood back from the rail, stood in the jostle, saw Cam again through the people. He was in light-grey suiting, elegant as a whippet. He took off his dark aviator glasses, put them in his top pocket. Then he turned his head, met my eyes, the lowering of the chin.

It was on.

Cam was looking elsewhere. The tiny nod again. I looked.

Cynthia, the commissioner, coming my way. I had the cash in my raincoat pockets, in packs, twenties and fifties, the totals written on the wrappers. Once Cynthia carried the money to the track, passed it to her team, people more closely vetted than judges and much more scared of retribution. But, one Wednesday, without meaning to, her daughter fingered her. Cynthia didn't know that, we hoped she never would. It would have added to the misery of losing 90 per cent of the sight in one eye. Her jaw, her nose, her cheekbones, they were repaired, almost as good as new, all the expenses met by Harry Strang.

So Cynthia didn't carry the money anymore. She wanted to, she was unafraid, but Harry wouldn't hear of it. What happened to her changed both of them, changed us all, probably.

Cynthia was wearing tinted glasses, not dark but close. She came up and stood facing me, elegant in black today, her costumes ranged from understated tweedy to a pink tracksuit and trainers. I took the packs from my pockets and glanced around as I fed them into the maw of the bag she held between us. No one looking at us that I could see.

'Don't know how this'll go,' Cynthia said. 'Strickland caught a few in the third, they'll be jumpy.'

'It goes, it goes,' I said.

She nodded and was gone, money to distribute to semi-retired hookers, redundant teachers, a sad-faced kleptomaniac, an aerobics instructor, the mother of the woman who did her hair.

In the yard, the jocks were all up, walking the horses around, ready to go to the line, all male, men sitting on other animals. Lost Legion was edgier and the sweating was more pronounced. Danny DiPiero would be happy to have the horse out of the confined space and on the track, riding it to the start, standing in the irons, letting it feel his weight and his hands, his confidence.

I took a walk, saw the very man Cynthia had mentioned, the punting trainer Robbie Strickland, stubbled head, dark glasses. He was talking to two men in suits, one fat, rolls over his collar. Robbie had one in this, Bold Voter, a nag of whom the tipsters today said, 'hard to follow'. Privately, they'd be putting a few bucks on it.

The bookies didn't need to be reminded that many of Robbie's cattle were hard to follow. There was no knowing what his horses would do: win, win, place, a few bad runs. Then a spell, perhaps another midfield performance or two, followed by a win out of nowhere, sitting off the pace before a sneaky rails run and, at the death, just a noble head and a few inches of cable-veined neck. For the insiders, the rewards were worth the wait: $10-plus on the TAB, around half that on course, and deliciously plump combinations.

From time to time, the stewards gave Robbie the please explain for poor showings that couldn't be blamed on missed starts, checks, runs blocked. They got the excuse note from his mother: didn't like the surface, off its feed, pulled up sore. In life, the easiest thing is to find reasons for failure. How many ways is it possible to lose? The bookies' sensible response was to ignore Robbie's explanations and the form and keep his horses short.

Exposed form, it was called: the public performances, factors you would take into account when making judgments. But, in racing as in other human endeavours, it was the things unexposed, the private trials, the secret times, the instructions to jockeys, that could decide outcomes.

On the stand, I took the latest device, the VE5000, out of its housing. I pressed buttons and then I was so close I had trouble finding Danny. When I did, I watched him walking the horse around, waiting his turn. Lost Legion looked happier, the sweat had dried.

'Favourite goes in, Fortunate Son, he's very short, shorter on course than the tote,' said the caller. 'There's money for Bold Voter, a trickle, an up and down performer. And support for Sum of Things, Queensland visitor, good form in lesser events, and Cold Callista, strong with her own sex, two wins out of three. Lost Legion's got some support, well named this horse, it's been a long while, years, since he had his few moments in the sun. Truly appalling record before he went off the radar. No first-up form ever, run a 2400 once for a fifth. Your mystery bet. Hard to see why he's in city class for his comeback. Hard to see why he's come back.'

Lost Legion was taking his place in the stalls. He went in placidly. I could see the jockey on Danny's right say something to him, shark mouth, full of teeth, Danny didn't look at him.

'Five or six to come in,' said the caller, 'money dumped on Bold Voter on course now, he's in to three, that's pushed the rest out.'

Whose money was that? Robbie Strickland's connections or ours? Harry never talked tactics to me but he loved to catch the bookies.

'Sum of Things is on eights,' said the caller. 'Lost Legion's attracting some support, he's shortened on the TAB, paying $12.60 now, in from forty-something a short while ago.'

I looked at what I could see of Lost Legion, his head gleaming, an alert eye, the ears electric, and I thought of the horse in the trodden paddock in Gippsland, hopeless, head down to the compacted mud, the rotten rug on his back, his fearful gaze.

I said to myself, a pledge: whatever happens here, this horse will live out his life in comfort. I will pay the feed bills.

Field of twelve, 2000 metres, drawn in gate number 4, a good position. It was a long run to the first bend and Legion needed to be off the rails, three wide would be fine, race just behind the front-runners, at the start of the long curve go for his life, lead them into the straight, 453 metres.

'Two to go in, money's come in for Lost Legion, hope it's not mug money. He's shortened to six dollars, $8.40 on the tote and shorter interstate, now someone's jumped in clothes and all in Queensland, this is taking on plunge proportions.'

They were all in their stalls, some still, some skittish. I saw Danny wipe a finger under his nose, along his cheek under the goggles. He knew Legion, he'd ridden him in a barrier trial, brought him in under a hold five lengths behind the winner, been on him for trackwork for a week.

'All in, light's flashing, come out in an even line,' said the caller.

Test number one passed. Legion had left the barrier. He was willing to race.

'Cobalt Heaven and Coadestone coming across from their wide barriers to take the lead, Benison's next on the rails, Tinto Rio outside him and Earth Summit makes a third. Eighteen hundred to go and there's no pace on, the favourite's lying five lengths back and inside him is Lost Legion on the rail.'

I throttled back the magnification of the VE5000 to see three lengths of horses, found Legion, Danny looked uncomfortable, he hadn't found his spot, he didn't want to be on the rail, he could be trapped in a pocket. Running along the river, no one was urgent, there was a long way to go, some hoop talking going on, Bold Voter's jockey was loquacious, so was the rider outside him. Danny's mouth was shut tight, I saw him glance to his right, he wasn't happy, he was being crowded, getting the verbal. Harry might have been wrong to give him the ride.

'At the 1600, Cobalt Heaven and Coadestone neck and

neck,' said the caller, 'Earth Summit wants to have a go now, he's gone up to them, the jockey's having a bit of a time with him. Sum of Things is moving up on the outside, he's four deep and Cold Callista's coming with him.'

There wasn't much Danny could do. He had two rows of horses in front of him, two outside him and a horse on his heels. I didn't like this much. The front-runners were no-hopers. When they wilted, they'd shunt Legion backwards.

'At the 1400 chute, getting some pace on now, Earth Summit's the leader, no one wants to go with him, Sum of Things getting a wriggle on, Benison's pushing his nose through on the rails, Coadestone's rider doesn't like his possie, Bold Voter and Lost Legion side by side, Cold Callista's outside the favourite and a gap's opened to the rest of the field.'

It stayed like this. The horse wasn't going to win from there. I was watching Danny. He didn't think so either, looking around.

'Lost Legion's drifting back in the field,' said the caller, 'this plunge is a fizzer all right, Bold Voter's forcing his way through the ranks, 1200 to go.'

I could see Lorna Halsey. Her hands were steepled in front of her face, index fingers against her lips. This wasn't her fault, it was Danny's, he placed the horse badly after the jump, the old hands pinned him.

'Lost Legion goes to the outside now, he's fifteen lengths off the pace, 900 to go, Bold Voter's through but Sum of Things turns on the power, moves to the front, shifts across, he's a length clear...'

This thing was over, all the time and effort and money wasted.

My mobile rang. I'd forgotten to switch it off.

'Jack?'

I had Danny's face full on. He was asking Legion for the impossible.

'Well, Lost Legion's not giving this away,' said the caller, 'DiPiero's gone for broke, don't know…'

'Jack?'

Barry Tregear, tobacco-rusted voice.

'Hang on,' I said. 'One minute.'

Lost Legion was at full stretch, running like a three-year-old sprinter. Danny hadn't touched him with the whip.

'Lost Legion's passed Cold Callista like she's stopped, Olley on Bold Voter looks back, goes for the whip now, this is a remarkable run, Lost Legion gets to him, he's got Sum of Things to go, a length clear at the 150.'

The boy was on the horse's neck, they were flying.

'Lost Legion and Sum of Things, can't separate them, fifty to go. Lost Legion, he's found more, he's in front, Lost Legion by a long neck, most incredible performance I've seen in a long day, this is a substantial plunge come off in the most spectacular way imaginable…'

'Jack?'

'They call me Happy Jack,' I said.

'Could be Happier Jack today,' he said. 'Your mate's taken an exit pass.'

'Which mate would that be?' I said. 'I've got a few of them out there.'

'Mate number one. Stedman got it in the weights room, there's sixteen-odd cunts didn't see a thing.'

I was also unseeing, looking at nothing, and then I came back to the world and saw an open sky, pale, blown free of dirt for the moment.

'He pissed on me.' I could not have said the words to anyone else on earth. 'He king hit me and then he pissed on me.'

A brief silence.

'Listen, son,' Barry said. 'You brood about it when they piss on you before they king hit you.'

The world righted itself. Lorna Halsey and her daughter were embracing. I caught sight of Harry, putting his binoculars away. He gave me a single nod, face blank.

In the car, me driving, Cam doing sums in the back, Harry said, 'Nice outin. Always sweet to stick it up Robbie Strickland too.' He looked out of the window, chewing on a dozen Smarties. 'Know what I reckon?'

'Tell me,' I said.

'This bloke'll run further.' He eyed me. 'The Queen Eliz, Jack, the Saab. How's that sound?'

'Exciting. But will it be sweeter than this day?'

'Never see this kind of sugar again,' said Cam. 'Six for dinner, Jack?'

'Six,' I said.

'We might pop a can of the Bolly first,' said Harry.

'Good timing,' said Drew. 'My informant says the seven o'clock news.'

'For Christ's sake don't ding this car,' I said. 'Promise me.'

'Relax. I'm not a denter, I'm a write-off man, I don't fuck around.'

Drew driving Linda's Alfa, the airport turnoff ahead, a slalom of deranged tradies, heartsick salesmen, tight-lipped women racing home to try to be mothers. For no good reason, he pulled out of the lane. I heard rubber pigsqueal behind us.

'So how long is this excursion?' he said.

'Open-ended,' I said. 'I don't just dent foreign travel, I'm a write-off man.'

'What, she loves you?'

'She's been sacked, she's cashed-up, she wants intelligence, wit, repartee, finely honed love-making techniques.'

'And your role?'

'Interview the candidates. I've got an instinct for human resources. Don't drive up this poor bastard's arse, please.'

'Speed lane, I'm reminding him. Put the radio on.'

I found the button, it took three punches to find the right station. News headlines, then: 'In a shock development today at the commission into the building industry, it was alleged that a notebook belonging to murdered Melbourne developer Michael Franklin revealed cash payments to contractors on a massive scale. Counsel assisting the inquiry, Kevin Carstairs QC, said huge sums of drug money were laundered though a company called Barras Holdings, linked with millionaire developer Anthony Haig. Mr Carstairs said drug money used to pay wages and other expenses was converted into property through complicated finance arrangements. Construction giant MassiBild was deeply involved, Mr Carstairs alleged.'

'Goodbye Saint Charlie,' said Drew.

'Barras,' I said. 'Hirer of the penthouse at the River Plaza. He gave Napoleon his big break.'

'What?'

'The Comte de Barras. He put Napoleon in charge of defending the French Convention. I never gave it a thought.'

Drew gave me the look. 'I'm surprised,' he said. 'First thing I thought of. Closer to ground level, the word is that Bernie Paech is giving up Haig in return for considerations. And Londregan's trying to do a deal on a lesser, shaft the much-missed Stedman, now tragically unable to defend himself.'

International departures. Drew parked, kissing the kerb, I winced. I got out and opened the back door to get the bag.

'Not much luggage,' he said.

'I'll be living off the land, making my own clothing from reindeer hide.'

'I suppose I should say I'm sorry I got you into all this terrible shit.'

'Why would you suppose that?'

He looked at me, the long face, the long nose. 'Why don't you just fuck off,' he said, 'and leave me to total this car?'

I went without a backward glance.